GIANT DAYS™

VOLUME ONE

DISCARD

Published by
BOOM! BOX™

Ross Richie	Chairman & Founder	Kenzie Rzonca	Assistant Editor
Jen Harned	CFO	Rey Netschke	Editorial Assistant
Matt Gagnon	Editor-in-Chief	Marie Krupina	Design Lead
Filip Sablik	President, Publishing & Marketing	Crystal White	Design Lead
Stephen Christy	President, Development	Grace Park	Design Coordinator
Lance Kreiter	Vice President, Licensing & Merchandising	Madison Goyette	Production Designer
Bryce Carlson	Vice President, Editorial & Creative Strategy	Veronica Gutierrez	Production Designer
Hunter Gorinson	Vice President, Business Development	Jessy Gould	Production Designer
Josh Hayes	Vice President, Sales	Nancy Mojica	Production Designer
Ryan Matsunaga	Director, Marketing	Samantha Knapp	Production Design Assistant
Stephanie Lazarski	Director, Operations	Esther Kim	Marketing Lead
Elyse Strandberg	Manager, Finance	Breanna Sarpy	Marketing Lead, Digital
Michelle Ankley	Manager, Production Design	Amanda Lawson	Marketing Coordinator
Cheryl Parker	Manager, Human Resources	Alex Lorenzen	Marketing Coordinator, Copywriter
Sierra Hahn	Executive Editor	Grecia Martinez	Marketing Assistant, Digital
Eric Harburn	Executive Editor	José Meza	Consumer Sales Lead
Dafna Pleban	Senior Editor	Ashley Troub	Consumer Sales Coordinator
Elizabeth Brei	Editor	Morgan Perry	Retail Sales Lead
Kathleen Wisneski	Editor	Harley Salbacka	Sales Coordinator
Sophie Philips-Roberts	Editor	Megan Christopher	Operations Lead
Allyson Gronowitz	Associate Editor	Rodrigo Hernandez	Operations Coordinator
Gavin Gronenthal	Assistant Editor	Jason Lee	Senior Accountant
Gwen Waller	Assistant Editor	Sabrina Lesin	Accounting Assistant
Ramiro Portnoy	Assistant Editor		

BOOM! BOX™

GIANT DAYS Volume One, July 2022. Published by BOOM! Box, a division of Boom Entertainment, Inc. Giant Days is ™ & © 2022 John Allison. Originally published in single magazine form as GIANT DAYS No. 1-4. ™ & © 2015 John Allison. All rights reserved. BOOM! Box™ and the BOOM! Box logo are trademarks of Boom Entertainment, Inc., registered in various countries and categories. All characters, events, and institutions depicted herein are fictional. Any similarity between any of the names, characters, persons, events, and/or institutions in this publication to actual names, characters, and persons, whether living or dead, events, and/or institutions is unintended and purely coincidental. BOOM! Studios does not read or accept unsolicited submissions of ideas, stories, or artwork.

BOOM! Studios, 5670 Wilshire Boulevard, Suite 400, Los Angeles, CA 90036-5679. Printed in China. Eighth Printing.

ISBN: 978-1-60886-789-9, eISBN: 978-1-61398-460-4

GIANT DAYS ORIENTATION #1

JOHN ALLISON

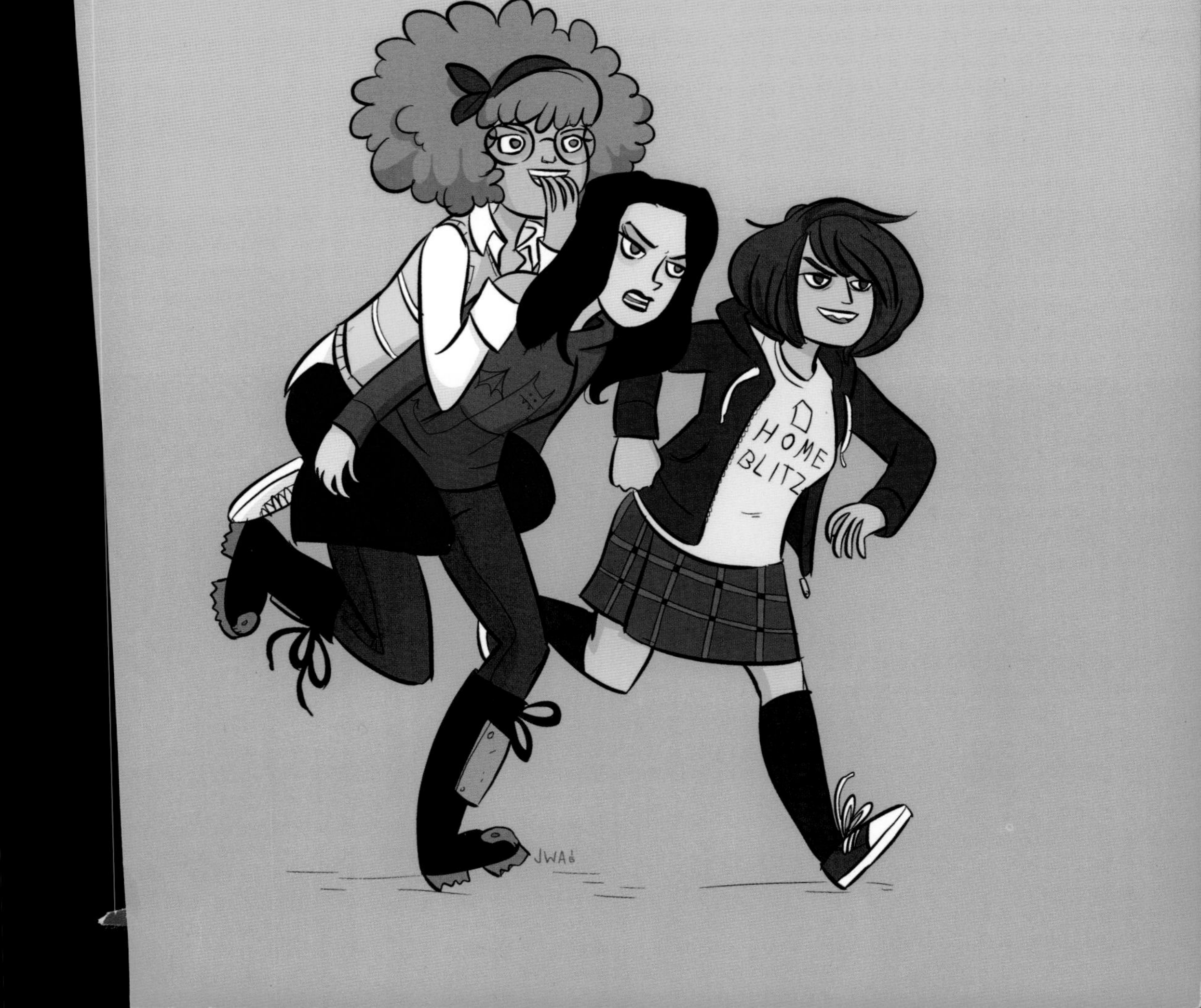
HOME
BLITZ

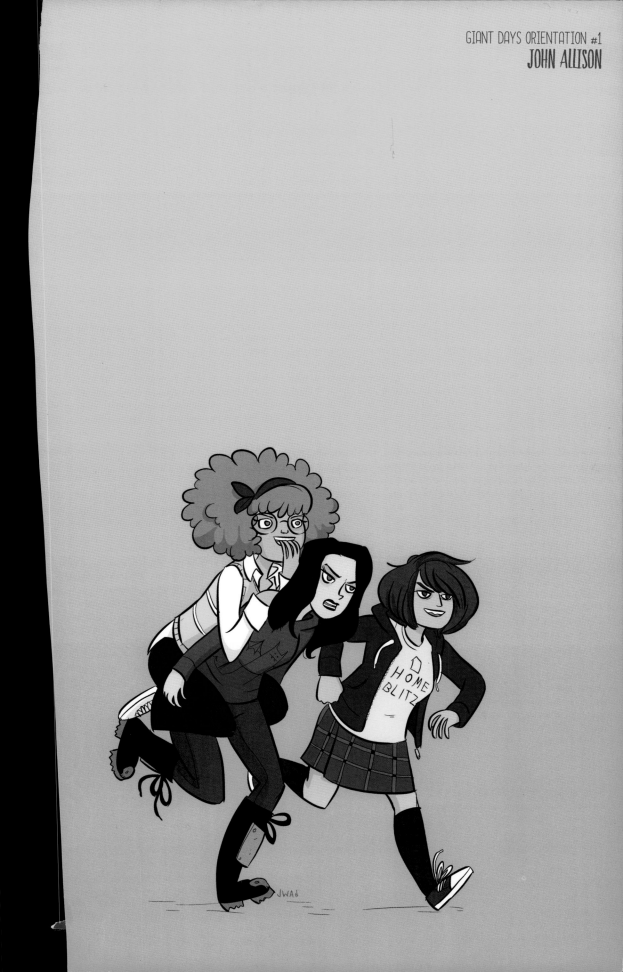

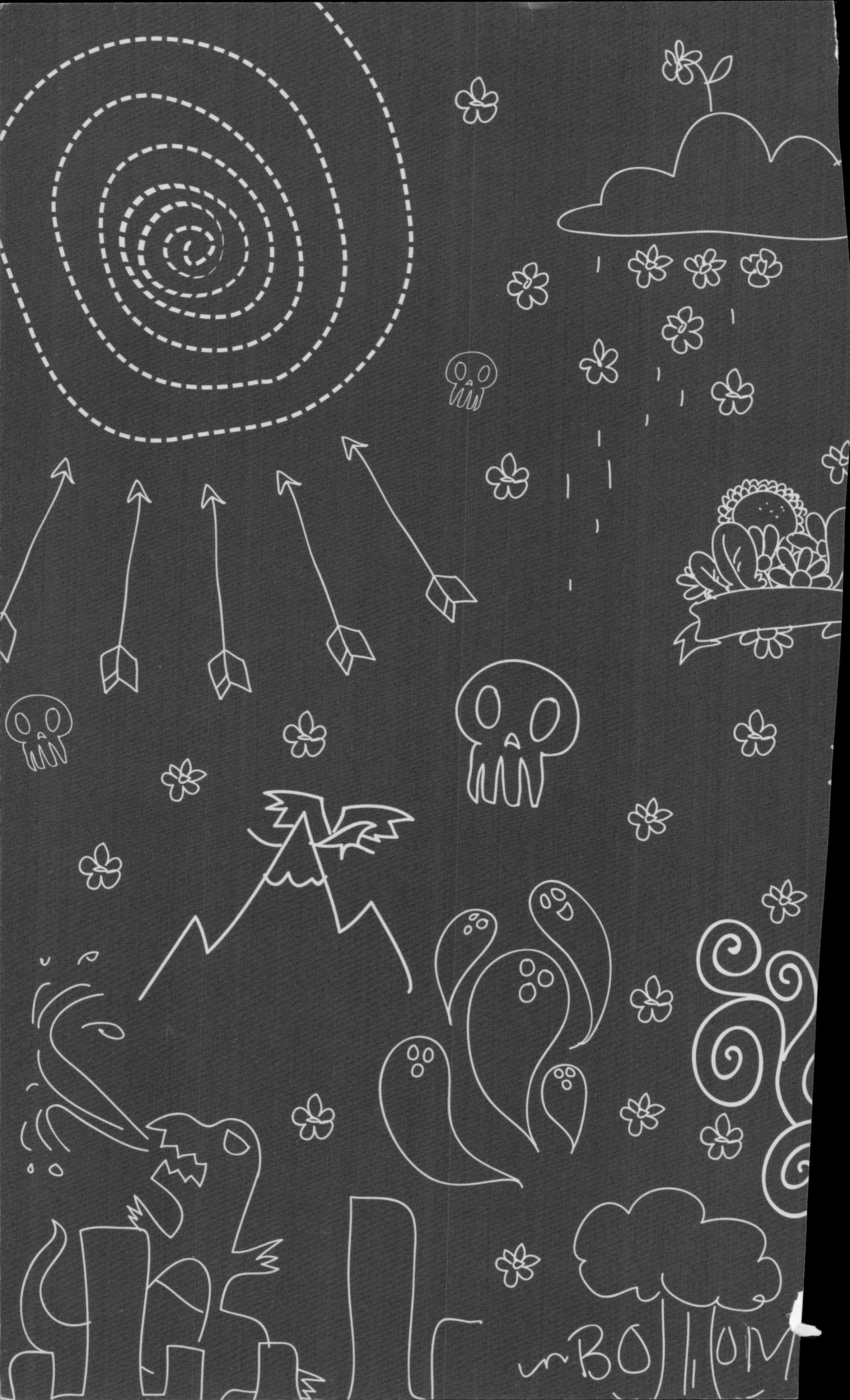

GIANT DAYS ™

CREATED + WRITTEN BY
JOHN ALLISON

ILLUSTRATED BY
LISSA TREIMAN

COLORS BY
WHITNEY COGAR

LETTERS BY
JIM CAMPBELL

COVER BY
LISSA TREIMAN

DESIGNER
BONES LEOPARD

EDITORS
SHANNON WATTERS + JASMINE AMIRI

CHAPTER ONE

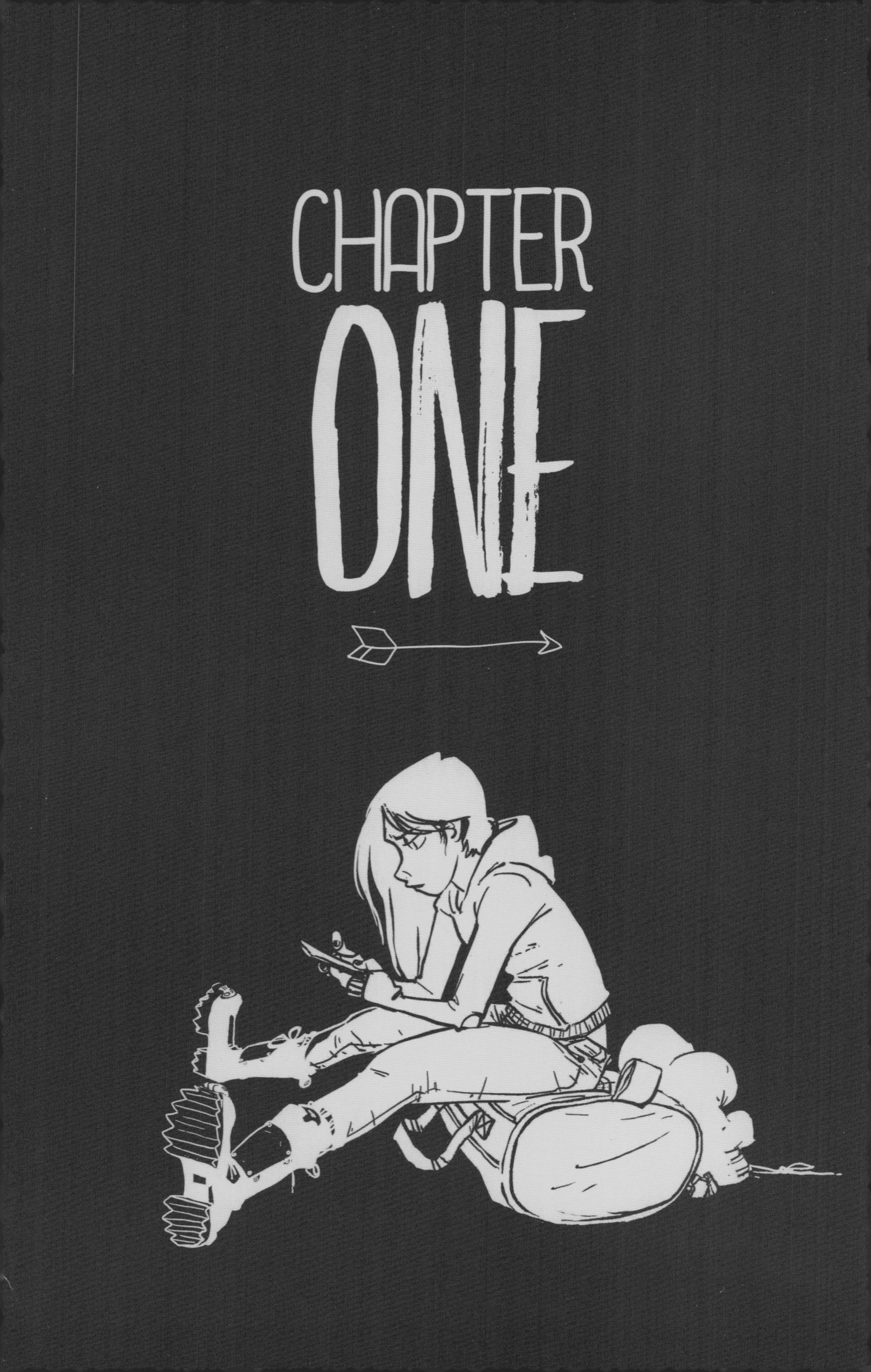

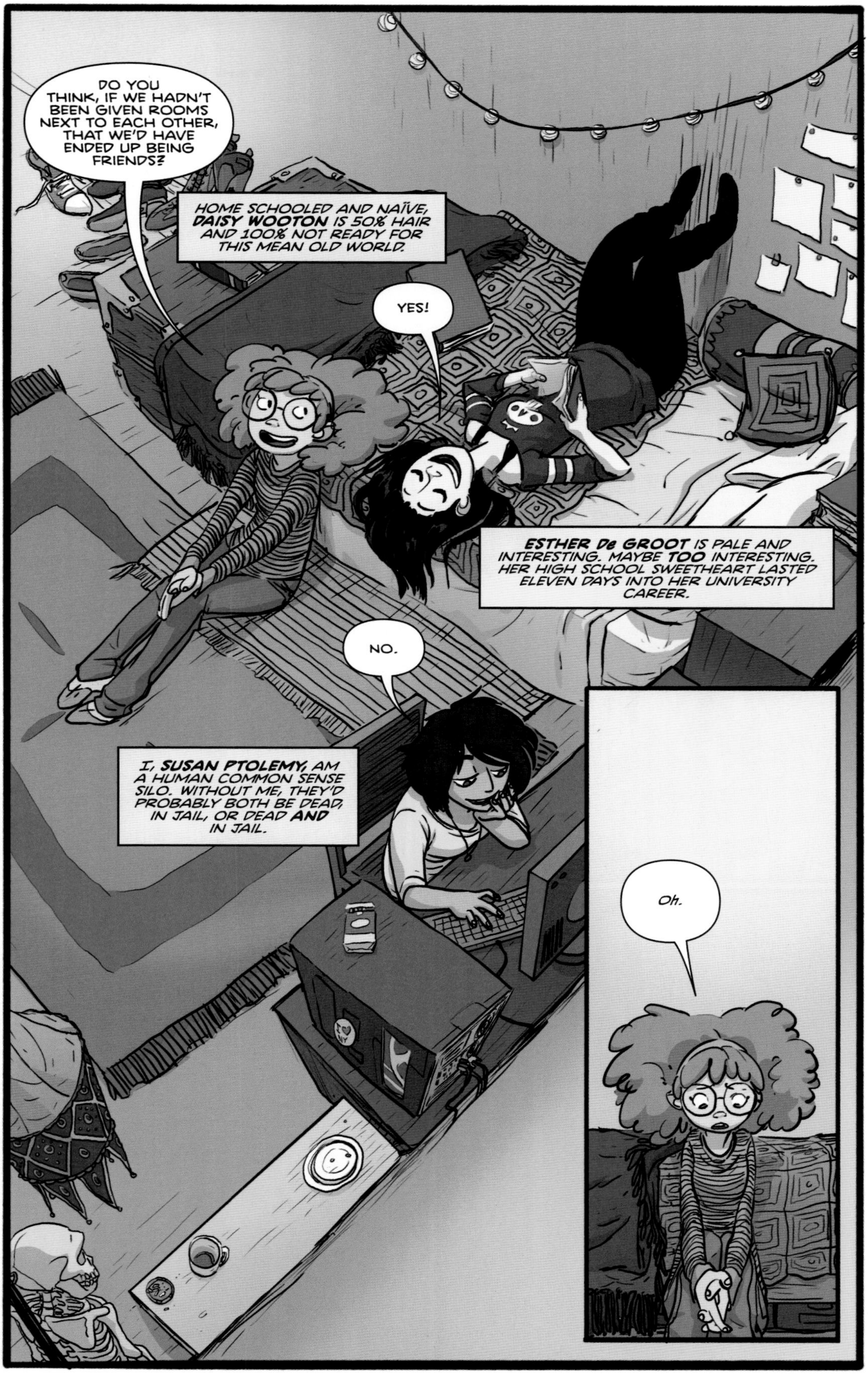
DO YOU THINK, IF WE HADN'T BEEN GIVEN ROOMS NEXT TO EACH OTHER, THAT WE'D HAVE ENDED UP BEING FRIENDS?
HOME SCHOOLED AND NAÏVE, DAISY WOOTON IS 50% HAIR AND 100% NOT READY FOR THIS MEAN OLD WORLD.
YES!
ESTHER De GROOT IS PALE AND INTERESTING. MAYBE TOO INTERESTING. HER HIGH SCHOOL SWEETHEART LASTED ELEVEN DAYS INTO HER UNIVERSITY CAREER.
NO.
I, SUSAN PTOLEMY, AM A HUMAN COMMON SENSE SILO. WITHOUT ME, THEY'D PROBABLY BOTH BE DEAD, IN JAIL, OR DEAD AND IN JAIL.
Oh.

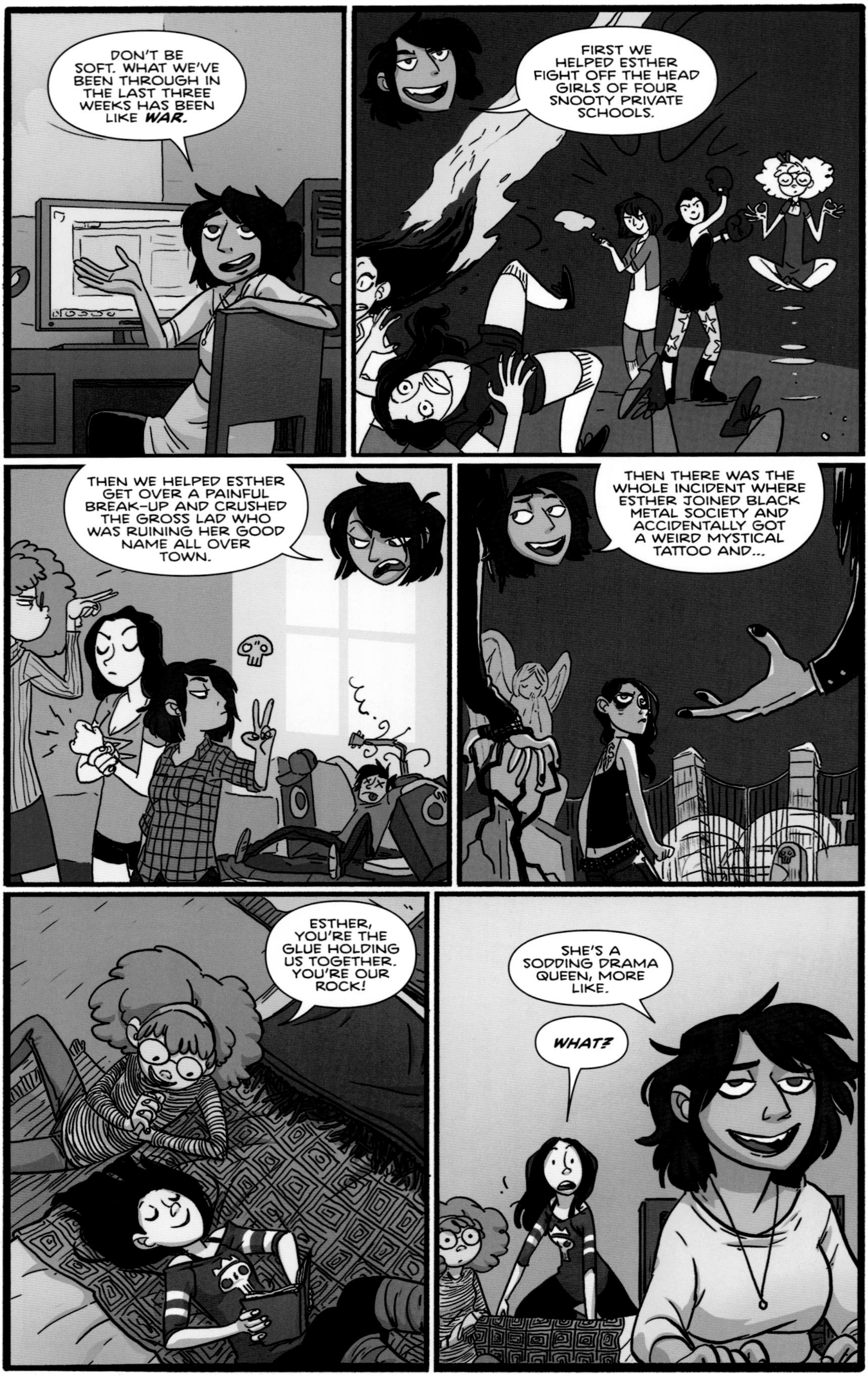
DON'T BE SOFT. WHAT WE'VE BEEN THROUGH IN THE LAST THREE WEEKS HAS BEEN LIKE WAR.
FIRST WE HELPED ESTHER FIGHT OFF THE HEAD GIRLS OF FOUR SNOOTY PRIVATE SCHOOLS.
THEN WE HELPED ESTHER GET OVER A PAINFUL BREAK-UP AND CRUSHED THE GROSS LAD WHO WAS RUINING HER GOOD NAME ALL OVER TOWN.
THEN THERE WAS THE WHOLE INCIDENT WHERE ESTHER JOINED BLACK METAL SOCIETY AND ACCIDENTALLY GOT A WEIRD MYSTICAL TATTOO AND...
ESTHER, YOU'RE THE GLUE HOLDING US TOGETHER. YOU'RE OUR ROCK!
SHE'S A SODDING DRAMA QUEEN, MORE LIKE.
WHAT?

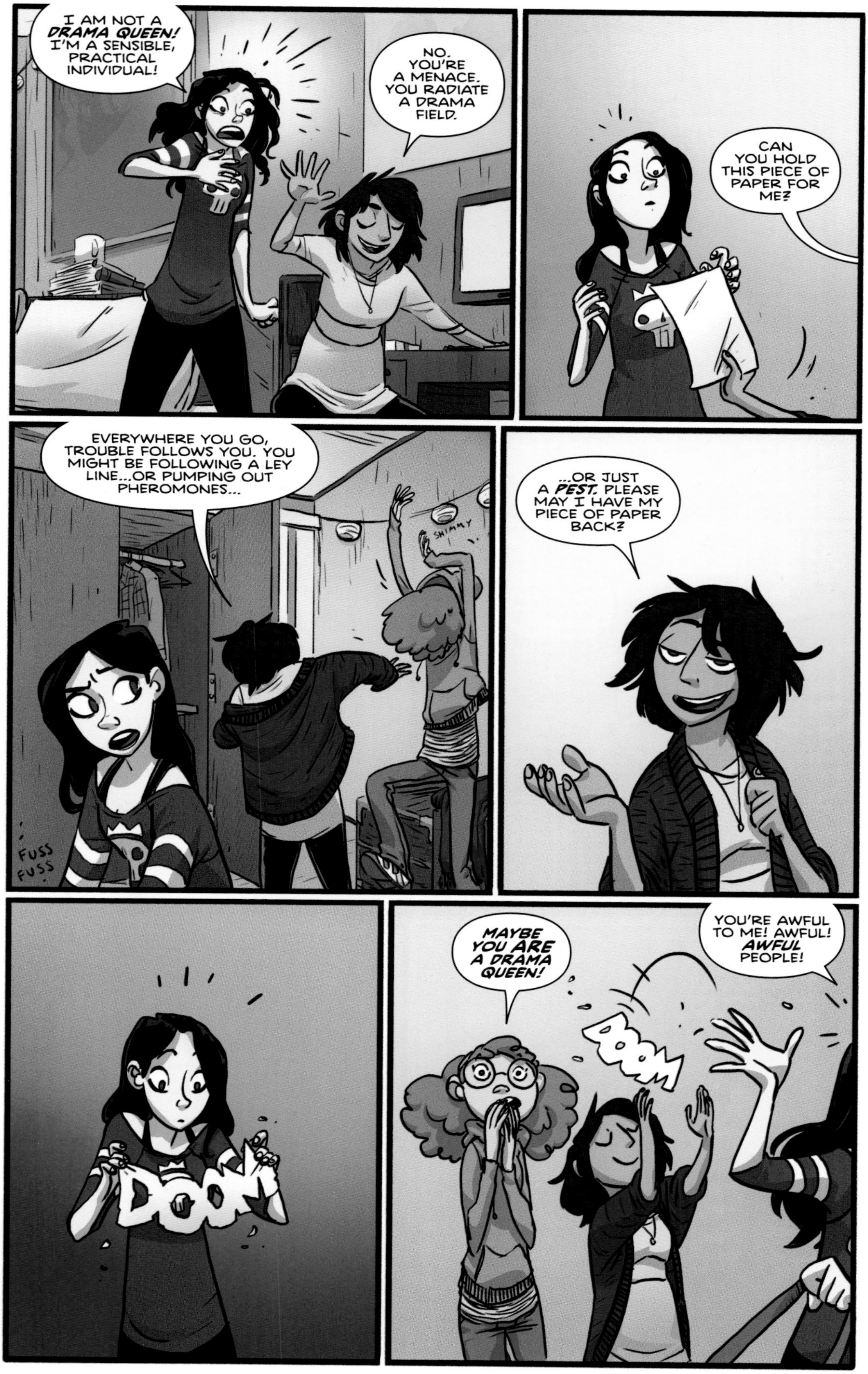
I AM NOT A DRAMA QUEEN! I'M A SENSIBLE, PRACTICAL INDIVIDUAL!
NO. YOU'RE A MENACE. YOU RADIATE A DRAMA FIELD.
CAN YOU HOLD THIS PIECE OF PAPER FOR ME?
EVERYWHERE YOU GO, TROUBLE FOLLOWS YOU. YOU MIGHT BE FOLLOWING A LEY LINE...OR PUMPING OUT PHEROMONES...
SHIMMY
FUSS FUSS
...OR JUST A PEST. PLEASE MAY I HAVE MY PIECE OF PAPER BACK?
DOOM
MAYBE YOU ARE A DRAMA QUEEN!
BOOM
YOU'RE AWFUL TO ME! AWFUL! AWFUL PEOPLE!

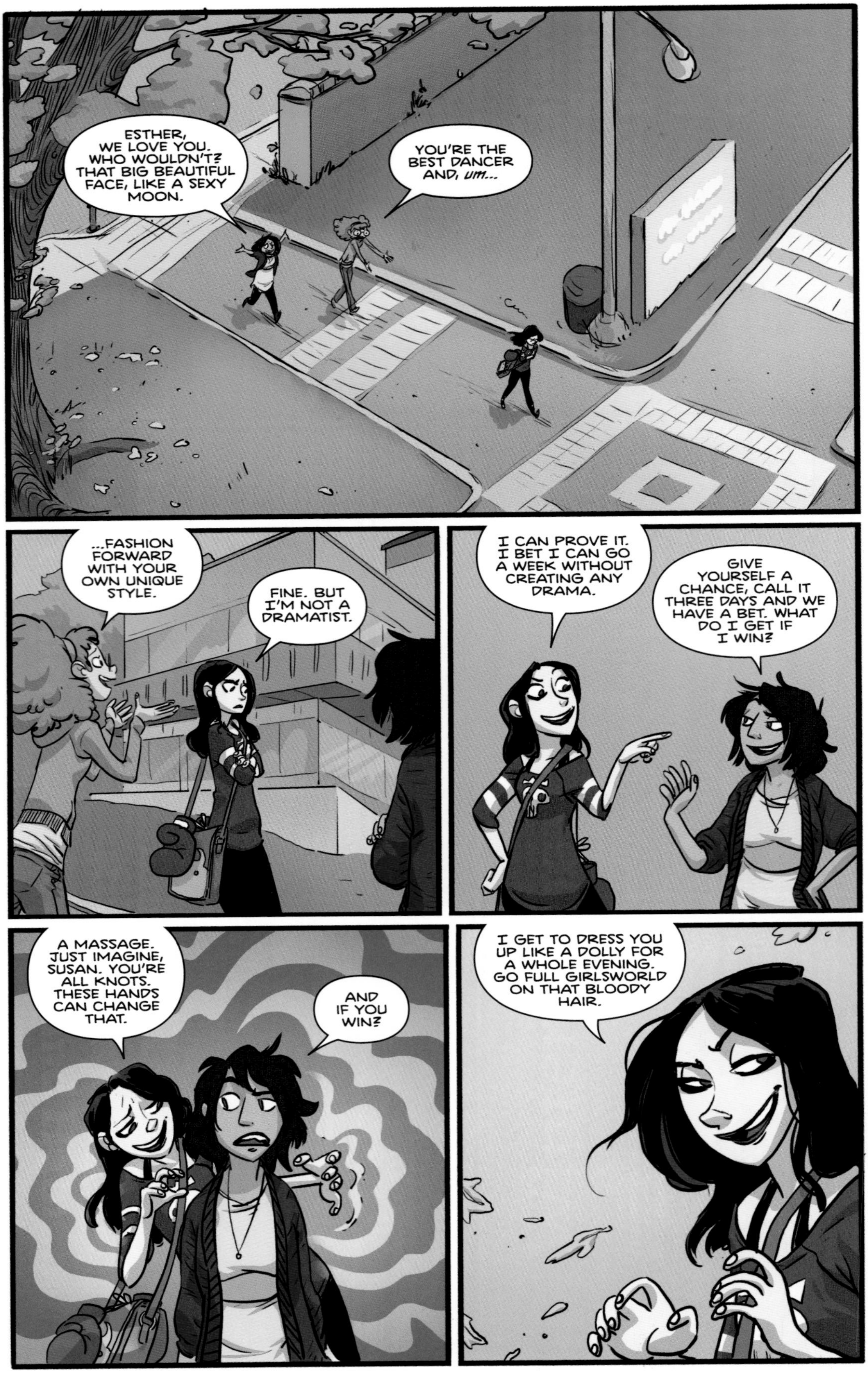
ESTHER, WE LOVE YOU. WHO WOULDN'T? THAT BIG BEAUTIFUL FACE, LIKE A SEXY MOON.
YOU'RE THE BEST DANCER AND, *UM...*
...FASHION FORWARD WITH YOUR OWN UNIQUE STYLE.
FINE. BUT I'M NOT A DRAMATIST.
I CAN PROVE IT. I BET I CAN GO A WEEK WITHOUT CREATING ANY DRAMA.
GIVE YOURSELF A CHANCE, CALL IT THREE DAYS AND WE HAVE A BET. WHAT DO I GET IF I WIN?
A MASSAGE. JUST IMAGINE, SUSAN. YOU'RE ALL KNOTS. THESE HANDS CAN CHANGE THAT.
AND IF YOU WIN?
I GET TO DRESS YOU UP LIKE A DOLLY FOR A WHOLE EVENING. GO FULL GIRLSWORLD ON THAT BLOODY HAIR.

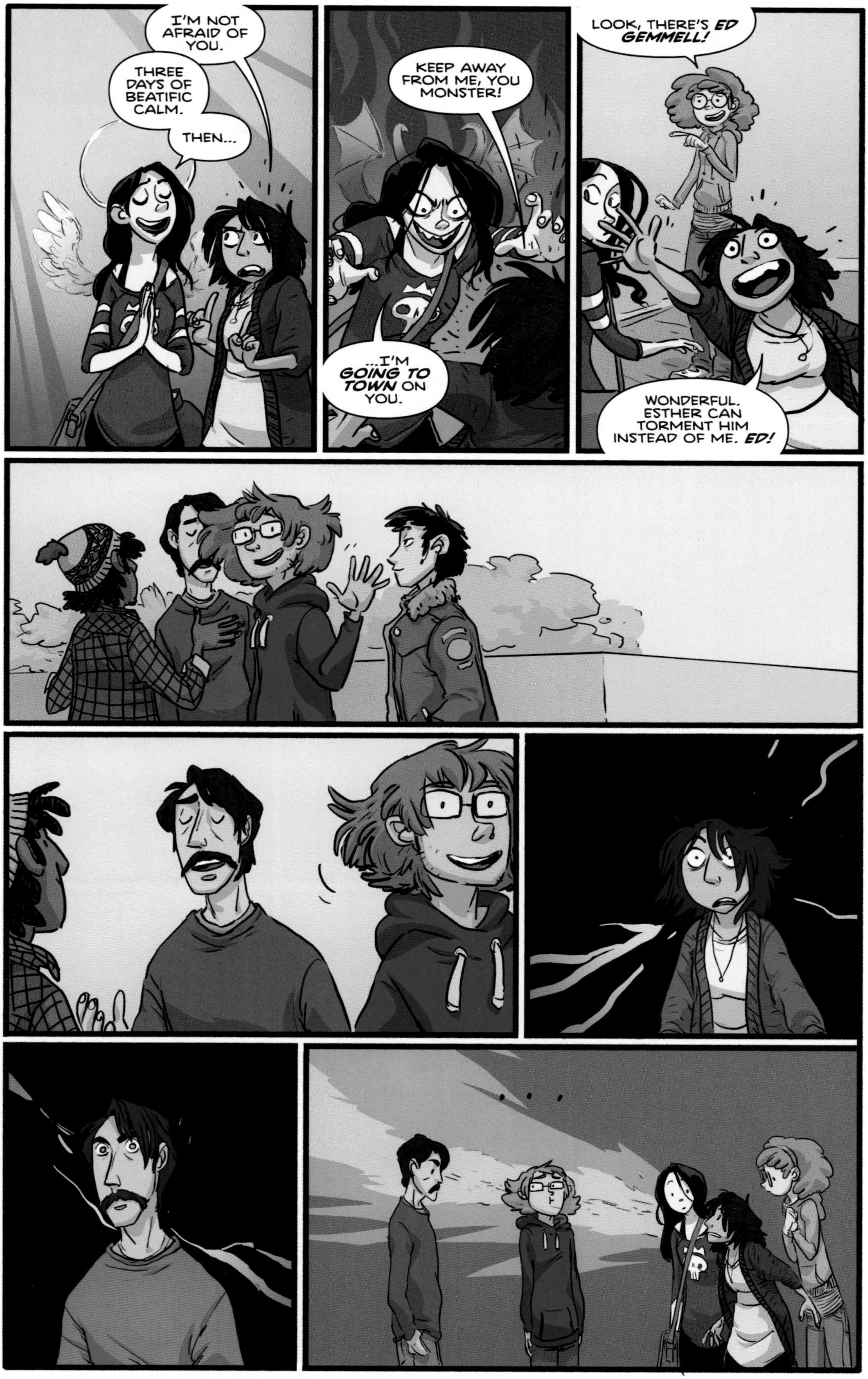
I'M NOT AFRAID OF YOU.
THREE DAYS OF BEATIFIC CALM.
THEN...
KEEP AWAY FROM ME, YOU MONSTER!
...I'M GOING TO TOWN ON YOU.
LOOK, THERE'S ED GEMMELL!
WONDERFUL. ESTHER CAN TORMENT HIM INSTEAD OF ME. ED!
...

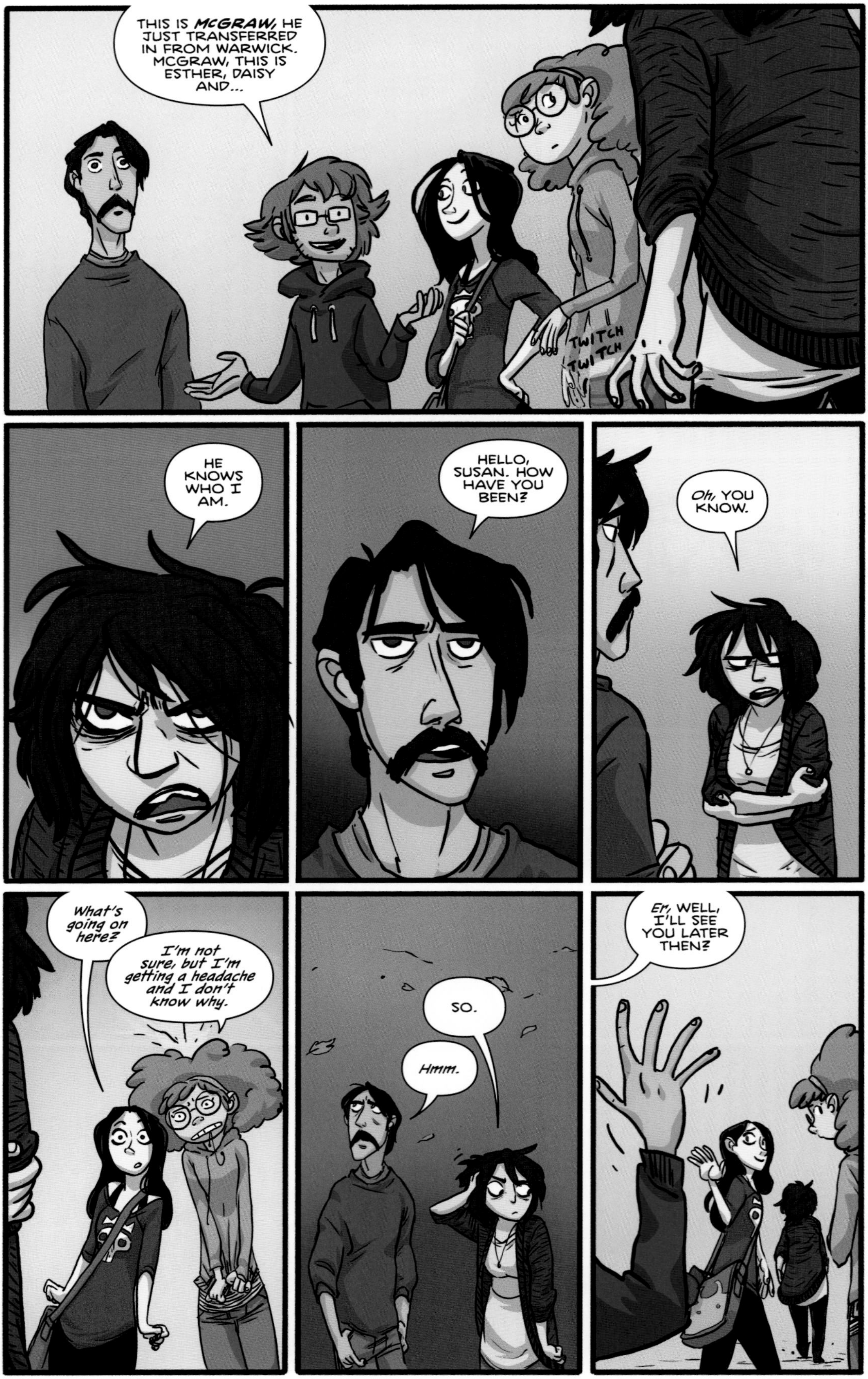
THIS IS McGRAW, HE JUST TRANSFERRED IN FROM WARWICK. MCGRAW, THIS IS ESTHER, DAISY AND...
TWITCH TWITCH
HE KNOWS WHO I AM.
HELLO, SUSAN. HOW HAVE YOU BEEN?
Oh, YOU KNOW.
What's going on here?
I'm not sure, but I'm getting a headache and I don't know why.
SO.
Hmm.
Er, WELL, I'LL SEE YOU LATER THEN?

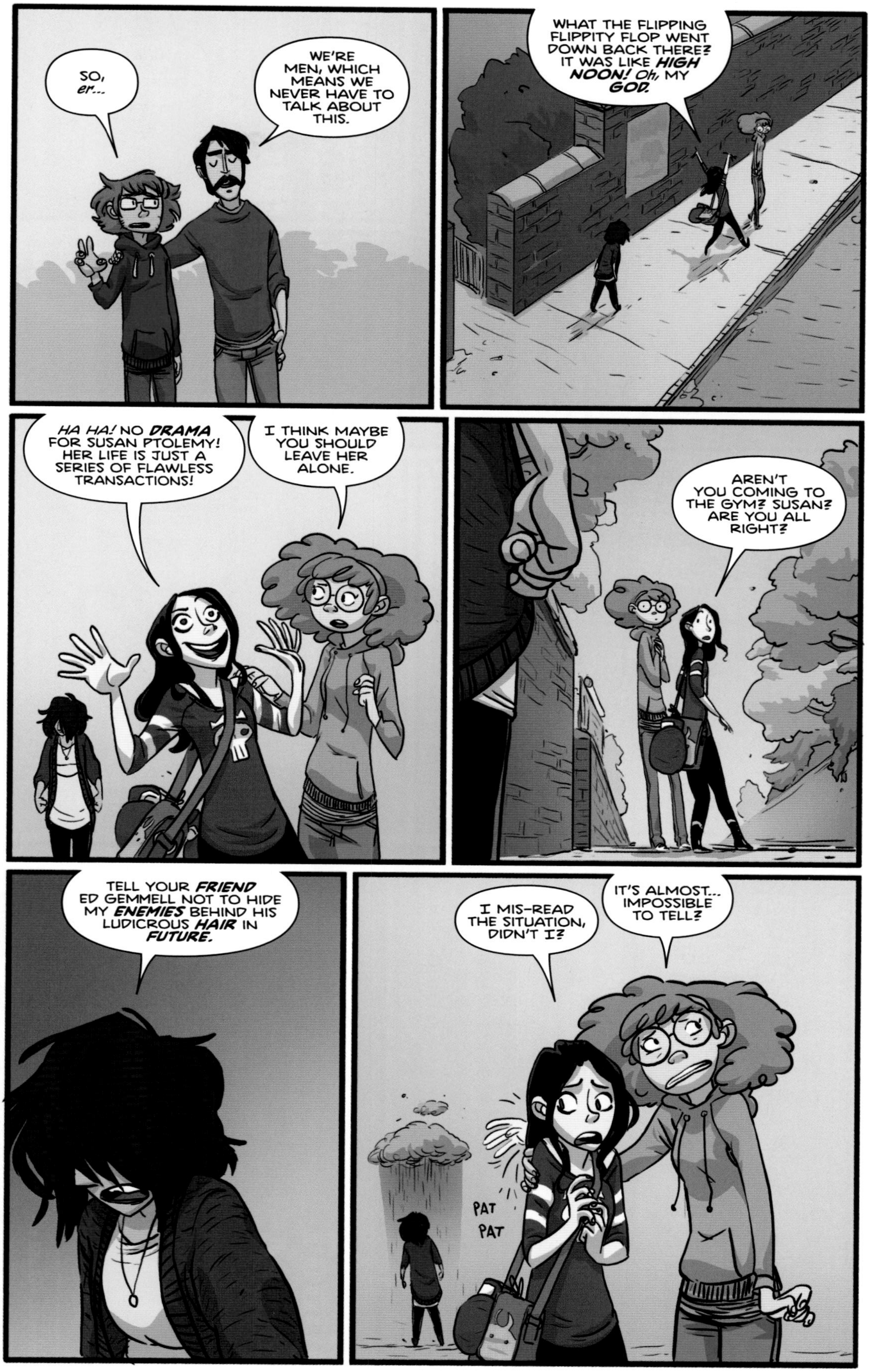
SO, er...
WE'RE MEN, WHICH MEANS WE NEVER HAVE TO TALK ABOUT THIS.
WHAT THE FLIPPING FLIPPITY FLOP WENT DOWN BACK THERE? IT WAS LIKE HIGH NOON! Oh, MY GOD.
HA HA! NO DRAMA FOR SUSAN PTOLEMY! HER LIFE IS JUST A SERIES OF FLAWLESS TRANSACTIONS!
I THINK MAYBE YOU SHOULD LEAVE HER ALONE.
AREN'T YOU COMING TO THE GYM? SUSAN? ARE YOU ALL RIGHT?
TELL YOUR FRIEND ED GEMMELL NOT TO HIDE MY ENEMIES BEHIND HIS LUDICROUS HAIR IN FUTURE.
I MIS-READ THE SITUATION, DIDN'T I?
IT'S ALMOST... IMPOSSIBLE TO TELL?
PAT
PAT

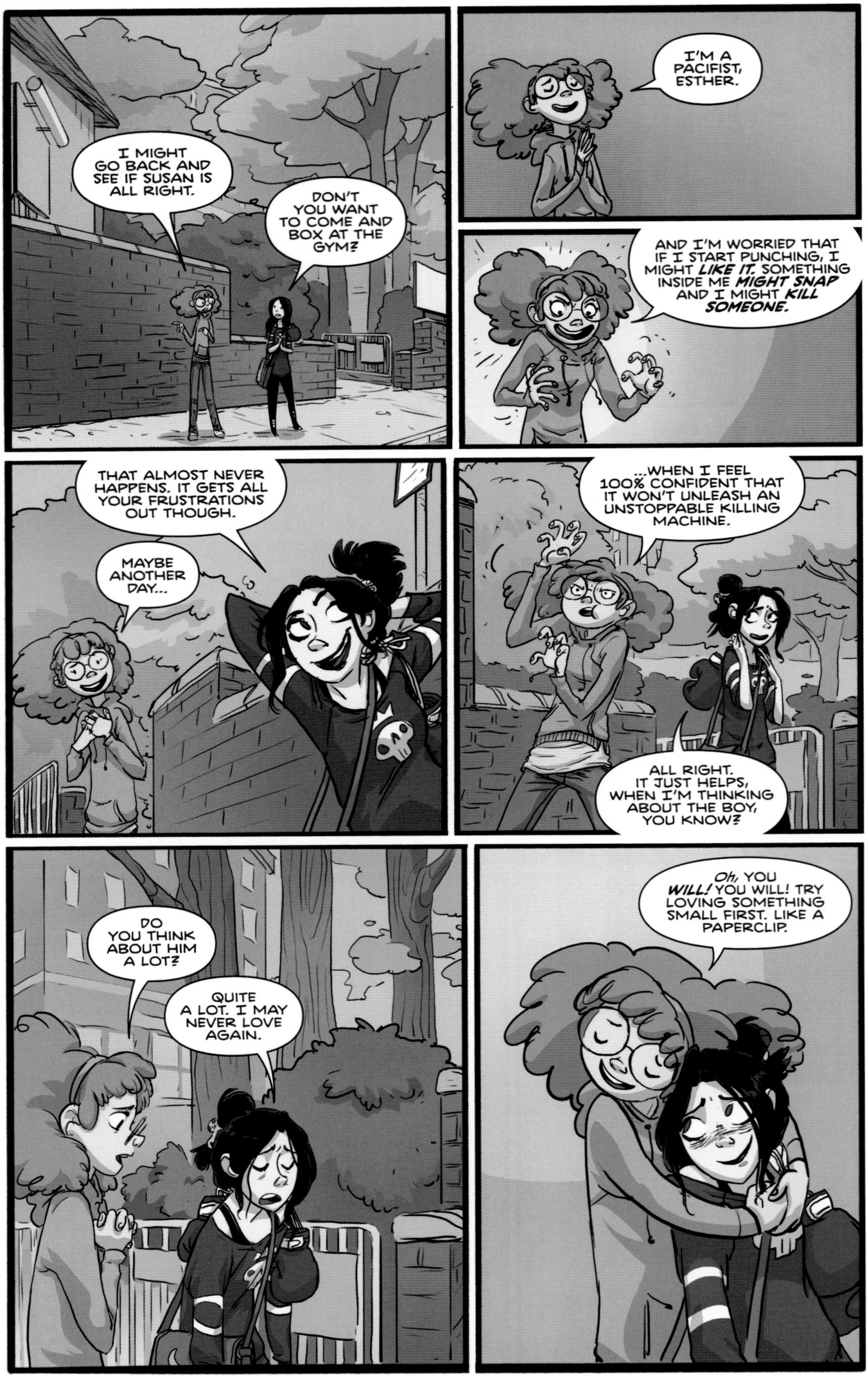
I MIGHT GO BACK AND SEE IF SUSAN IS ALL RIGHT.
DON'T YOU WANT TO COME AND BOX AT THE GYM?
I'M A PACIFIST, ESTHER.
AND I'M WORRIED THAT IF I START PUNCHING, I MIGHT *LIKE IT.* SOMETHING INSIDE ME *MIGHT SNAP* AND I MIGHT *KILL SOMEONE.*
THAT ALMOST NEVER HAPPENS. IT GETS ALL YOUR FRUSTRATIONS OUT THOUGH.
MAYBE ANOTHER DAY...
...WHEN I FEEL 100% CONFIDENT THAT IT WON'T UNLEASH AN UNSTOPPABLE KILLING MACHINE.
ALL RIGHT. IT JUST HELPS, WHEN I'M THINKING ABOUT THE BOY, YOU KNOW?
DO YOU THINK ABOUT HIM A LOT?
QUITE A LOT. I MAY NEVER LOVE AGAIN.
Oh, YOU *WILL!* YOU WILL! TRY LOVING SOMETHING SMALL FIRST. LIKE A PAPERCLIP.

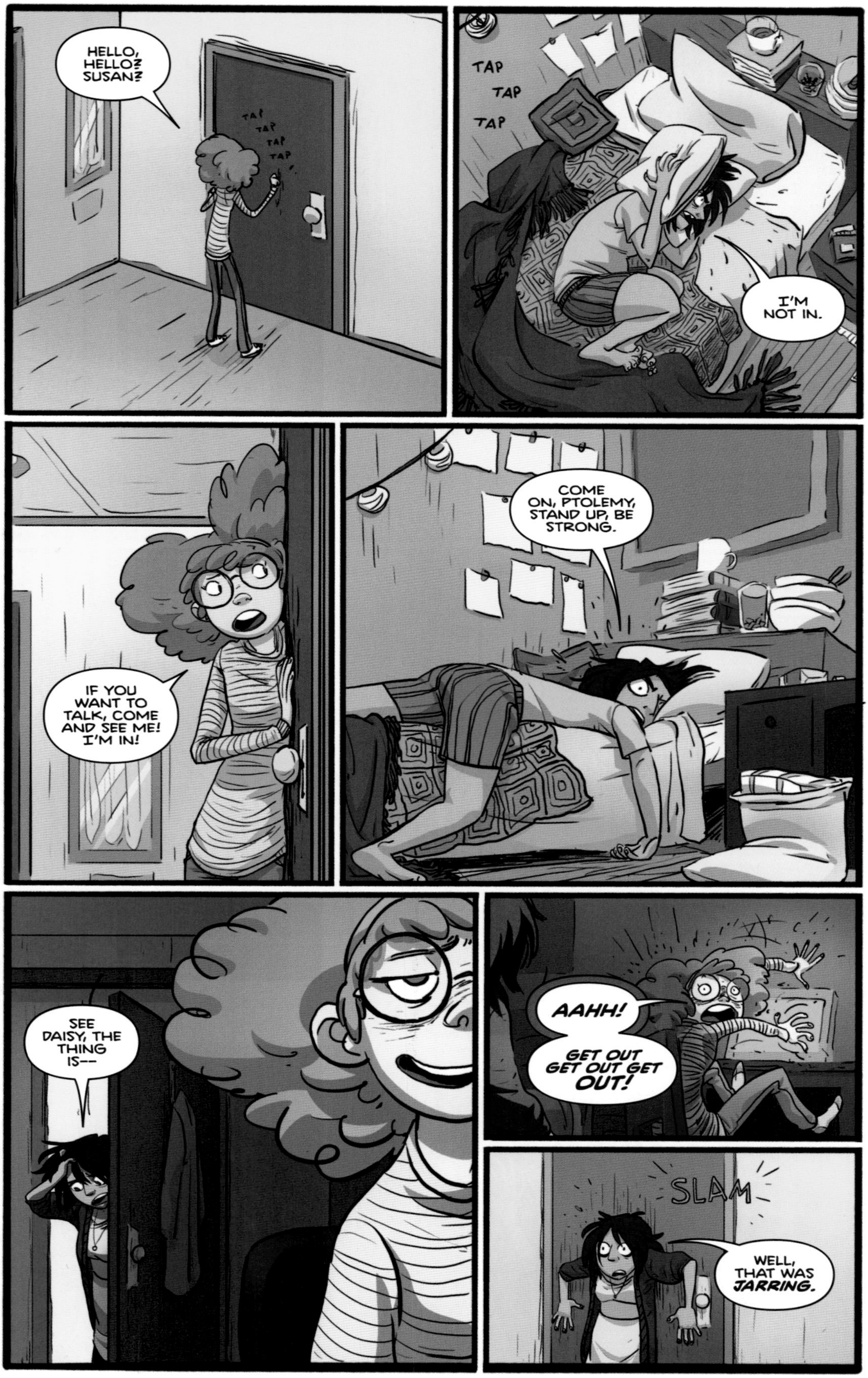
HELLO, HELLO? SUSAN?
TAP TAP TAP TAP
TAP TAP TAP
I'M NOT IN.
IF YOU WANT TO TALK, COME AND SEE ME! I'M IN!
COME ON, PTOLEMY, STAND UP, BE STRONG.
SEE DAISY, THE THING IS--
AAHH!
GET OUT GET OUT GET OUT!
SLAM
WELL, THAT WAS JARRING.

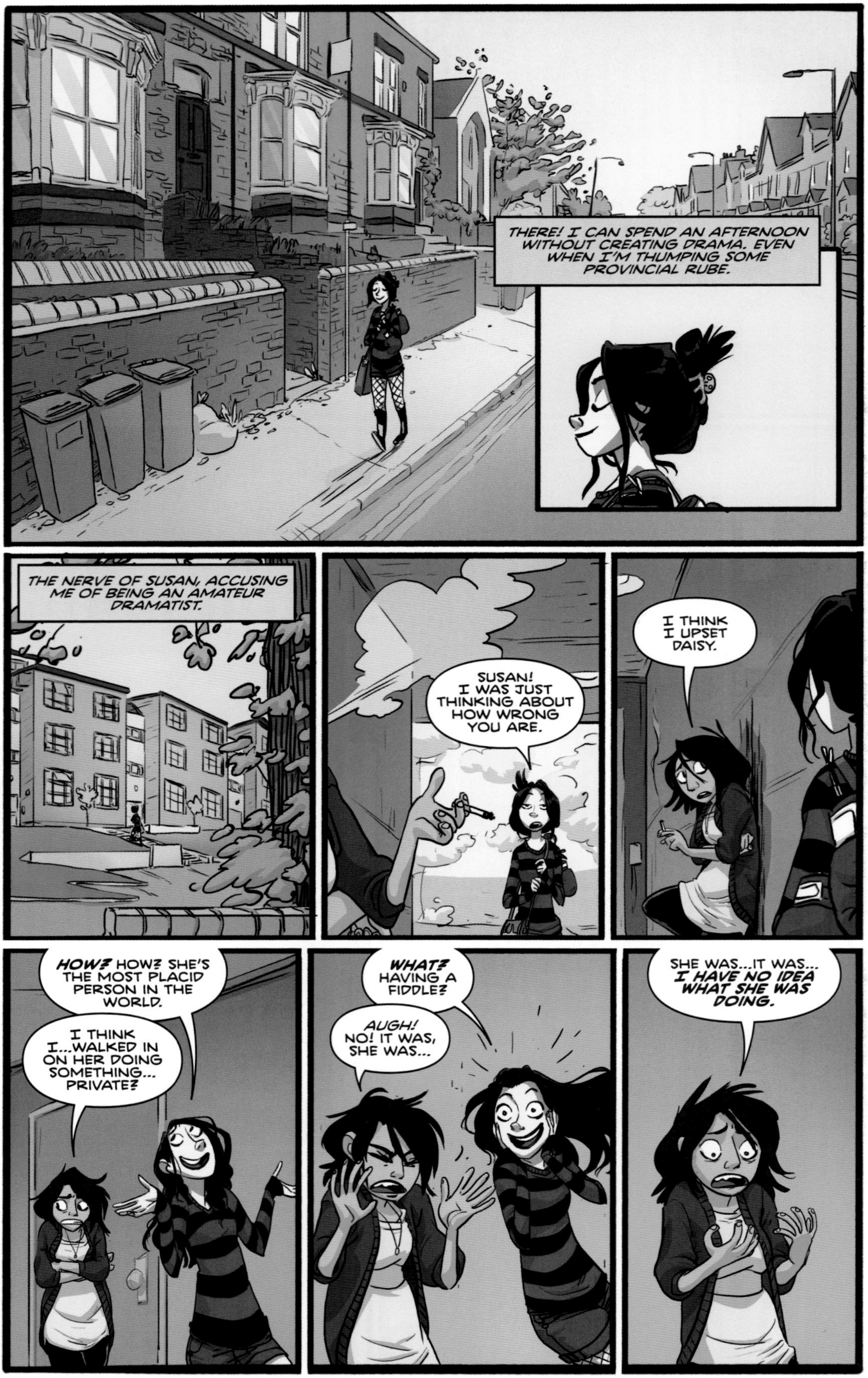
THERE! I CAN SPEND AN AFTERNOON WITHOUT CREATING DRAMA. EVEN WHEN I'M THUMPING SOME PROVINCIAL RUBE.
THE NERVE OF SUSAN, ACCUSING ME OF BEING AN AMATEUR DRAMATIST.
SUSAN! I WAS JUST THINKING ABOUT HOW WRONG YOU ARE.
I THINK I UPSET DAISY.
HOW? HOW? SHE'S THE MOST PLACID PERSON IN THE WORLD.
I THINK I...WALKED IN ON HER DOING SOMETHING... PRIVATE?
WHAT? HAVING A FIDDLE?
AUGH! NO! IT WAS, SHE WAS...
SHE WAS...IT WAS... I HAVE NO IDEA WHAT SHE WAS DOING.

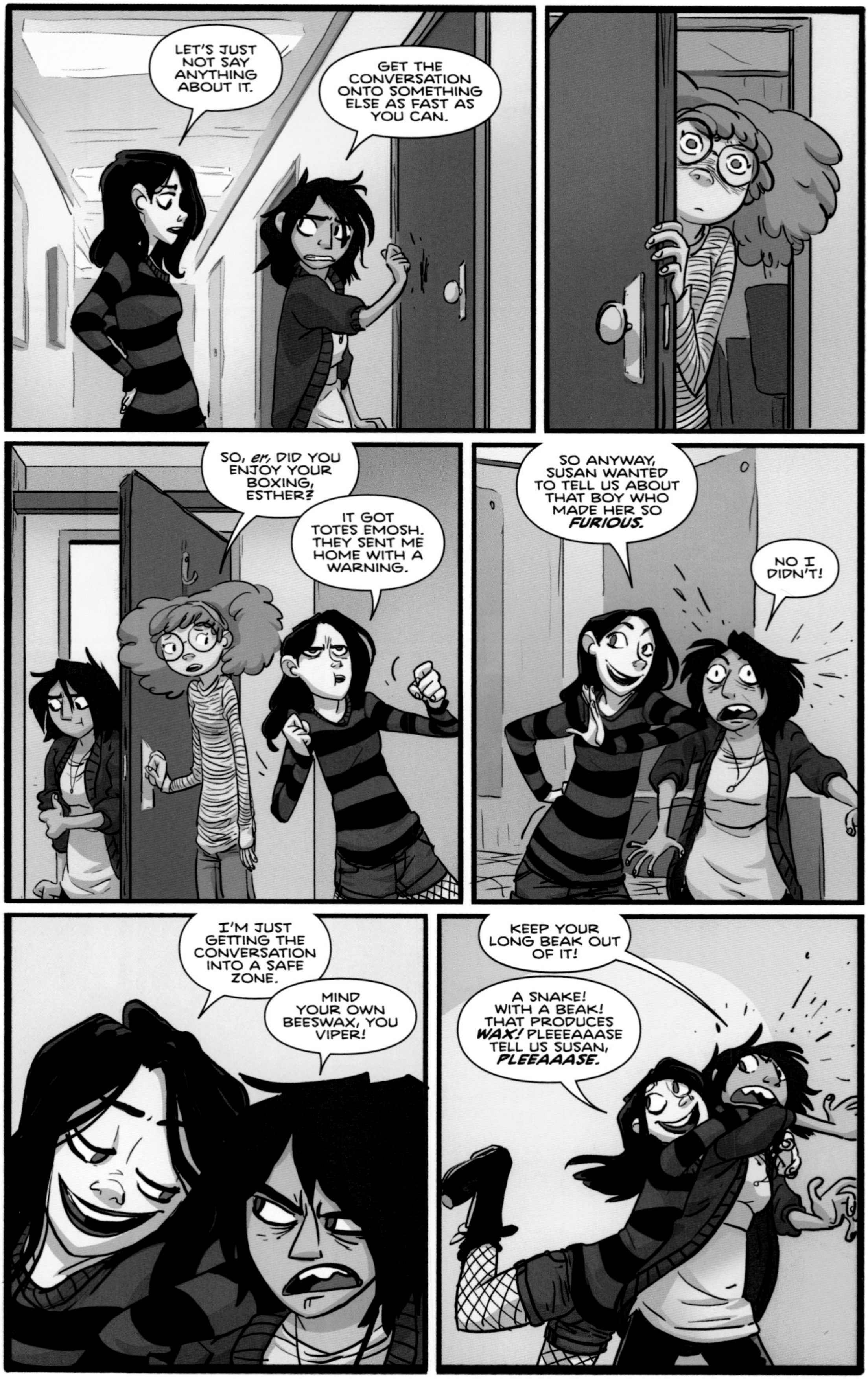
LET'S JUST NOT SAY ANYTHING ABOUT IT.
GET THE CONVERSATION ONTO SOMETHING ELSE AS FAST AS YOU CAN.
SO, *ER*, DID YOU ENJOY YOUR BOXING, ESTHER?
IT GOT TOTES EMOSH. THEY SENT ME HOME WITH A WARNING.
SO ANYWAY, SUSAN WANTED TO TELL US ABOUT THAT BOY WHO MADE HER SO ***FURIOUS.***
NO I DIDN'T!
I'M JUST GETTING THE CONVERSATION INTO A SAFE ZONE.
MIND YOUR OWN BEESWAX, YOU VIPER!
KEEP YOUR LONG BEAK OUT OF IT!
A SNAKE! WITH A BEAK! THAT PRODUCES ***WAX!*** PLEEEAAASE TELL US SUSAN, ***PLEEAAAASE.***

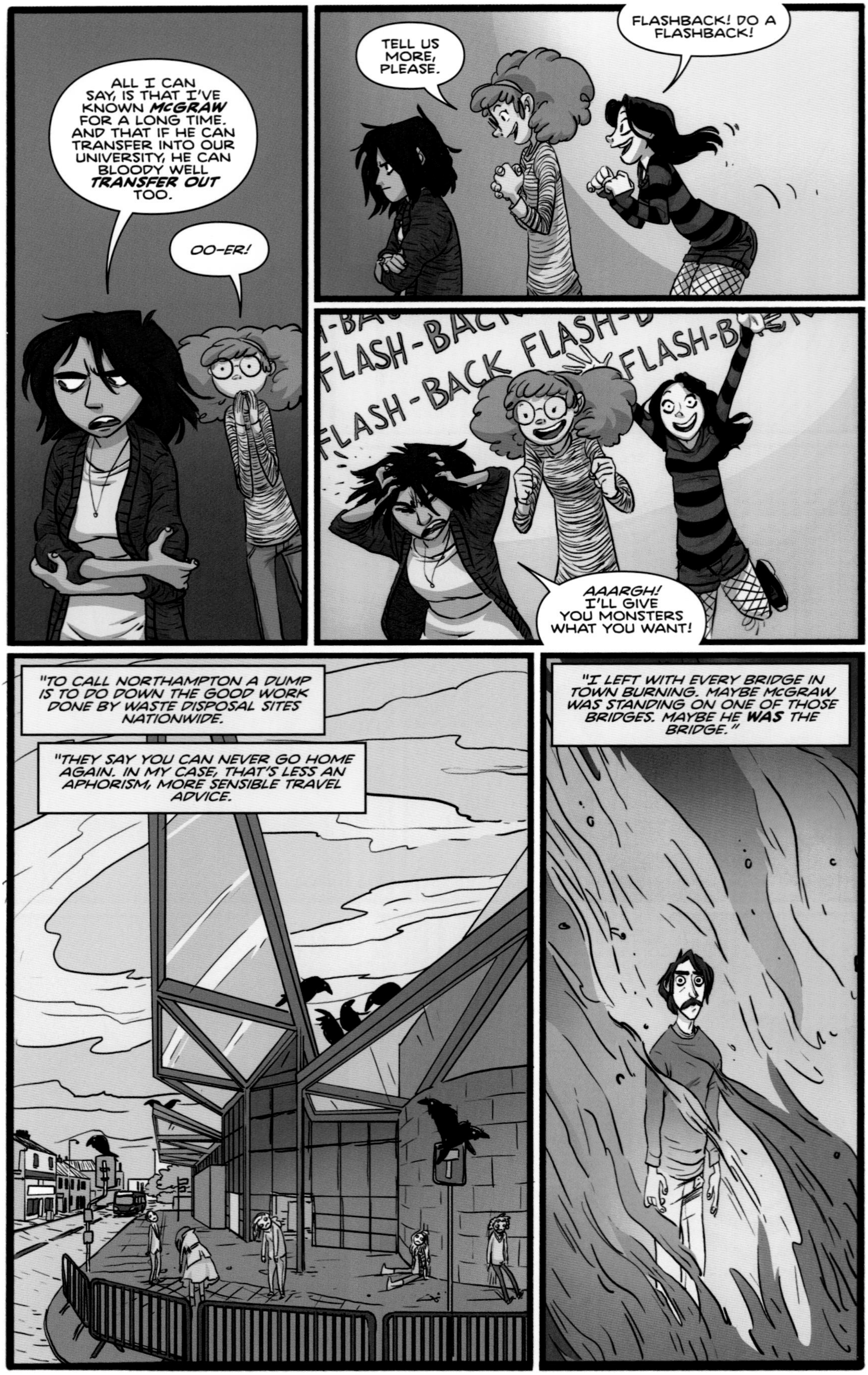
ALL I CAN SAY, IS THAT I'VE KNOWN MCGRAW FOR A LONG TIME. AND THAT IF HE CAN TRANSFER INTO OUR UNIVERSITY, HE CAN BLOODY WELL TRANSFER OUT TOO.
OO-ER!
TELL US MORE, PLEASE.
FLASHBACK! DO A FLASHBACK!
FLASH-BACK FLASH-BACK FLASH-BACK
AAARGH! I'LL GIVE YOU MONSTERS WHAT YOU WANT!
"TO CALL NORTHAMPTON A DUMP IS TO DO DOWN THE GOOD WORK DONE BY WASTE DISPOSAL SITES NATIONWIDE.
"THEY SAY YOU CAN NEVER GO HOME AGAIN. IN MY CASE, THAT'S LESS AN APHORISM, MORE SENSIBLE TRAVEL ADVICE.
"I LEFT WITH EVERY BRIDGE IN TOWN BURNING. MAYBE MCGRAW WAS STANDING ON ONE OF THOSE BRIDGES. MAYBE HE WAS THE BRIDGE."

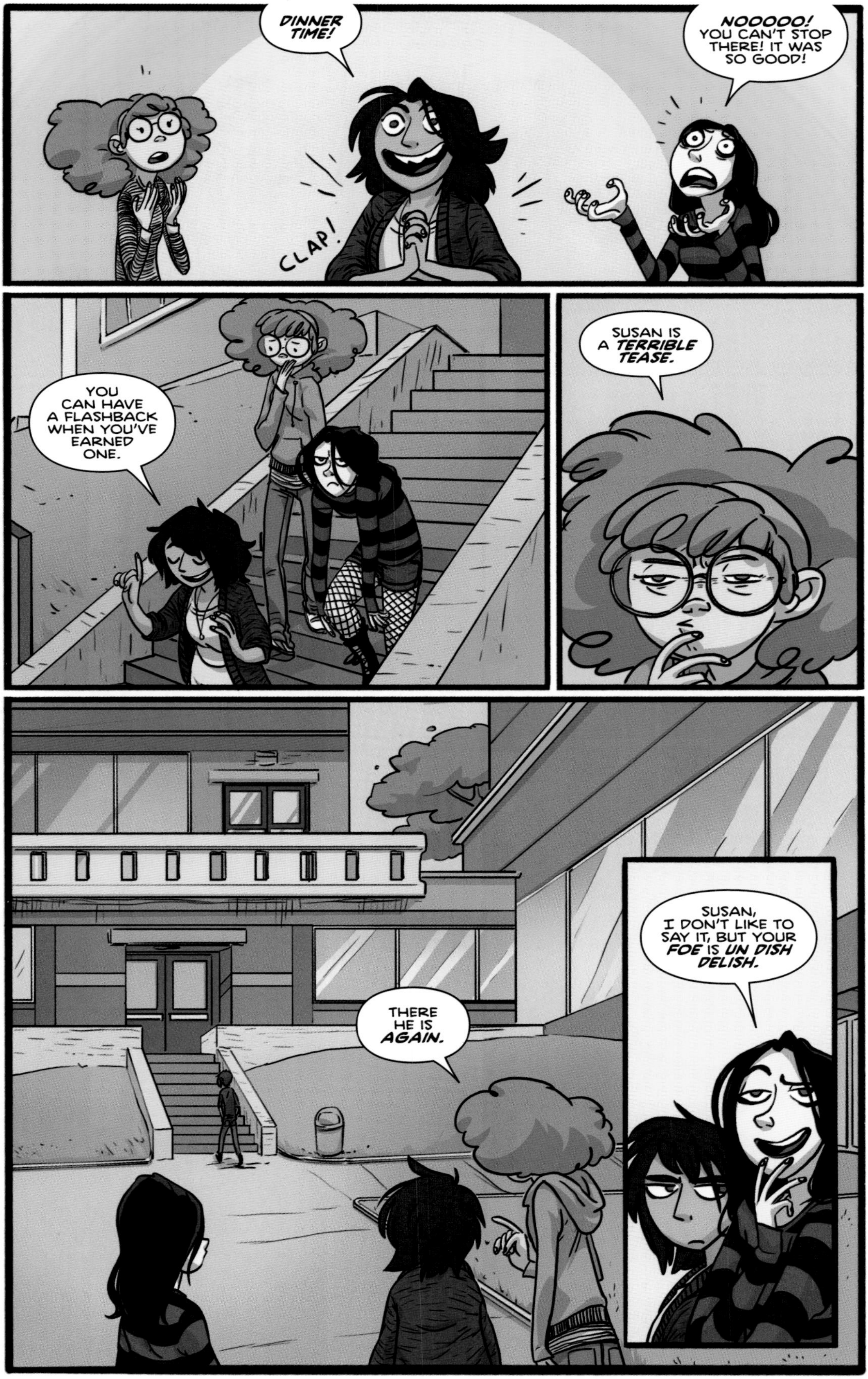
DINNER TIME!
NOOOOO! YOU CAN'T STOP THERE! IT WAS SO GOOD!
CLAP!
YOU CAN HAVE A FLASHBACK WHEN YOU'VE EARNED ONE.
SUSAN IS A TERRIBLE TEASE.
THERE HE IS AGAIN.
SUSAN, I DON'T LIKE TO SAY IT, BUT YOUR FOE IS UN DISH DELISH.

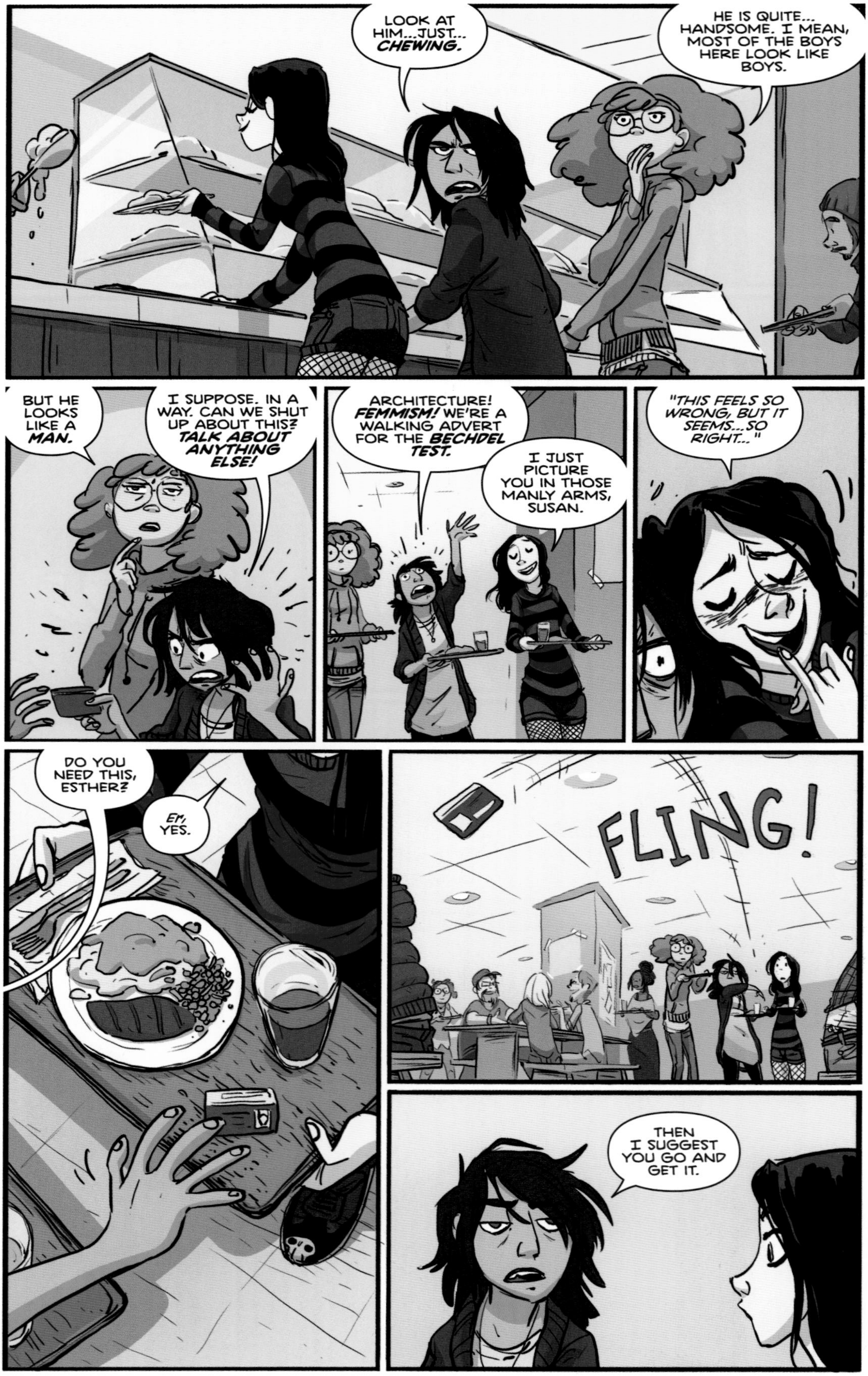
LOOK AT HIM... JUST... CHEWING.
HE IS QUITE... HANDSOME. I MEAN, MOST OF THE BOYS HERE LOOK LIKE BOYS.
BUT HE LOOKS LIKE A MAN.
I SUPPOSE. IN A WAY. CAN WE SHUT UP ABOUT THIS? TALK ABOUT ANYTHING ELSE!
ARCHITECTURE! FEMMISM! WE'RE A WALKING ADVERT FOR THE BECHDEL TEST.
I JUST PICTURE YOU IN THOSE MANLY ARMS, SUSAN.
"THIS FEELS SO WRONG, BUT IT SEEMS... SO RIGHT..."
DO YOU NEED THIS, ESTHER?
EM, YES.
FLING!
THEN I SUGGEST YOU GO AND GET IT.

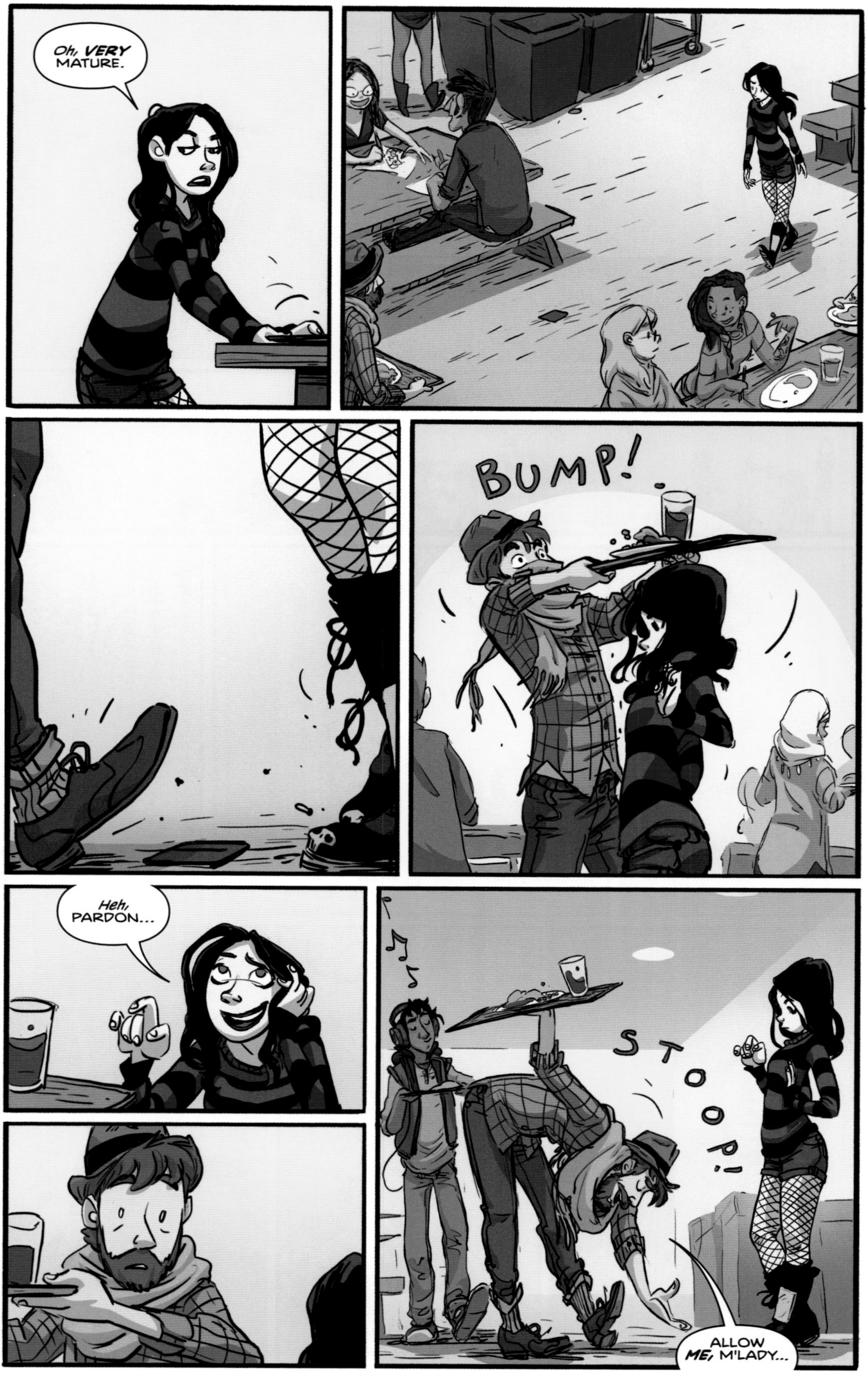
Oh, VERY MATURE.
BUMP!
Heh, PARDON...
STOOP!
ALLOW ME, M'LADY...

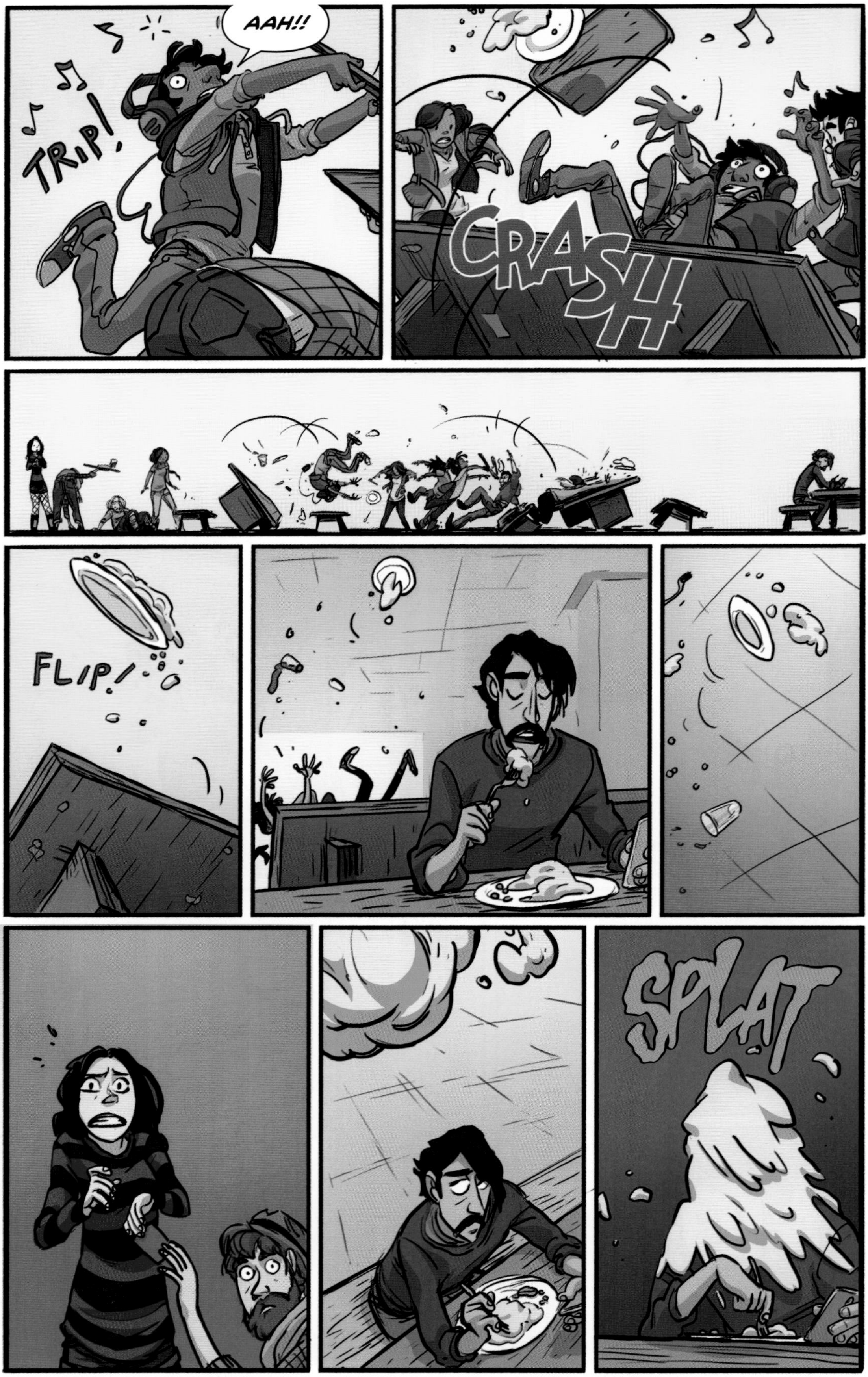
AAH!!
TRIP!
CRASH
FLIP!
SPLAT

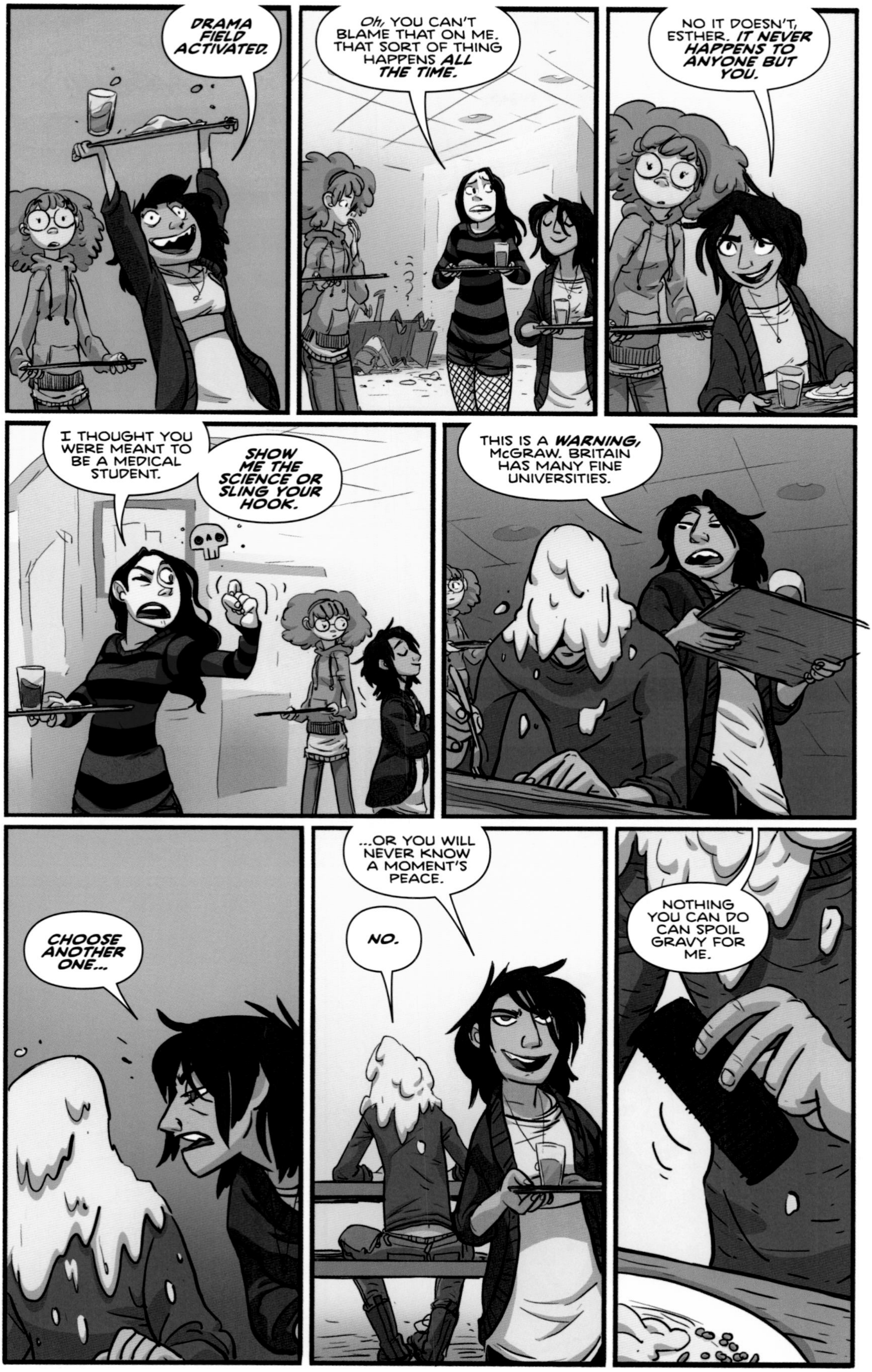
DRAMA FIELD ACTIVATED.
Oh, YOU CAN'T BLAME THAT ON ME. THAT SORT OF THING HAPPENS ALL THE TIME.
NO IT DOESN'T, ESTHER. IT NEVER HAPPENS TO ANYONE BUT YOU.
I THOUGHT YOU WERE MEANT TO BE A MEDICAL STUDENT.
SHOW ME THE SCIENCE OR SLING YOUR HOOK.
THIS IS A WARNING, McGRAW. BRITAIN HAS MANY FINE UNIVERSITIES.
CHOOSE ANOTHER ONE...
...OR YOU WILL NEVER KNOW A MOMENT'S PEACE.
NO.
NOTHING YOU CAN DO CAN SPOIL GRAVY FOR ME.

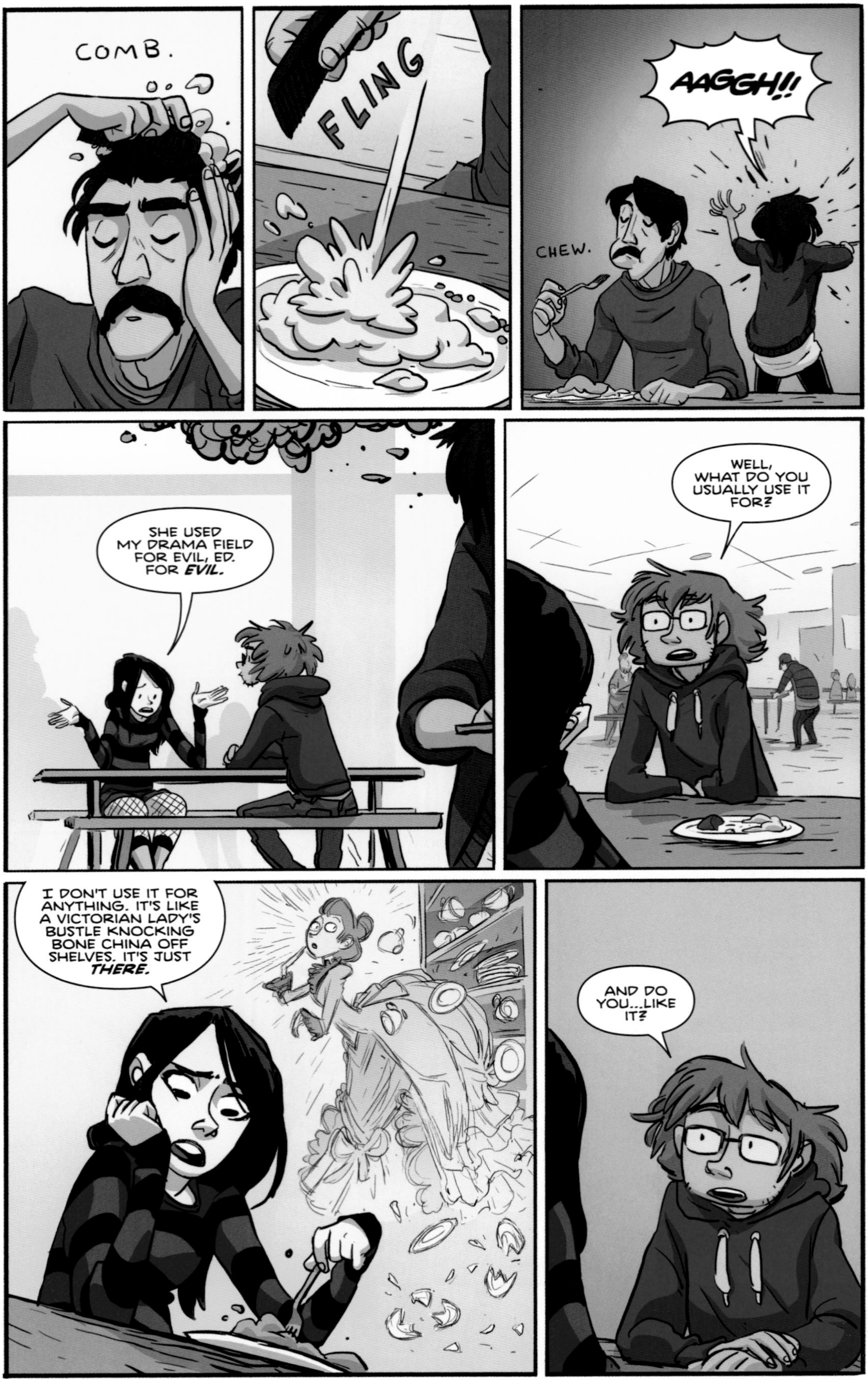
COMB.
FLING
AAGGH!!
CHEW.
SHE USED MY DRAMA FIELD FOR EVIL, ED. FOR *EVIL.*
WELL, WHAT DO YOU USUALLY USE IT FOR?
I DON'T USE IT FOR ANYTHING. IT'S LIKE A VICTORIAN LADY'S BUSTLE KNOCKING BONE CHINA OFF SHELVES. IT'S JUST *THERE.*
AND DO YOU...LIKE IT?

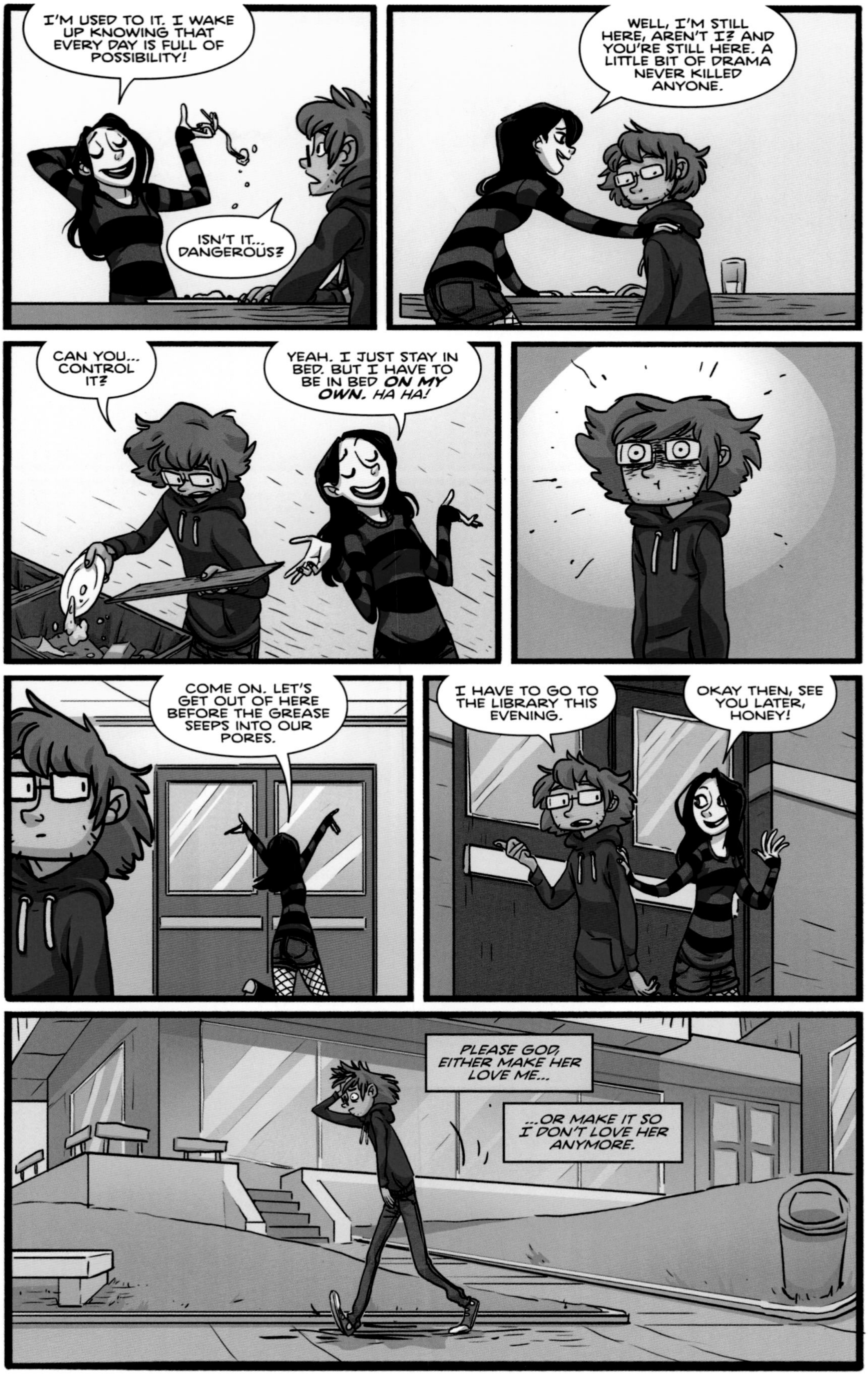
I'M USED TO IT. I WAKE UP KNOWING THAT EVERY DAY IS FULL OF POSSIBILITY!
ISN'T IT... DANGEROUS?
WELL, I'M STILL HERE, AREN'T I? AND YOU'RE STILL HERE. A LITTLE BIT OF DRAMA NEVER KILLED ANYONE.
CAN YOU... CONTROL IT?
YEAH. I JUST STAY IN BED. BUT I HAVE TO BE IN BED *ON MY OWN.* HA HA!
COME ON. LET'S GET OUT OF HERE BEFORE THE GREASE SEEPS INTO OUR PORES.
I HAVE TO GO TO THE LIBRARY THIS EVENING.
OKAY THEN, SEE YOU LATER, HONEY!
PLEASE GOD, EITHER MAKE HER LOVE ME...
...OR MAKE IT SO I DON'T LOVE HER ANYMORE.

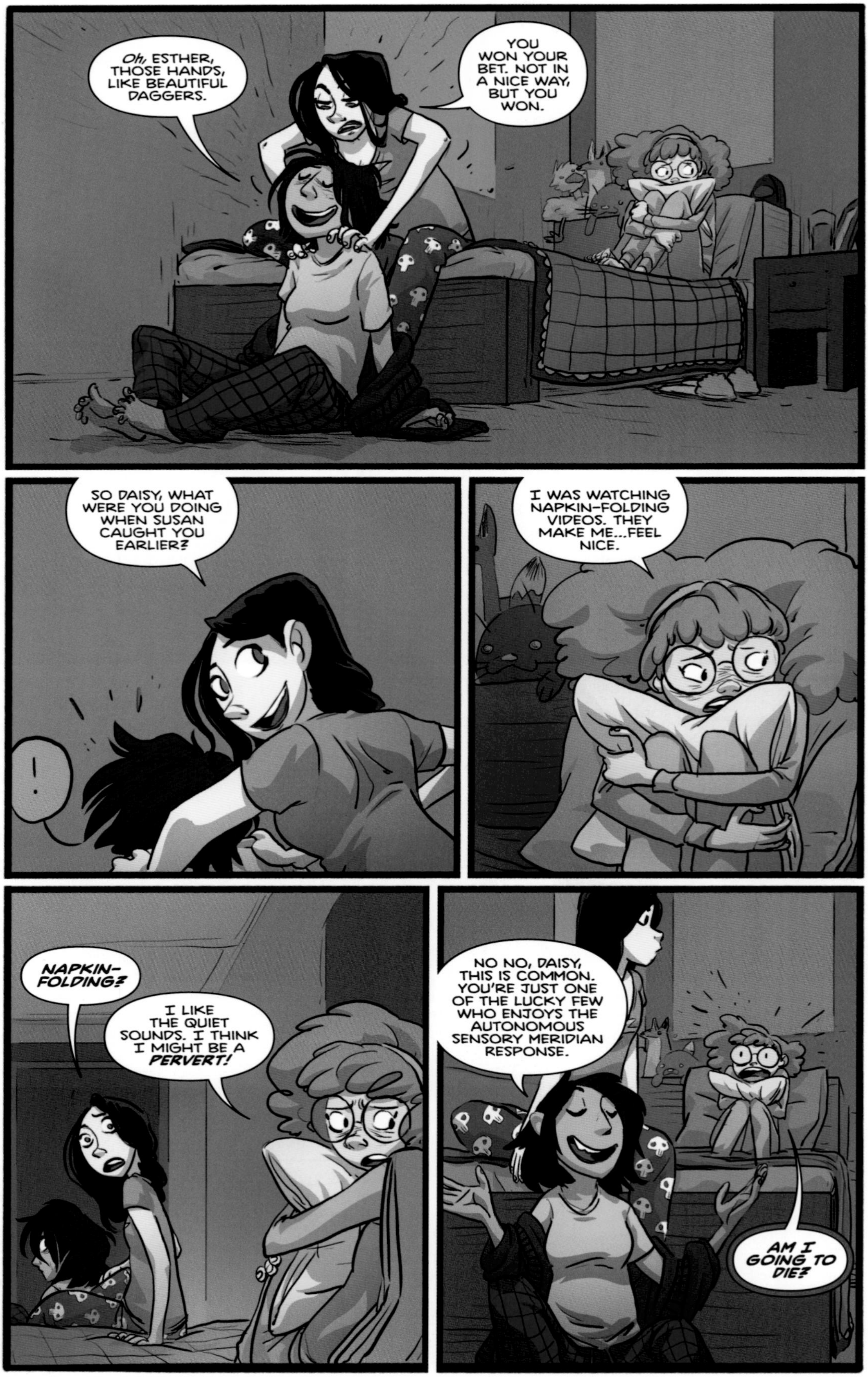

Oh, ESTHER, THOSE HANDS, LIKE BEAUTIFUL DAGGERS.
YOU WON YOUR BET. NOT IN A NICE WAY, BUT YOU WON.
SO DAISY, WHAT WERE YOU DOING WHEN SUSAN CAUGHT YOU EARLIER?
!
I WAS WATCHING NAPKIN-FOLDING VIDEOS. THEY MAKE ME...FEEL NICE.
NAPKIN-FOLDING?
I LIKE THE QUIET SOUNDS. I THINK I MIGHT BE A ***PERVERT!***
NO NO, DAISY, THIS IS COMMON. YOU'RE JUST ONE OF THE LUCKY FEW WHO ENJOYS THE AUTONOMOUS SENSORY MERIDIAN RESPONSE.
AM I GOING TO DIE?

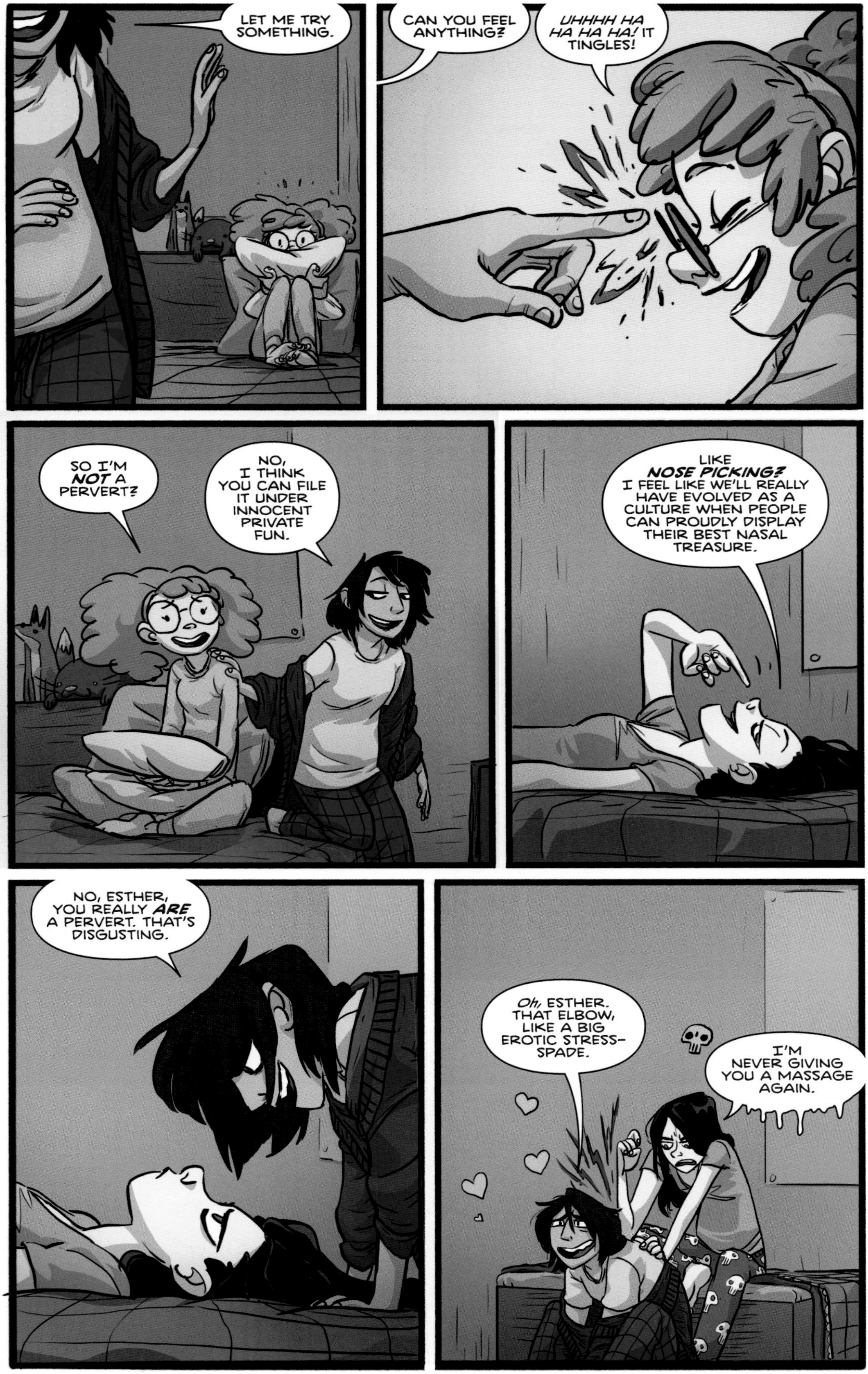
LET ME TRY SOMETHING.
CAN YOU FEEL ANYTHING?
UHHHH HA HA HA HA! IT TINGLES!
SO I'M NOT A PERVERT?
NO, I THINK YOU CAN FILE IT UNDER INNOCENT PRIVATE FUN.
LIKE NOSE PICKING? I FEEL LIKE WE'LL REALLY HAVE EVOLVED AS A CULTURE WHEN PEOPLE CAN PROUDLY DISPLAY THEIR BEST NASAL TREASURE.
NO, ESTHER, YOU REALLY ARE A PERVERT. THAT'S DISGUSTING.
Oh, ESTHER. THAT ELBOW, LIKE A BIG EROTIC STRESS-SPADE.
I'M NEVER GIVING YOU A MASSAGE AGAIN.

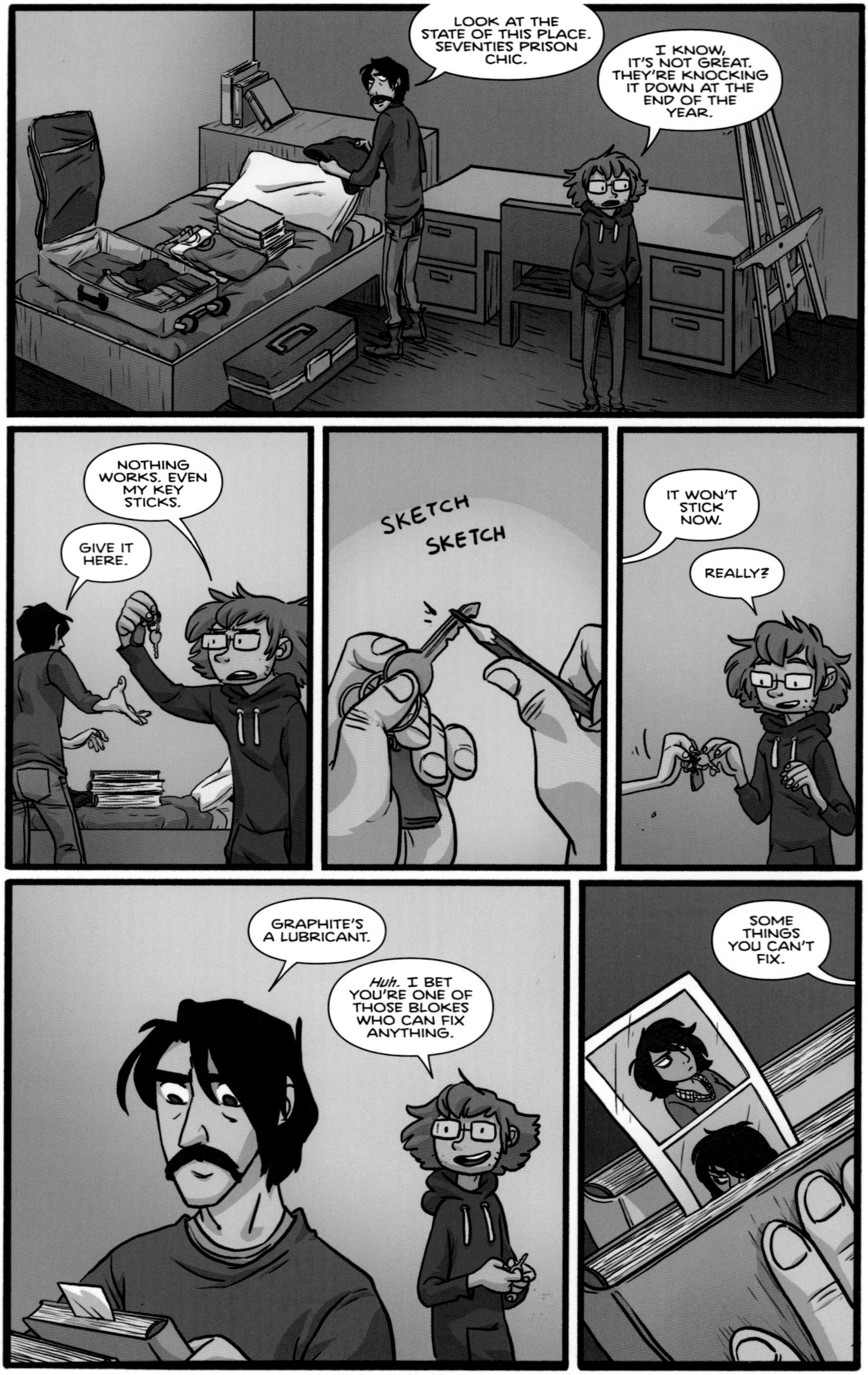

LOOK AT THE STATE OF THIS PLACE. SEVENTIES PRISON CHIC.
I KNOW, IT'S NOT GREAT. THEY'RE KNOCKING IT DOWN AT THE END OF THE YEAR.
NOTHING WORKS. EVEN MY KEY STICKS.
GIVE IT HERE.
SKETCH
SKETCH
IT WON'T STICK NOW.
REALLY?
GRAPHITE'S A LUBRICANT.
Huh. I BET YOU'RE ONE OF THOSE BLOKES WHO CAN FIX ANYTHING.
SOME THINGS YOU CAN'T FIX.

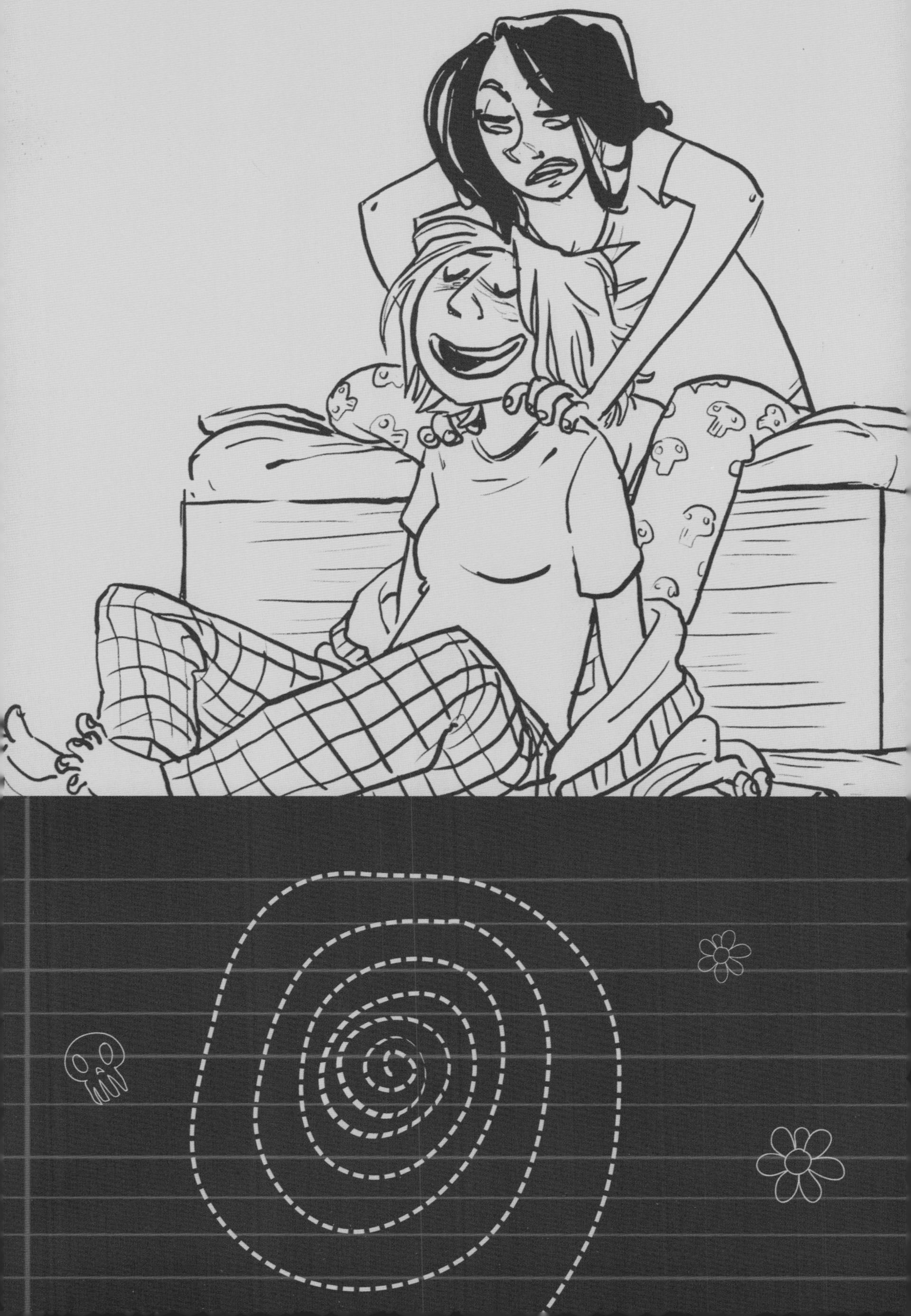

CHAPTER TWO

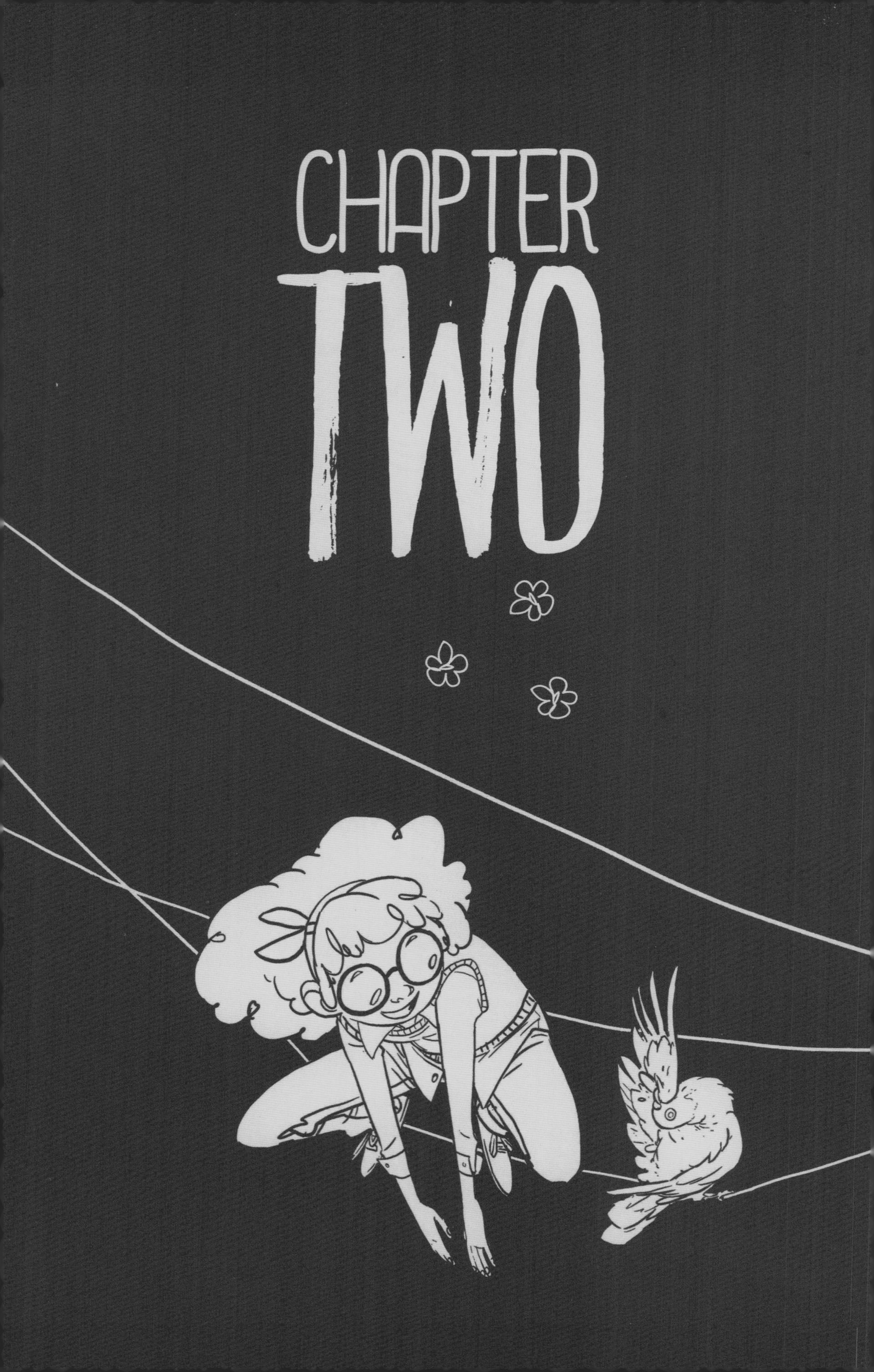

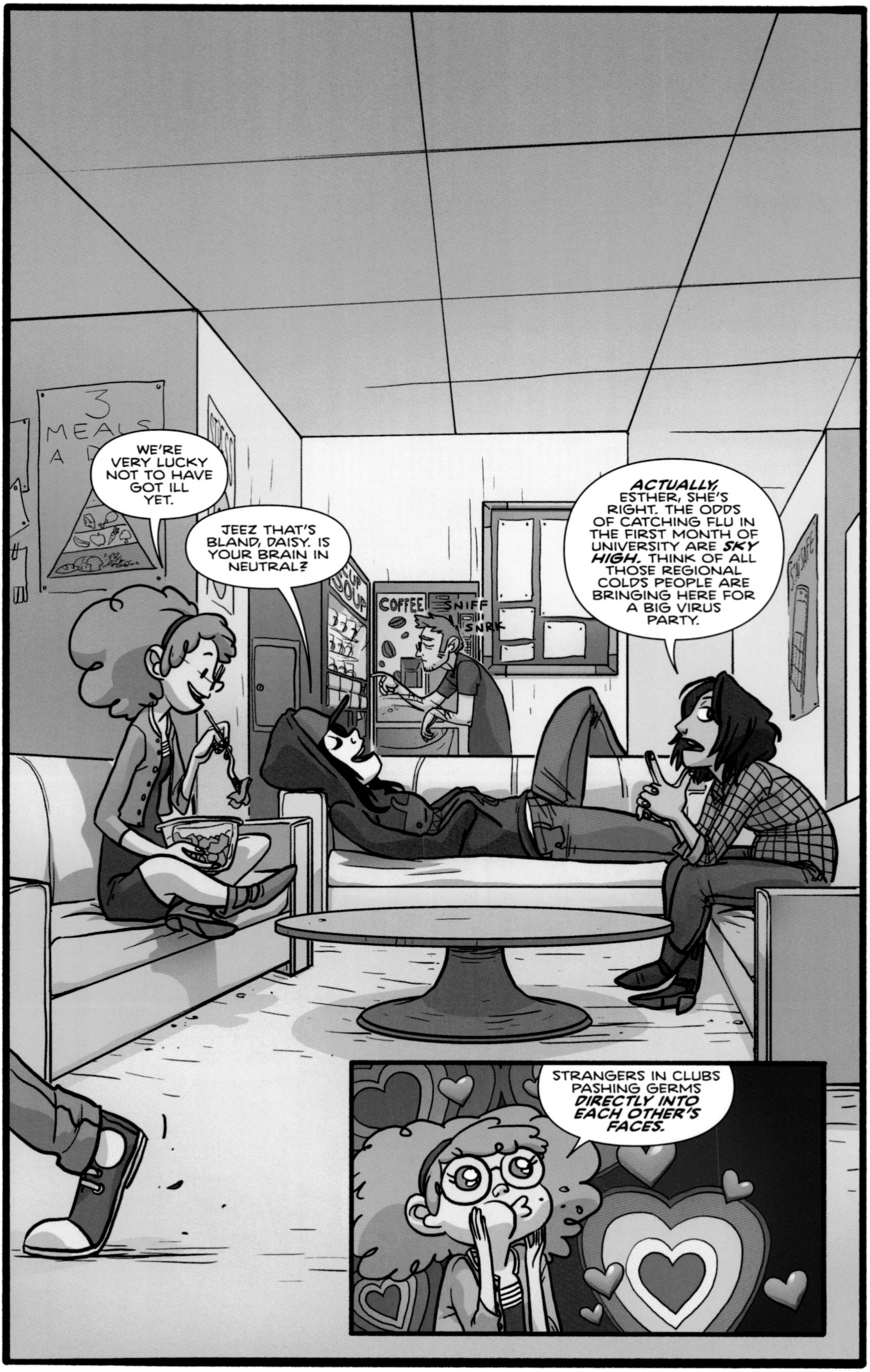
3 MEALS A D
WE'RE VERY LUCKY NOT TO HAVE GOT ILL YET.
JEEZ THAT'S BLAND, DAISY. IS YOUR BRAIN IN NEUTRAL?
CUP SOUP
COFFEE
SNIFF
SNRK
ACTUALLY, ESTHER, SHE'S RIGHT. THE ODDS OF CATCHING FLU IN THE FIRST MONTH OF UNIVERSITY ARE ***SKY HIGH.*** THINK OF ALL THOSE REGIONAL COLDS PEOPLE ARE BRINGING HERE FOR A BIG VIRUS PARTY.
STRANGERS IN CLUBS PASHING GERMS ***DIRECTLY INTO EACH OTHER'S FACES.***

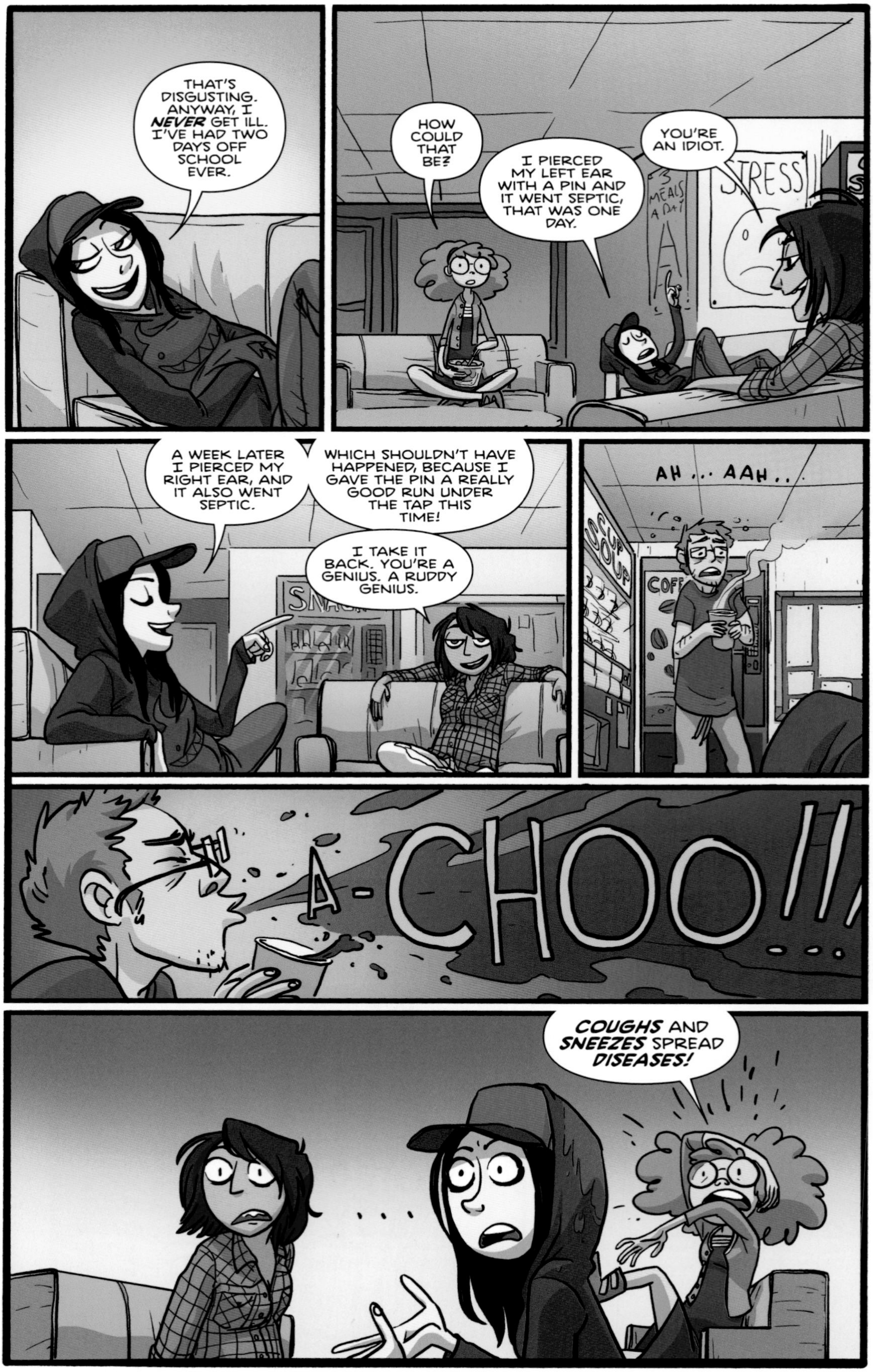
THAT'S DISGUSTING. ANYWAY, I *NEVER* GET ILL. I'VE HAD TWO DAYS OFF SCHOOL EVER.
HOW COULD THAT BE?
I PIERCED MY LEFT EAR WITH A PIN AND IT WENT SEPTIC, THAT WAS ONE DAY.
YOU'RE AN IDIOT.
3 MEALS A DAY
STRESS
A WEEK LATER I PIERCED MY RIGHT EAR, AND IT ALSO WENT SEPTIC.
WHICH SHOULDN'T HAVE HAPPENED, BECAUSE I GAVE THE PIN A REALLY GOOD RUN UNDER THE TAP THIS TIME!
I TAKE IT BACK. YOU'RE A GENIUS. A RUDDY GENIUS.
AH ... AAH ..
CUP SOUP
COFF
A-CHOO!!
COUGHS AND SNEEZES SPREAD DISEASES!
...

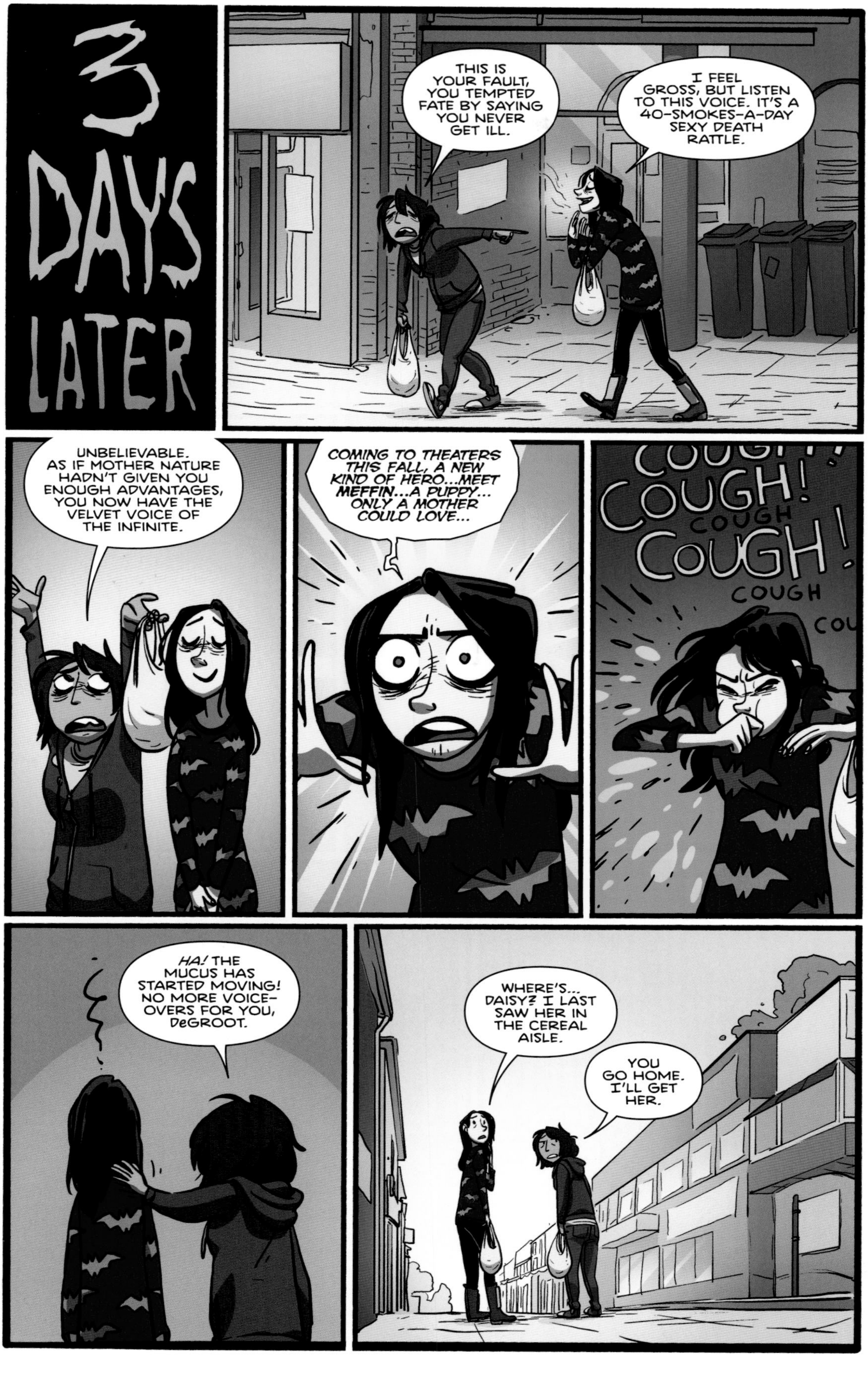
3 DAYS LATER
THIS IS YOUR FAULT, YOU TEMPTED FATE BY SAYING YOU NEVER GET ILL.
I FEEL GROSS, BUT LISTEN TO THIS VOICE. IT'S A 40-SMOKES-A-DAY SEXY DEATH RATTLE.
UNBELIEVABLE. AS IF MOTHER NATURE HADN'T GIVEN YOU ENOUGH ADVANTAGES, YOU NOW HAVE THE VELVET VOICE OF THE INFINITE.
COMING TO THEATERS THIS FALL, A NEW KIND OF HERO...MEET MEFFIN...A PUPPY... ONLY A MOTHER COULD LOVE...
COUGH! COUGH! COUGH COUGH! COUGH
HA! THE MUCUS HAS STARTED MOVING! NO MORE VOICE-OVERS FOR YOU, DeGROOT.
WHERE'S... DAISY? I LAST SAW HER IN THE CEREAL AISLE.
YOU GO HOME. I'LL GET HER.

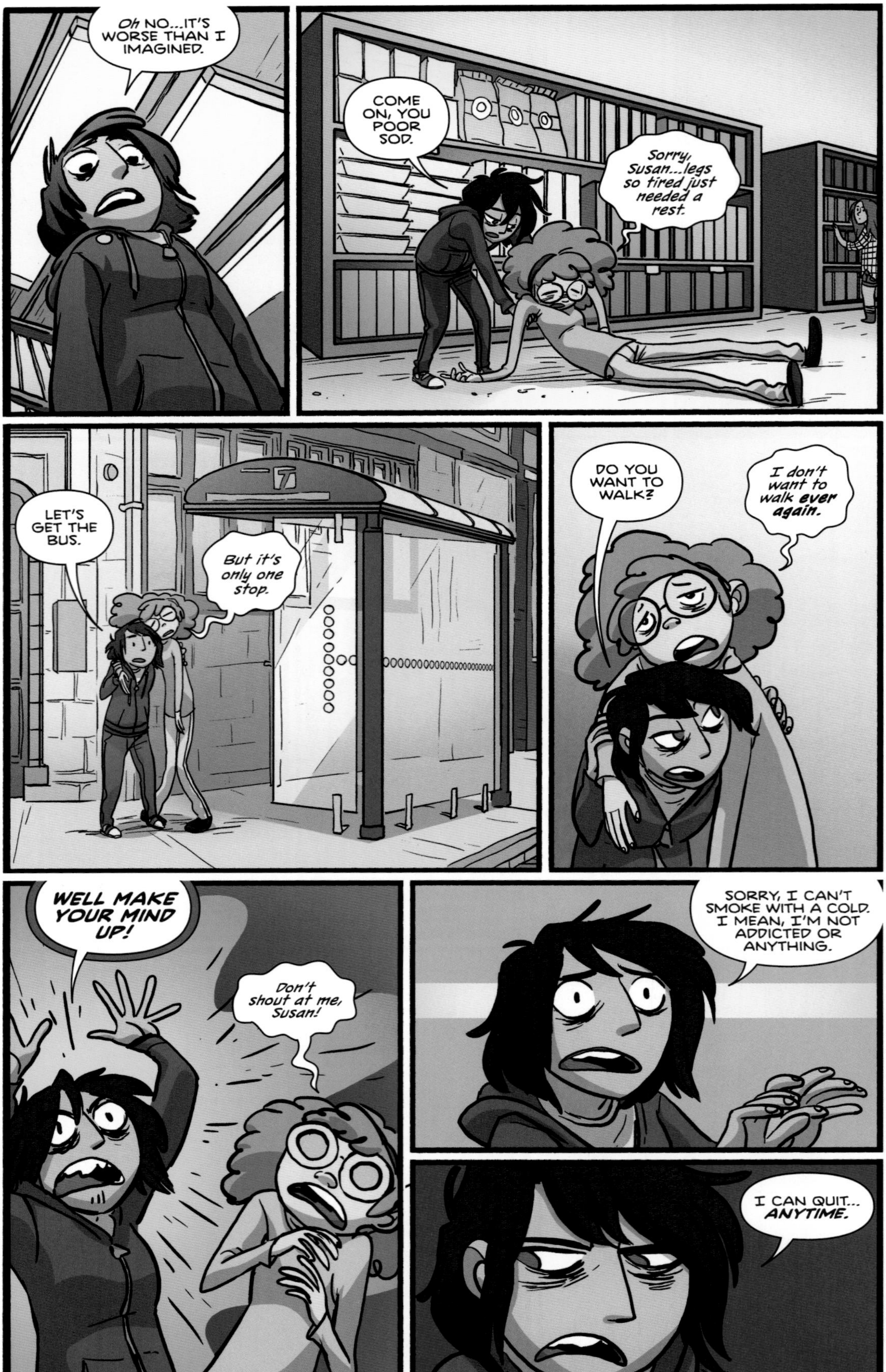
Oh NO...IT'S WORSE THAN I IMAGINED.
COME ON, YOU POOR SOD.
Sorry, Susan...legs so tired just needed a rest.
LET'S GET THE BUS.
But it's only one stop.
DO YOU WANT TO WALK?
I don't want to walk ever again.
WELL MAKE YOUR MIND UP!
Don't shout at me, Susan!
SORRY, I CAN'T SMOKE WITH A COLD. I MEAN, I'M NOT ADDICTED OR ANYTHING.
I CAN QUIT... ANYTIME.

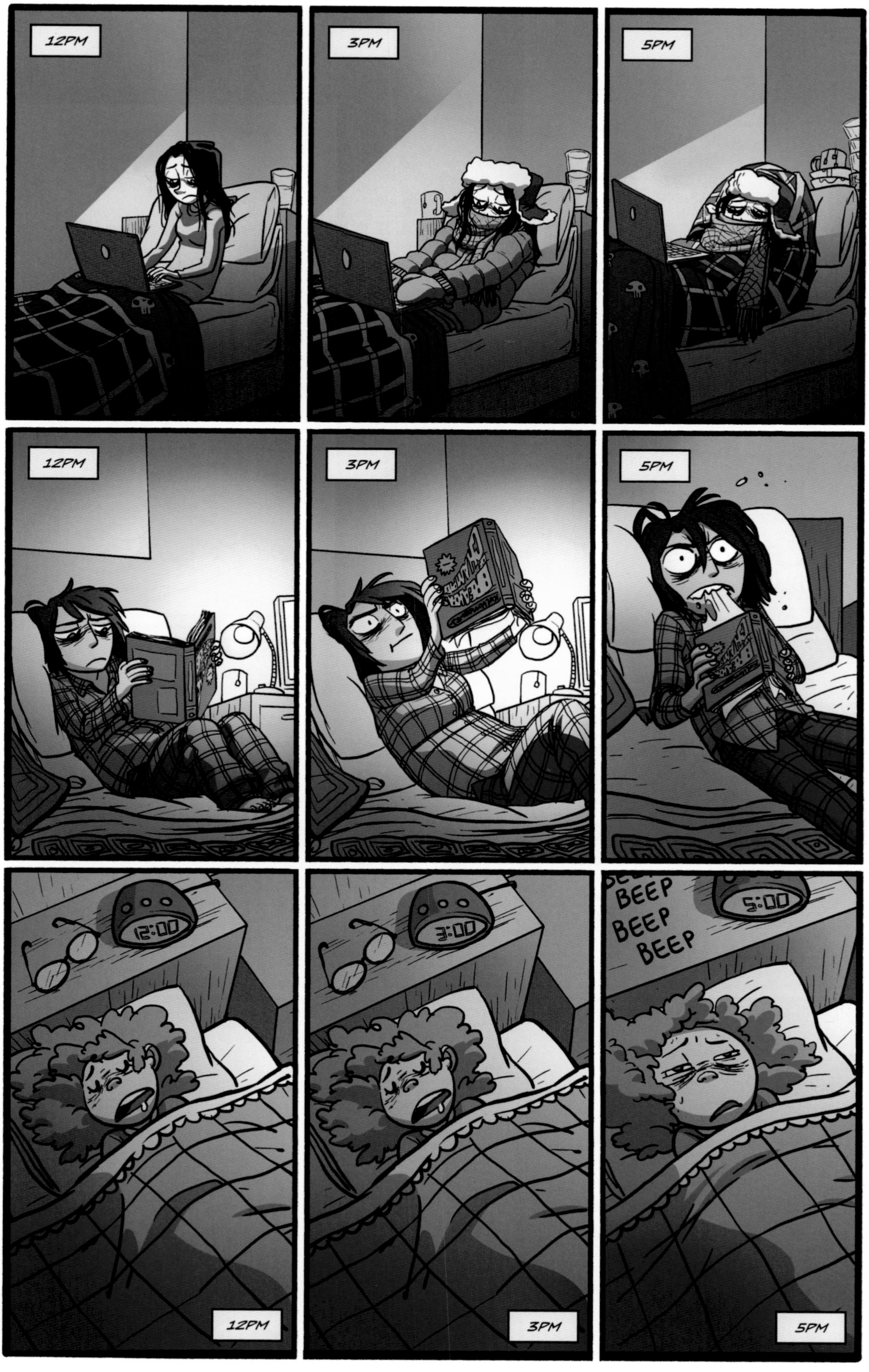

12PM
3PM
5PM
12PM
3PM
5PM
12:00
3:00
BEEP
BEEP
BEEP
BEEP
5:00
12PM
3PM
5PM

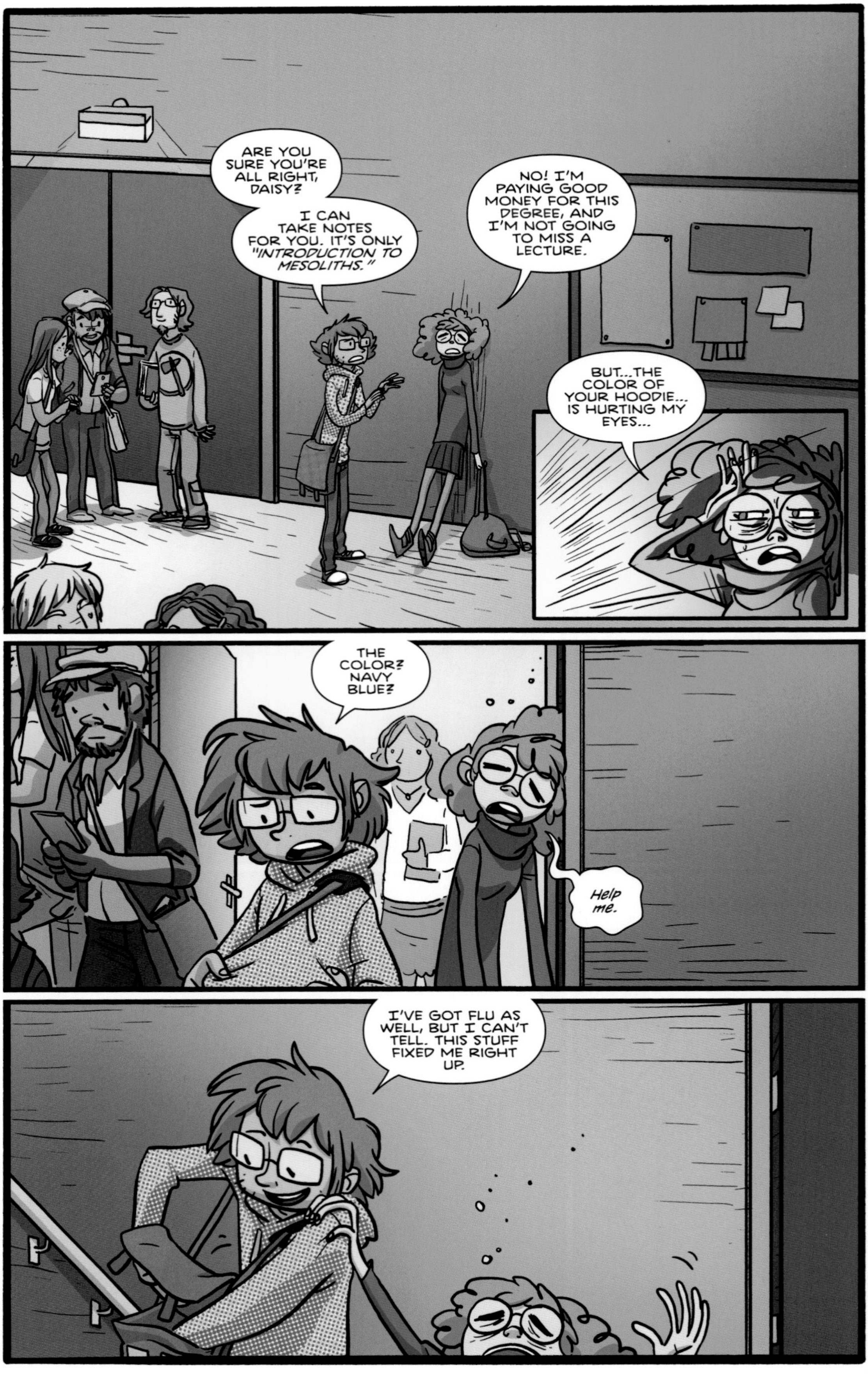
ARE YOU SURE YOU'RE ALL RIGHT, DAISY?
I CAN TAKE NOTES FOR YOU. IT'S ONLY *"INTRODUCTION TO MESOLITHS."*
NO! I'M PAYING GOOD MONEY FOR THIS DEGREE, AND I'M NOT GOING TO MISS A LECTURE.
BUT...THE COLOR OF YOUR HOODIE... IS HURTING MY EYES...
THE COLOR? NAVY BLUE?
Help me.
I'VE GOT FLU AS WELL, BUT I CAN'T TELL. THIS STUFF FIXED ME RIGHT UP.

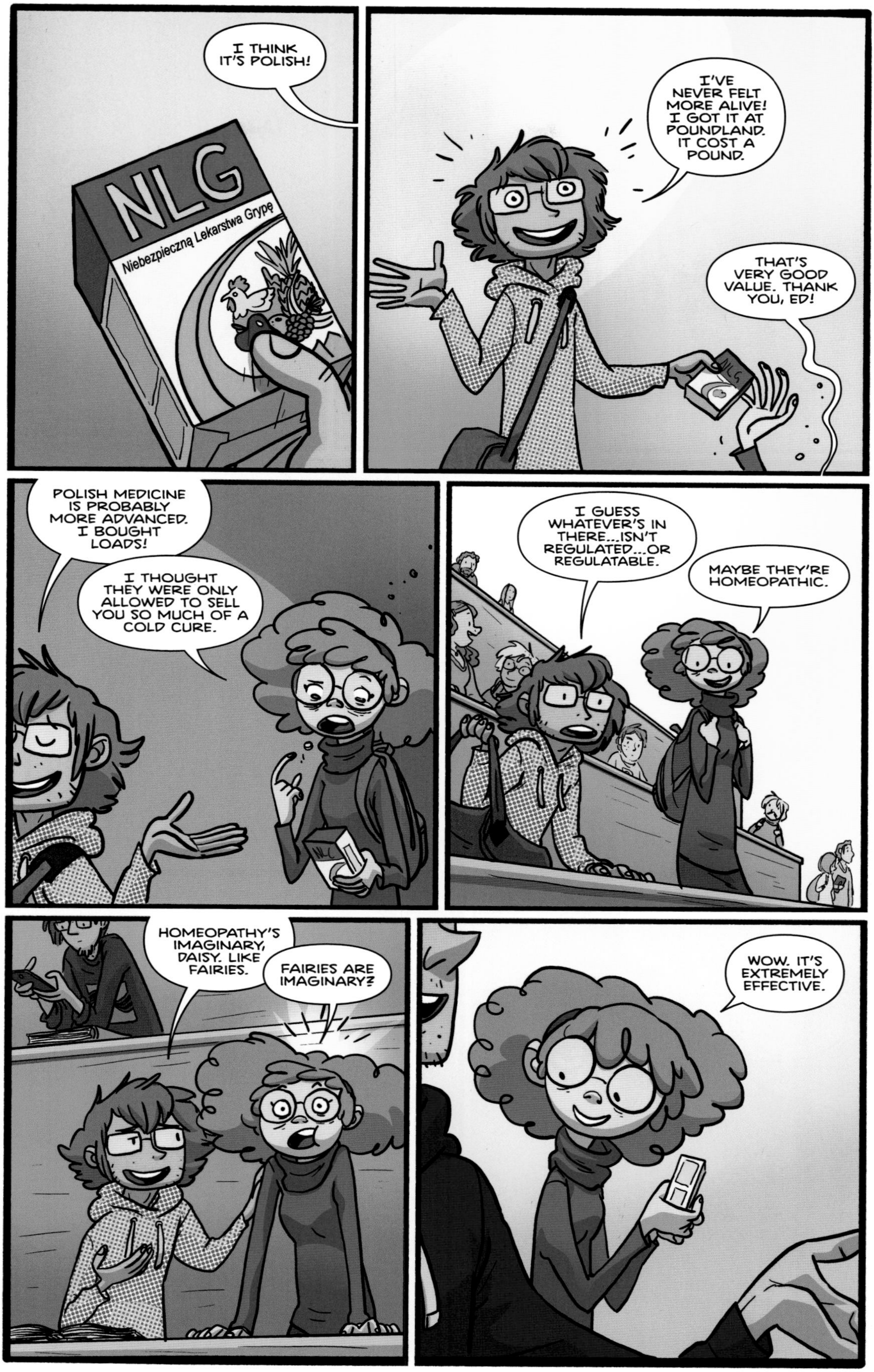
I THINK IT'S POLISH!
NLG
Niebezpieczną Lekarstwa Grypę
I'VE NEVER FELT MORE ALIVE! I GOT IT AT POUNDLAND. IT COST A POUND.
THAT'S VERY GOOD VALUE. THANK YOU, ED!
POLISH MEDICINE IS PROBABLY MORE ADVANCED. I BOUGHT LOADS!
I THOUGHT THEY WERE ONLY ALLOWED TO SELL YOU SO MUCH OF A COLD CURE.
I GUESS WHATEVER'S IN THERE...ISN'T REGULATED...OR REGULATABLE.
MAYBE THEY'RE HOMEOPATHIC.
HOMEOPATHY'S IMAGINARY, DAISY. LIKE FAIRIES.
FAIRIES ARE IMAGINARY?
WOW. IT'S EXTREMELY EFFECTIVE.

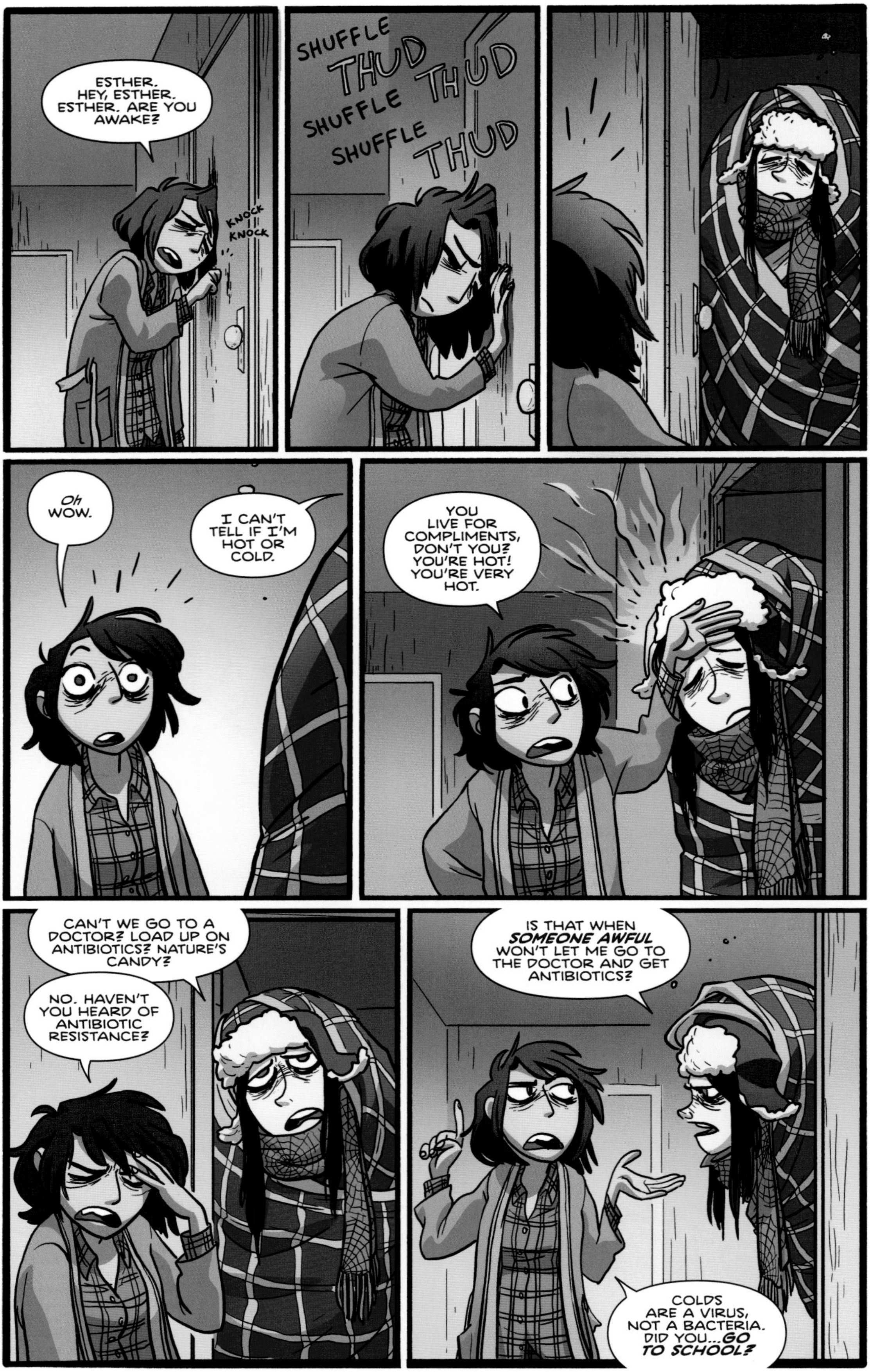
ESTHER. HEY, ESTHER. ESTHER. ARE YOU AWAKE?
KNOCK KNOCK
SHUFFLE THUD SHUFFLE THUD SHUFFLE THUD
Oh WOW.
I CAN'T TELL IF I'M HOT OR COLD.
YOU LIVE FOR COMPLIMENTS, DON'T YOU? YOU'RE HOT! YOU'RE VERY HOT.
CAN'T WE GO TO A DOCTOR? LOAD UP ON ANTIBIOTICS? NATURE'S CANDY?
NO. HAVEN'T YOU HEARD OF ANTIBIOTIC RESISTANCE?
IS THAT WHEN SOMEONE AWFUL WON'T LET ME GO TO THE DOCTOR AND GET ANTIBIOTICS?
COLDS ARE A VIRUS, NOT A BACTERIA. DID YOU...GO TO SCHOOL?

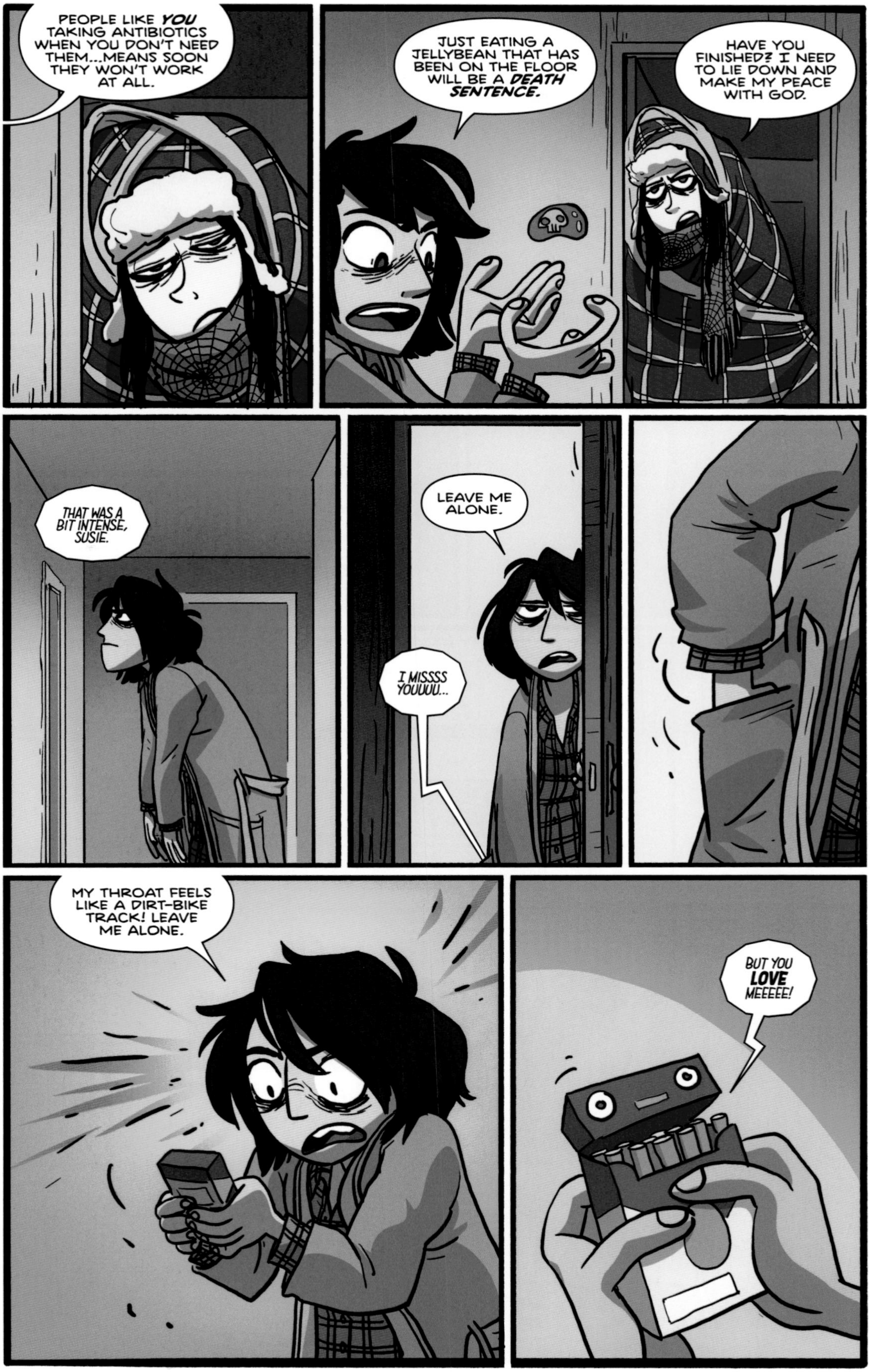
PEOPLE LIKE **YOU** TAKING ANTIBIOTICS WHEN YOU DON'T NEED THEM...MEANS SOON THEY WON'T WORK AT ALL.
JUST EATING A JELLYBEAN THAT HAS BEEN ON THE FLOOR WILL BE A **DEATH SENTENCE.**
HAVE YOU FINISHED? I NEED TO LIE DOWN AND MAKE MY PEACE WITH GOD.
THAT WAS A BIT INTENSE, SUSIE.
LEAVE ME ALONE.
I MISSSS YOUUUU...
MY THROAT FEELS LIKE A DIRT-BIKE TRACK! LEAVE ME ALONE.
BUT YOU **LOVE** MEEEEE!

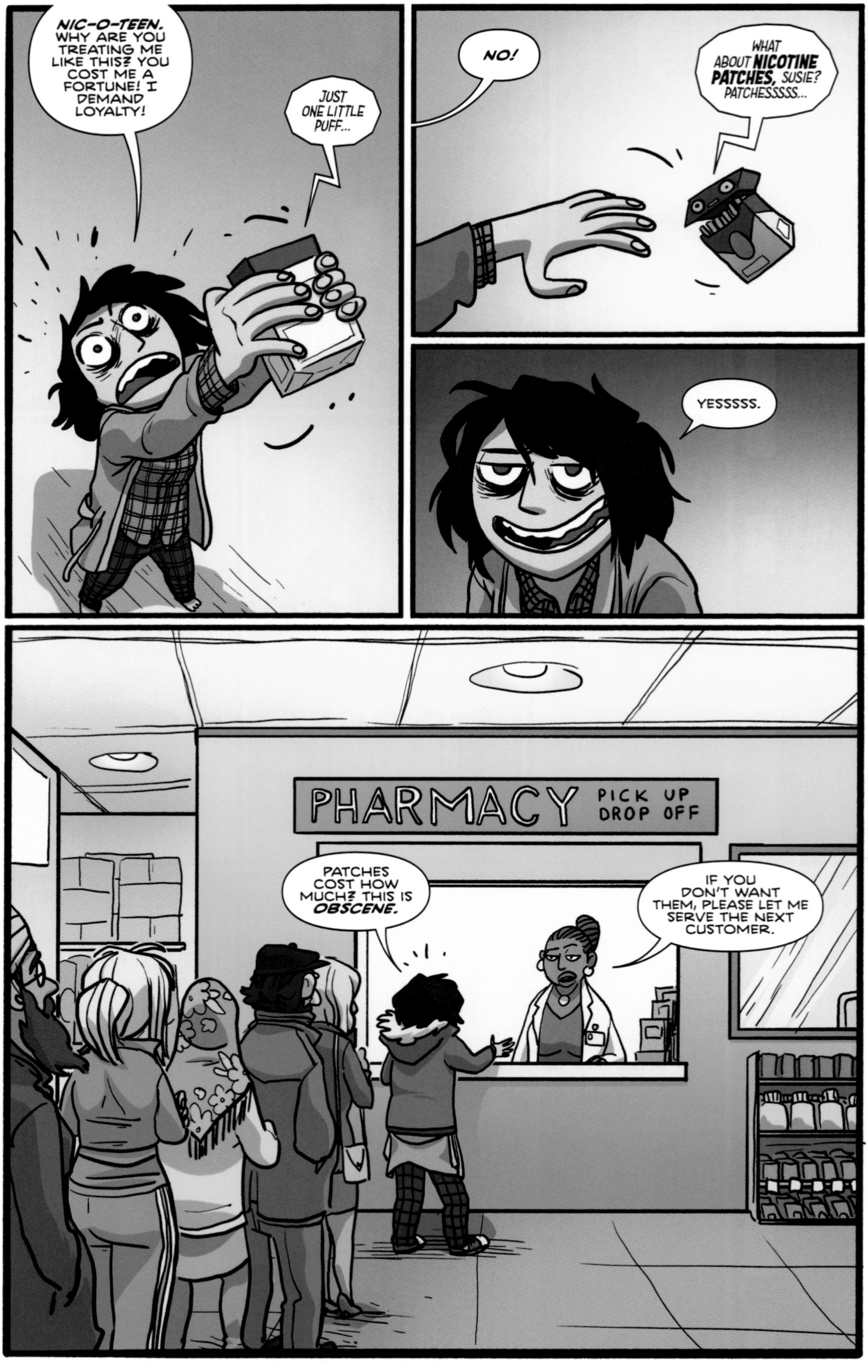
NIC-O-TEEN. WHY ARE YOU TREATING ME LIKE THIS? YOU COST ME A FORTUNE! I DEMAND LOYALTY!
JUST ONE LITTLE PUFF...
NO!
WHAT ABOUT NICOTINE PATCHES, SUSIE? PATCHESSSSS...
YESSSSS.
PHARMACY PICK UP DROP OFF
PATCHES COST HOW MUCH? THIS IS OBSCENE.
IF YOU DON'T WANT THEM, PLEASE LET ME SERVE THE NEXT CUSTOMER.

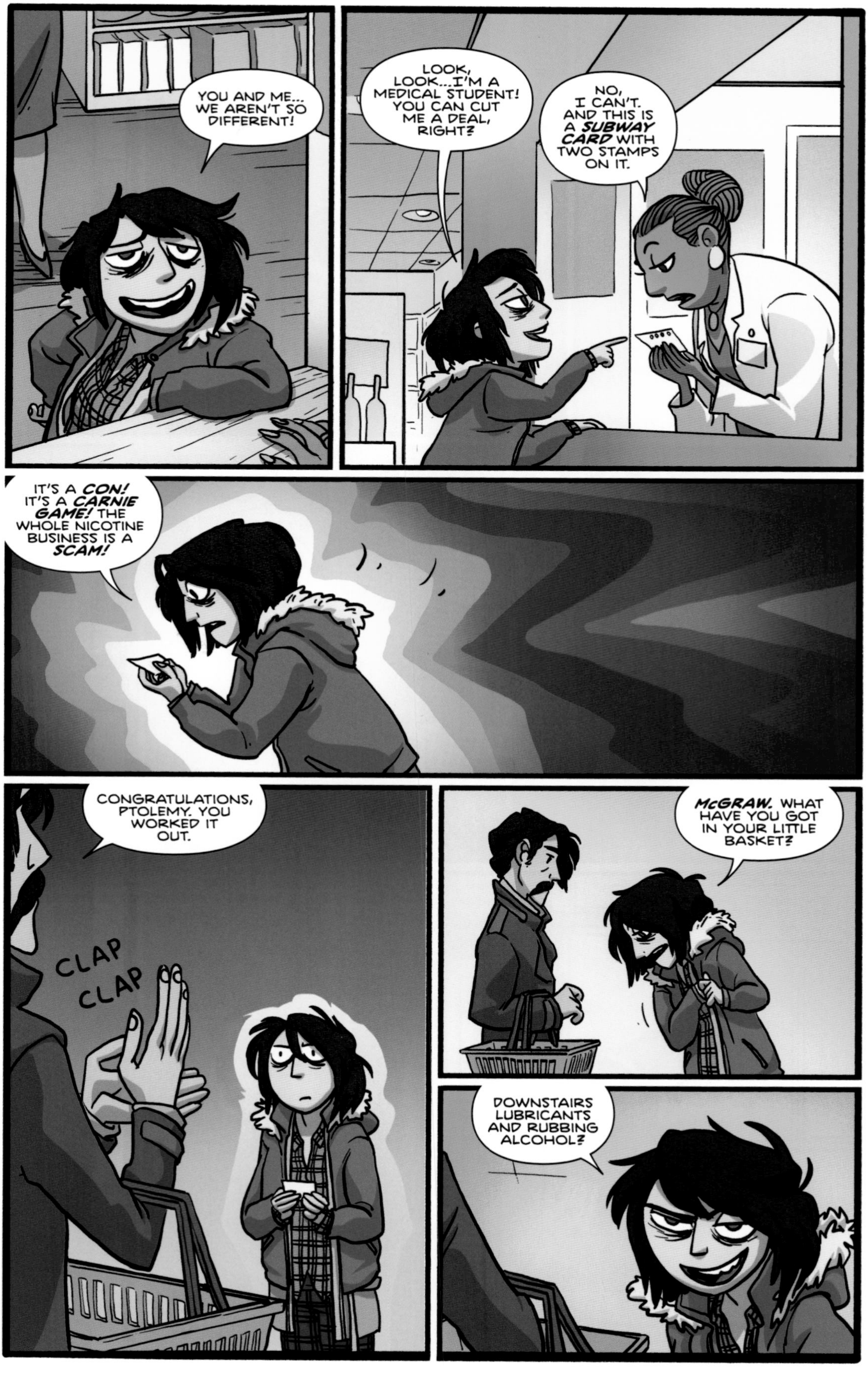
YOU AND ME... WE AREN'T SO DIFFERENT!
LOOK, LOOK...I'M A MEDICAL STUDENT! YOU CAN CUT ME A DEAL, RIGHT?
NO, I CAN'T. AND THIS IS A SUBWAY CARD WITH TWO STAMPS ON IT.
IT'S A CON! IT'S A CARNIE GAME! THE WHOLE NICOTINE BUSINESS IS A SCAM!
CONGRATULATIONS, PTOLEMY. YOU WORKED IT OUT.
CLAP
CLAP
McGRAW. WHAT HAVE YOU GOT IN YOUR LITTLE BASKET?
DOWNSTAIRS LUBRICANTS AND RUBBING ALCOHOL?

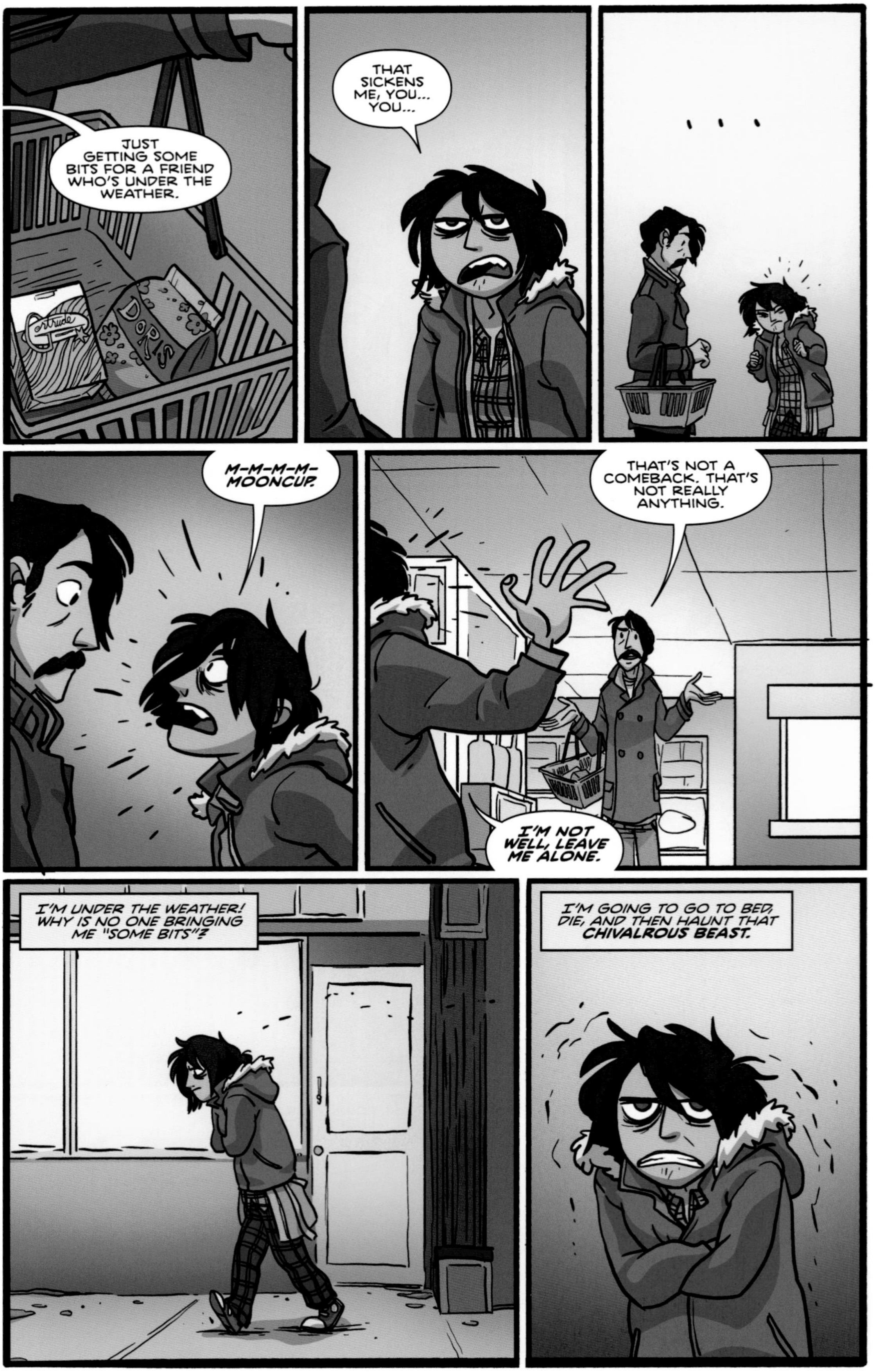
JUST GETTING SOME BITS FOR A FRIEND WHO'S UNDER THE WEATHER.
THAT SICKENS ME, YOU... YOU...
. . .
M-M-M-M-MOONCUP.
THAT'S NOT A COMEBACK. THAT'S NOT REALLY ANYTHING.
I'M NOT WELL, LEAVE ME ALONE.
I'M UNDER THE WEATHER! WHY IS NO ONE BRINGING ME "SOME BITS"?
I'M GOING TO GO TO BED, DIE, AND THEN HAUNT THAT CHIVALROUS BEAST.

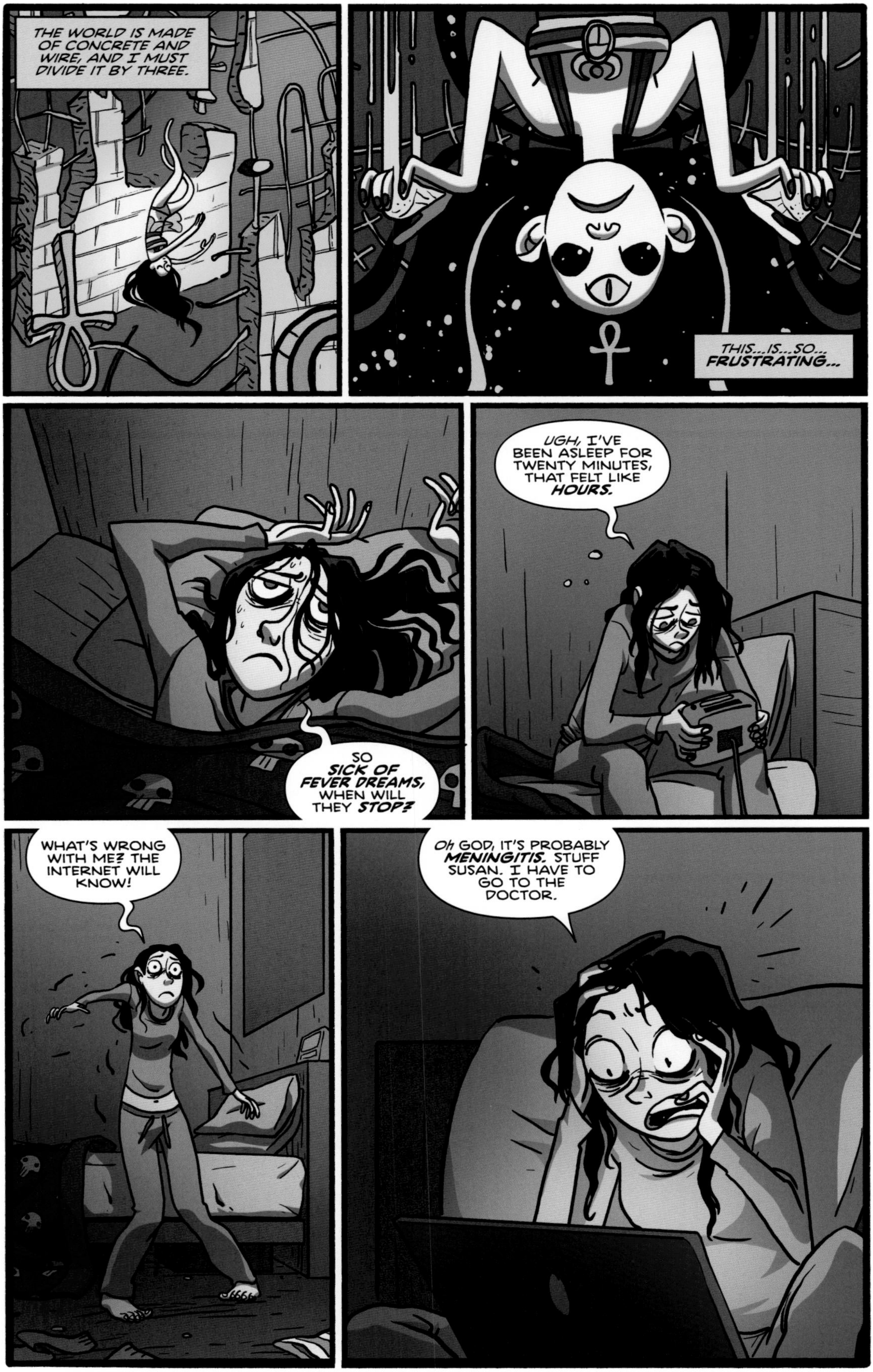
THE WORLD IS MADE OF CONCRETE AND WIRE, AND I MUST DIVIDE IT BY THREE.
THIS... IS... SO... FRUSTRATING...
SO SICK OF FEVER DREAMS, WHEN WILL THEY STOP?
UGH, I'VE BEEN ASLEEP FOR TWENTY MINUTES, THAT FELT LIKE HOURS.
WHAT'S WRONG WITH ME? THE INTERNET WILL KNOW!
OH GOD, IT'S PROBABLY MENINGITIS. STUFF SUSAN. I HAVE TO GO TO THE DOCTOR.

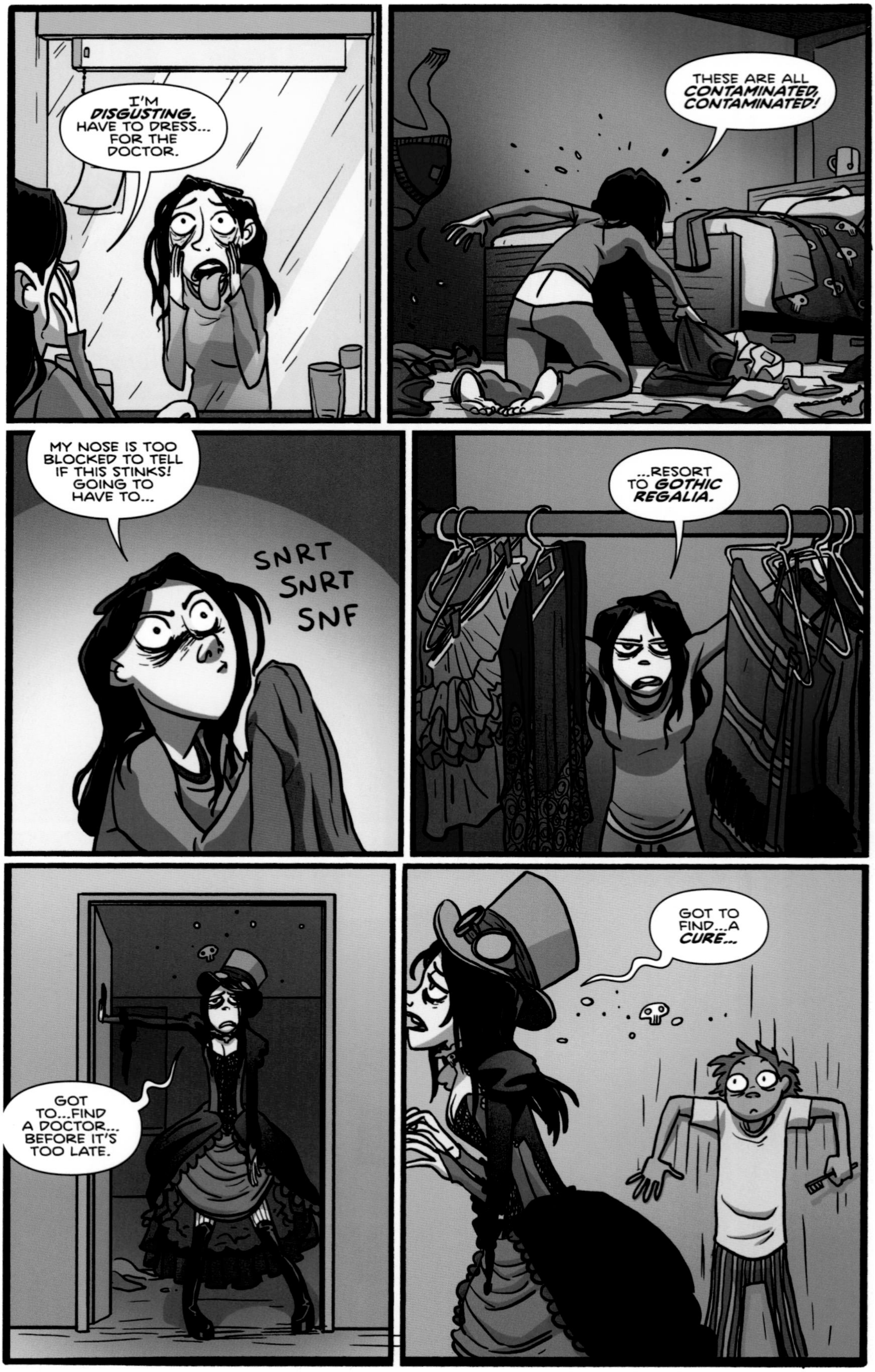
I'M DISGUSTING. HAVE TO DRESS... FOR THE DOCTOR.
THESE ARE ALL CONTAMINATED, CONTAMINATED!
MY NOSE IS TOO BLOCKED TO TELL IF THIS STINKS! GOING TO HAVE TO...
SNRT SNRT SNF
...RESORT TO GOTHIC REGALIA.
GOT TO...FIND A DOCTOR... BEFORE IT'S TOO LATE.
GOT TO FIND...A CURE...

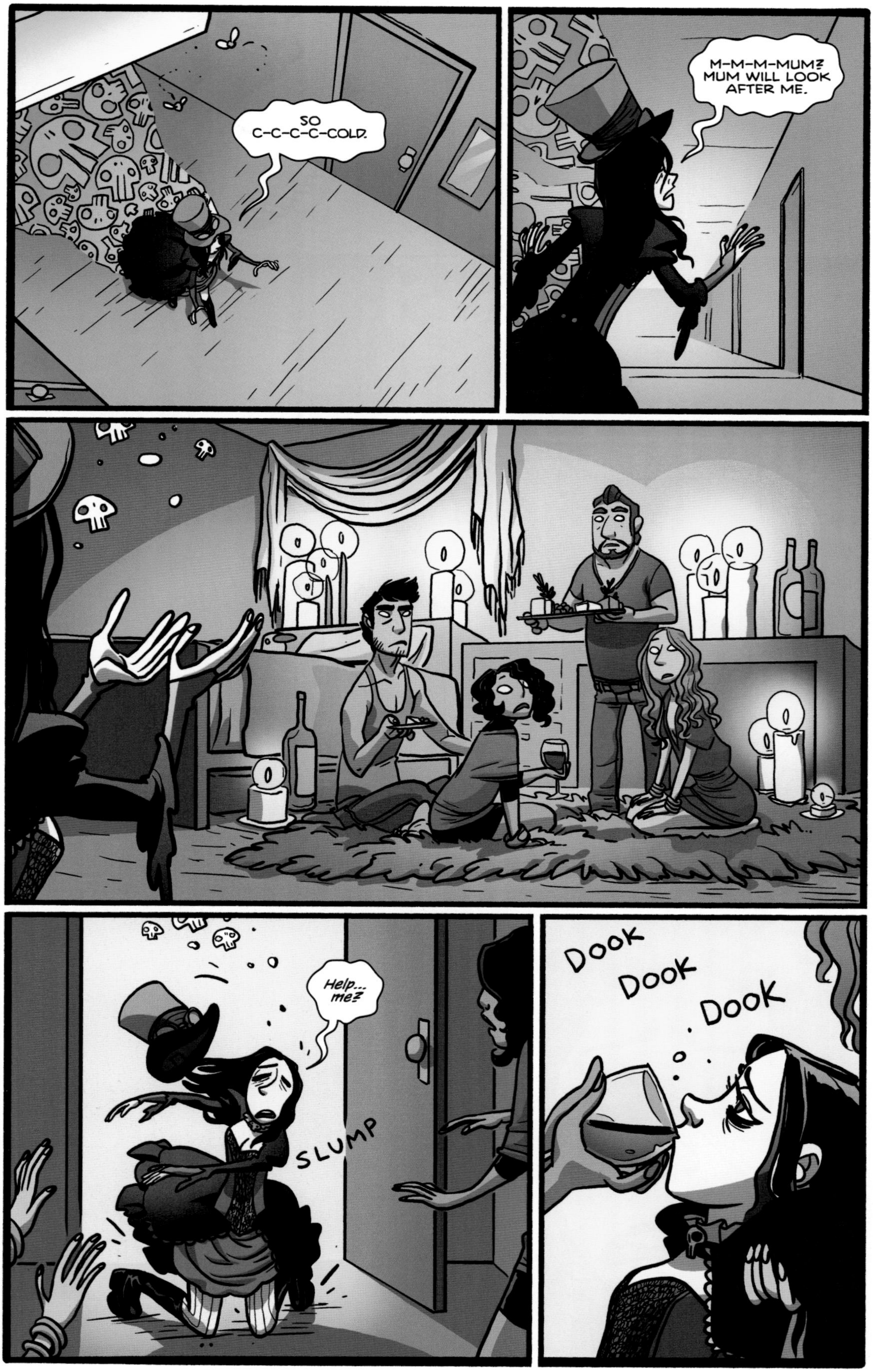

SO C-C-C-C-COLD.
M-M-M-MUM? MUM WILL LOOK AFTER ME.
Help... me?
SLUMP
DOOK
DOOK
DOOK

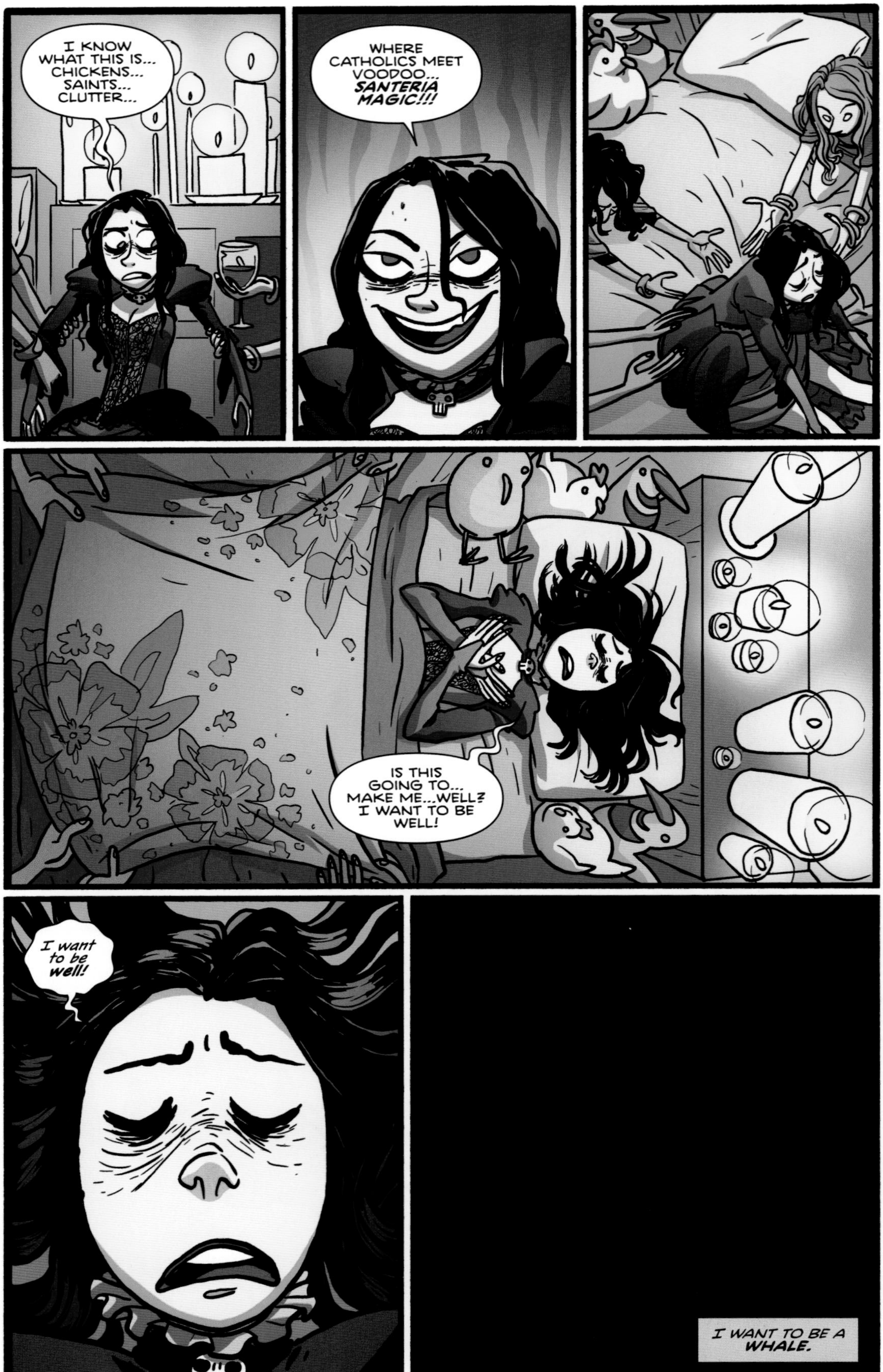
I KNOW WHAT THIS IS... CHICKENS... SAINTS... CLUTTER...
WHERE CATHOLICS MEET VOODOO... SANTERIA MAGIC!!!
IS THIS GOING TO... MAKE ME...WELL? I WANT TO BE WELL!
I want to be well!
I WANT TO BE A WHALE.

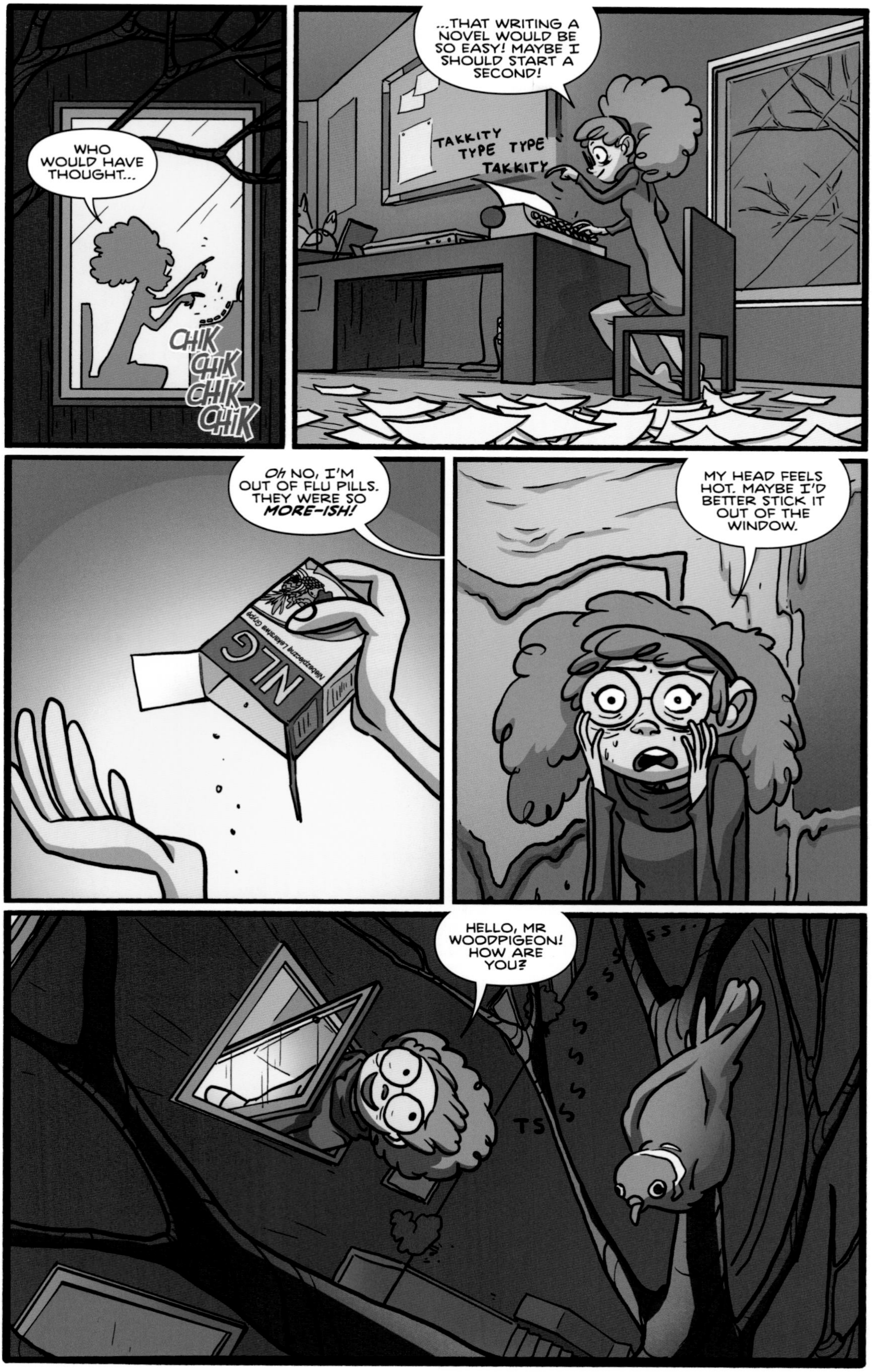
WHO WOULD HAVE THOUGHT...
CHIK CHIK CHIK CHIK
...THAT WRITING A NOVEL WOULD BE SO EASY! MAYBE I SHOULD START A SECOND!
TAKKITY TYPE TYPE TAKKITY
OH NO, I'M OUT OF FLU PILLS. THEY WERE SO MORE-ISH!
NLG
MY HEAD FEELS HOT. MAYBE I'D BETTER STICK IT OUT OF THE WINDOW.
HELLO, MR WOODPIGEON! HOW ARE YOU?
TSSSSSSSSS

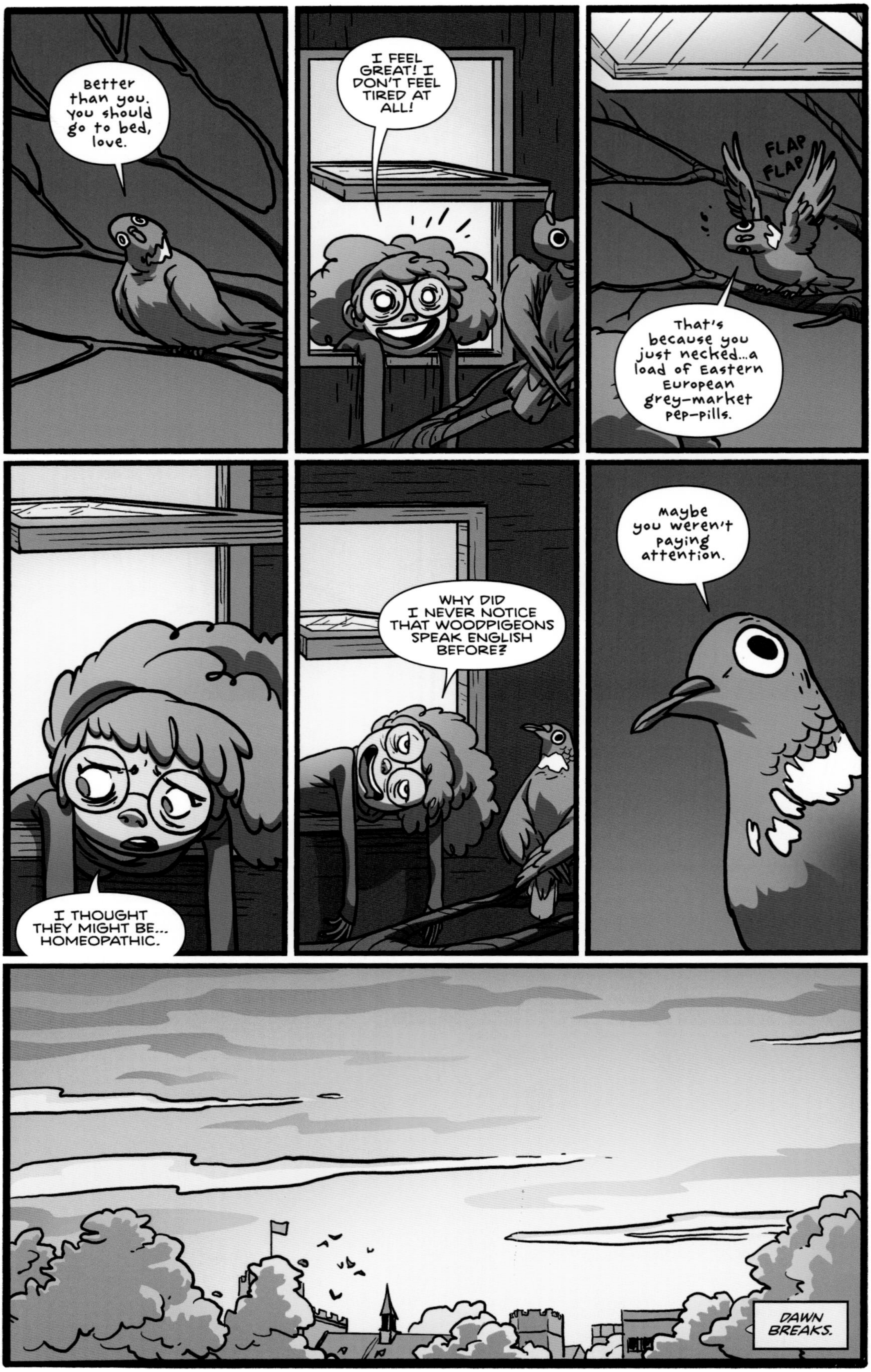
Better than you. You should go to bed, love.
I FEEL GREAT! I DON'T FEEL TIRED AT ALL!
FLAP FLAP
That's because you just necked...a load of Eastern European grey-market pep-pills.
I THOUGHT THEY MIGHT BE... HOMEOPATHIC.
WHY DID I NEVER NOTICE THAT WOODPIGEONS SPEAK ENGLISH BEFORE?
Maybe you weren't paying attention.
DAWN BREAKS.

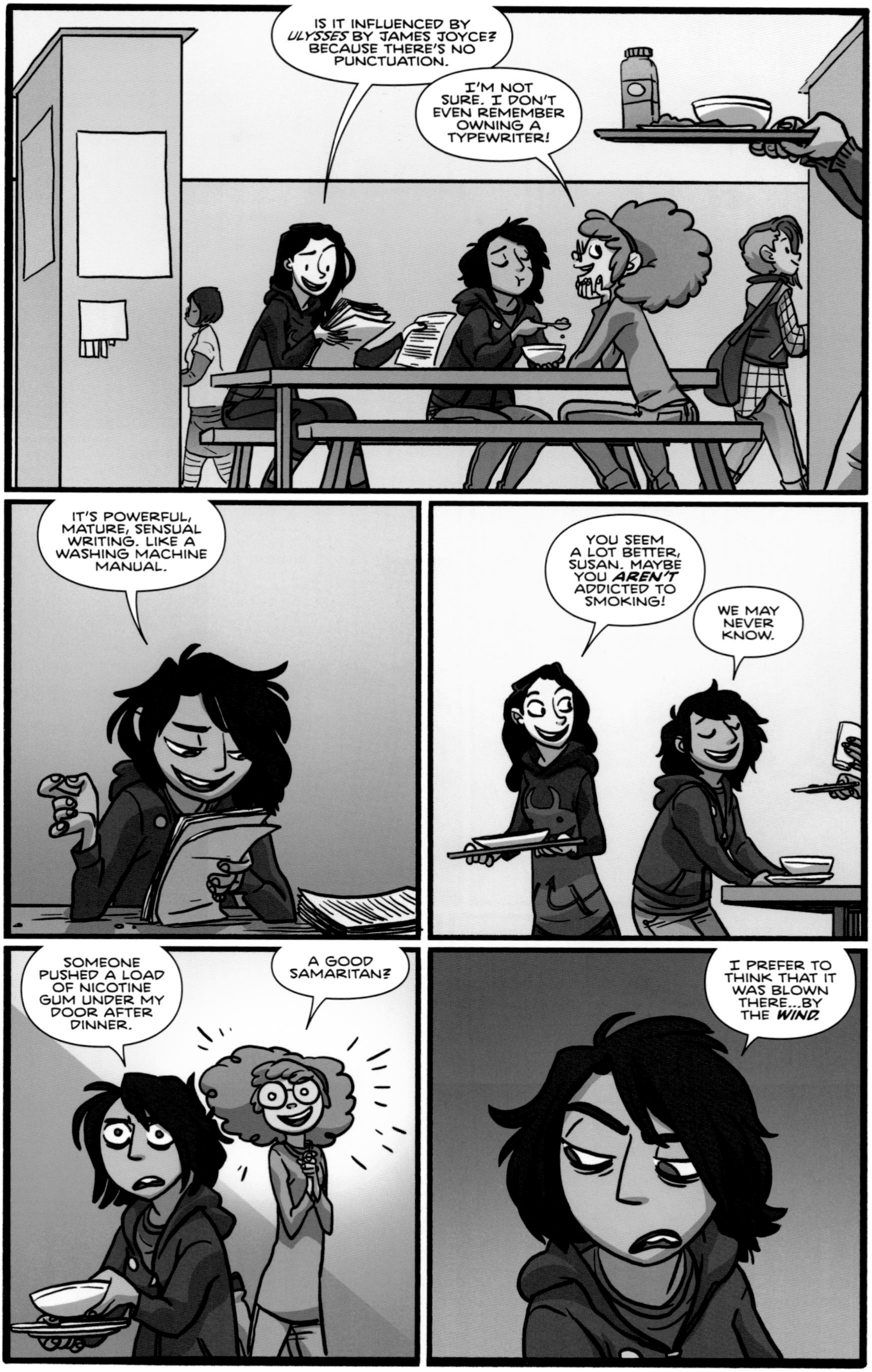
IS IT INFLUENCED BY *ULYSSES* BY JAMES JOYCE? BECAUSE THERE'S NO PUNCTUATION.
I'M NOT SURE. I DON'T EVEN REMEMBER OWNING A TYPEWRITER!
IT'S POWERFUL, MATURE, SENSUAL WRITING. LIKE A WASHING MACHINE MANUAL.
YOU SEEM A LOT BETTER, SUSAN. MAYBE YOU ***AREN'T*** ADDICTED TO SMOKING!
WE MAY NEVER KNOW.
SOMEONE PUSHED A LOAD OF NICOTINE GUM UNDER MY DOOR AFTER DINNER.
A GOOD SAMARITAN?
I PREFER TO THINK THAT IT WAS BLOWN THERE...BY THE ***WIND.***

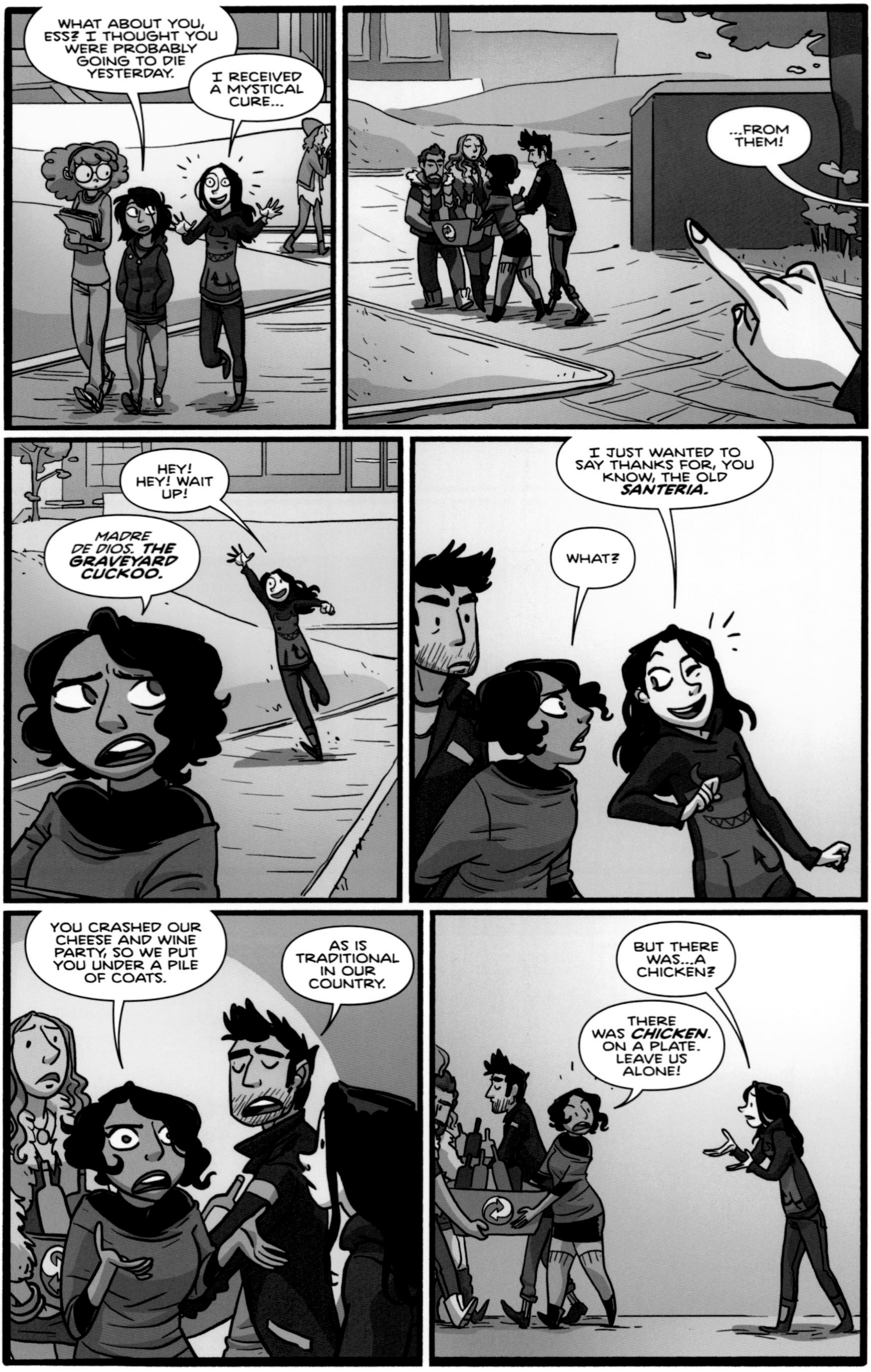
WHAT ABOUT YOU, ESS? I THOUGHT YOU WERE PROBABLY GOING TO DIE YESTERDAY.
I RECEIVED A MYSTICAL CURE...
...FROM THEM!
HEY! HEY! WAIT UP!
MADRE DE DIOS. THE GRAVEYARD CUCKOO.
I JUST WANTED TO SAY THANKS FOR, YOU KNOW, THE OLD SANTERIA.
WHAT?
YOU CRASHED OUR CHEESE AND WINE PARTY, SO WE PUT YOU UNDER A PILE OF COATS.
AS IS TRADITIONAL IN OUR COUNTRY.
BUT THERE WAS...A CHICKEN?
THERE WAS CHICKEN. ON A PLATE. LEAVE US ALONE!

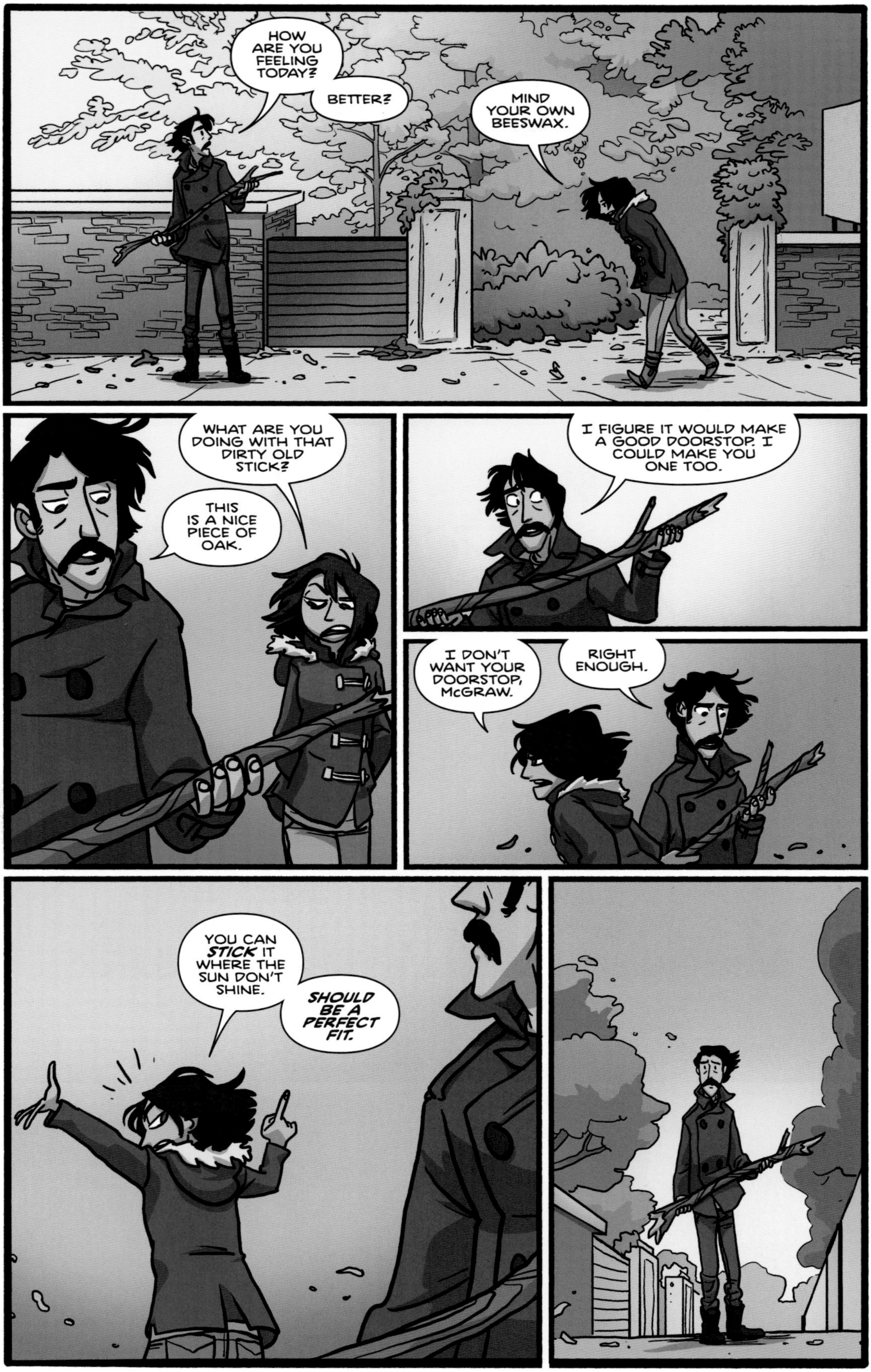
HOW ARE YOU FEELING TODAY?
BETTER?
MIND YOUR OWN BEESWAX.
WHAT ARE YOU DOING WITH THAT DIRTY OLD STICK?
THIS IS A NICE PIECE OF OAK.
I FIGURE IT WOULD MAKE A GOOD DOORSTOP. I COULD MAKE YOU ONE TOO.
I DON'T WANT YOUR DOORSTOP, McGRAW.
RIGHT ENOUGH.
YOU CAN STICK IT WHERE THE SUN DON'T SHINE.
SHOULD BE A PERFECT FIT.

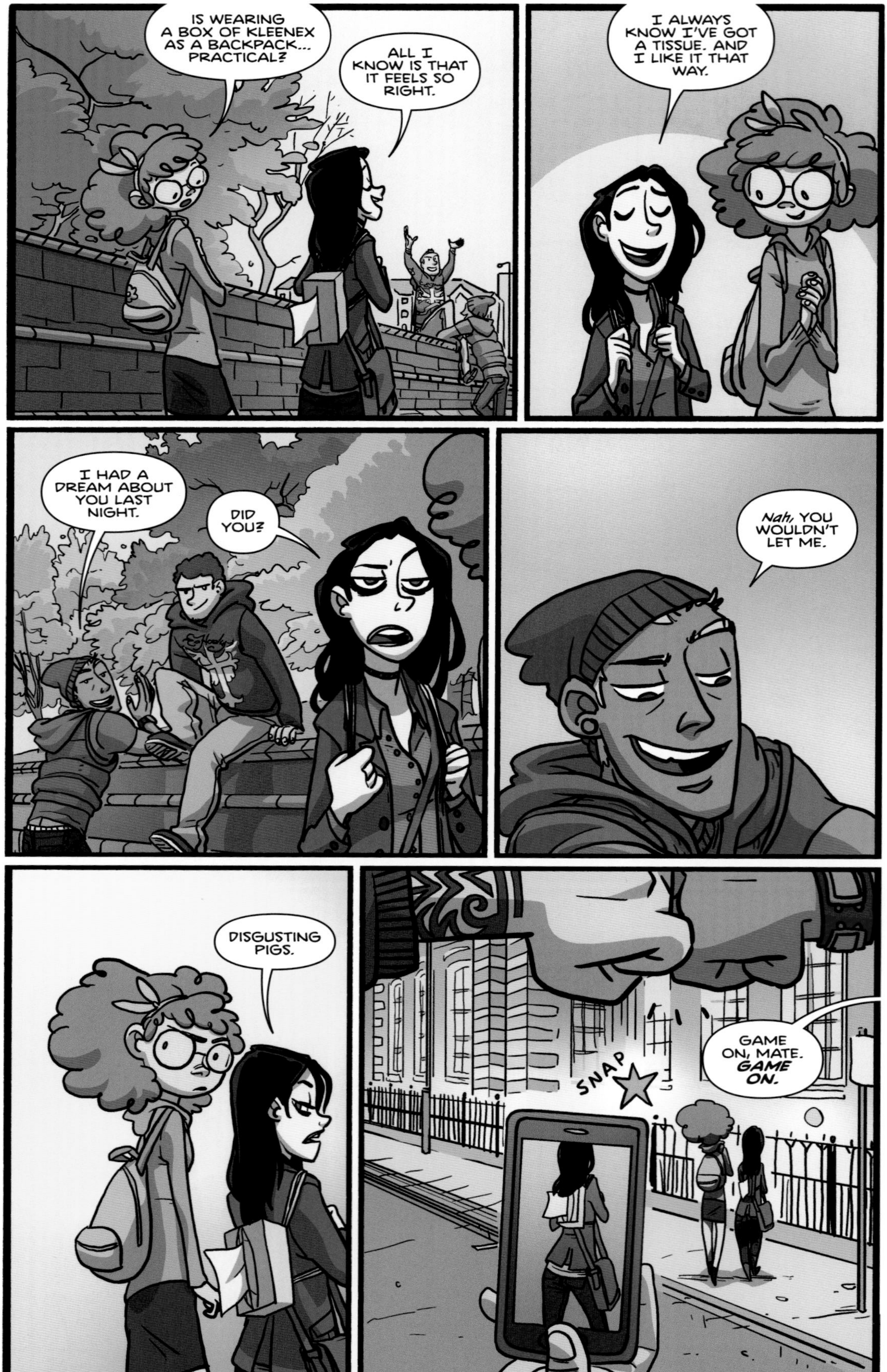
IS WEARING A BOX OF KLEENEX AS A BACKPACK... PRACTICAL?
ALL I KNOW IS THAT IT FEELS SO RIGHT.
I ALWAYS KNOW I'VE GOT A TISSUE. AND I LIKE IT THAT WAY.
I HAD A DREAM ABOUT YOU LAST NIGHT.
DID YOU?
Nah, YOU WOULDN'T LET ME.
DISGUSTING PIGS.
SNAP
GAME ON, MATE. ***GAME ON.***

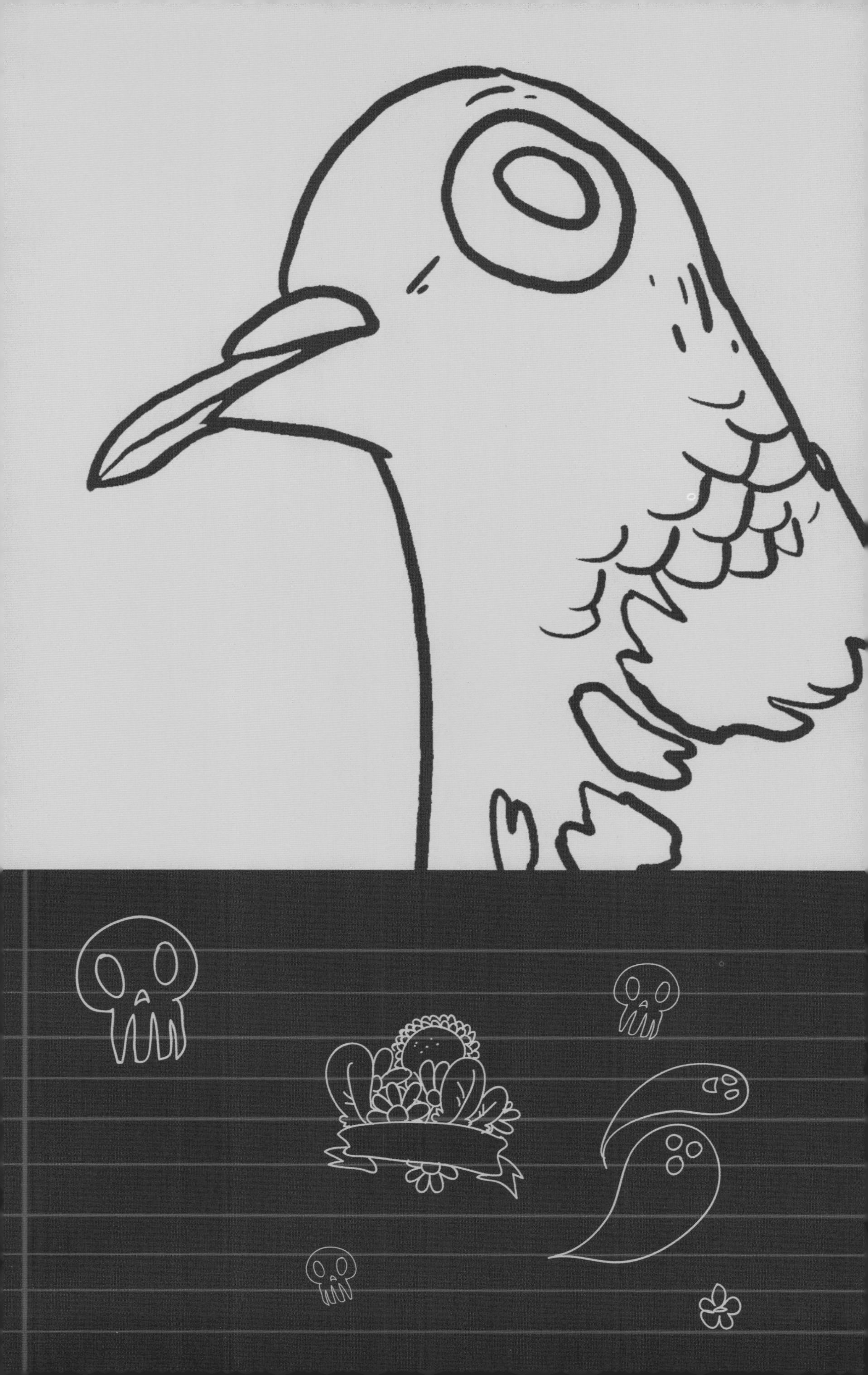

CHAPTER THREE

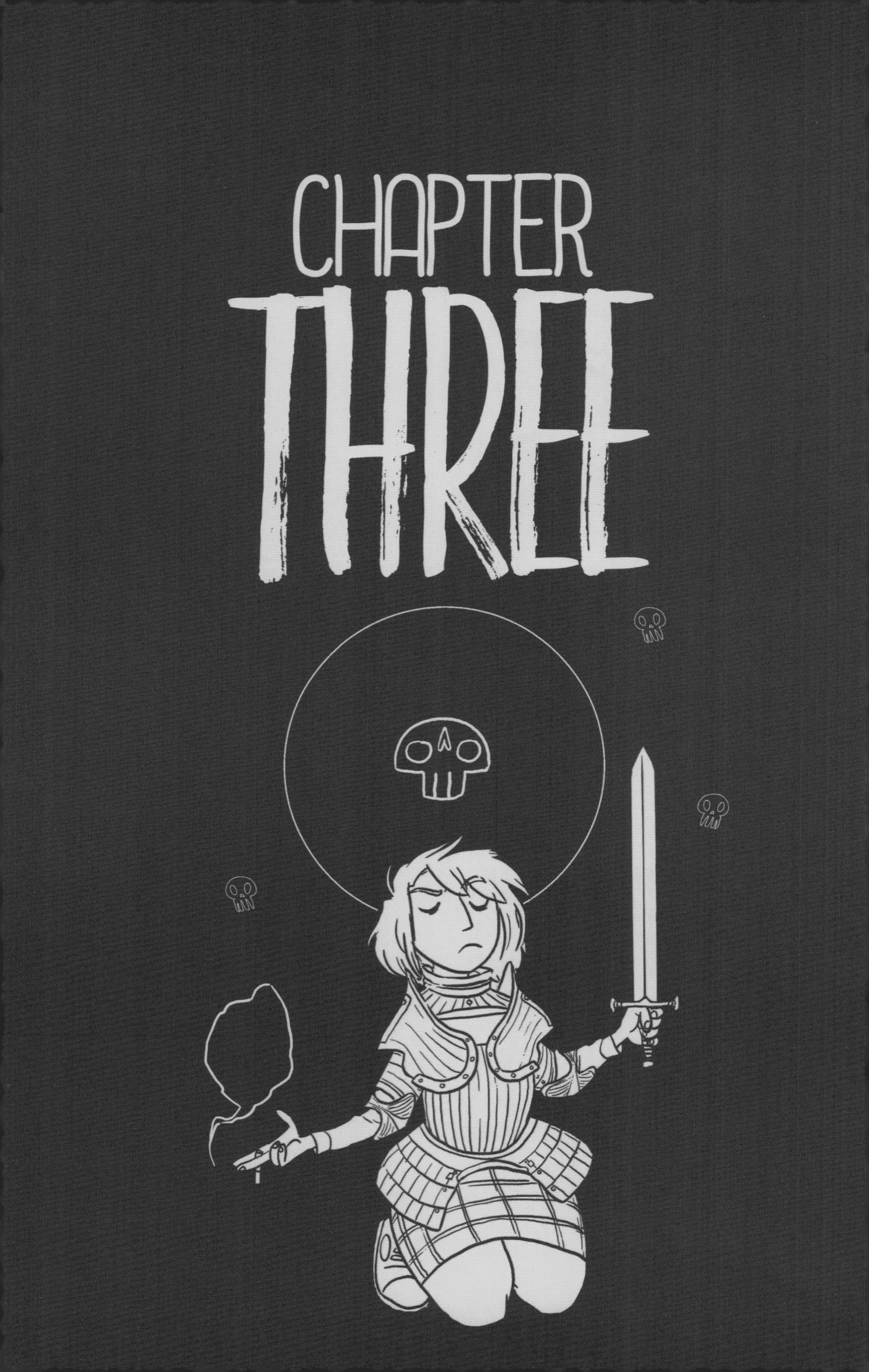

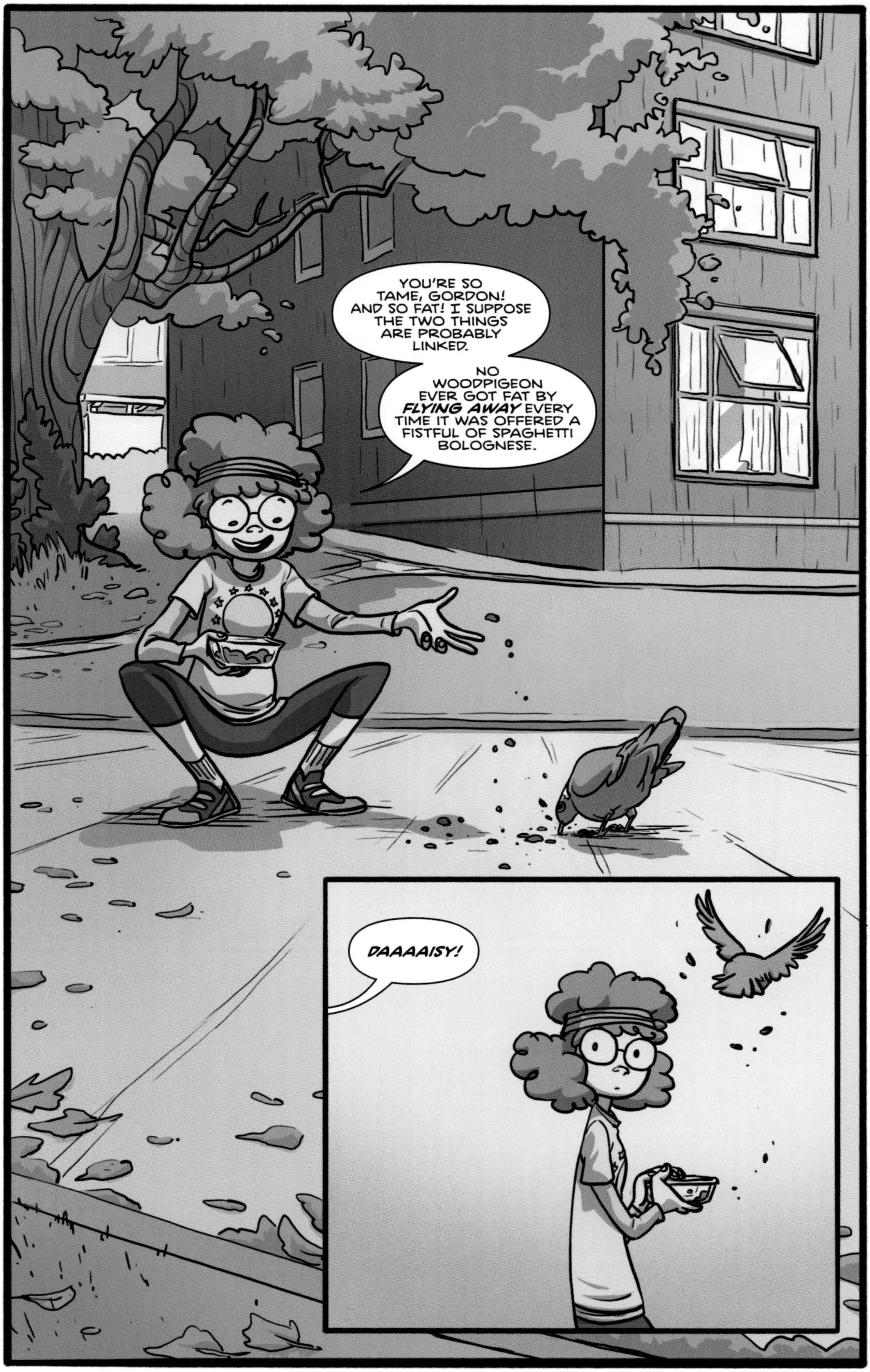
YOU'RE SO TAME, GORDON! AND SO FAT! I SUPPOSE THE TWO THINGS ARE PROBABLY LINKED.
NO WOODPIGEON EVER GOT FAT BY FLYING AWAY EVERY TIME IT WAS OFFERED A FISTFUL OF SPAGHETTI BOLOGNESE.
DAAAAISY!

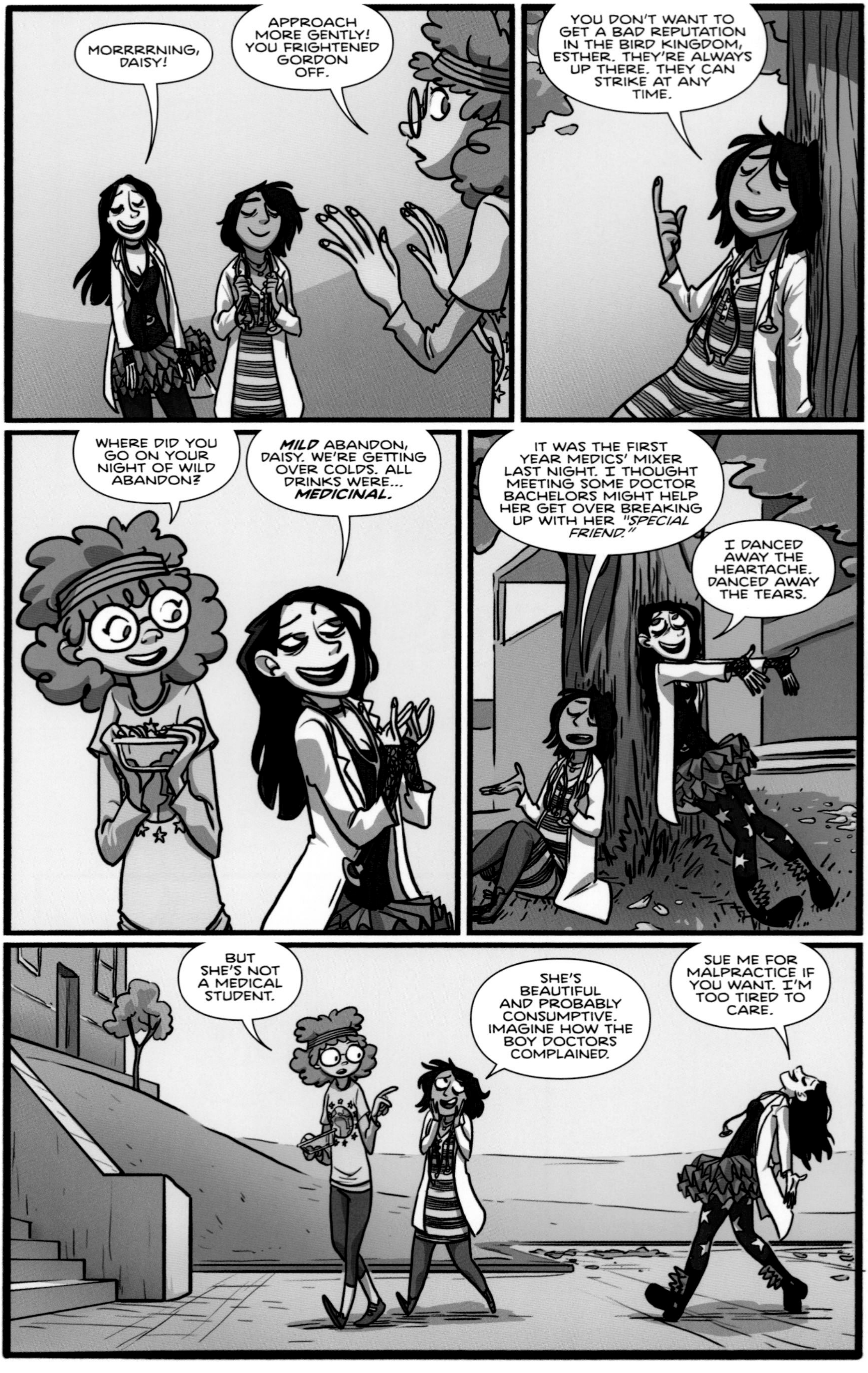
MORRRRNING, DAISY!
APPROACH MORE GENTLY! YOU FRIGHTENED GORDON OFF.
YOU DON'T WANT TO GET A BAD REPUTATION IN THE BIRD KINGDOM, ESTHER. THEY'RE ALWAYS UP THERE. THEY CAN STRIKE AT ANY TIME.
WHERE DID YOU GO ON YOUR NIGHT OF WILD ABANDON?
MILD ABANDON, DAISY. WE'RE GETTING OVER COLDS. ALL DRINKS WERE... ***MEDICINAL.***
IT WAS THE FIRST YEAR MEDICS' MIXER LAST NIGHT. I THOUGHT MEETING SOME DOCTOR BACHELORS MIGHT HELP HER GET OVER BREAKING UP WITH HER *"SPECIAL FRIEND."*
I DANCED AWAY THE HEARTACHE. DANCED AWAY THE TEARS.
BUT SHE'S NOT A MEDICAL STUDENT.
SHE'S BEAUTIFUL AND PROBABLY CONSUMPTIVE. IMAGINE HOW THE BOY DOCTORS COMPLAINED.
SUE ME FOR MALPRACTICE IF YOU WANT. I'M TOO TIRED TO CARE.

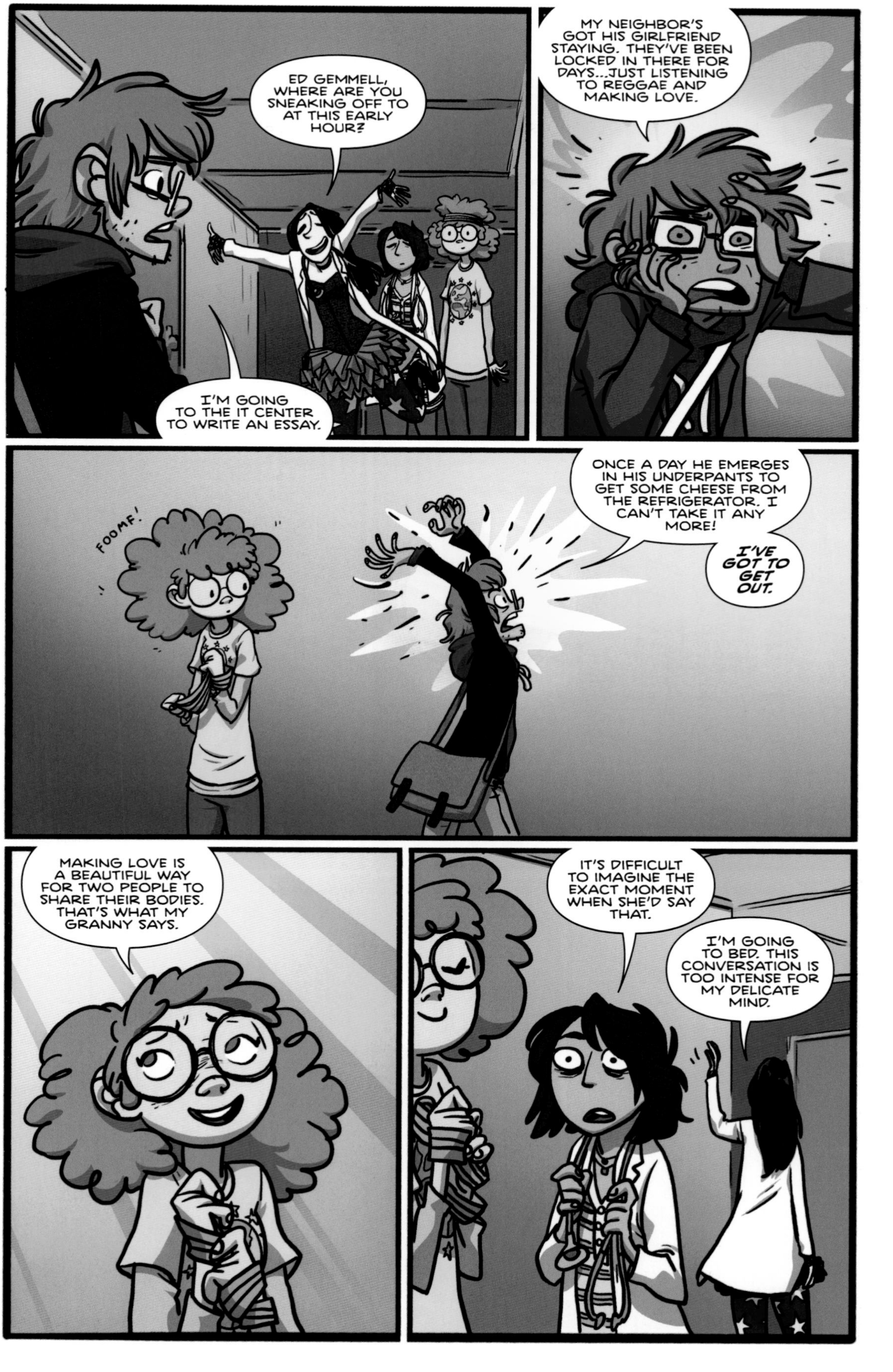
ED GEMMELL, WHERE ARE YOU SNEAKING OFF TO AT THIS EARLY HOUR?
I'M GOING TO THE IT CENTER TO WRITE AN ESSAY.
MY NEIGHBOR'S GOT HIS GIRLFRIEND STAYING. THEY'VE BEEN LOCKED IN THERE FOR DAYS...JUST LISTENING TO REGGAE AND MAKING LOVE.
ONCE A DAY HE EMERGES IN HIS UNDERPANTS TO GET SOME CHEESE FROM THE REFRIGERATOR. I CAN'T TAKE IT ANY MORE!
I'VE GOT TO GET OUT.
FOOMF!
MAKING LOVE IS A BEAUTIFUL WAY FOR TWO PEOPLE TO SHARE THEIR BODIES. THAT'S WHAT MY GRANNY SAYS.
IT'S DIFFICULT TO IMAGINE THE EXACT MOMENT WHEN SHE'D SAY THAT.
I'M GOING TO BED. THIS CONVERSATION IS TOO INTENSE FOR MY DELICATE MIND.

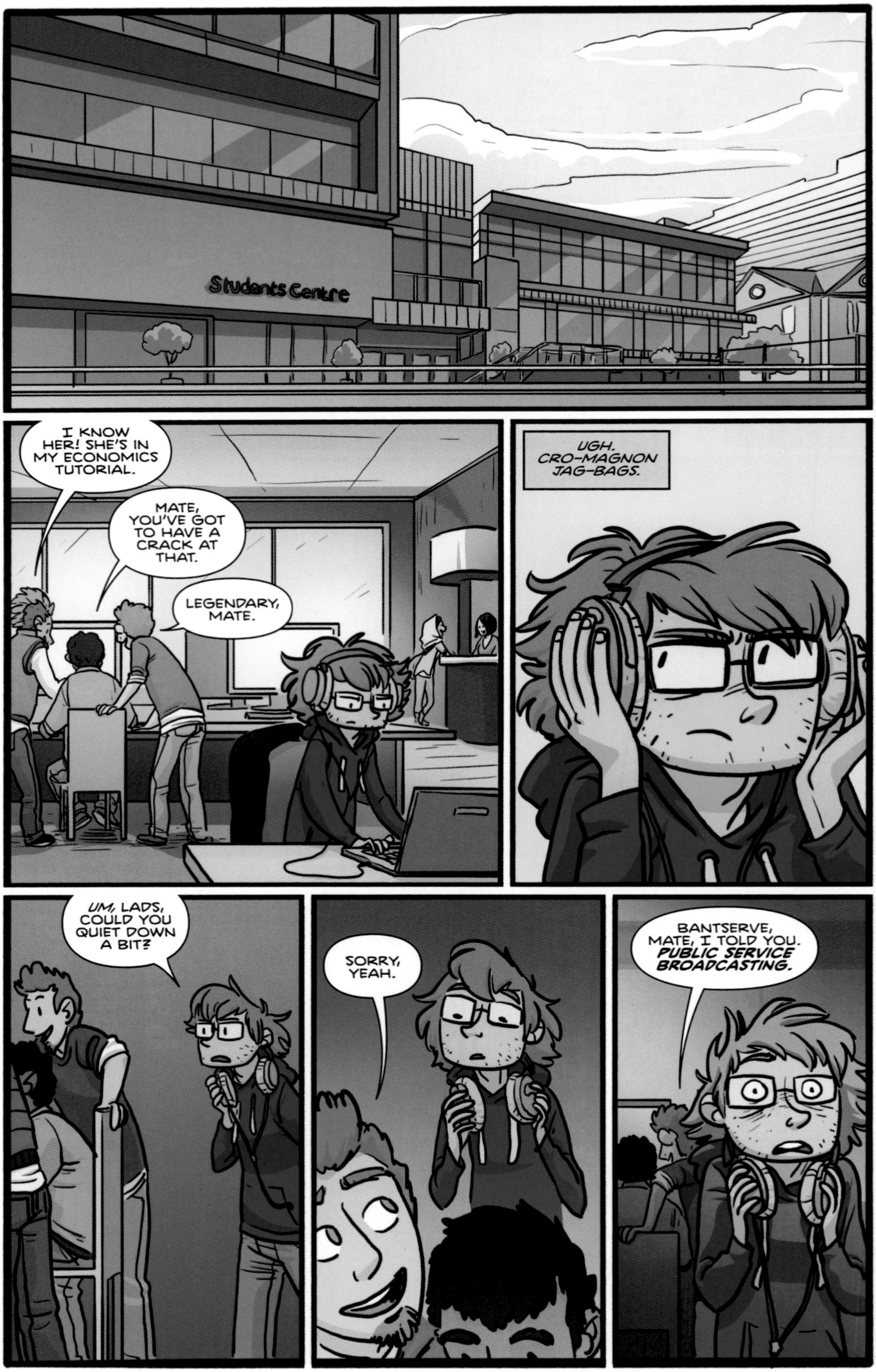
Students Centre
I KNOW HER! SHE'S IN MY ECONOMICS TUTORIAL.
MATE, YOU'VE GOT TO HAVE A CRACK AT THAT.
LEGENDARY, MATE.
UGH. CRO-MAGNON JAG-BAGS.
UM, LADS, COULD YOU QUIET DOWN A BIT?
SORRY, YEAH.
BANTSERVE, MATE, I TOLD YOU. PUBLIC SERVICE BROADCASTING.

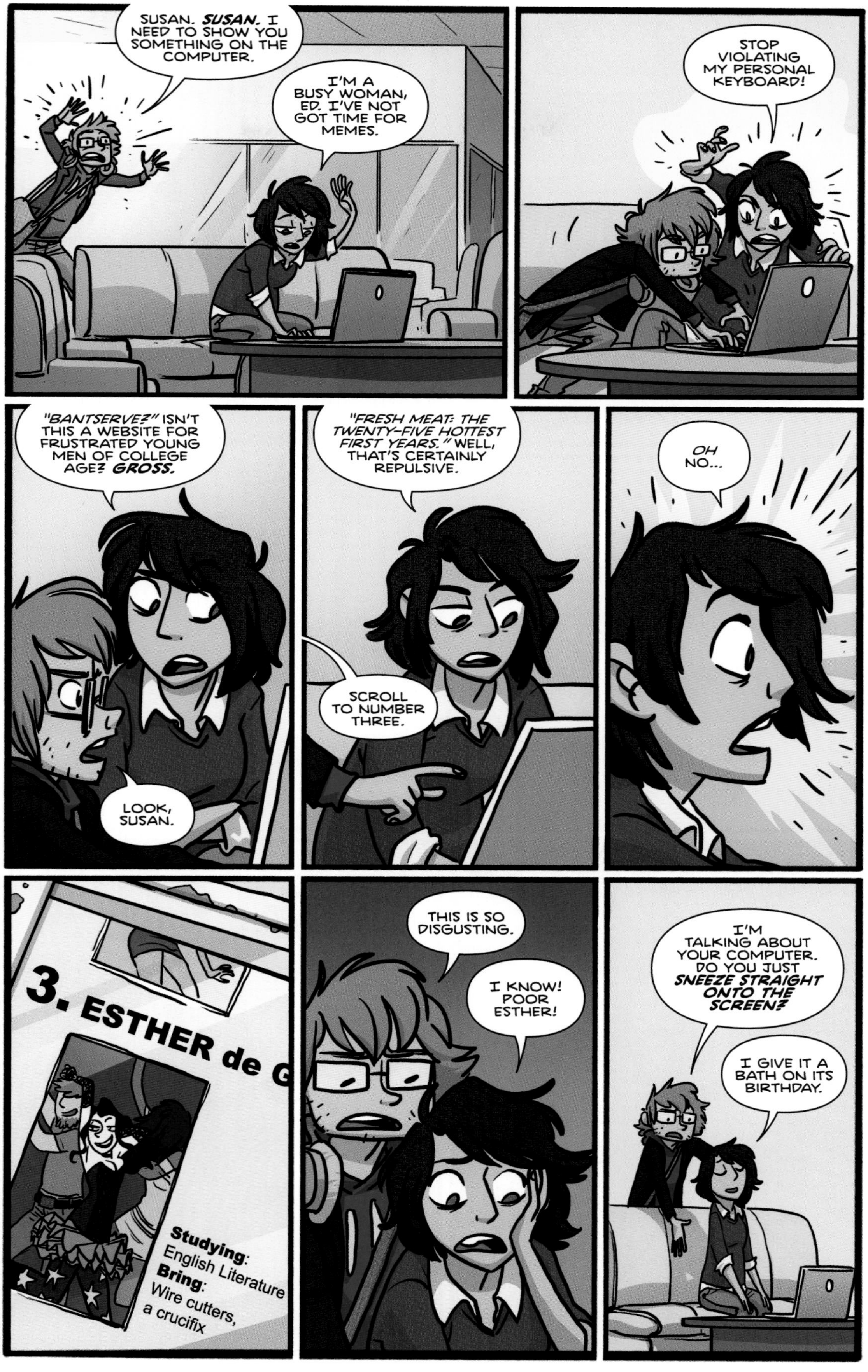
SUSAN. SUSAN. I NEED TO SHOW YOU SOMETHING ON THE COMPUTER.
I'M A BUSY WOMAN, ED. I'VE NOT GOT TIME FOR MEMES.
STOP VIOLATING MY PERSONAL KEYBOARD!
"BANTSERVE?" ISN'T THIS A WEBSITE FOR FRUSTRATED YOUNG MEN OF COLLEGE AGE? GROSS.
LOOK, SUSAN.
"FRESH MEAT: THE TWENTY-FIVE HOTTEST FIRST YEARS." WELL, THAT'S CERTAINLY REPULSIVE.
SCROLL TO NUMBER THREE.
OH NO...
3. ESTHER de G
Studying: English Literature
Bring: Wire cutters, a crucifix
THIS IS SO DISGUSTING.
I KNOW! POOR ESTHER!
I'M TALKING ABOUT YOUR COMPUTER. DO YOU JUST SNEEZE STRAIGHT ONTO THE SCREEN?
I GIVE IT A BATH ON ITS BIRTHDAY.

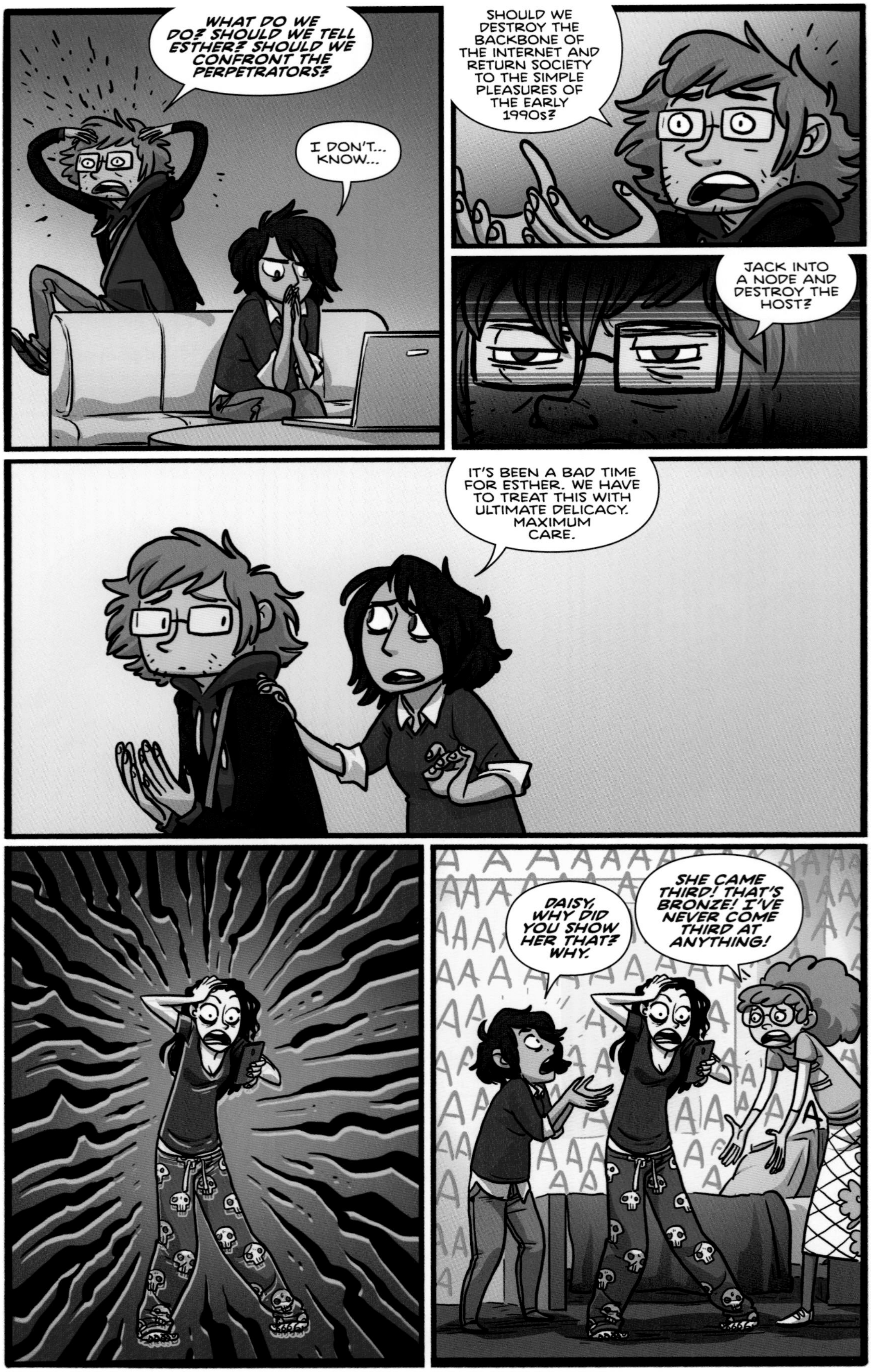
WHAT DO WE DO? SHOULD WE TELL ESTHER? SHOULD WE CONFRONT THE PERPETRATORS?
I DON'T... KNOW...
SHOULD WE DESTROY THE BACKBONE OF THE INTERNET AND RETURN SOCIETY TO THE SIMPLE PLEASURES OF THE EARLY 1990s?
JACK INTO A NODE AND DESTROY THE HOST?
IT'S BEEN A BAD TIME FOR ESTHER. WE HAVE TO TREAT THIS WITH ULTIMATE DELICACY. MAXIMUM CARE.
DAISY, WHY DID YOU SHOW HER THAT? WHY.
SHE CAME THIRD! THAT'S BRONZE! I'VE NEVER COME THIRD AT ANYTHING!

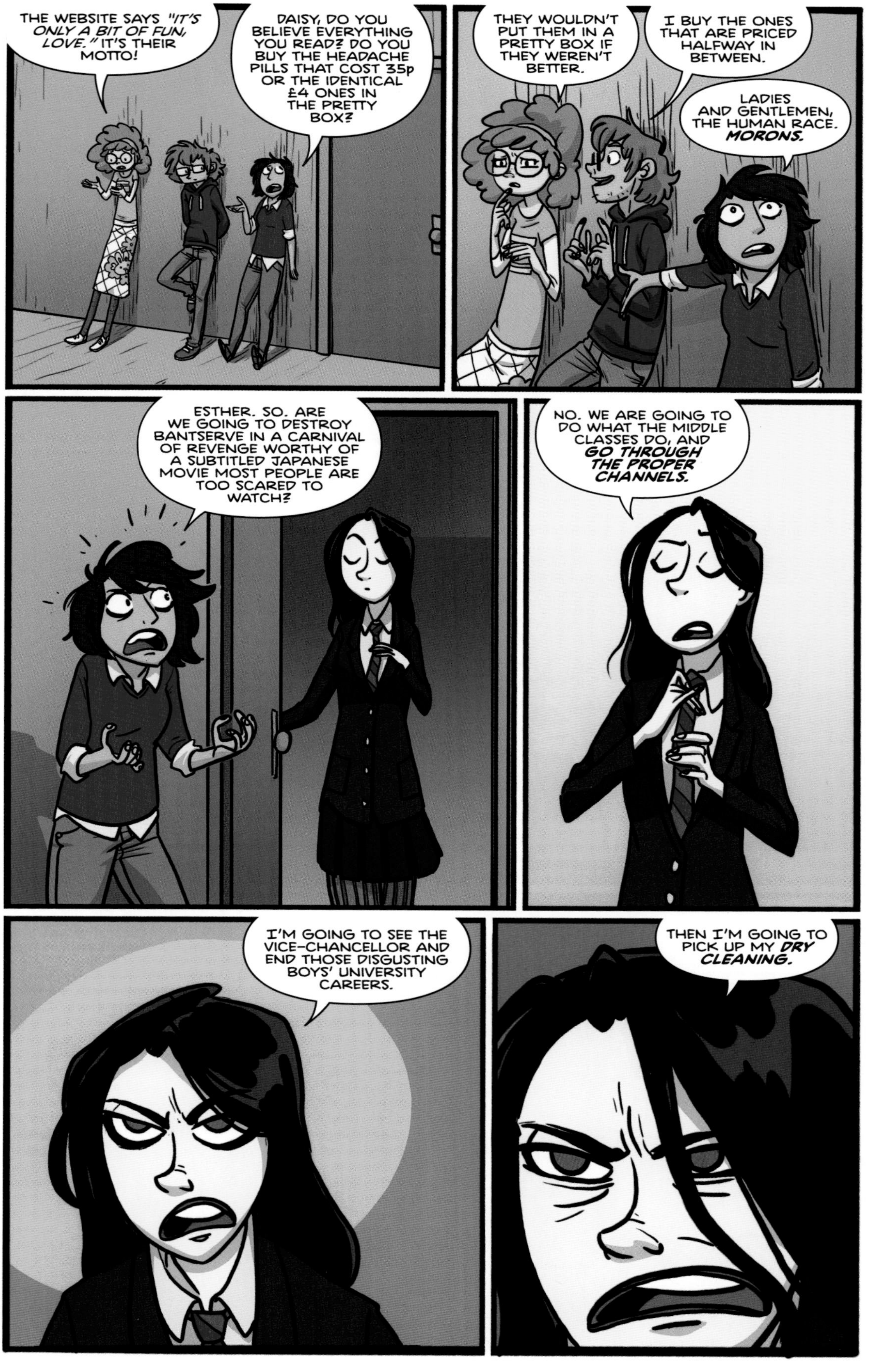
THE WEBSITE SAYS *"IT'S ONLY A BIT OF FUN, LOVE."* IT'S THEIR MOTTO!
DAISY, DO YOU BELIEVE EVERYTHING YOU READ? DO YOU BUY THE HEADACHE PILLS THAT COST 35p OR THE IDENTICAL £4 ONES IN THE PRETTY BOX?
THEY WOULDN'T PUT THEM IN A PRETTY BOX IF THEY WEREN'T BETTER.
I BUY THE ONES THAT ARE PRICED HALFWAY IN BETWEEN.
LADIES AND GENTLEMEN, THE HUMAN RACE. ***MORONS.***
ESTHER. SO. ARE WE GOING TO DESTROY BANTSERVE IN A CARNIVAL OF REVENGE WORTHY OF A SUBTITLED JAPANESE MOVIE MOST PEOPLE ARE TOO SCARED TO WATCH?
NO. WE ARE GOING TO DO WHAT THE MIDDLE CLASSES DO, AND ***GO THROUGH THE PROPER CHANNELS.***
I'M GOING TO SEE THE VICE-CHANCELLOR AND END THOSE DISGUSTING BOYS' UNIVERSITY CAREERS.
THEN I'M GOING TO PICK UP MY ***DRY CLEANING.***

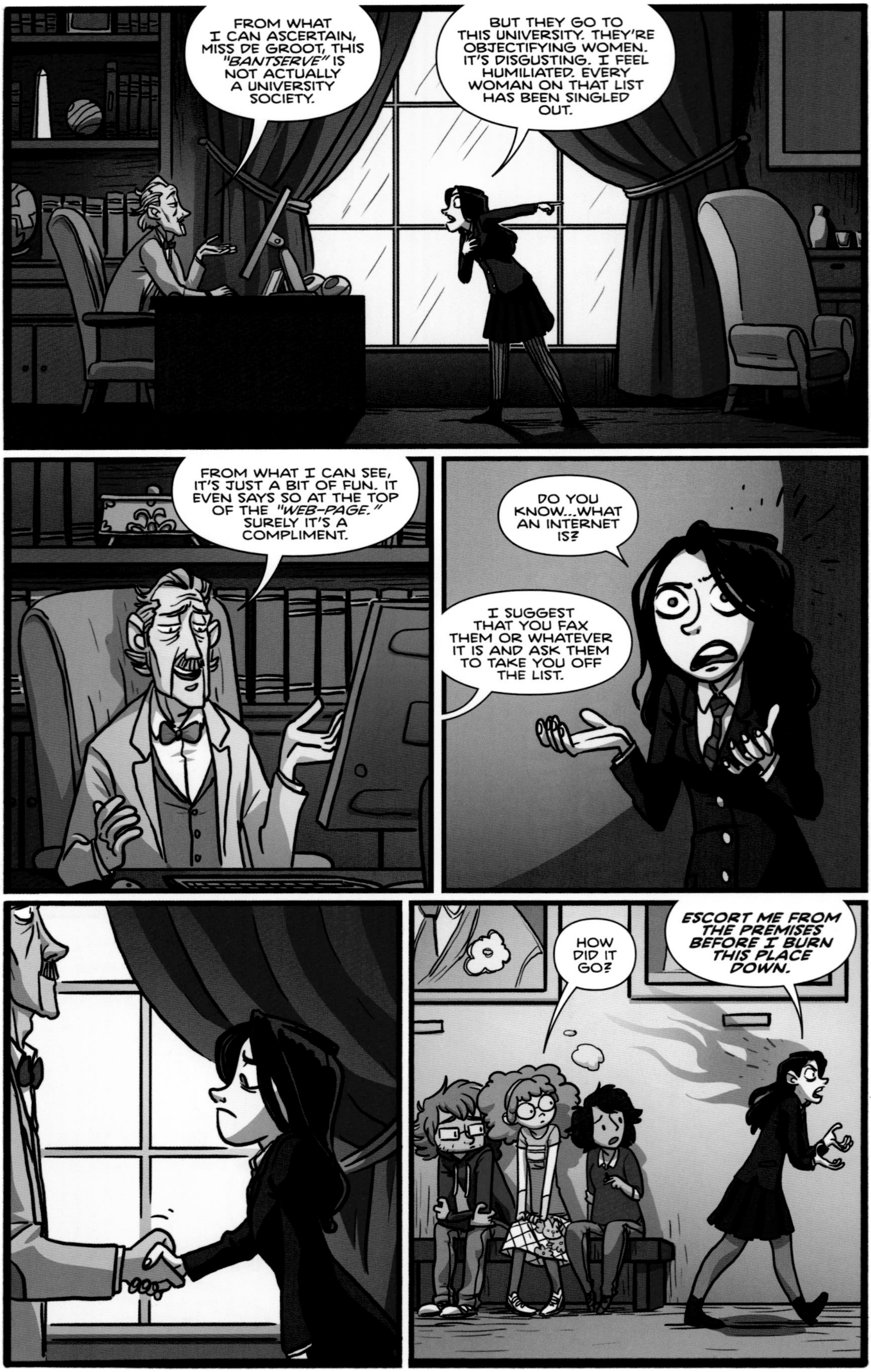
FROM WHAT I CAN ASCERTAIN, MISS DE GROOT, THIS "BANTSERVE" IS NOT ACTUALLY A UNIVERSITY SOCIETY.
BUT THEY GO TO THIS UNIVERSITY. THEY'RE OBJECTIFYING WOMEN. IT'S DISGUSTING. I FEEL HUMILIATED. EVERY WOMAN ON THAT LIST HAS BEEN SINGLED OUT.
FROM WHAT I CAN SEE, IT'S JUST A BIT OF FUN. IT EVEN SAYS SO AT THE TOP OF THE "WEB-PAGE." SURELY IT'S A COMPLIMENT.
DO YOU KNOW...WHAT AN INTERNET IS?
I SUGGEST THAT YOU FAX THEM OR WHATEVER IT IS AND ASK THEM TO TAKE YOU OFF THE LIST.
HOW DID IT GO?
ESCORT ME FROM THE PREMISES BEFORE I BURN THIS PLACE DOWN.

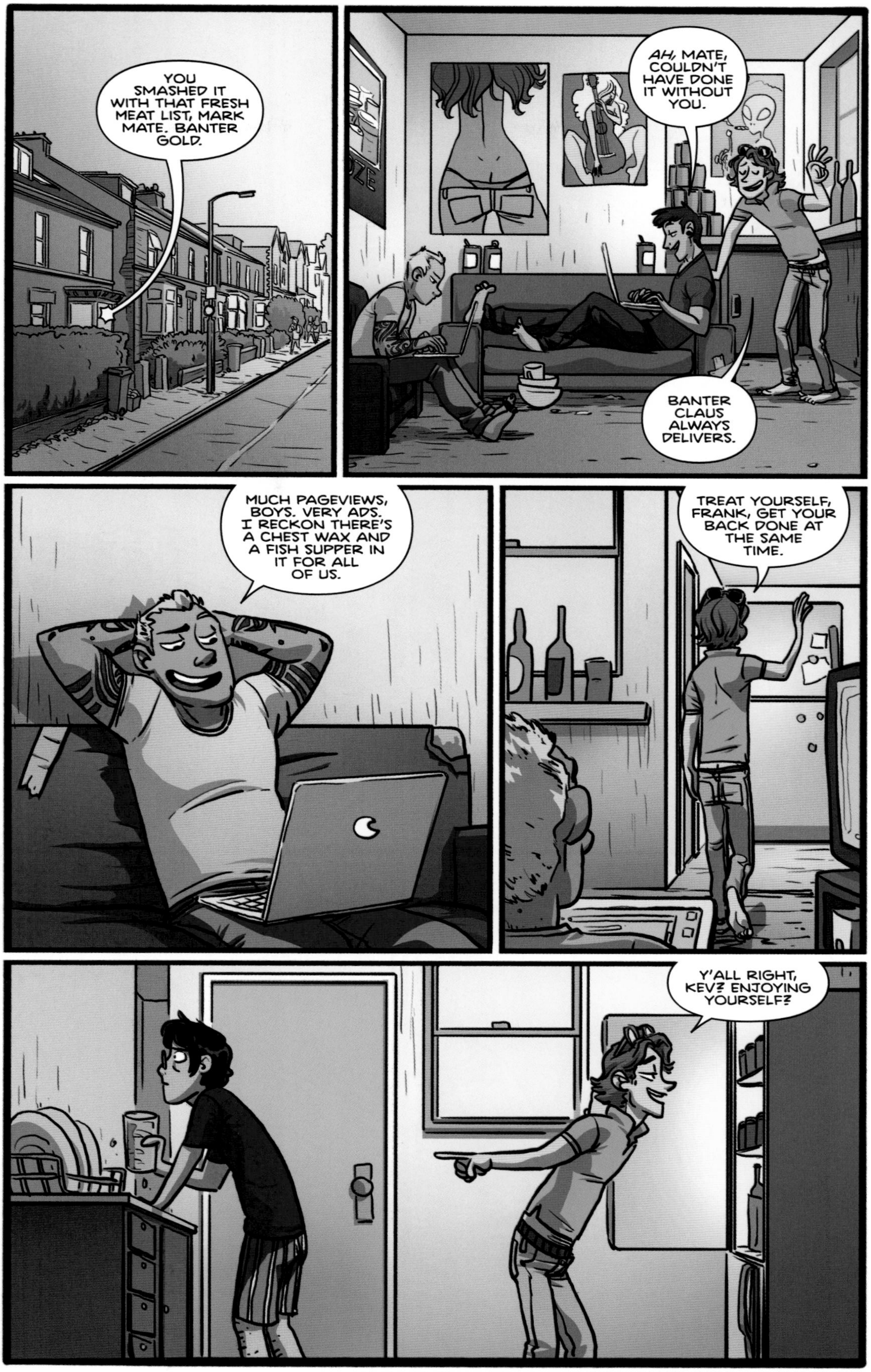
YOU SMASHED IT WITH THAT FRESH MEAT LIST, MARK MATE. BANTER GOLD.
AH, MATE, COULDN'T HAVE DONE IT WITHOUT YOU.
BANTER CLAUS ALWAYS DELIVERS.
MUCH PAGEVIEWS, BOYS. VERY ADS. I RECKON THERE'S A CHEST WAX AND A FISH SUPPER IN IT FOR ALL OF US.
TREAT YOURSELF, FRANK, GET YOUR BACK DONE AT THE SAME TIME.
Y'ALL RIGHT, KEV? ENJOYING YOURSELF?

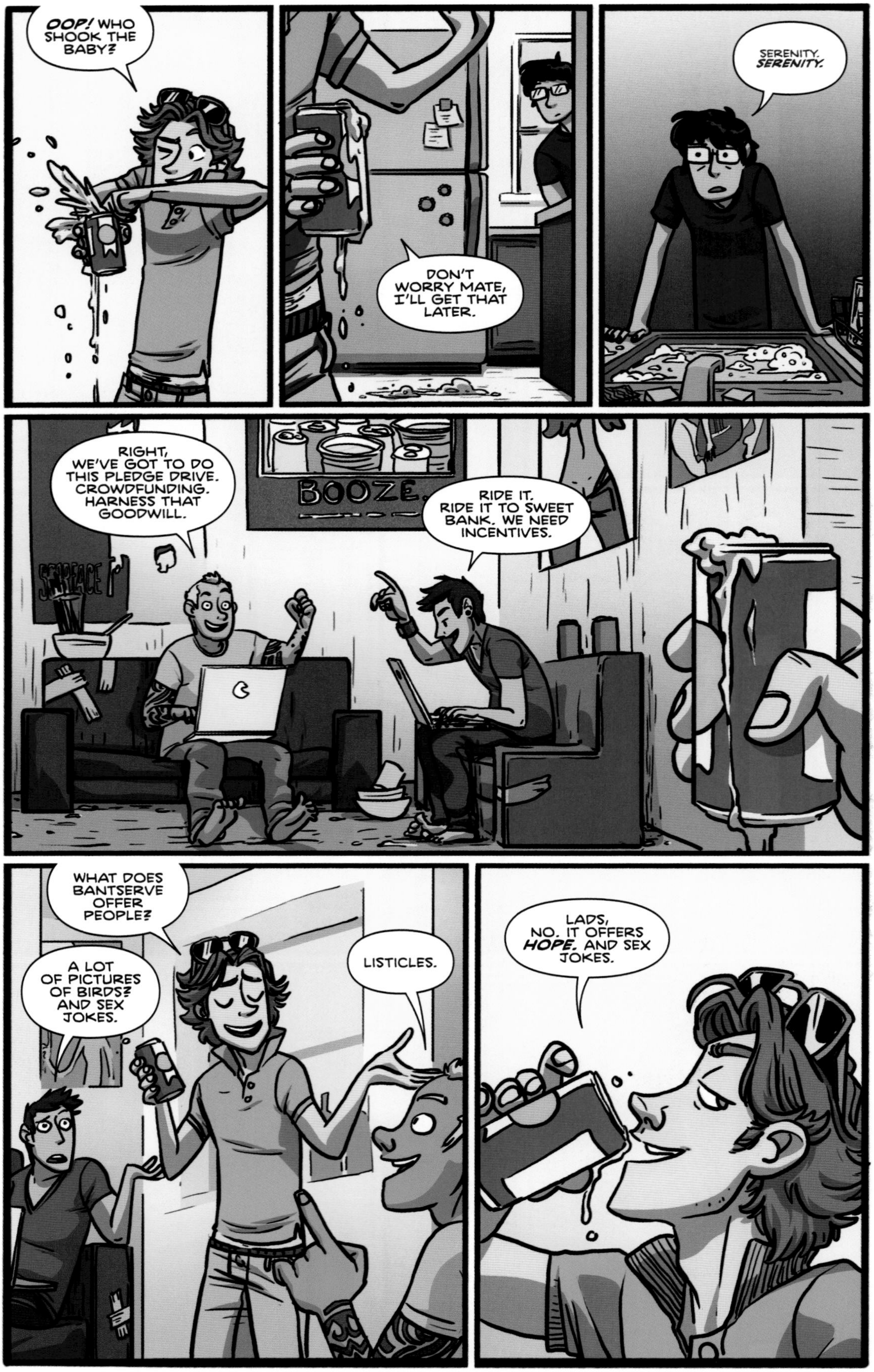

OOP! WHO SHOOK THE BABY?
DON'T WORRY MATE, I'LL GET THAT LATER.
SERENITY. SERENITY.
BOOZE.
RIGHT, WE'VE GOT TO DO THIS PLEDGE DRIVE. CROWDFUNDING. HARNESS THAT GOODWILL.
RIDE IT. RIDE IT TO SWEET BANK. WE NEED INCENTIVES.
WHAT DOES BANTSERVE OFFER PEOPLE?
A LOT OF PICTURES OF BIRDS? AND SEX JOKES.
LISTICLES.
LADS, NO. IT OFFERS HOPE. AND SEX JOKES.

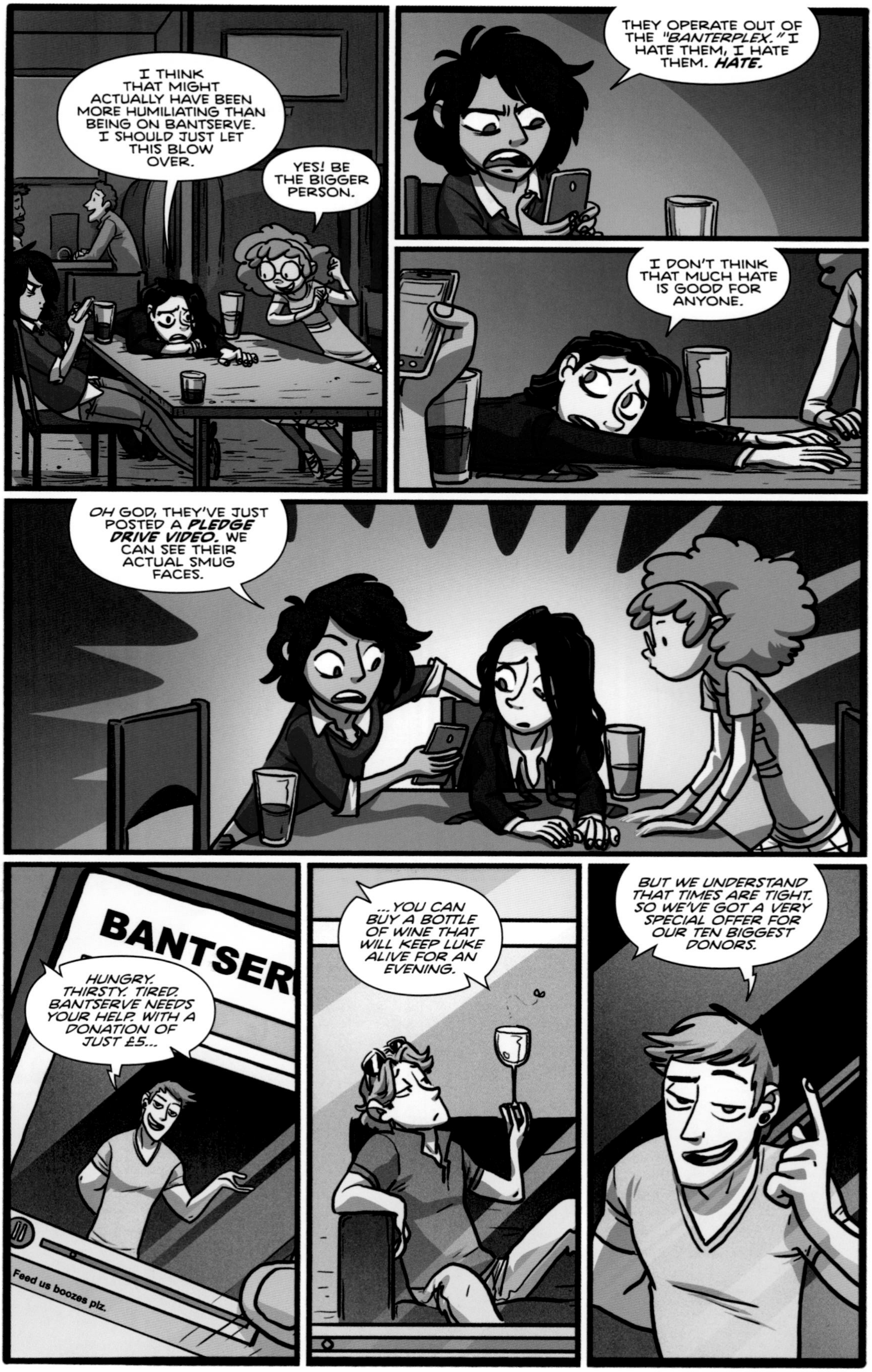
I THINK THAT MIGHT ACTUALLY HAVE BEEN MORE HUMILIATING THAN BEING ON BANTSERVE. I SHOULD JUST LET THIS BLOW OVER.
YES! BE THE BIGGER PERSON.
THEY OPERATE OUT OF THE "BANTERPLEX." I HATE THEM, I HATE THEM. HATE.
I DON'T THINK THAT MUCH HATE IS GOOD FOR ANYONE.
OH GOD, THEY'VE JUST POSTED A PLEDGE DRIVE VIDEO. WE CAN SEE THEIR ACTUAL SMUG FACES.
BANTSER
HUNGRY. THIRSTY. TIRED. BANTSERVE NEEDS YOUR HELP. WITH A DONATION OF JUST £5...
Feed us boozes plz.
...YOU CAN BUY A BOTTLE OF WINE THAT WILL KEEP LUKE ALIVE FOR AN EVENING.
BUT WE UNDERSTAND THAT TIMES ARE TIGHT. SO WE'VE GOT A VERY SPECIAL OFFER FOR OUR TEN BIGGEST DONORS.

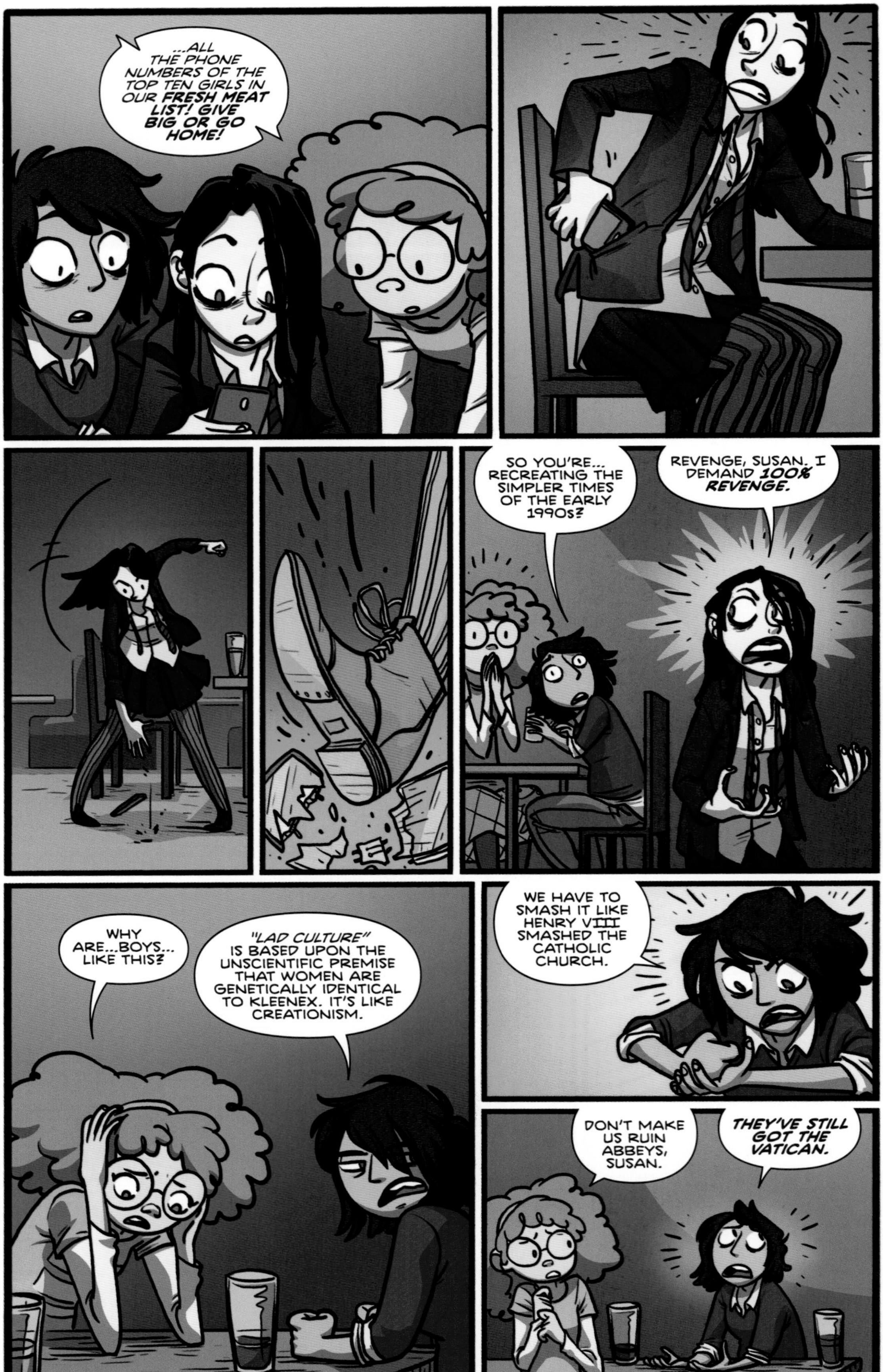
...ALL THE PHONE NUMBERS OF THE TOP TEN GIRLS IN OUR FRESH MEAT LIST! GIVE BIG OR GO HOME!
SO YOU'RE... RECREATING THE SIMPLER TIMES OF THE EARLY 1990s?
REVENGE, SUSAN. I DEMAND 100% REVENGE.
WHY ARE...BOYS... LIKE THIS?
"LAD CULTURE" IS BASED UPON THE UNSCIENTIFIC PREMISE THAT WOMEN ARE GENETICALLY IDENTICAL TO KLEENEX. IT'S LIKE CREATIONISM.
WE HAVE TO SMASH IT LIKE HENRY VIII SMASHED THE CATHOLIC CHURCH.
DON'T MAKE US RUIN ABBEYS, SUSAN.
THEY'VE STILL GOT THE VATICAN.

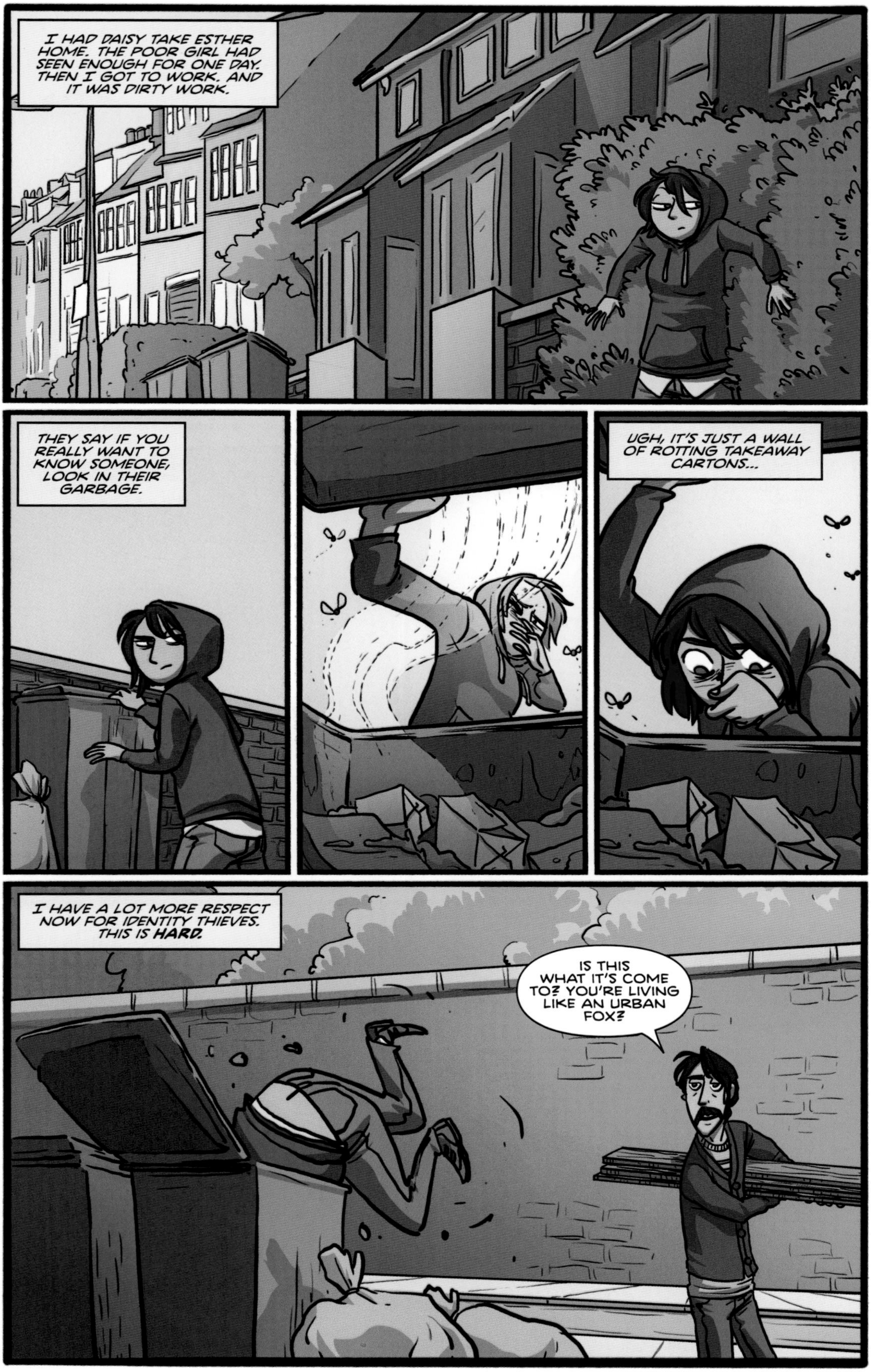
I HAD DAISY TAKE ESTHER HOME. THE POOR GIRL HAD SEEN ENOUGH FOR ONE DAY. THEN I GOT TO WORK. AND IT WAS DIRTY WORK.
THEY SAY IF YOU REALLY WANT TO KNOW SOMEONE, LOOK IN THEIR GARBAGE.
UGH, IT'S JUST A WALL OF ROTTING TAKEAWAY CARTONS...
I HAVE A LOT MORE RESPECT NOW FOR IDENTITY THIEVES. THIS IS **HARD.**
IS THIS WHAT IT'S COME TO? YOU'RE LIVING LIKE AN URBAN FOX?

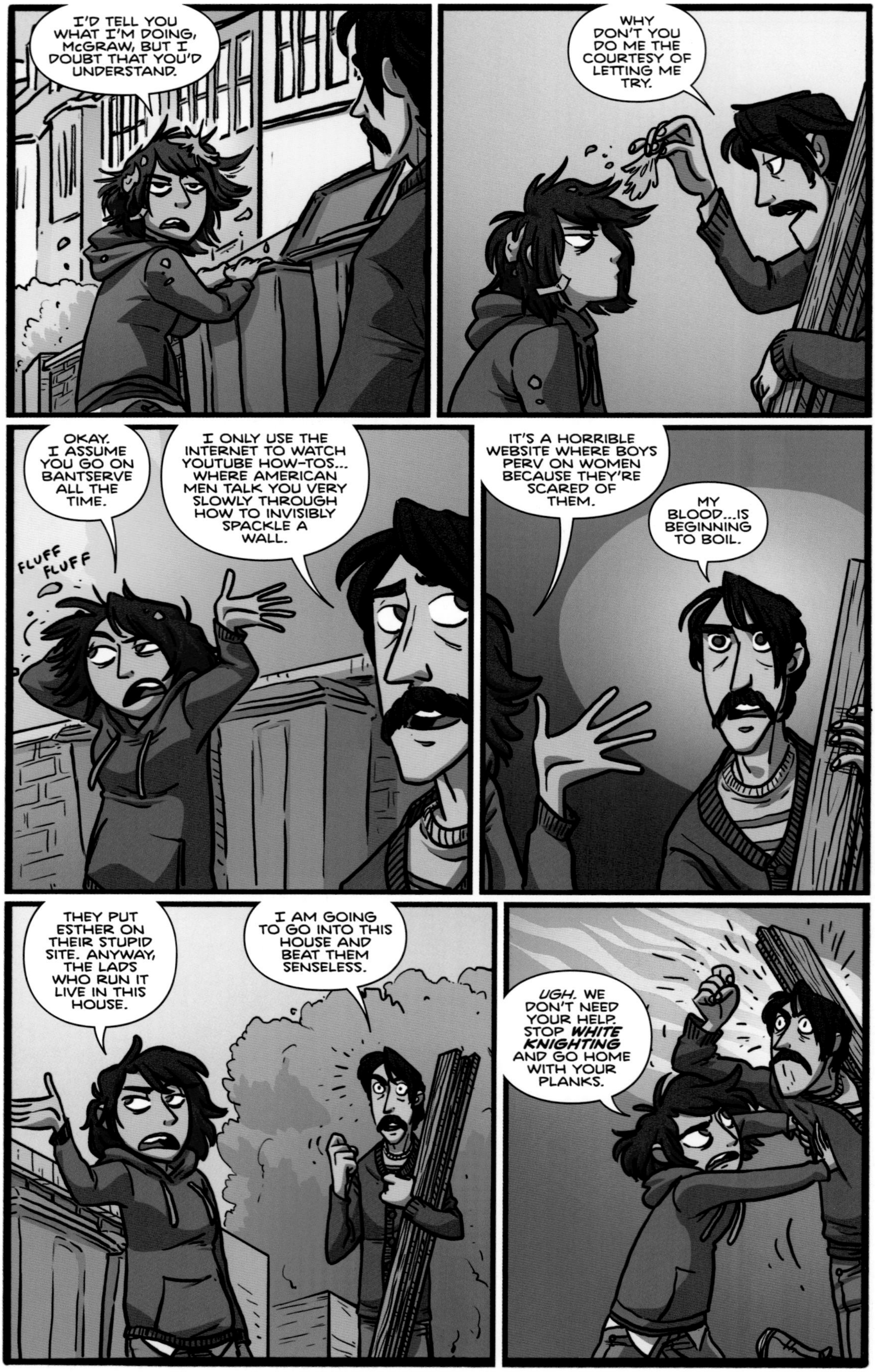
I'D TELL YOU WHAT I'M DOING, McGRAW, BUT I DOUBT THAT YOU'D UNDERSTAND.
WHY DON'T YOU DO ME THE COURTESY OF LETTING ME TRY.
OKAY. I ASSUME YOU GO ON BANTSERVE ALL THE TIME.
I ONLY USE THE INTERNET TO WATCH YOUTUBE HOW-TOS... WHERE AMERICAN MEN TALK YOU VERY SLOWLY THROUGH HOW TO INVISIBLY SPACKLE A WALL.
FLUFF FLUFF
IT'S A HORRIBLE WEBSITE WHERE BOYS PERV ON WOMEN BECAUSE THEY'RE SCARED OF THEM.
MY BLOOD...IS BEGINNING TO BOIL.
THEY PUT ESTHER ON THEIR STUPID SITE. ANYWAY, THE LADS WHO RUN IT LIVE IN THIS HOUSE.
I AM GOING TO GO INTO THIS HOUSE AND BEAT THEM SENSELESS.
UGH. WE DON'T NEED YOUR HELP. STOP ***WHITE KNIGHTING*** AND GO HOME WITH YOUR PLANKS.

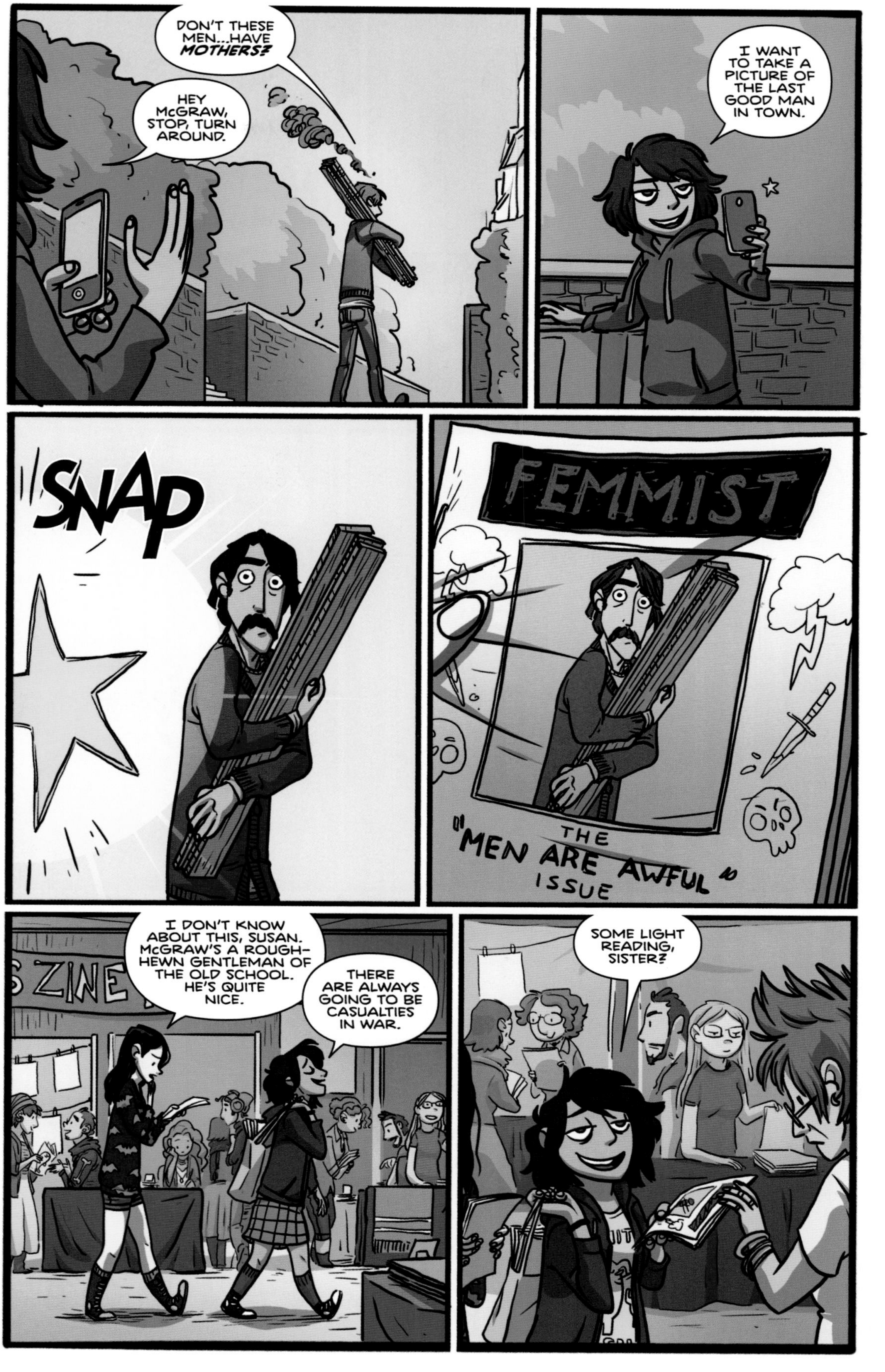
DON'T THESE MEN...HAVE *MOTHERS?*
HEY McGRAW, STOP, TURN AROUND.
I WANT TO TAKE A PICTURE OF THE LAST GOOD MAN IN TOWN.
SNAP
FEMMIST
"THE MEN ARE AWFUL ISSUE"
I DON'T KNOW ABOUT THIS, SUSAN. McGRAW'S A ROUGH-HEWN GENTLEMAN OF THE OLD SCHOOL. HE'S QUITE NICE.
THERE ARE ALWAYS GOING TO BE CASUALTIES IN WAR.
SOME LIGHT READING, SISTER?

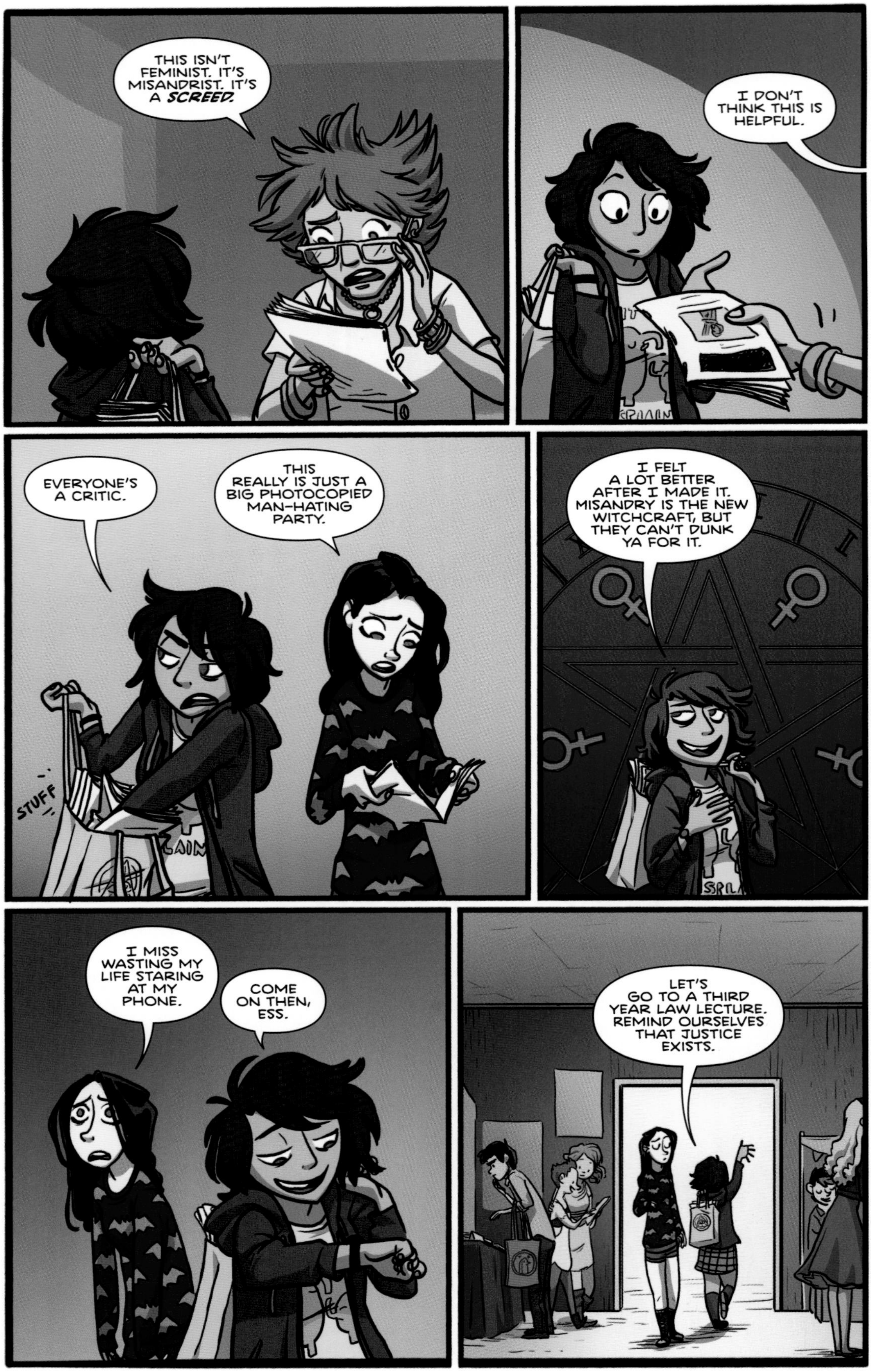
THIS ISN'T FEMINIST. IT'S MISANDRIST. IT'S A SCREED.
I DON'T THINK THIS IS HELPFUL.
EVERYONE'S A CRITIC.
THIS REALLY IS JUST A BIG PHOTOCOPIED MAN-HATING PARTY.
STUFF
I FELT A LOT BETTER AFTER I MADE IT. MISANDRY IS THE NEW WITCHCRAFT, BUT THEY CAN'T DUNK YA FOR IT.
I MISS WASTING MY LIFE STARING AT MY PHONE.
COME ON THEN, ESS.
LET'S GO TO A THIRD YEAR LAW LECTURE. REMIND OURSELVES THAT JUSTICE EXISTS.

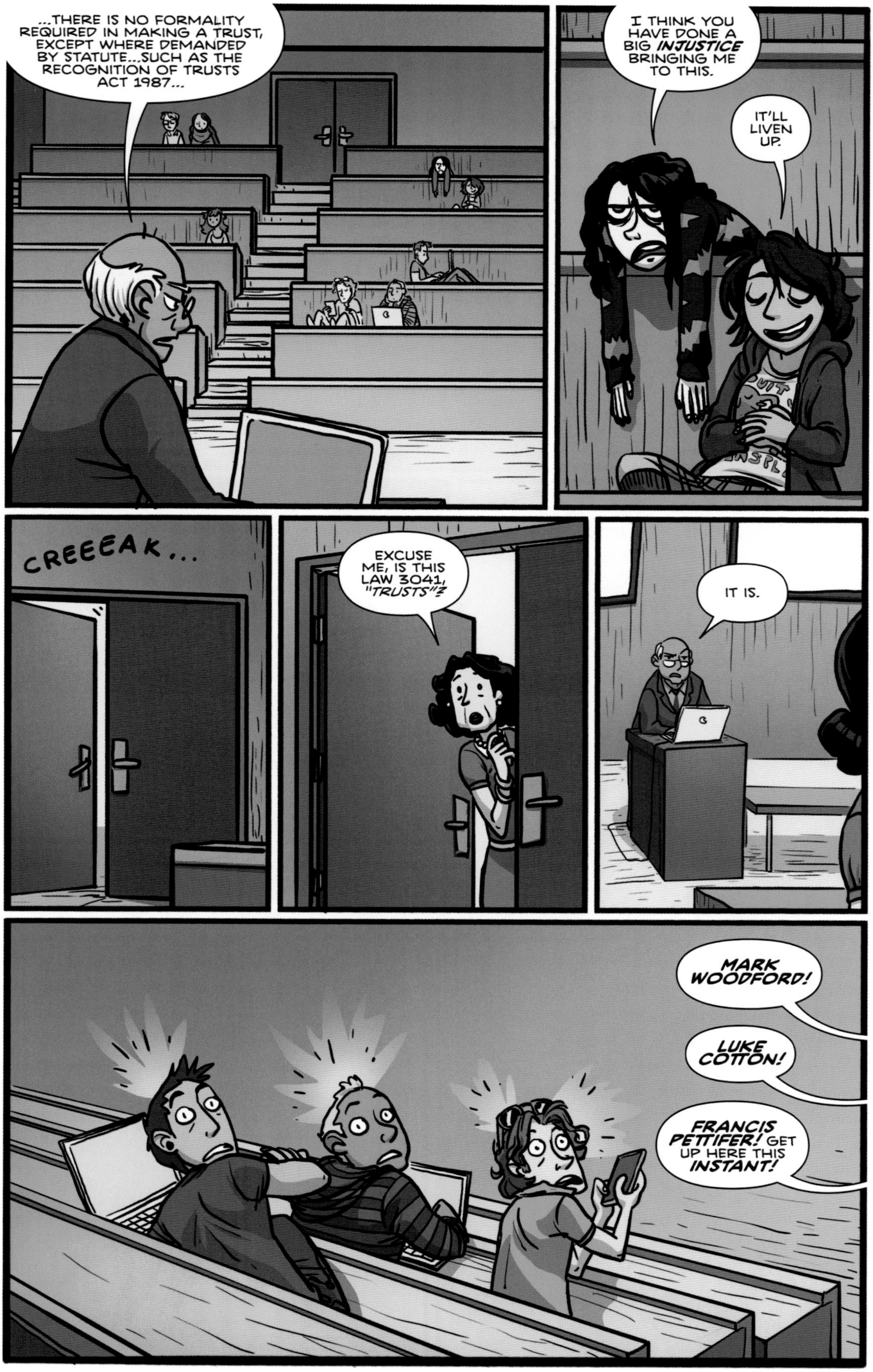
...THERE IS NO FORMALITY REQUIRED IN MAKING A TRUST, EXCEPT WHERE DEMANDED BY STATUTE...SUCH AS THE RECOGNITION OF TRUSTS ACT 1987...
I THINK YOU HAVE DONE A BIG INJUSTICE BRINGING ME TO THIS.
IT'LL LIVEN UP.
CREEEAK...
EXCUSE ME, IS THIS LAW 3041, "TRUSTS"?
IT IS.
MARK WOODFORD!
LUKE COTTON!
FRANCIS PETTIFER! GET UP HERE THIS INSTANT!

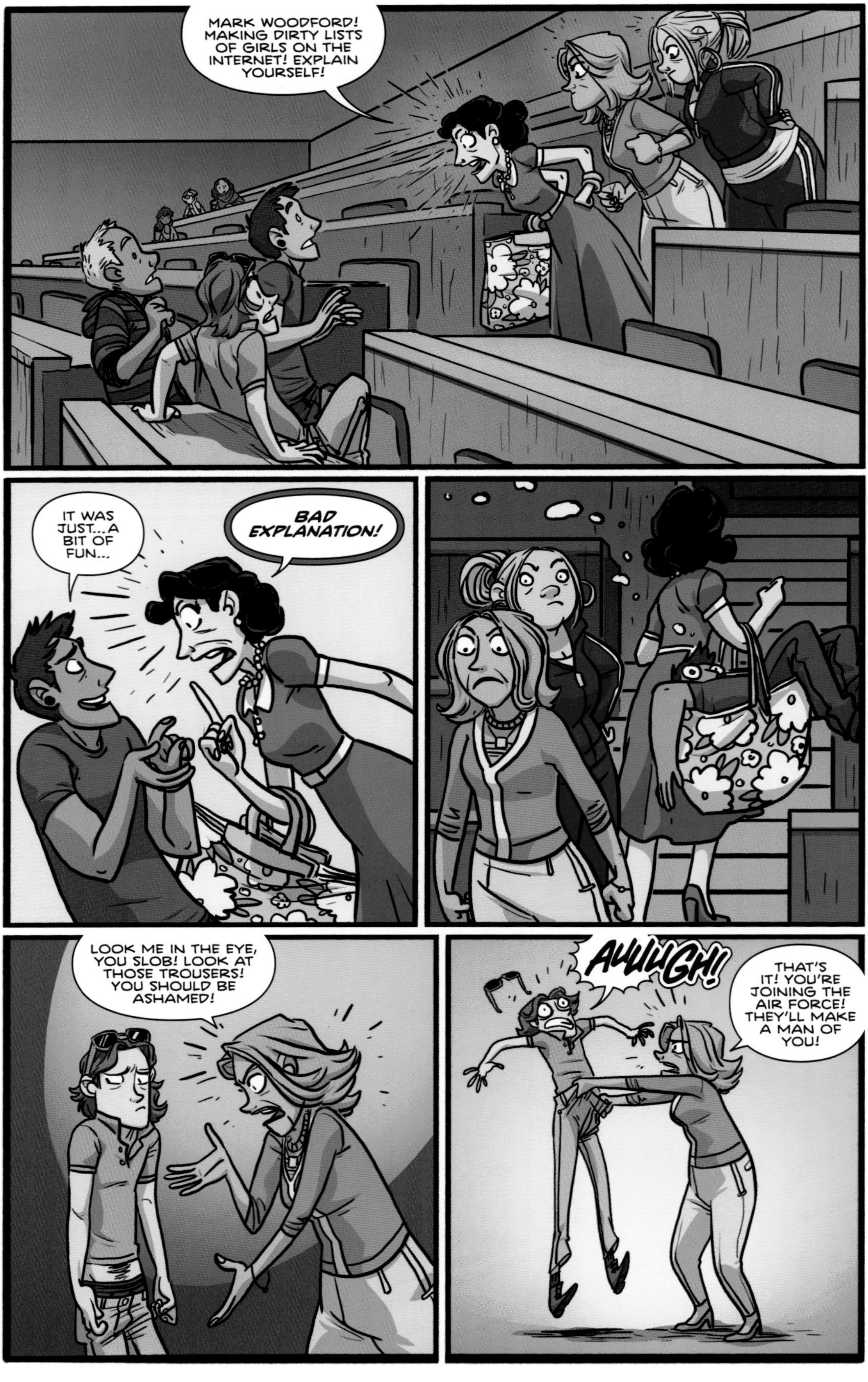
MARK WOODFORD! MAKING DIRTY LISTS OF GIRLS ON THE INTERNET! EXPLAIN YOURSELF!
IT WAS JUST... A BIT OF FUN...
BAD EXPLANATION!
LOOK ME IN THE EYE, YOU SLOB! LOOK AT THOSE TROUSERS! YOU SHOULD BE ASHAMED!
AUUUGH!
THAT'S IT! YOU'RE JOINING THE AIR FORCE! THEY'LL MAKE A MAN OF YOU!

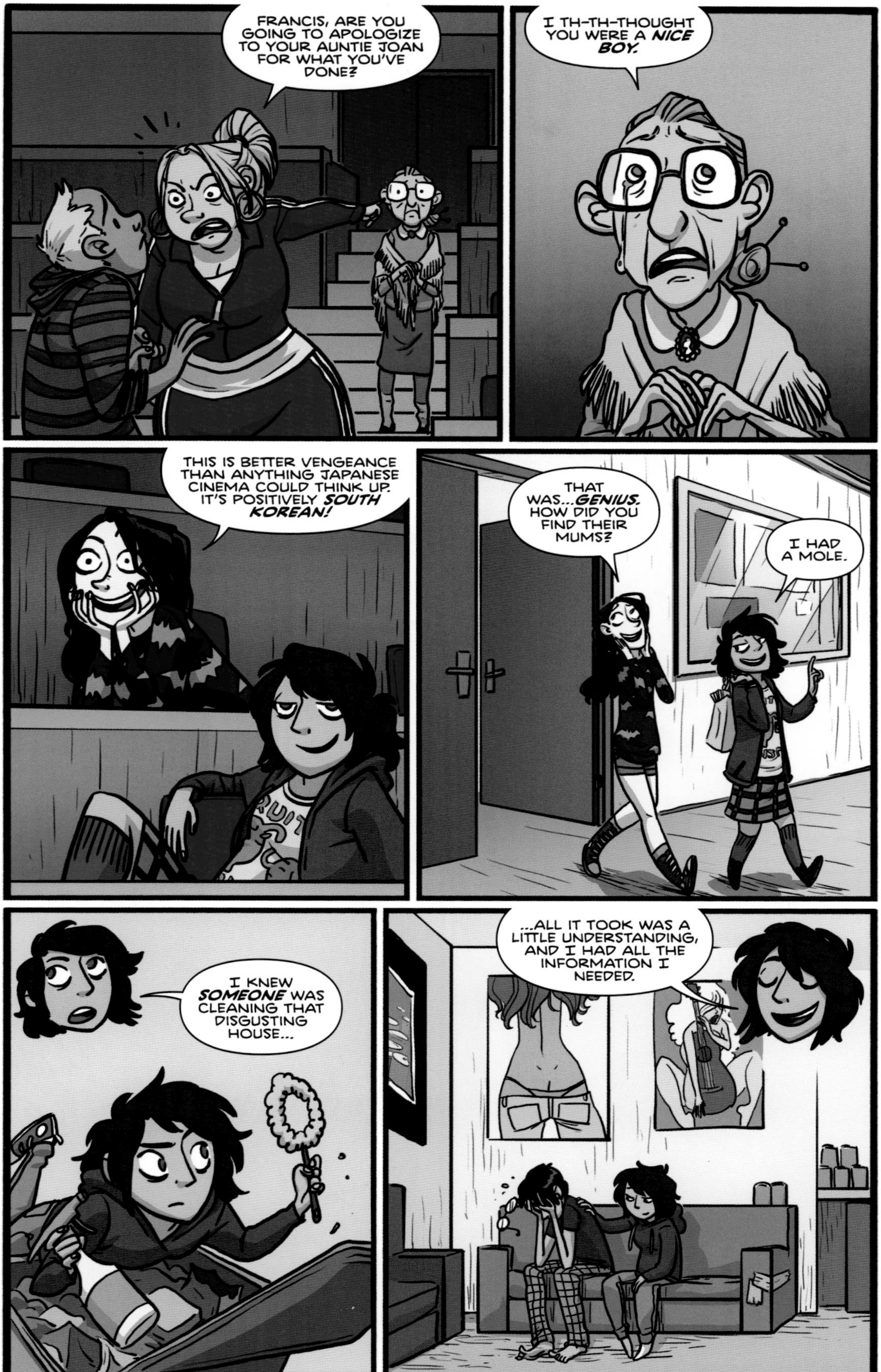

FRANCIS, ARE YOU GOING TO APOLOGIZE TO YOUR AUNTIE JOAN FOR WHAT YOU'VE DONE?
I TH-TH-THOUGHT YOU WERE A NICE BOY.
THIS IS BETTER VENGEANCE THAN ANYTHING JAPANESE CINEMA COULD THINK UP. IT'S POSITIVELY SOUTH KOREAN!
THAT WAS... GENIUS. HOW DID YOU FIND THEIR MUMS?
I HAD A MOLE.
I KNEW SOMEONE WAS CLEANING THAT DISGUSTING HOUSE...
...ALL IT TOOK WAS A LITTLE UNDERSTANDING, AND I HAD ALL THE INFORMATION I NEEDED.

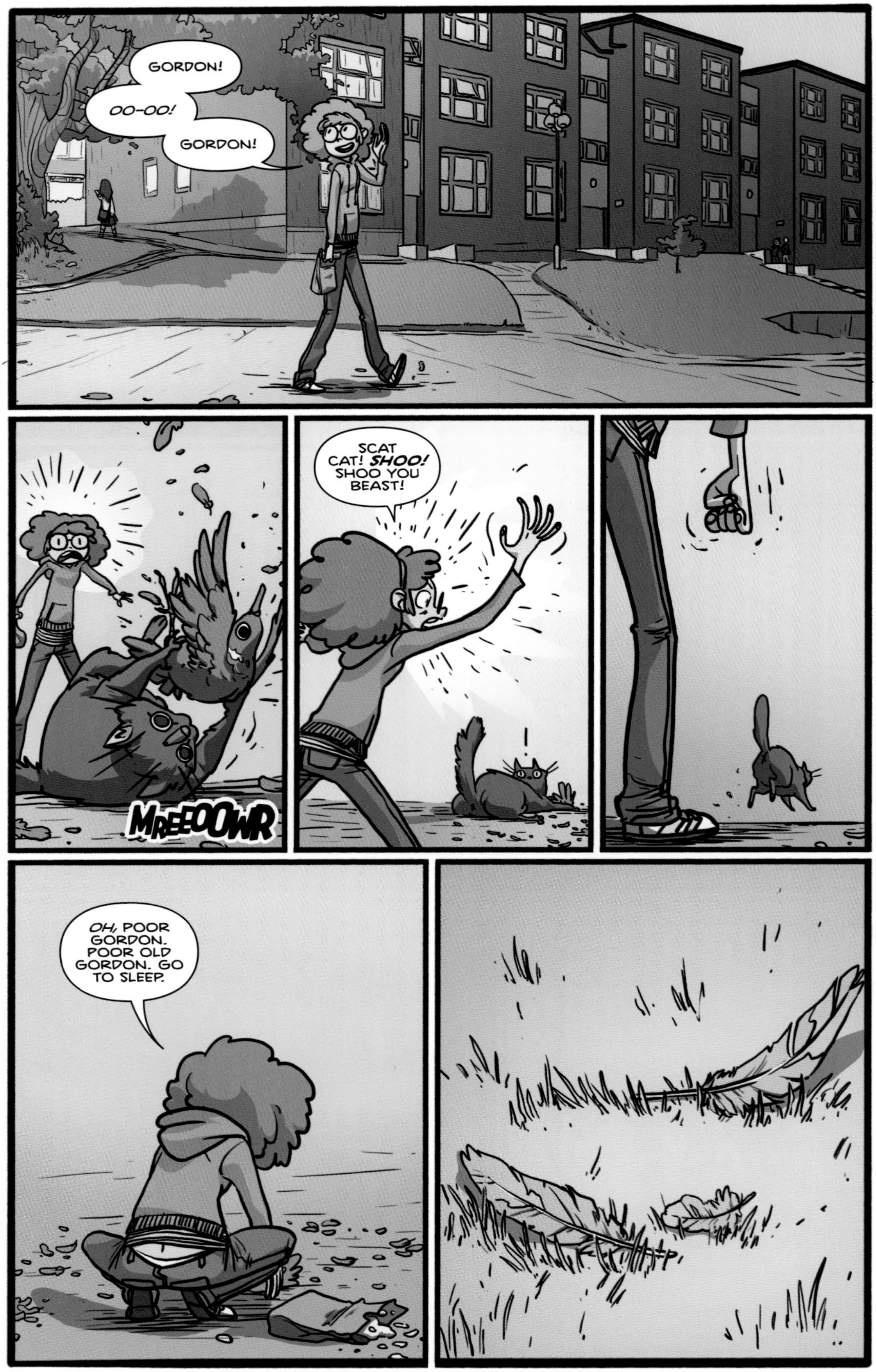
GORDON!
OO-OO!
GORDON!
MREEOOWR
SCAT CAT! SHOO! SHOO YOU BEAST!
OH, POOR GORDON. POOR OLD GORDON. GO TO SLEEP.

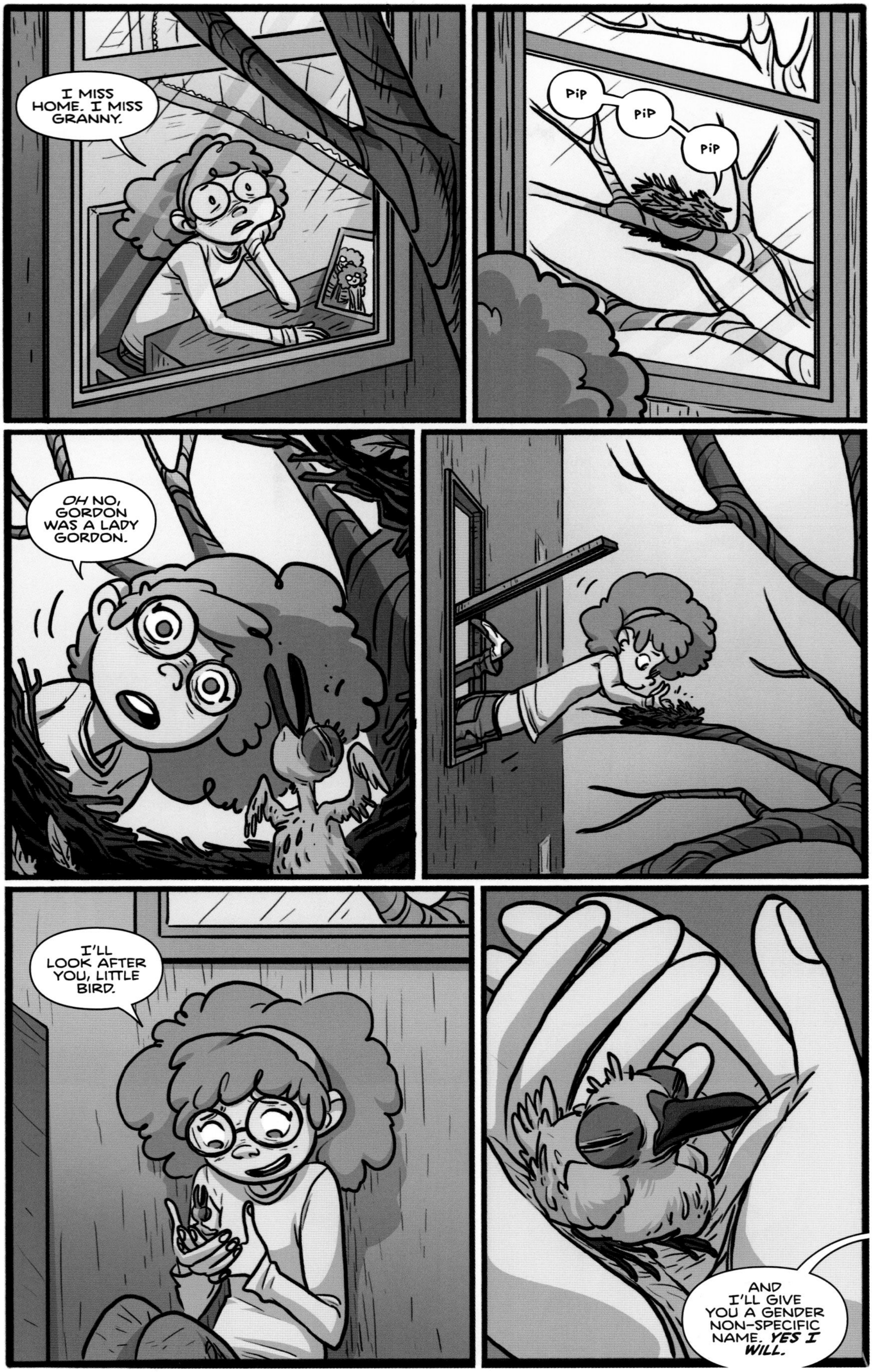
I MISS HOME. I MISS GRANNY.
PIP
PIP
PIP
OH NO, GORDON WAS A LADY GORDON.
I'LL LOOK AFTER YOU, LITTLE BIRD.
AND I'LL GIVE YOU A GENDER NON-SPECIFIC NAME. ***YES I WILL.***

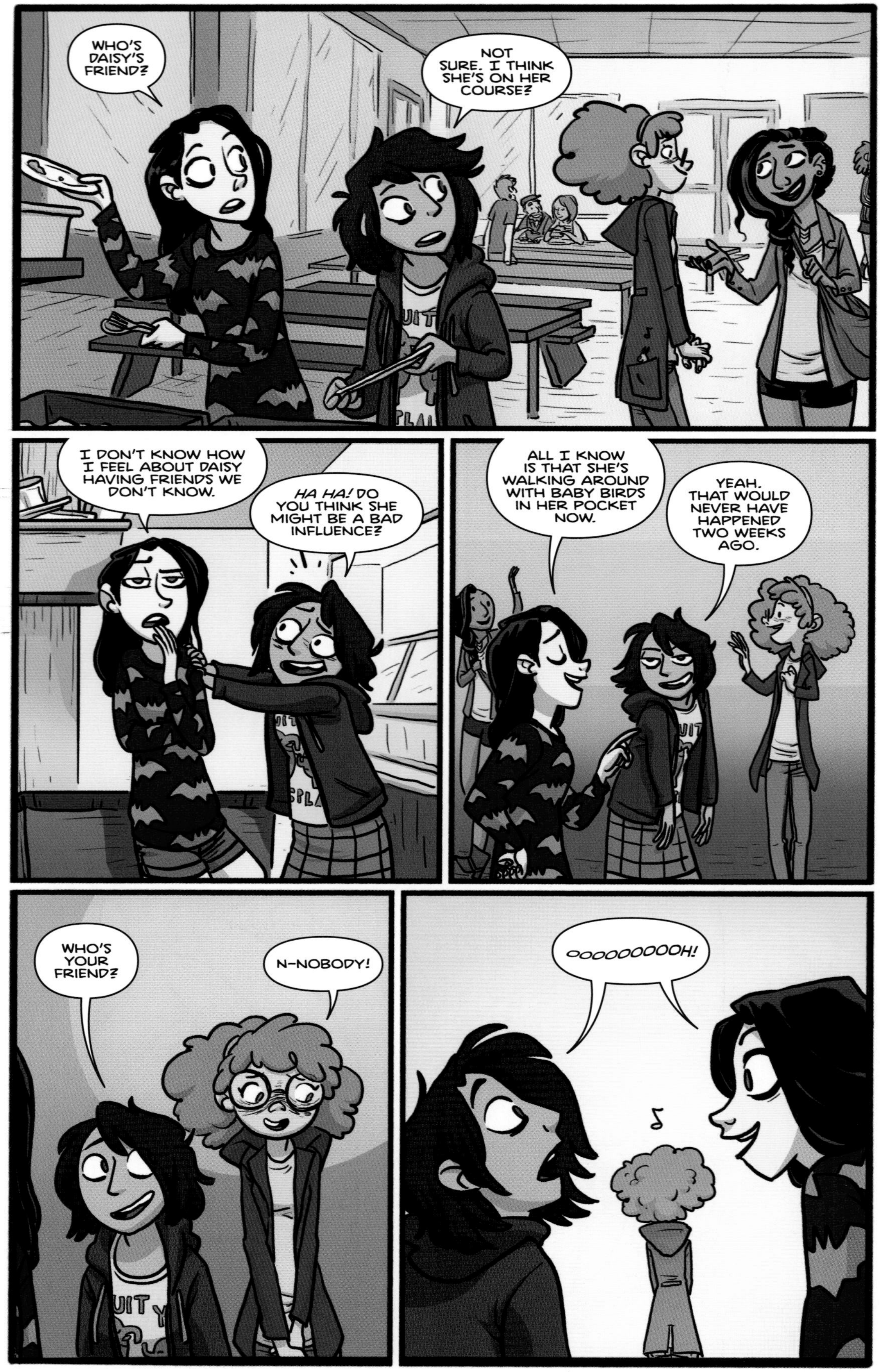
WHO'S DAISY'S FRIEND?
NOT SURE. I THINK SHE'S ON HER COURSE?
I DON'T KNOW HOW I FEEL ABOUT DAISY HAVING FRIENDS WE DON'T KNOW.
HA HA! DO YOU THINK SHE MIGHT BE A BAD INFLUENCE?
ALL I KNOW IS THAT SHE'S WALKING AROUND WITH BABY BIRDS IN HER POCKET NOW.
YEAH. THAT WOULD NEVER HAVE HAPPENED TWO WEEKS AGO.
WHO'S YOUR FRIEND?
N-NOBODY!
OOOOOOOOOH!

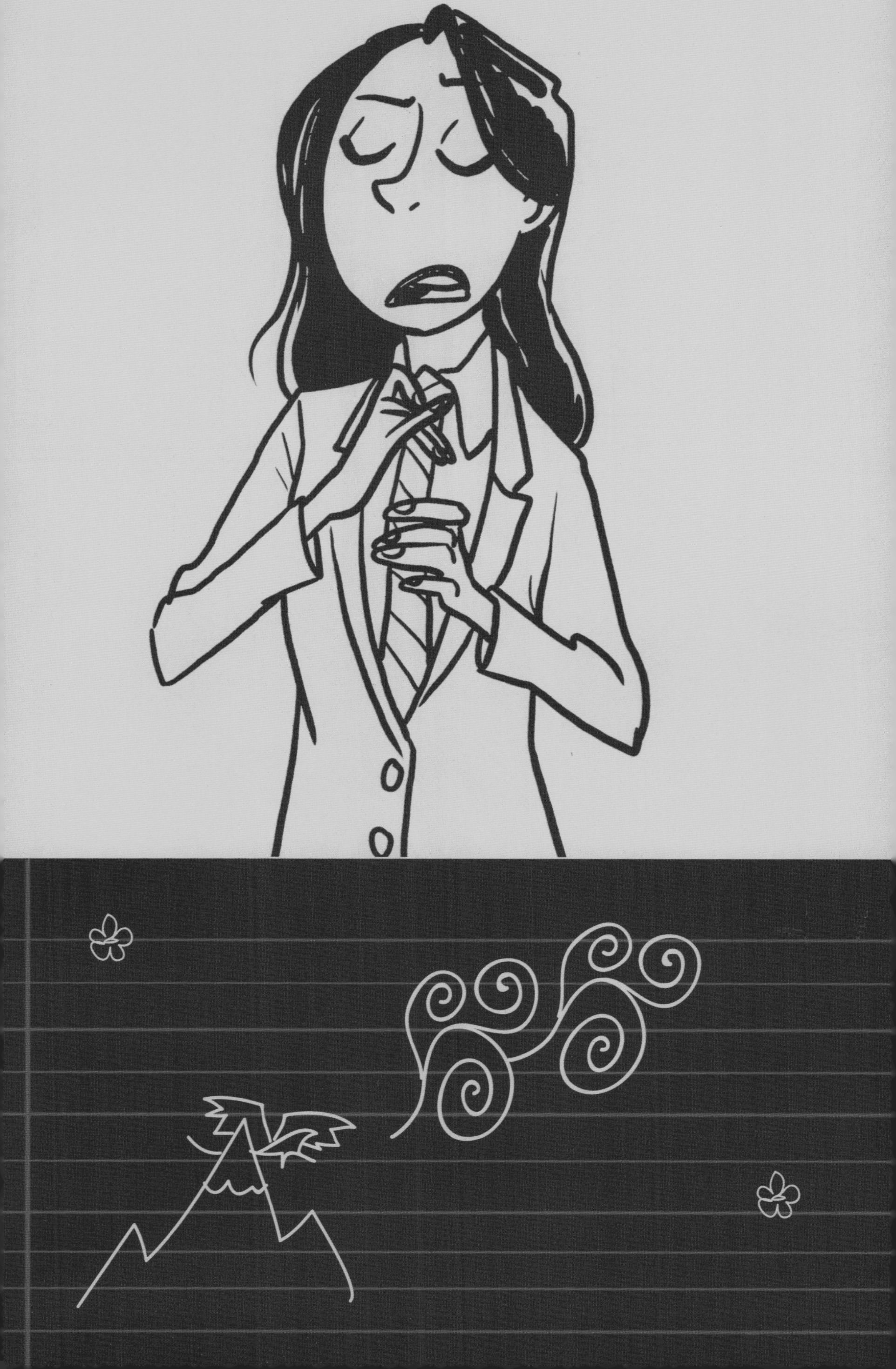

CHAPTER
FOUR

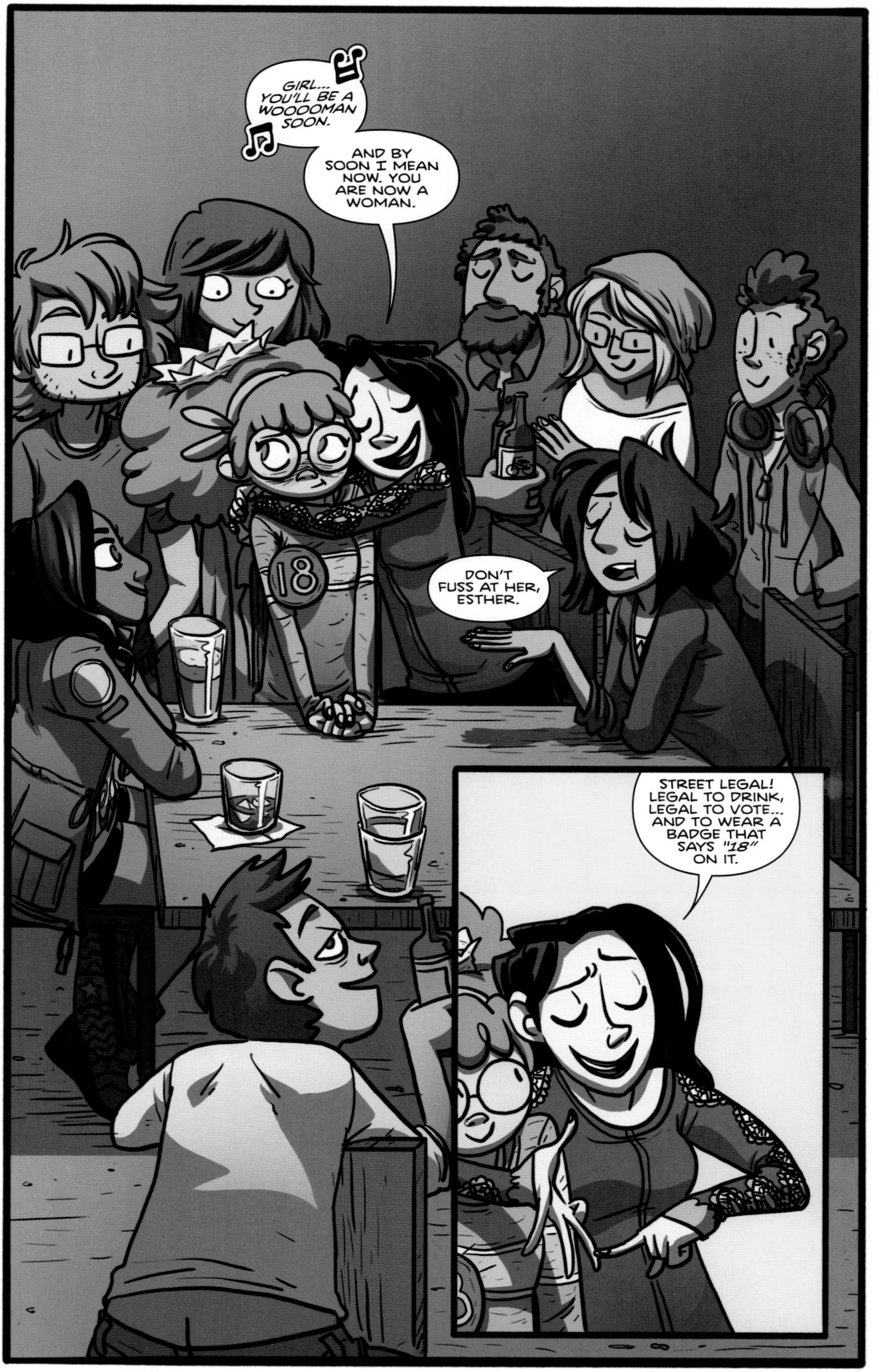
GIRL... YOU'LL BE A WOOOOMAN SOON.
AND BY SOON I MEAN NOW. YOU ARE NOW A WOMAN.
DON'T FUSS AT HER, ESTHER.
18
STREET LEGAL! LEGAL TO DRINK, LEGAL TO VOTE... AND TO WEAR A BADGE THAT SAYS "18" ON IT.

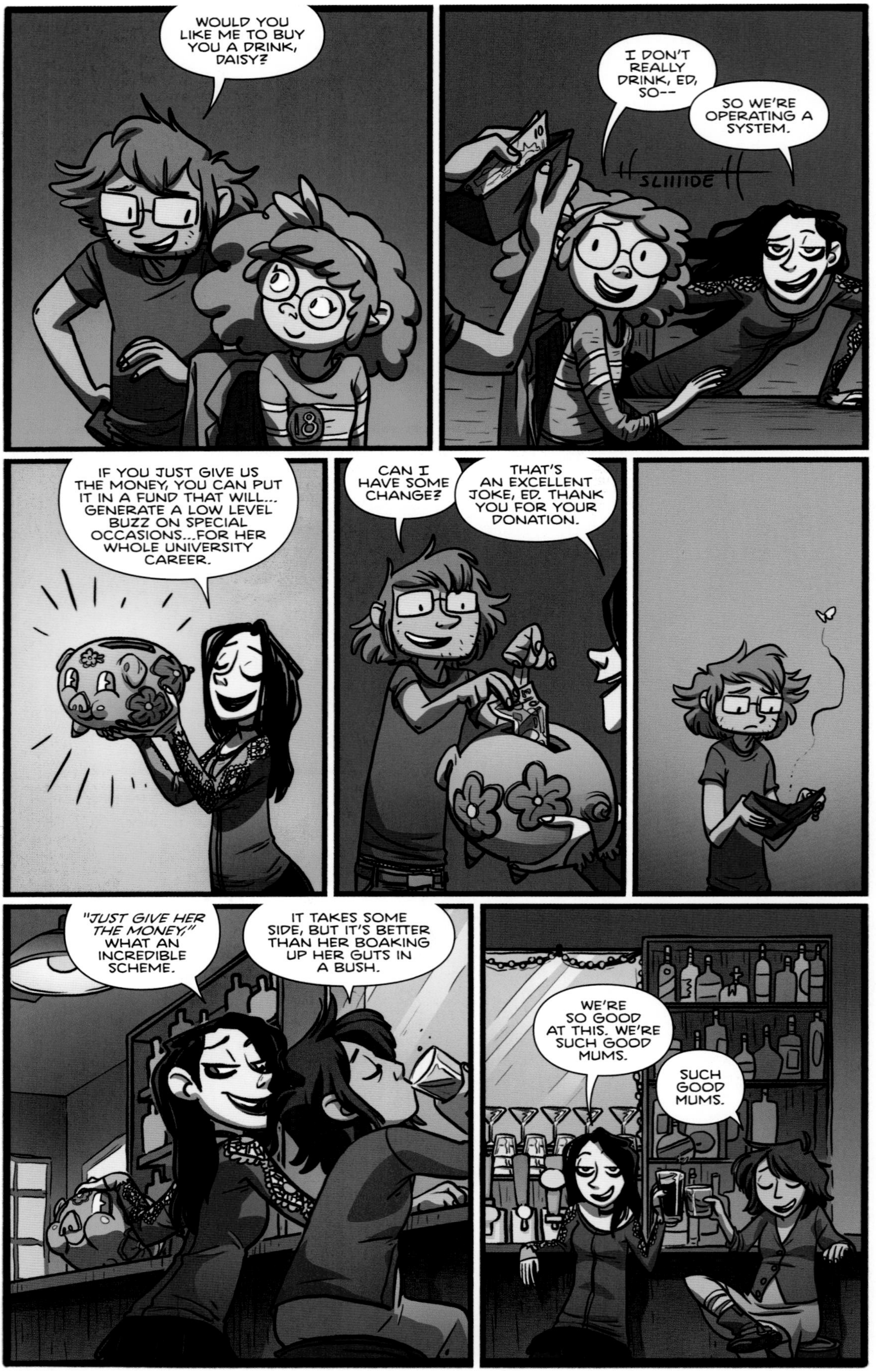
WOULD YOU LIKE ME TO BUY YOU A DRINK, DAISY?
I DON'T REALLY DRINK, ED, SO--
SO WE'RE OPERATING A SYSTEM.
SLIIIIDE
IF YOU JUST GIVE US THE MONEY, YOU CAN PUT IT IN A FUND THAT WILL... GENERATE A LOW LEVEL BUZZ ON SPECIAL OCCASIONS...FOR HER WHOLE UNIVERSITY CAREER.
CAN I HAVE SOME CHANGE?
THAT'S AN EXCELLENT JOKE, ED. THANK YOU FOR YOUR DONATION.
"JUST GIVE HER THE MONEY," WHAT AN INCREDIBLE SCHEME.
IT TAKES SOME SIDE, BUT IT'S BETTER THAN HER BOAKING UP HER GUTS IN A BUSH.
WE'RE SO GOOD AT THIS. WE'RE SUCH GOOD MUMS.
SUCH GOOD MUMS.

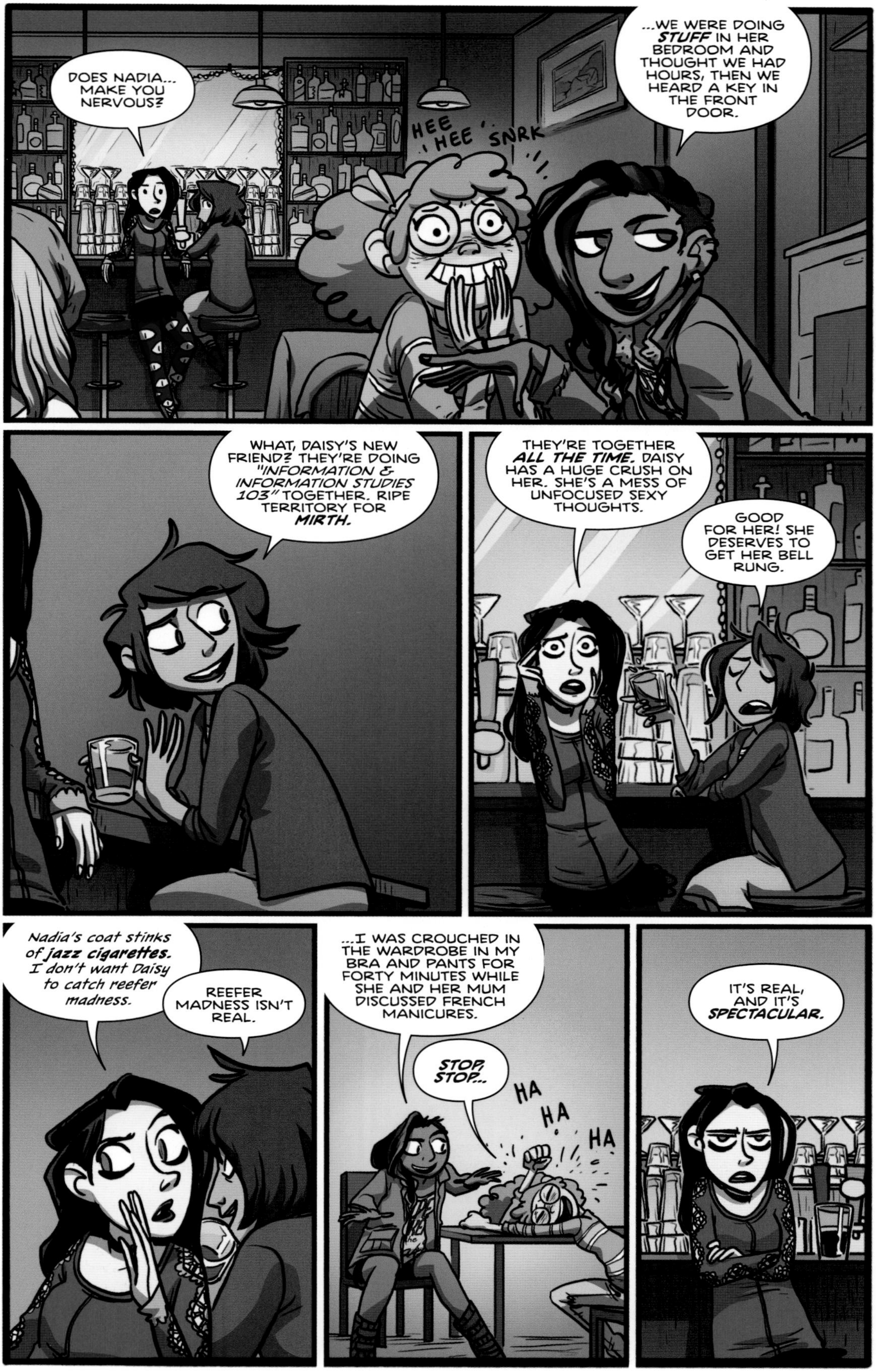
DOES NADIA... MAKE YOU NERVOUS?
HEE HEE SNRK
...WE WERE DOING STUFF IN HER BEDROOM AND THOUGHT WE HAD HOURS, THEN WE HEARD A KEY IN THE FRONT DOOR.
WHAT, DAISY'S NEW FRIEND? THEY'RE DOING "INFORMATION & INFORMATION STUDIES 103" TOGETHER. RIPE TERRITORY FOR MIRTH.
THEY'RE TOGETHER ALL THE TIME. DAISY HAS A HUGE CRUSH ON HER. SHE'S A MESS OF UNFOCUSED SEXY THOUGHTS.
GOOD FOR HER! SHE DESERVES TO GET HER BELL RUNG.
Nadia's coat stinks of jazz cigarettes. I don't want Daisy to catch reefer madness.
REEFER MADNESS ISN'T REAL.
...I WAS CROUCHED IN THE WARDROBE IN MY BRA AND PANTS FOR FORTY MINUTES WHILE SHE AND HER MUM DISCUSSED FRENCH MANICURES.
STOP, STOP...
HA HA HA
IT'S REAL, AND IT'S SPECTACULAR.

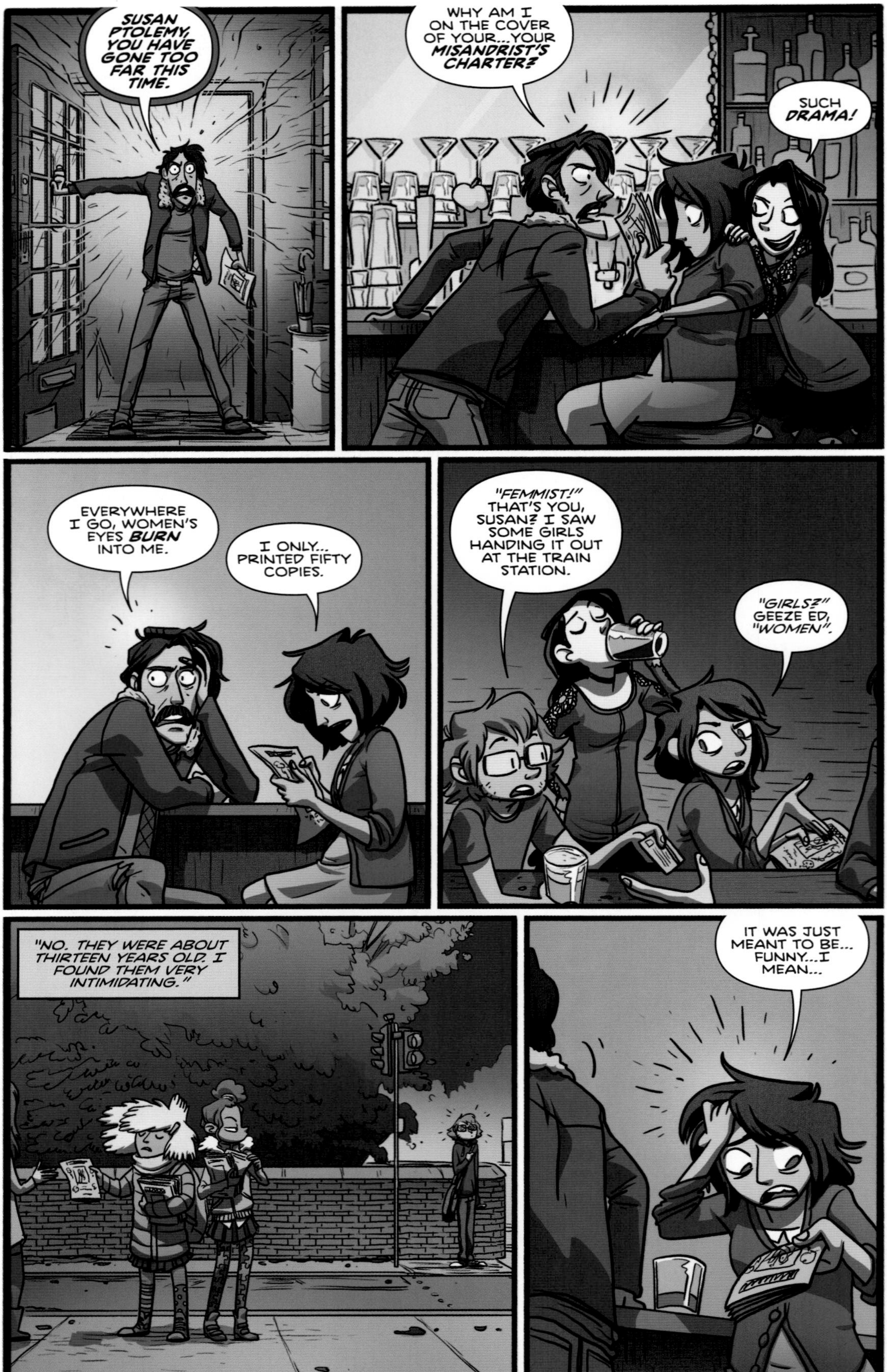
SUSAN PTOLEMY, YOU HAVE GONE TOO FAR THIS TIME.
WHY AM I ON THE COVER OF YOUR...YOUR MISANDRIST'S CHARTER?
SUCH DRAMA!
EVERYWHERE I GO, WOMEN'S EYES BURN INTO ME.
I ONLY... PRINTED FIFTY COPIES.
"FEMMIST!" THAT'S YOU, SUSAN? I SAW SOME GIRLS HANDING IT OUT AT THE TRAIN STATION.
"GIRLS?" GEEZE ED, "WOMEN".
"NO. THEY WERE ABOUT THIRTEEN YEARS OLD. I FOUND THEM VERY INTIMIDATING."
IT WAS JUST MEANT TO BE... FUNNY...I MEAN...

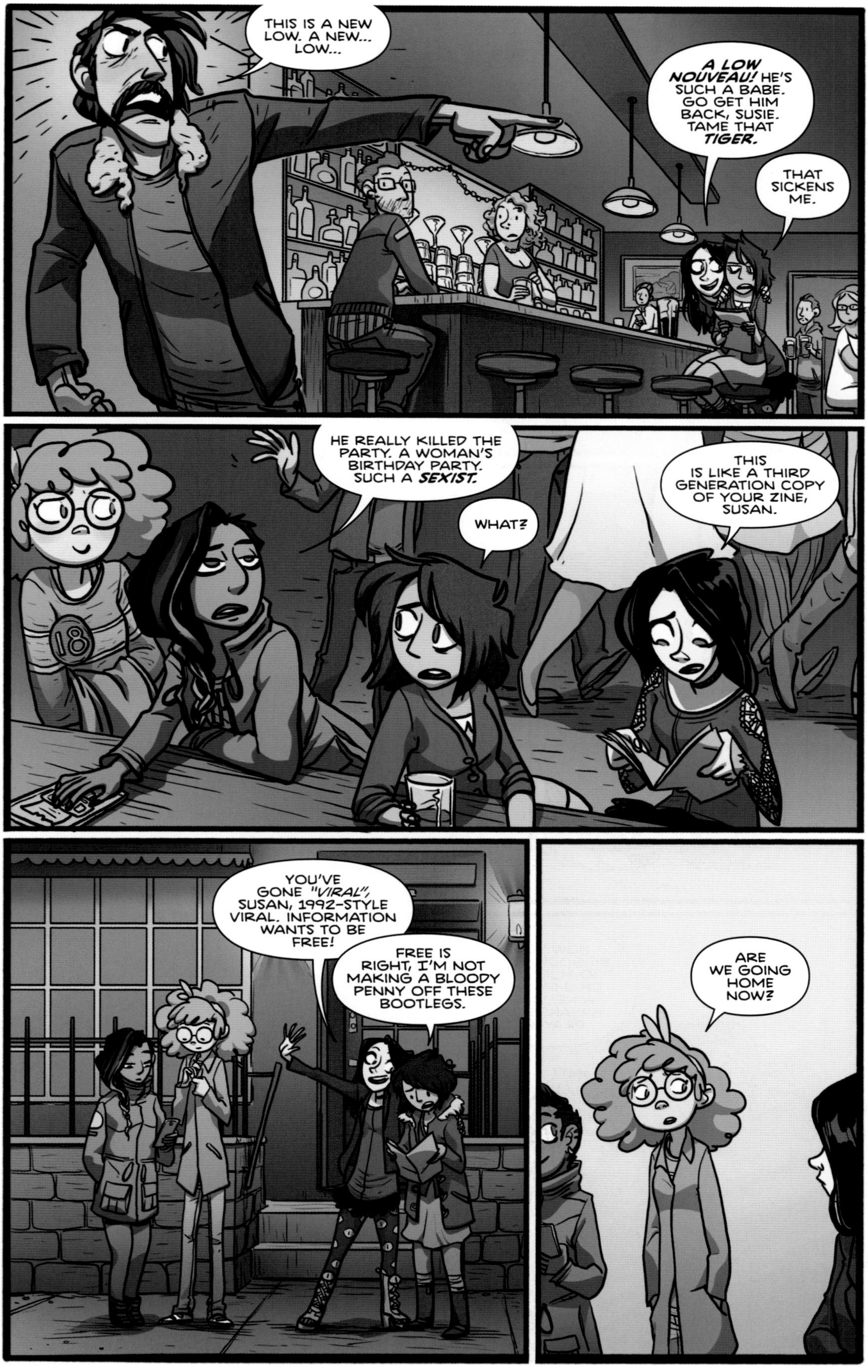
THIS IS A NEW LOW. A NEW... LOW...
A LOW NOUVEAU! HE'S SUCH A BABE. GO GET HIM BACK, SUSIE. TAME THAT TIGER.
THAT SICKENS ME.
HE REALLY KILLED THE PARTY. A WOMAN'S BIRTHDAY PARTY. SUCH A SEXIST.
WHAT?
THIS IS LIKE A THIRD GENERATION COPY OF YOUR ZINE, SUSAN.
18
YOU'VE GONE "VIRAL", SUSAN, 1992-STYLE VIRAL. INFORMATION WANTS TO BE FREE!
FREE IS RIGHT, I'M NOT MAKING A BLOODY PENNY OFF THESE BOOTLEGS.
ARE WE GOING HOME NOW?

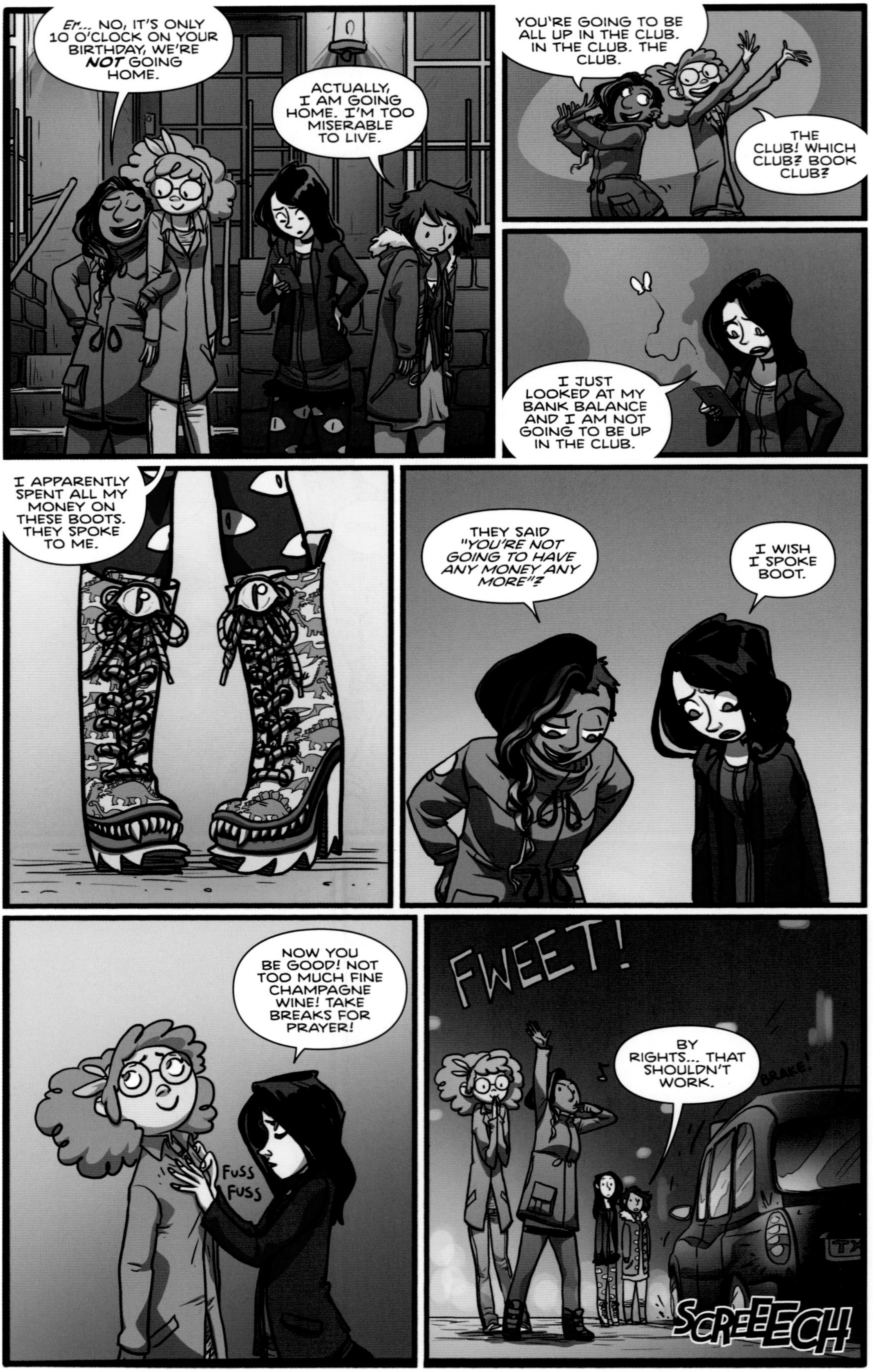
Er... NO, IT'S ONLY 10 O'CLOCK ON YOUR BIRTHDAY, WE'RE **NOT** GOING HOME.
ACTUALLY, I AM GOING HOME. I'M TOO MISERABLE TO LIVE.
YOU'RE GOING TO BE ALL UP IN THE CLUB. IN THE CLUB. THE CLUB.
THE CLUB! WHICH CLUB? BOOK CLUB?
I JUST LOOKED AT MY BANK BALANCE AND I AM NOT GOING TO BE UP IN THE CLUB.
I APPARENTLY SPENT ALL MY MONEY ON THESE BOOTS. THEY SPOKE TO ME.
THEY SAID *"YOU'RE NOT GOING TO HAVE ANY MONEY ANY MORE"?*
I WISH I SPOKE BOOT.
NOW YOU BE GOOD! NOT TOO MUCH FINE CHAMPAGNE WINE! TAKE BREAKS FOR PRAYER!
FUSS FUSS
FWEET!
BY RIGHTS... THAT SHOULDN'T WORK.
BRAKE!
SCREEECH

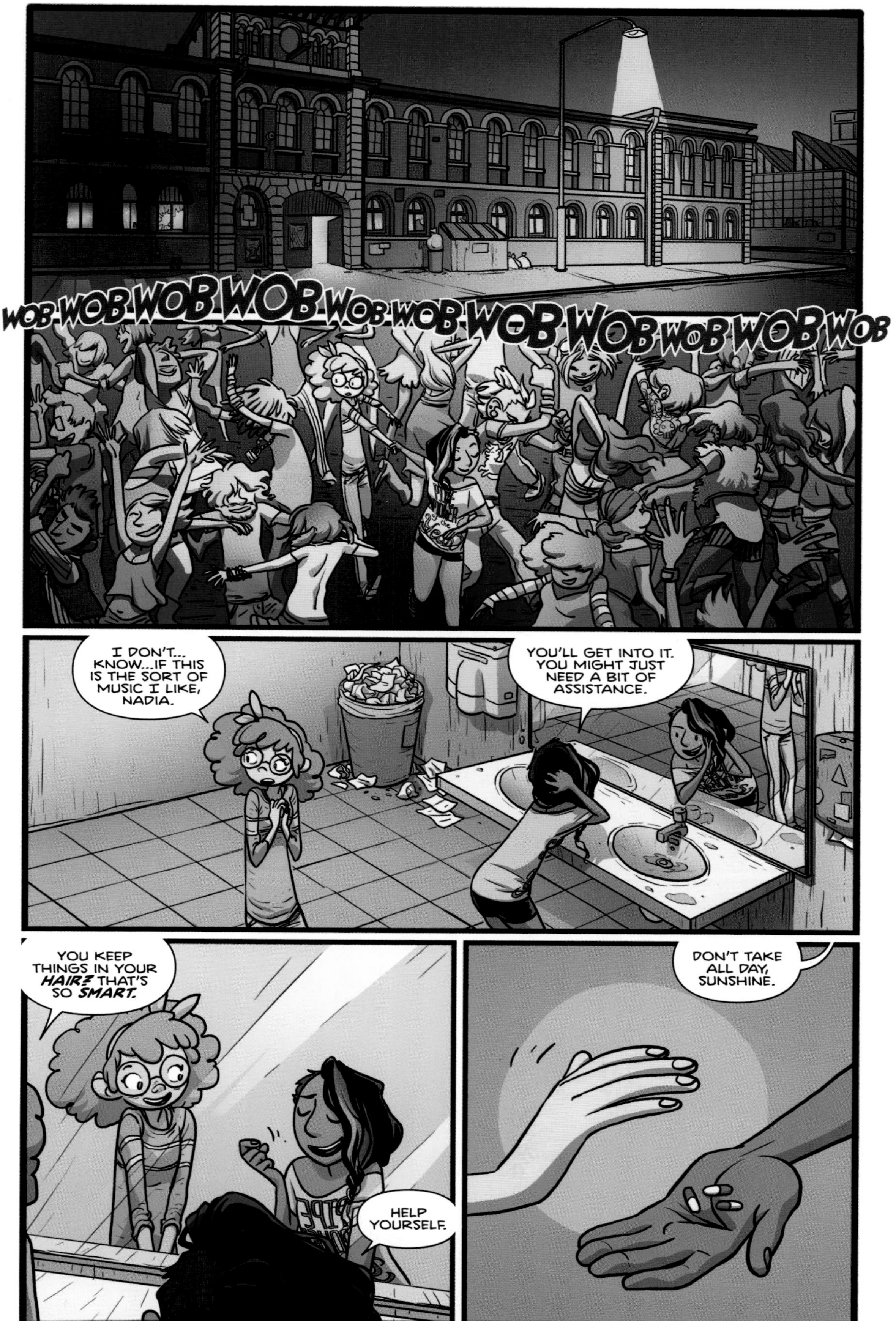
WOB WOB WOB WOB WOB WOB WOB WOB WOB WOB WOB WOB
I DON'T... KNOW...IF THIS IS THE SORT OF MUSIC I LIKE, NADIA.
YOU'LL GET INTO IT. YOU MIGHT JUST NEED A BIT OF ASSISTANCE.
YOU KEEP THINGS IN YOUR HAIR? THAT'S SO SMART.
HELP YOURSELF.
DON'T TAKE ALL DAY, SUNSHINE.

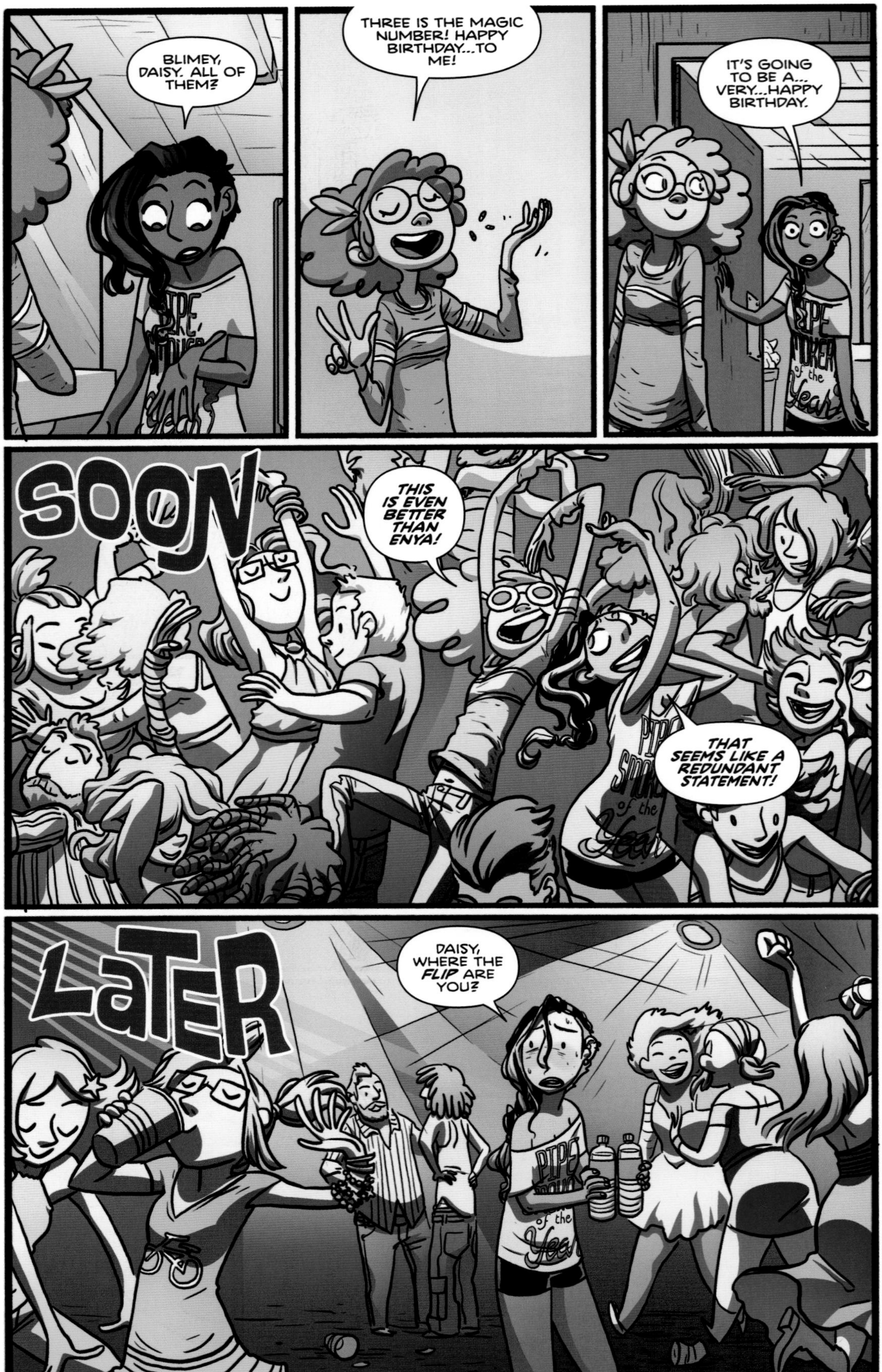
BLIMEY, DAISY. ALL OF THEM?
THREE IS THE MAGIC NUMBER! HAPPY BIRTHDAY...TO ME!
IT'S GOING TO BE A... VERY...HAPPY BIRTHDAY.
PIPE SMOKER of the Year
SOON
THIS IS EVEN BETTER THAN ENYA!
THAT SEEMS LIKE A REDUNDANT STATEMENT!
LaTER
DAISY, WHERE THE FLIP ARE YOU?

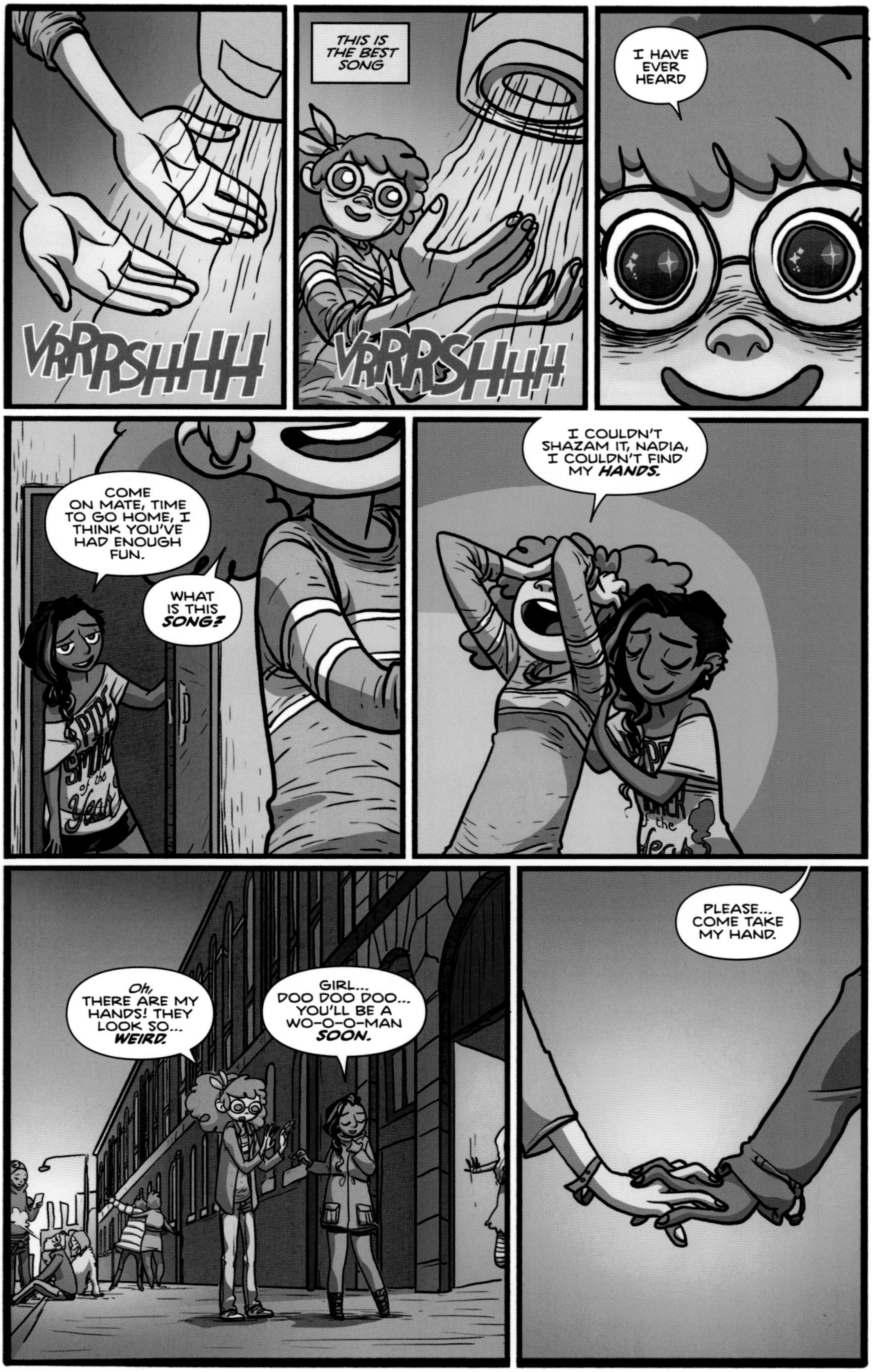
VRRRSHHHH
THIS IS THE BEST SONG
VRRRSHHHH
I HAVE EVER HEARD
COME ON MATE, TIME TO GO HOME, I THINK YOU'VE HAD ENOUGH FUN.
WHAT IS THIS SONG?
I COULDN'T SHAZAM IT, NADIA, I COULDN'T FIND MY HANDS.
Oh, THERE ARE MY HANDS! THEY LOOK SO... WEIRD.
GIRL... DOO DOO DOO... YOU'LL BE A WO-O-O-MAN SOON.
PLEASE... COME TAKE MY HAND.

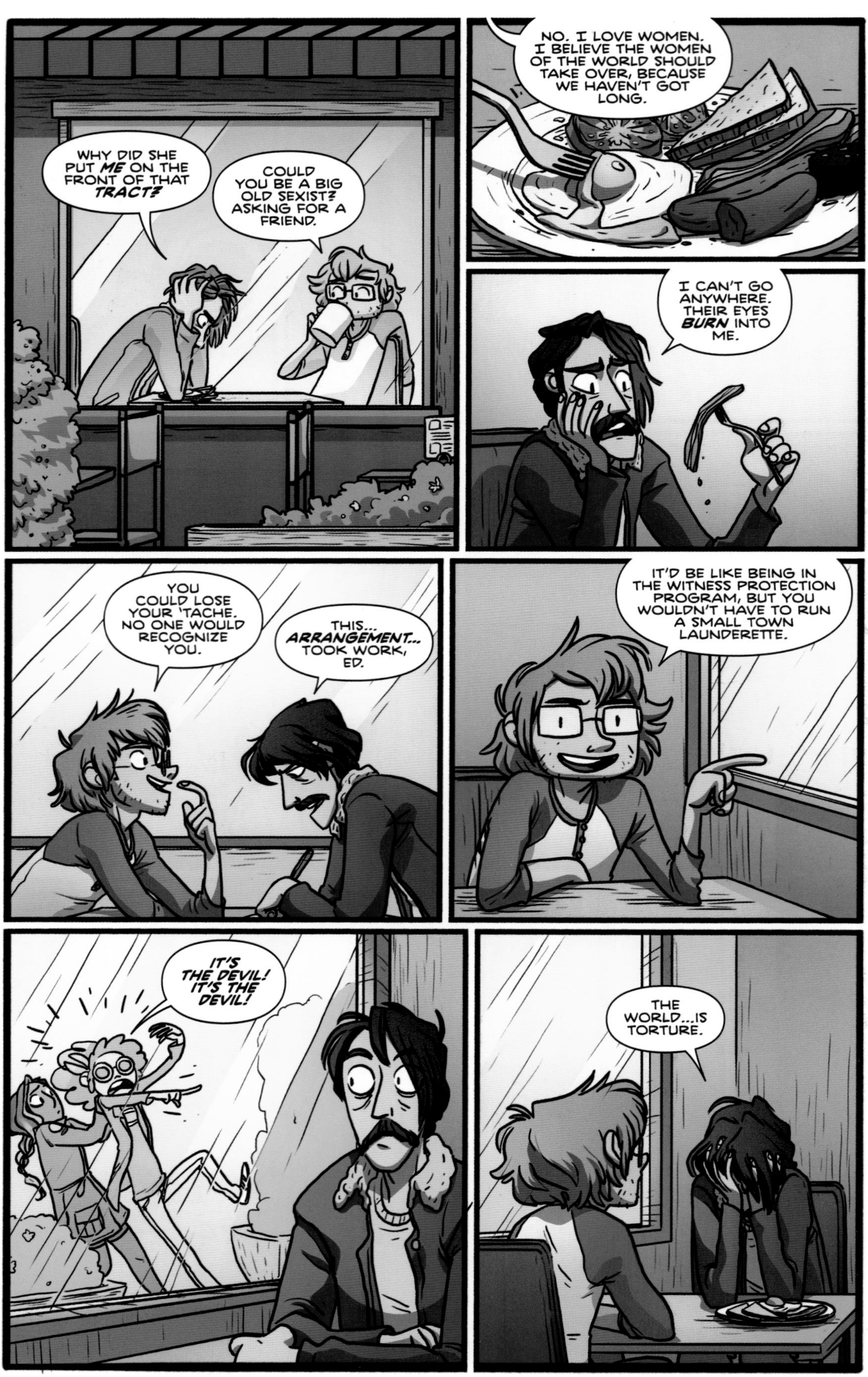
WHY DID SHE PUT *ME* ON THE FRONT OF THAT *TRACT?*
COULD YOU BE A BIG OLD SEXIST? ASKING FOR A FRIEND.
NO. I LOVE WOMEN. I BELIEVE THE WOMEN OF THE WORLD SHOULD TAKE OVER, BECAUSE WE HAVEN'T GOT LONG.
I CAN'T GO ANYWHERE. THEIR EYES *BURN* INTO ME.
YOU COULD LOSE YOUR 'TACHE. NO ONE WOULD RECOGNIZE YOU.
THIS... *ARRANGEMENT...* TOOK WORK, ED.
IT'D BE LIKE BEING IN THE WITNESS PROTECTION PROGRAM, BUT YOU WOULDN'T HAVE TO RUN A SMALL TOWN LAUNDERETTE.
IT'S THE DEVIL! IT'S THE DEVIL!
THE WORLD...IS TORTURE.

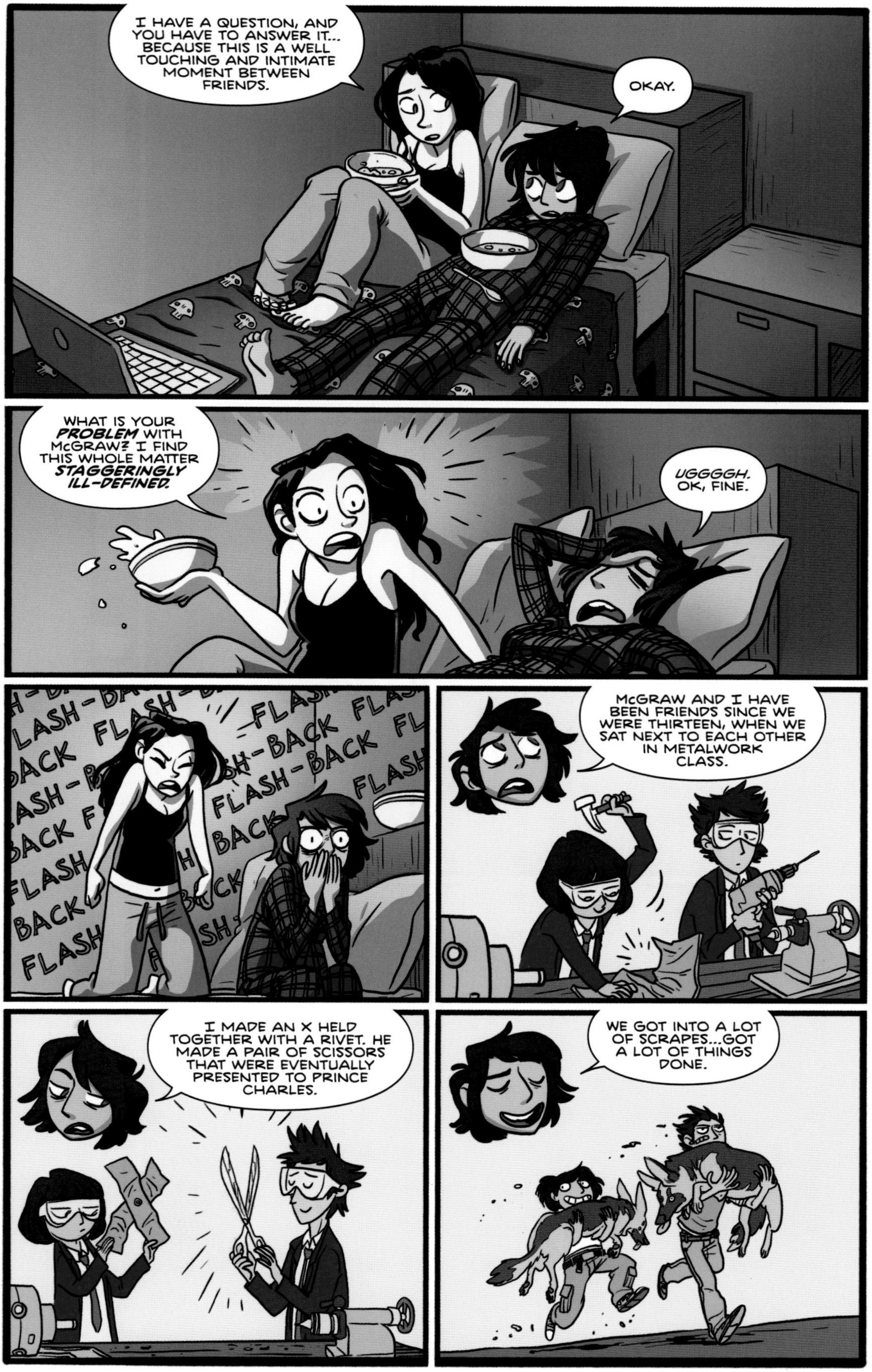
I HAVE A QUESTION, AND YOU HAVE TO ANSWER IT... BECAUSE THIS IS A WELL TOUCHING AND INTIMATE MOMENT BETWEEN FRIENDS.
OKAY.
WHAT IS YOUR PROBLEM WITH McGRAW? I FIND THIS WHOLE MATTER STAGGERINGLY ILL-DEFINED.
UGGGGH. OK, FINE.
FLASH-BACK FLASH-BACK FLASH-BACK
McGRAW AND I HAVE BEEN FRIENDS SINCE WE WERE THIRTEEN, WHEN WE SAT NEXT TO EACH OTHER IN METALWORK CLASS.
I MADE AN X HELD TOGETHER WITH A RIVET. HE MADE A PAIR OF SCISSORS THAT WERE EVENTUALLY PRESENTED TO PRINCE CHARLES.
WE GOT INTO A LOT OF SCRAPES...GOT A LOT OF THINGS DONE.

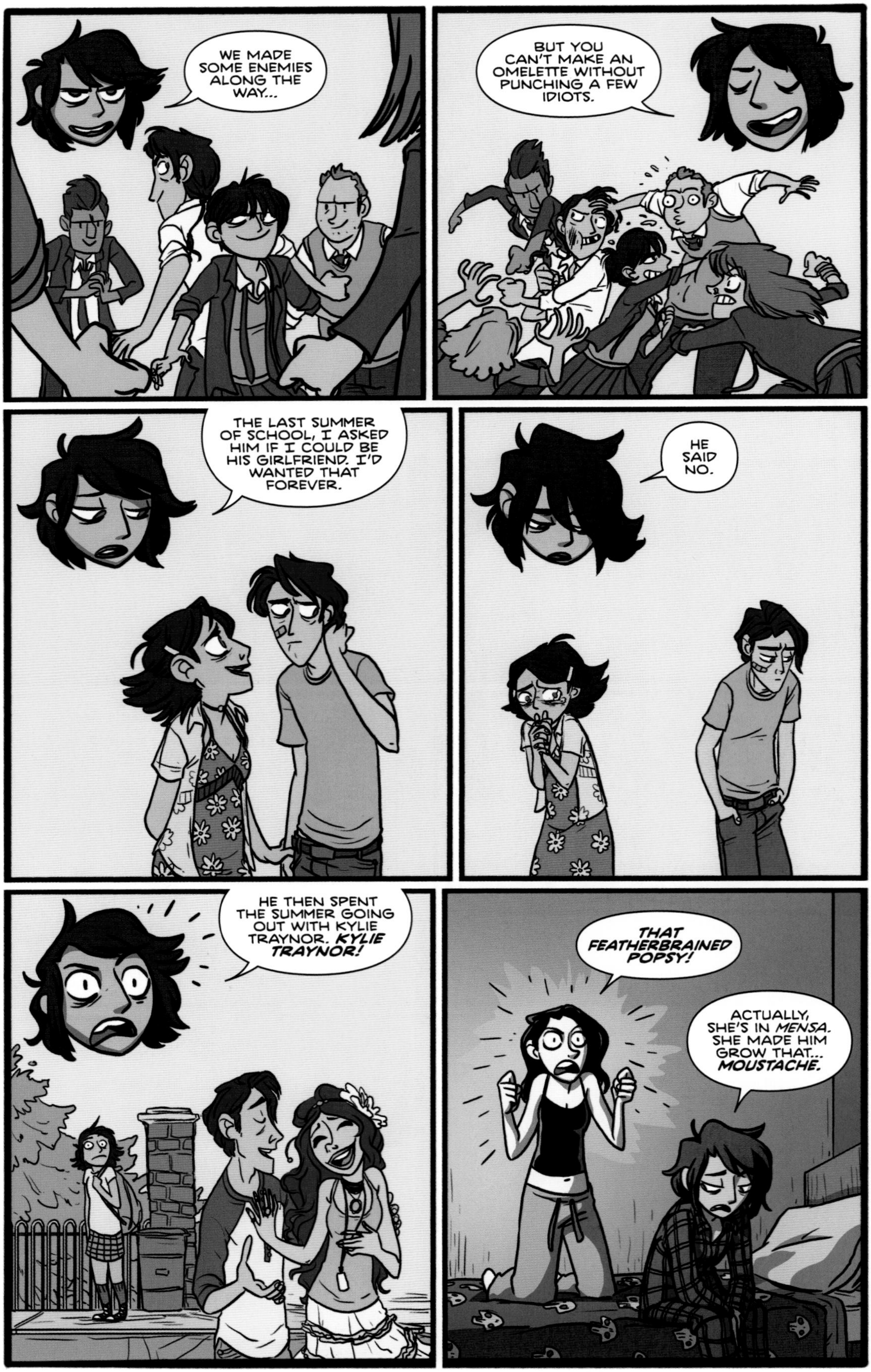
WE MADE SOME ENEMIES ALONG THE WAY...
BUT YOU CAN'T MAKE AN OMELETTE WITHOUT PUNCHING A FEW IDIOTS.
THE LAST SUMMER OF SCHOOL, I ASKED HIM IF I COULD BE HIS GIRLFRIEND. I'D WANTED THAT FOREVER.
HE SAID NO.
HE THEN SPENT THE SUMMER GOING OUT WITH KYLIE TRAYNOR. *KYLIE TRAYNOR!*
THAT FEATHERBRAINED POPSY!
ACTUALLY, SHE'S IN *MENSA.* SHE MADE HIM GROW THAT... *MOUSTACHE.*

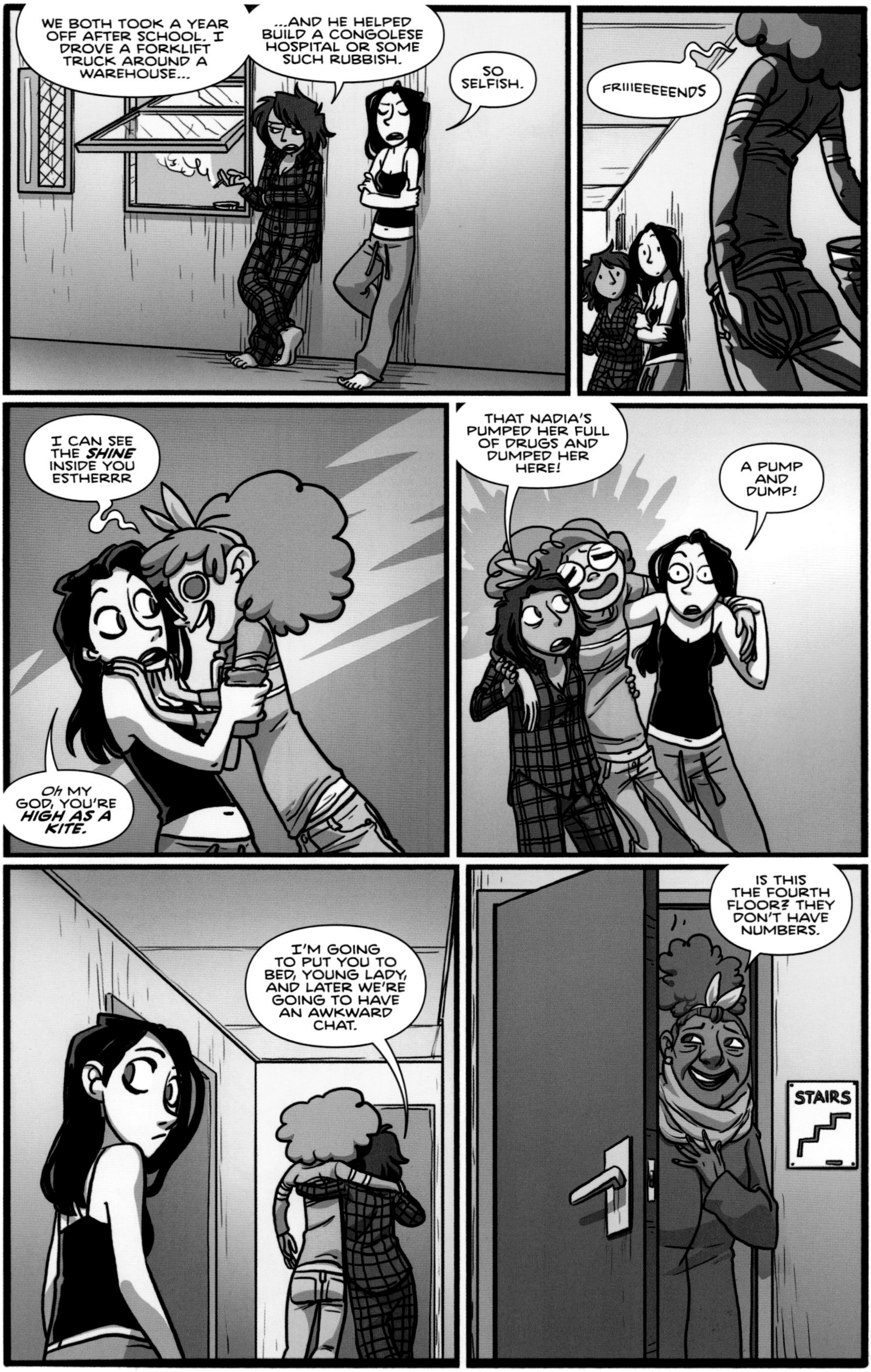
WE BOTH TOOK A YEAR OFF AFTER SCHOOL. I DROVE A FORKLIFT TRUCK AROUND A WAREHOUSE...
...AND HE HELPED BUILD A CONGOLESE HOSPITAL OR SOME SUCH RUBBISH.
SO SELFISH.
FRIIIEEEEEENDS
I CAN SEE THE *SHINE* INSIDE YOU ESTHERRR
Oh MY GOD, YOU'RE ***HIGH AS A KITE.***
THAT NADIA'S PUMPED HER FULL OF DRUGS AND DUMPED HER HERE!
A PUMP AND DUMP!
I'M GOING TO PUT YOU TO BED, YOUNG LADY, AND LATER WE'RE GOING TO HAVE AN AWKWARD CHAT.
IS THIS THE FOURTH FLOOR? THEY DON'T HAVE NUMBERS.
STAIRS

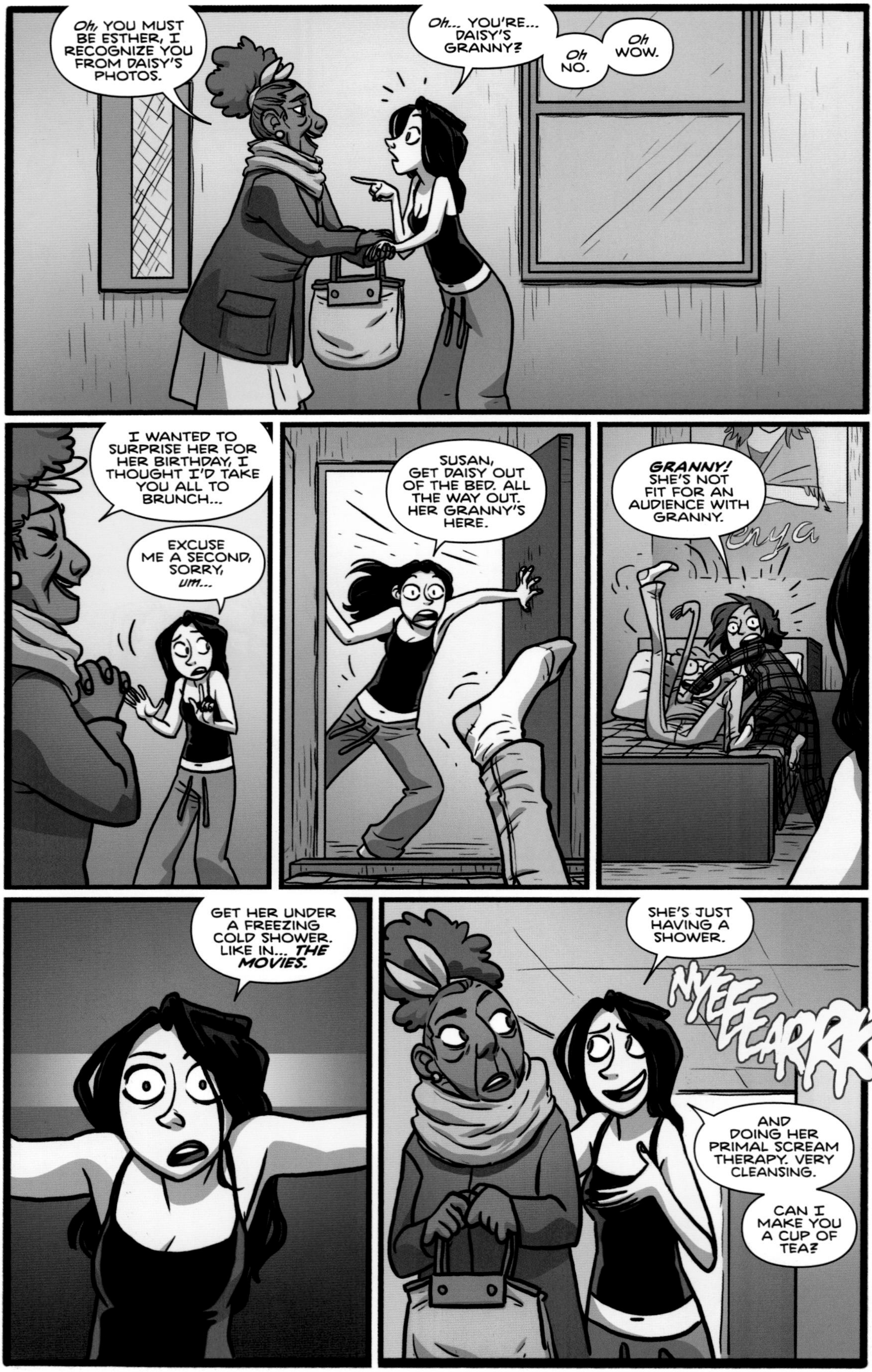
Oh, YOU MUST BE ESTHER, I RECOGNIZE YOU FROM DAISY'S PHOTOS.
Oh... YOU'RE... DAISY'S GRANNY?
Oh NO.
Oh WOW.
I WANTED TO SURPRISE HER FOR HER BIRTHDAY, I THOUGHT I'D TAKE YOU ALL TO BRUNCH...
EXCUSE ME A SECOND, SORRY, UM...
SUSAN, GET DAISY OUT OF THE BED. ALL THE WAY OUT. HER GRANNY'S HERE.
GRANNY! SHE'S NOT FIT FOR AN AUDIENCE WITH GRANNY.
GET HER UNDER A FREEZING COLD SHOWER. LIKE IN... THE MOVIES.
SHE'S JUST HAVING A SHOWER.
NYEEEEARRK
AND DOING HER PRIMAL SCREAM THERAPY. VERY CLEANSING.
CAN I MAKE YOU A CUP OF TEA?

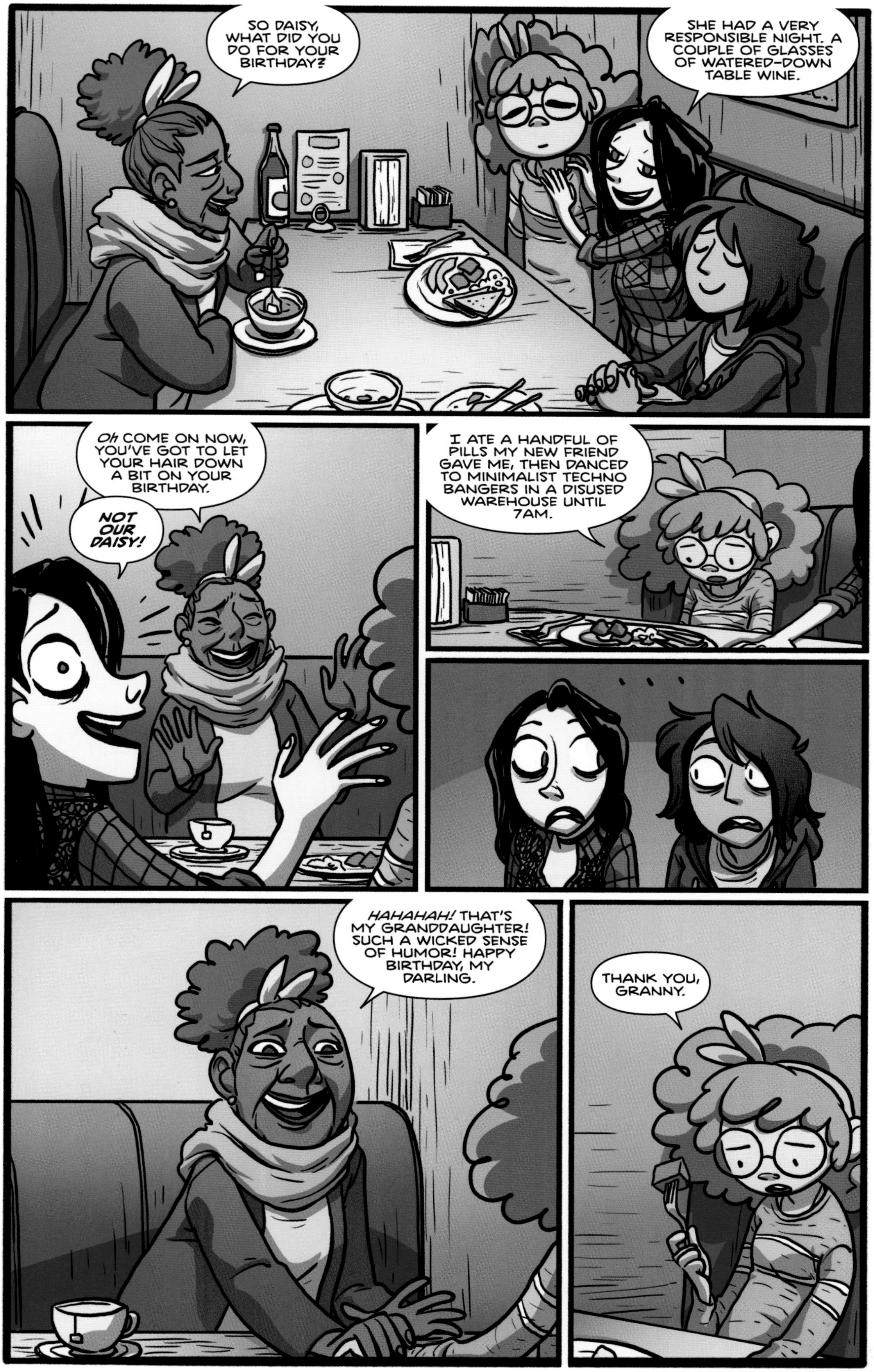
SO DAISY, WHAT DID YOU DO FOR YOUR BIRTHDAY?
SHE HAD A VERY RESPONSIBLE NIGHT. A COUPLE OF GLASSES OF WATERED-DOWN TABLE WINE.
Oh COME ON NOW, YOU'VE GOT TO LET YOUR HAIR DOWN A BIT ON YOUR BIRTHDAY.
NOT OUR DAISY!
I ATE A HANDFUL OF PILLS MY NEW FRIEND GAVE ME, THEN DANCED TO MINIMALIST TECHNO BANGERS IN A DISUSED WAREHOUSE UNTIL 7AM.
HAHAHAH! THAT'S MY GRANDDAUGHTER! SUCH A WICKED SENSE OF HUMOR! HAPPY BIRTHDAY, MY DARLING.
THANK YOU, GRANNY.

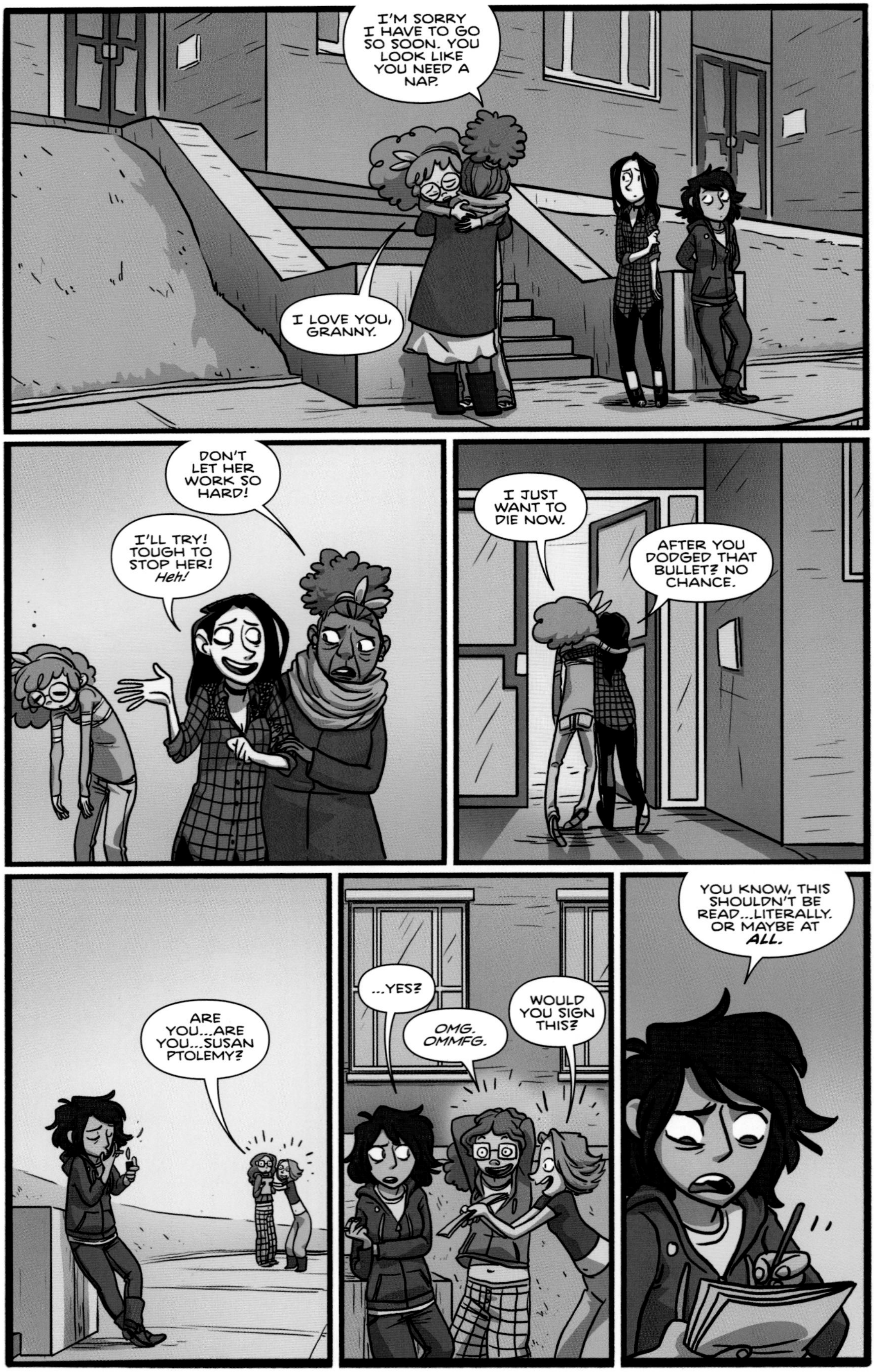
I'M SORRY I HAVE TO GO SO SOON. YOU LOOK LIKE YOU NEED A NAP.
I LOVE YOU, GRANNY.
DON'T LET HER WORK SO HARD!
I'LL TRY! TOUGH TO STOP HER! *Heh!*
I JUST WANT TO DIE NOW.
AFTER YOU DODGED THAT BULLET? NO CHANCE.
ARE YOU...ARE YOU...SUSAN PTOLEMY?
...YES?
OMG. OMMFG.
WOULD YOU SIGN THIS?
YOU KNOW, THIS SHOULDN'T BE READ...LITERALLY. OR MAYBE AT **ALL.**

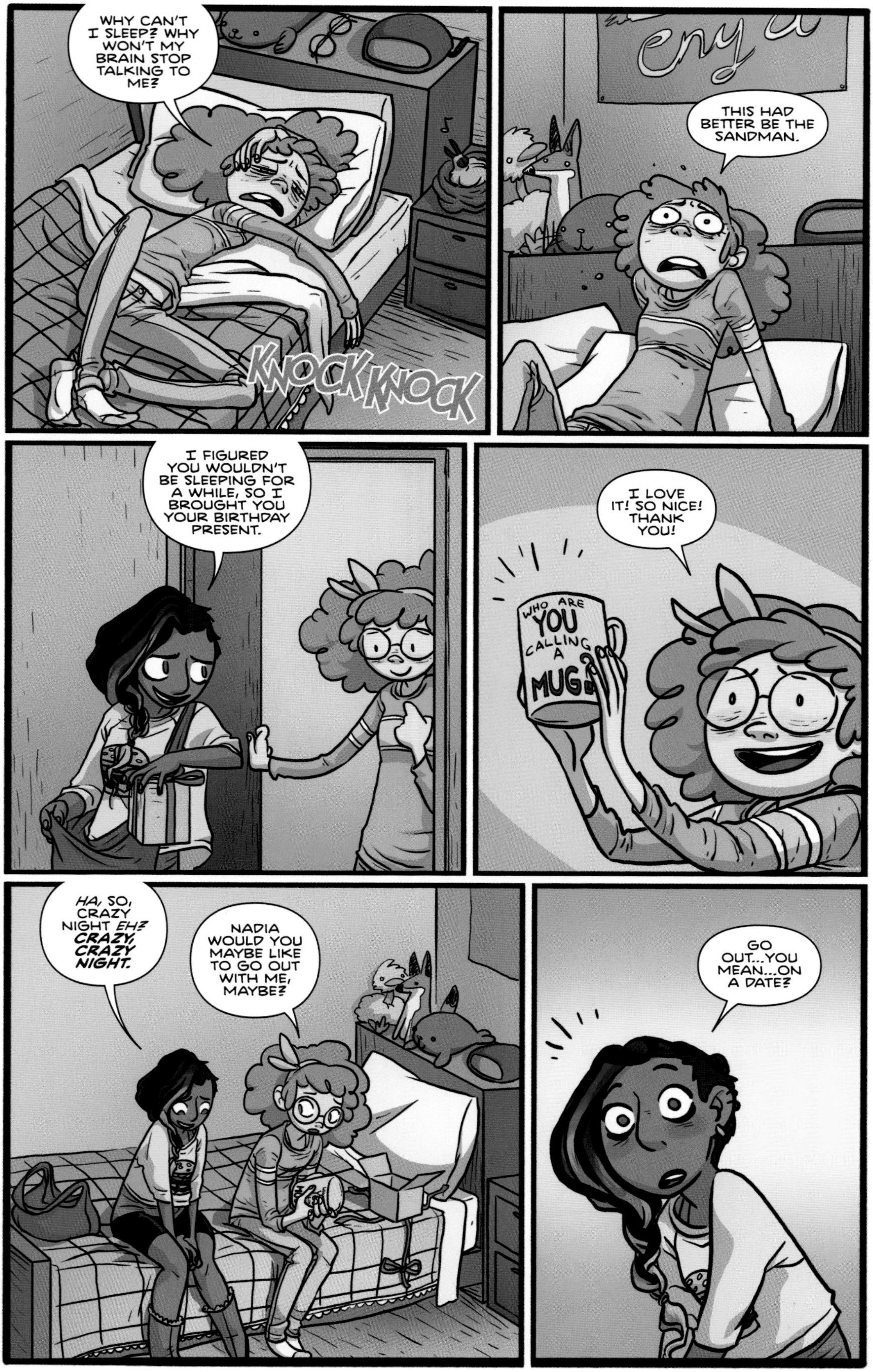
WHY CAN'T I SLEEP? WHY WON'T MY BRAIN STOP TALKING TO ME?
KNOCK KNOCK
THIS HAD BETTER BE THE SANDMAN.
I FIGURED YOU WOULDN'T BE SLEEPING FOR A WHILE, SO I BROUGHT YOU YOUR BIRTHDAY PRESENT.
I LOVE IT! SO NICE! THANK YOU!
WHO ARE YOU CALLING A MUG?
HA, SO, CRAZY NIGHT EH? CRAZY, CRAZY NIGHT.
NADIA WOULD YOU MAYBE LIKE TO GO OUT WITH ME, MAYBE?
GO OUT...YOU MEAN...ON A DATE?

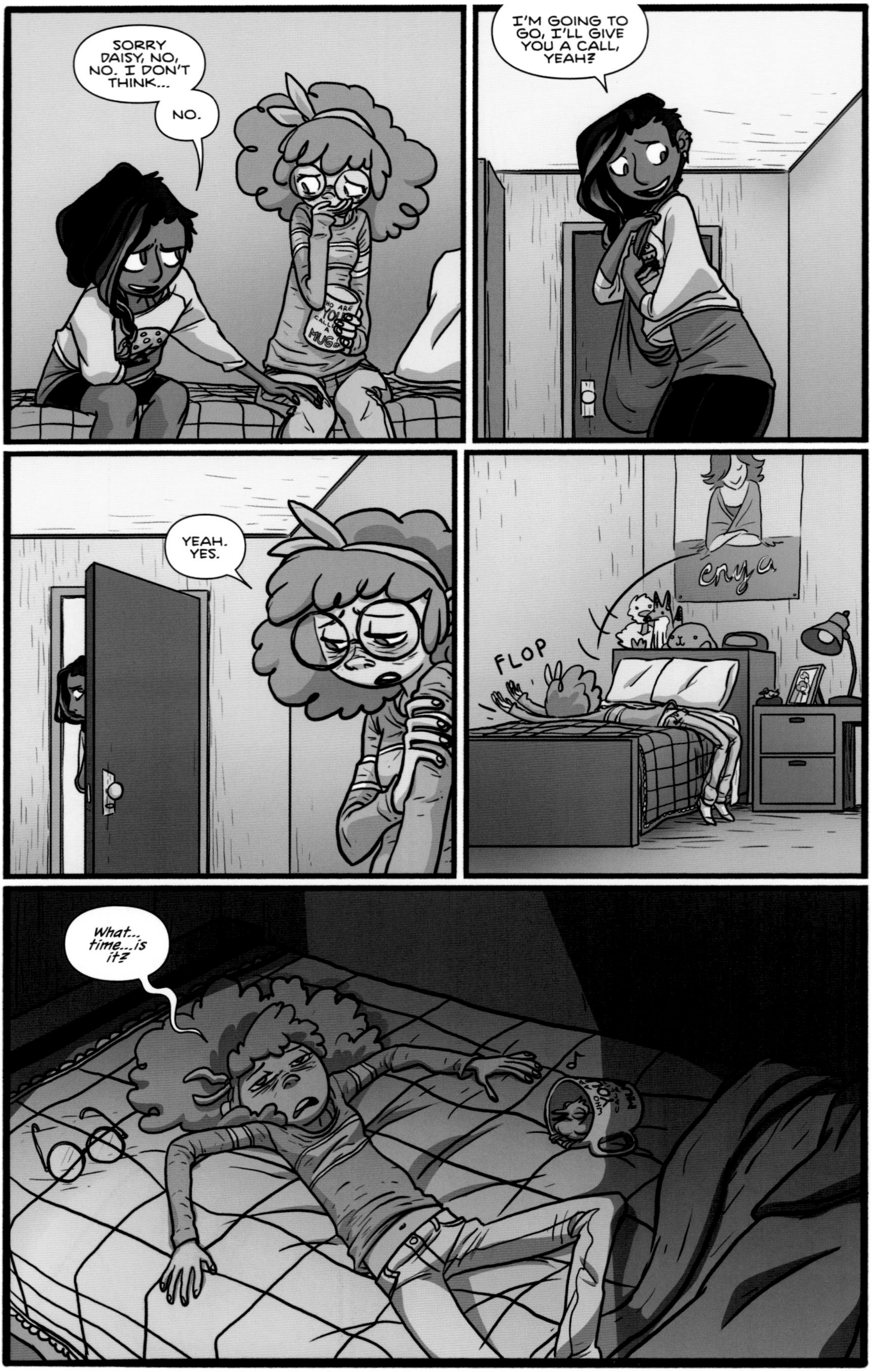
SORRY DAISY, NO, NO. I DON'T THINK...
NO.
WHO ARE YOU CALLING A MUG?
I'M GOING TO GO, I'LL GIVE YOU A CALL, YEAH?
YEAH. YES.
enya
FLOP
What... time... is it?

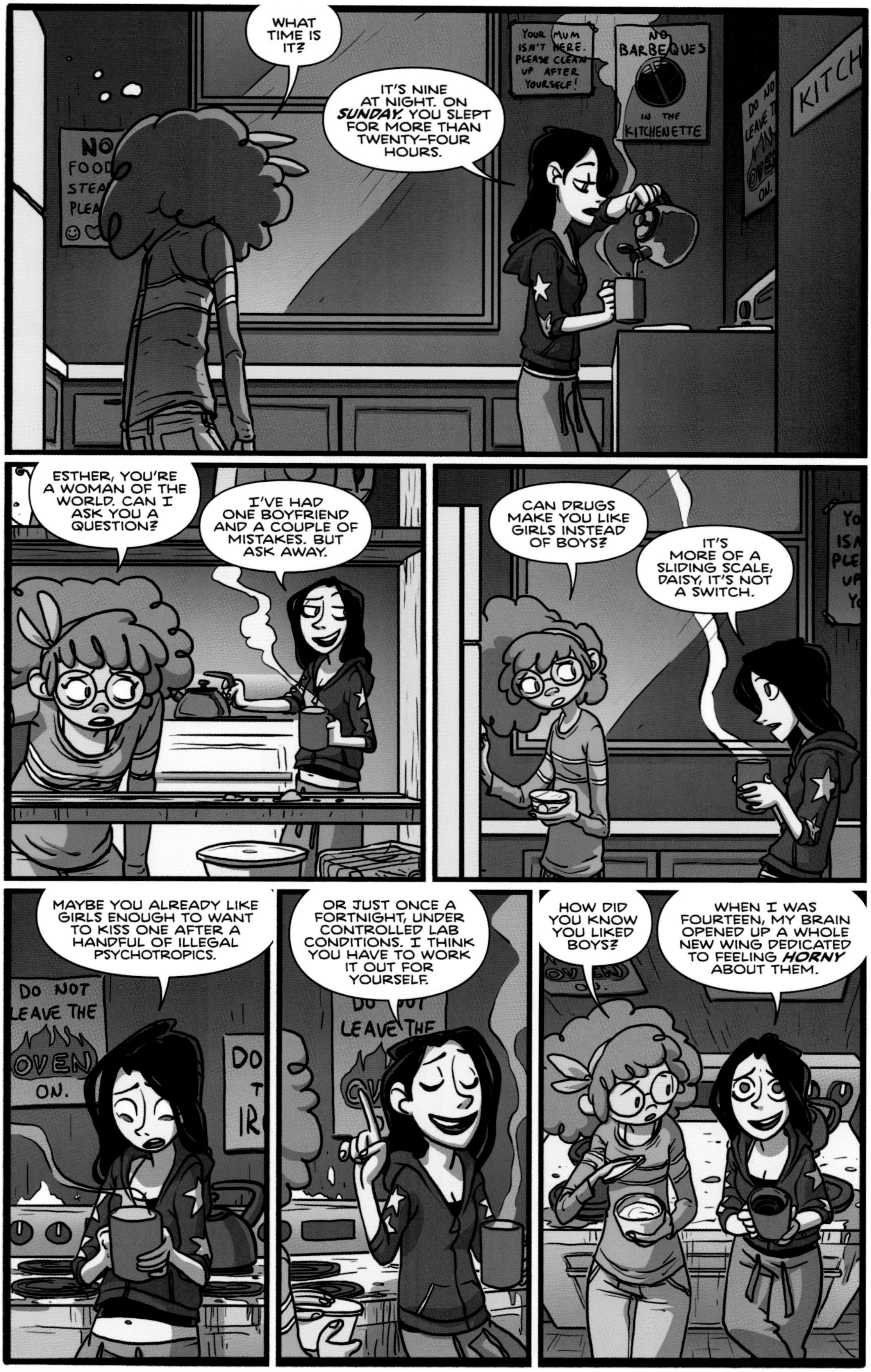

WHAT TIME IS IT?
IT'S NINE AT NIGHT. ON SUNDAY. YOU SLEPT FOR MORE THAN TWENTY-FOUR HOURS.
YOUR MUM ISN'T HERE. PLEASE CLEAN UP AFTER YOURSELF!
NO BARBEQUES IN THE KITCHENETTE
KITCH
NO FOOD STEA PLEA
ESTHER, YOU'RE A WOMAN OF THE WORLD. CAN I ASK YOU A QUESTION?
I'VE HAD ONE BOYFRIEND AND A COUPLE OF MISTAKES. BUT ASK AWAY.
CAN DRUGS MAKE YOU LIKE GIRLS INSTEAD OF BOYS?
IT'S MORE OF A SLIDING SCALE, DAISY, IT'S NOT A SWITCH.
MAYBE YOU ALREADY LIKE GIRLS ENOUGH TO WANT TO KISS ONE AFTER A HANDFUL OF ILLEGAL PSYCHOTROPICS.
DO NOT LEAVE THE OVEN ON.
OR JUST ONCE A FORTNIGHT, UNDER CONTROLLED LAB CONDITIONS. I THINK YOU HAVE TO WORK IT OUT FOR YOURSELF.
HOW DID YOU KNOW YOU LIKED BOYS?
WHEN I WAS FOURTEEN, MY BRAIN OPENED UP A WHOLE NEW WING DEDICATED TO FEELING HORNY ABOUT THEM.

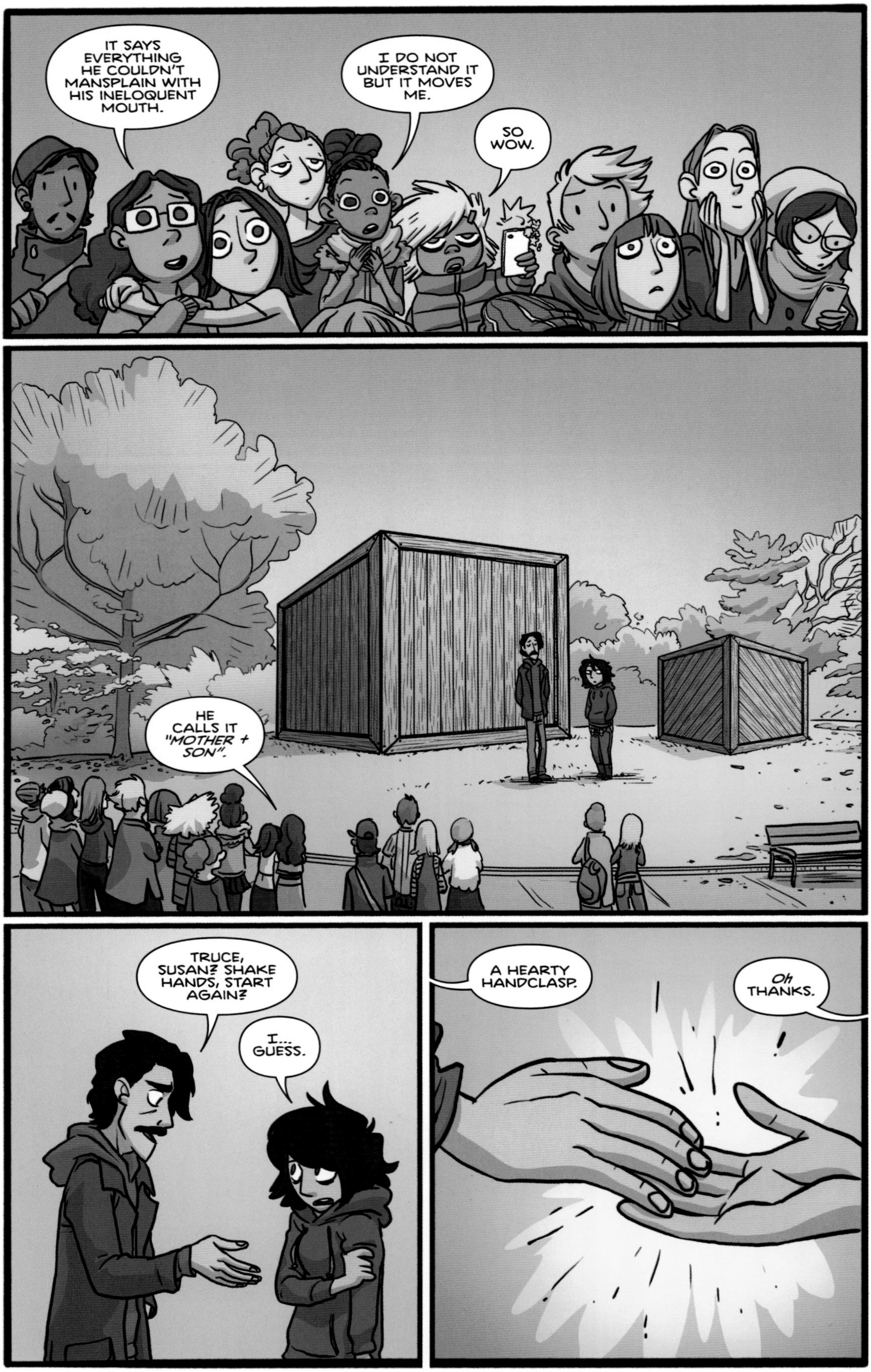
IT SAYS EVERYTHING HE COULDN'T MANSPLAIN WITH HIS INELOQUENT MOUTH.
I DO NOT UNDERSTAND IT BUT IT MOVES ME.
SO WOW.
HE CALLS IT "MOTHER + SON".
TRUCE, SUSAN? SHAKE HANDS, START AGAIN?
I... GUESS.
A HEARTY HANDCLASP.
Oh THANKS.

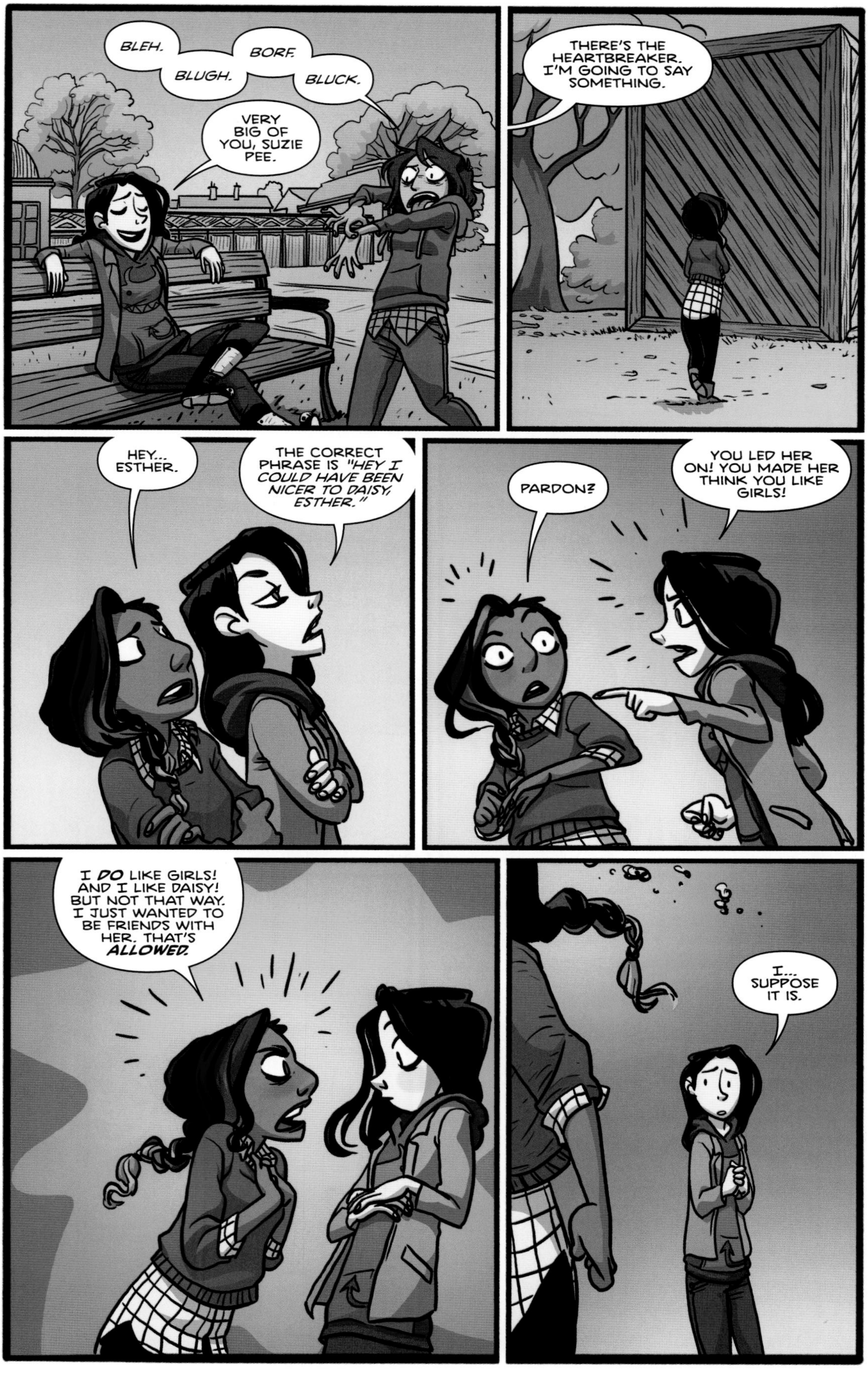
BLEH.
BLUGH.
BORF.
BLUCK.
VERY BIG OF YOU, SUZIE PEE.
THERE'S THE HEARTBREAKER. I'M GOING TO SAY SOMETHING.
HEY... ESTHER.
THE CORRECT PHRASE IS "HEY I COULD HAVE BEEN NICER TO DAISY, ESTHER."
PARDON?
YOU LED HER ON! YOU MADE HER THINK YOU LIKE GIRLS!
I DO LIKE GIRLS! AND I LIKE DAISY! BUT NOT THAT WAY. I JUST WANTED TO BE FRIENDS WITH HER. THAT'S ALLOWED.
I... SUPPOSE IT IS.

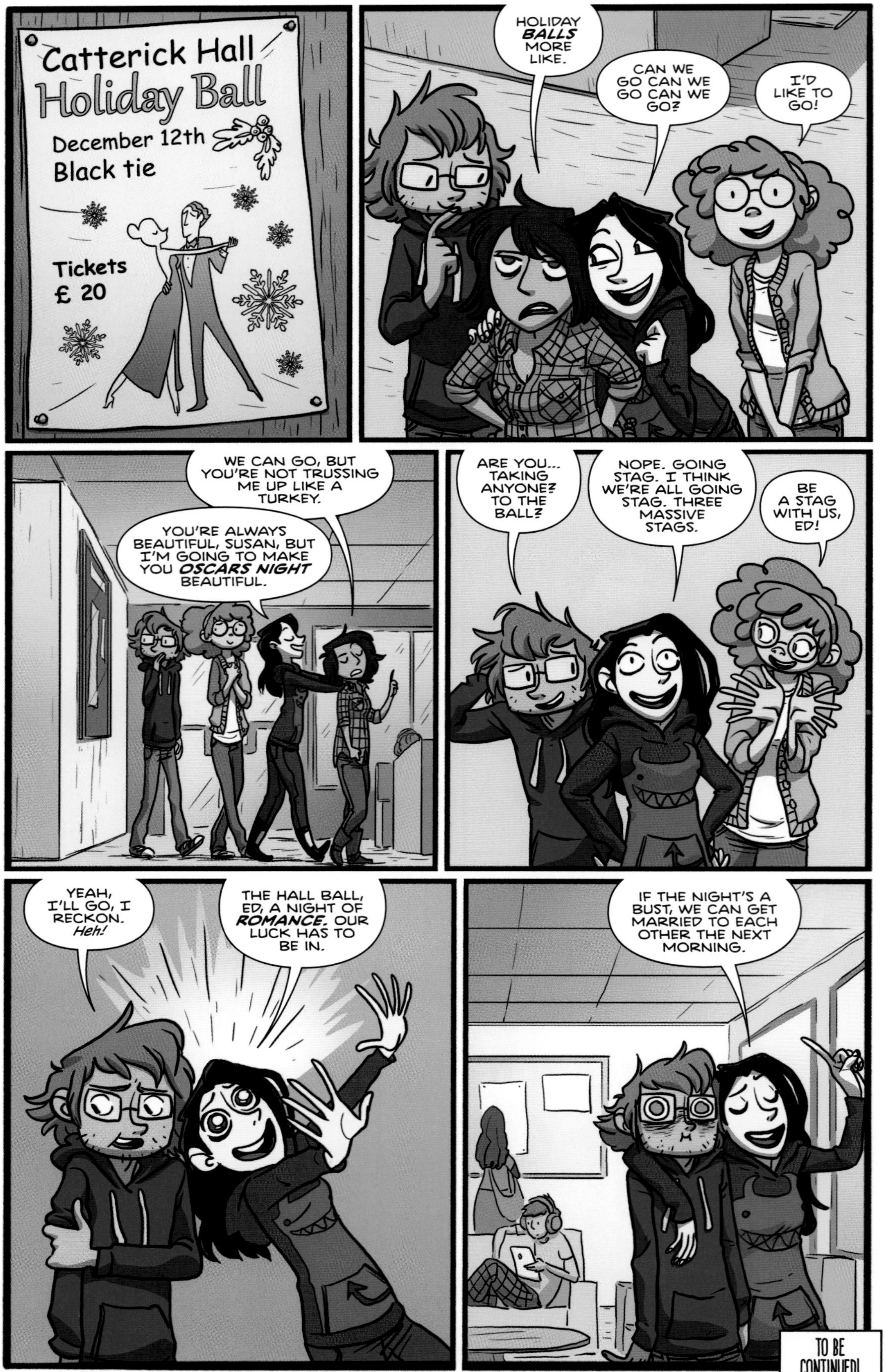
Catterick Hall
Holiday Ball
December 12th
Black tie
Tickets
£ 20
HOLIDAY *BALLS* MORE LIKE.
CAN WE GO CAN WE GO CAN WE GO?
I'D LIKE TO GO!
WE CAN GO, BUT YOU'RE NOT TRUSSING ME UP LIKE A TURKEY.
YOU'RE ALWAYS BEAUTIFUL, SUSAN, BUT I'M GOING TO MAKE YOU *OSCARS NIGHT* BEAUTIFUL.
ARE YOU... TAKING ANYONE? TO THE BALL?
NOPE. GOING STAG. I THINK WE'RE ALL GOING STAG. THREE MASSIVE STAGS.
BE A STAG WITH US, ED!
YEAH, I'LL GO, I RECKON. *Heh!*
THE HALL BALL, ED, A NIGHT OF *ROMANCE.* OUR LUCK HAS TO BE IN.
IF THE NIGHT'S A BUST, WE CAN GET MARRIED TO EACH OTHER THE NEXT MORNING.
TO BE CONTINUED!

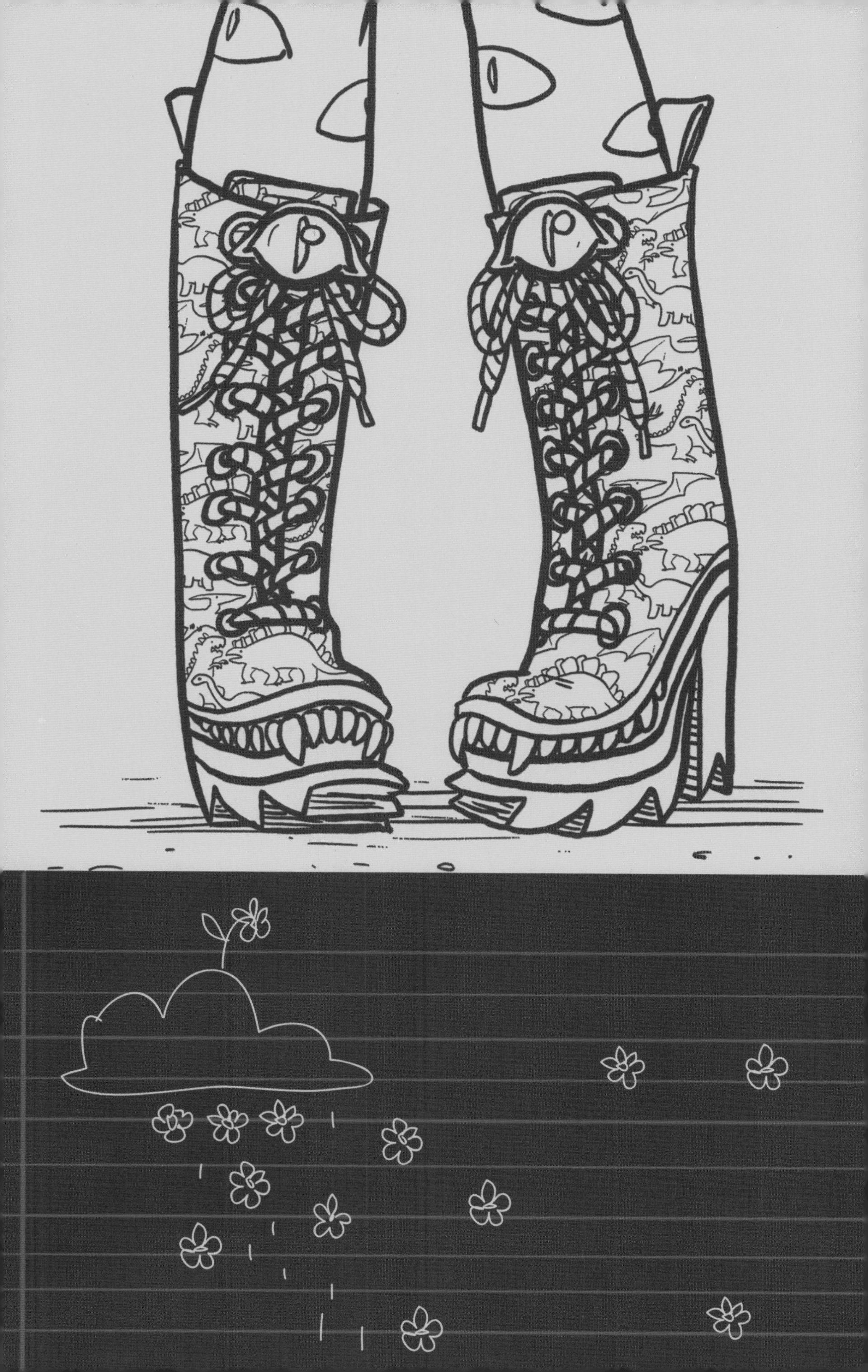

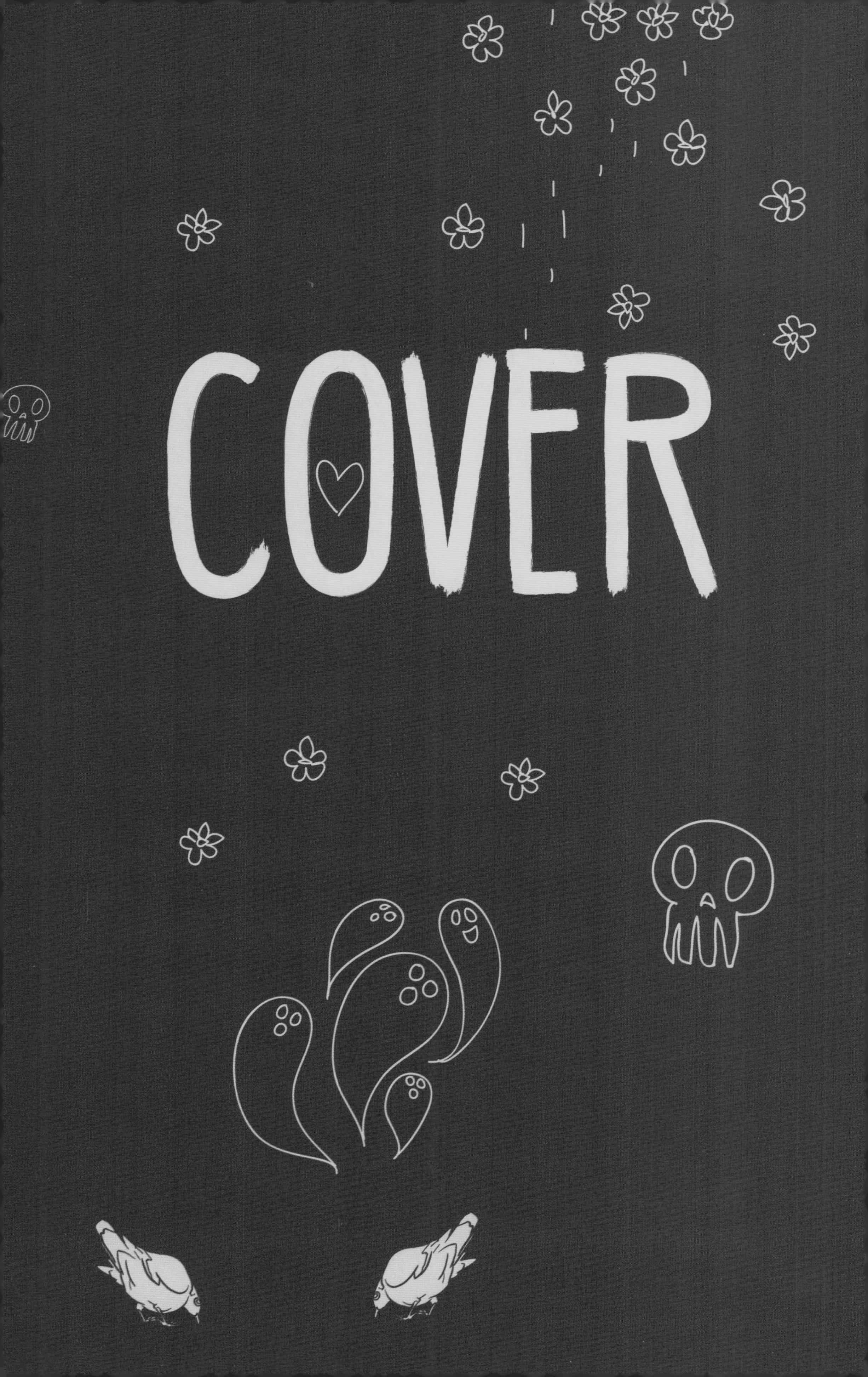
COVER

GALLERY

ISSUE #1 COVER A
LISSA TREIMAN

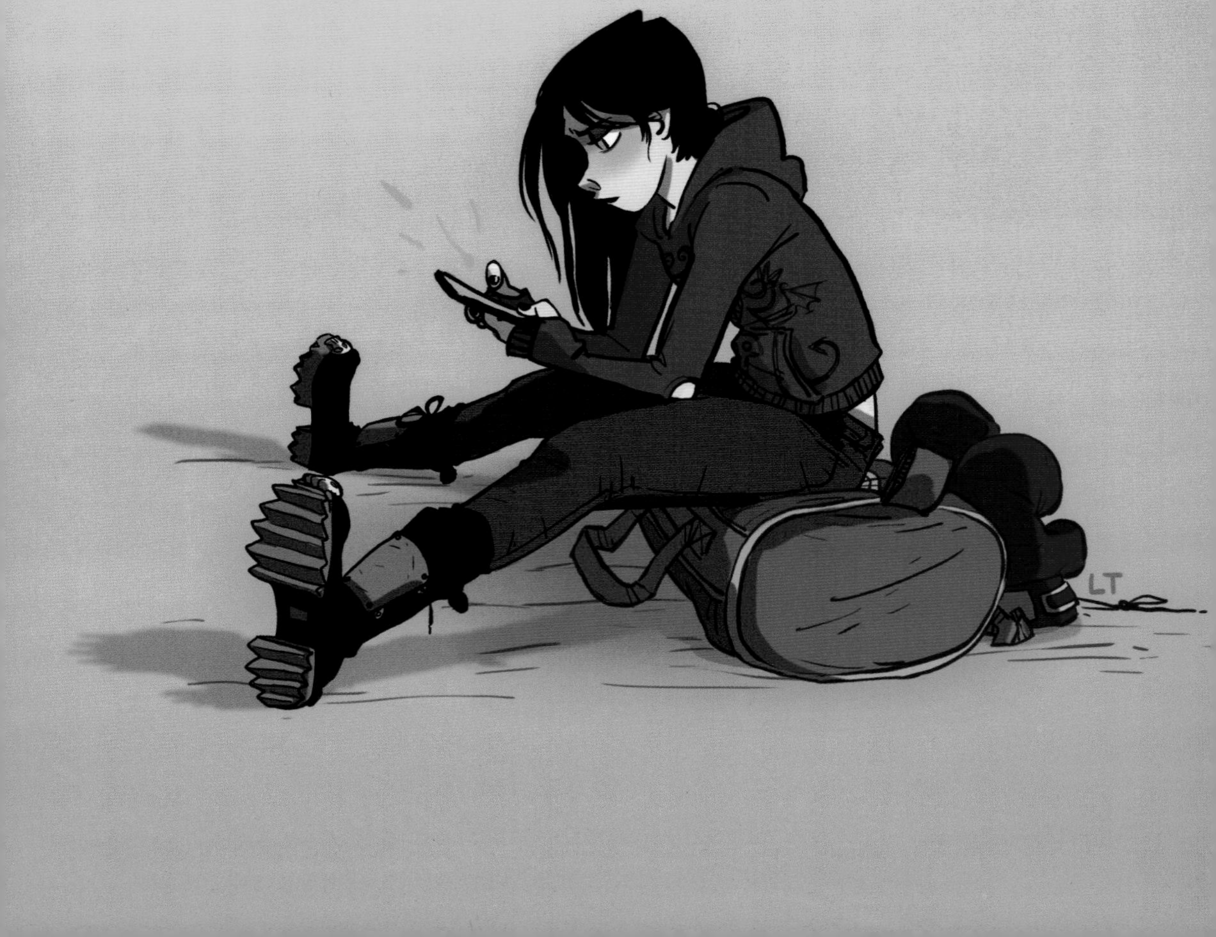
LT

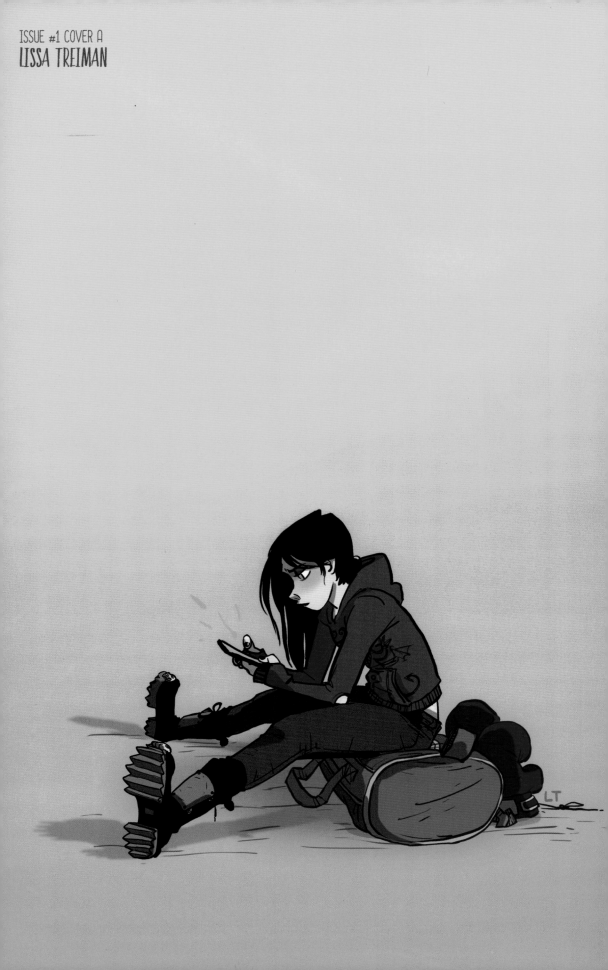

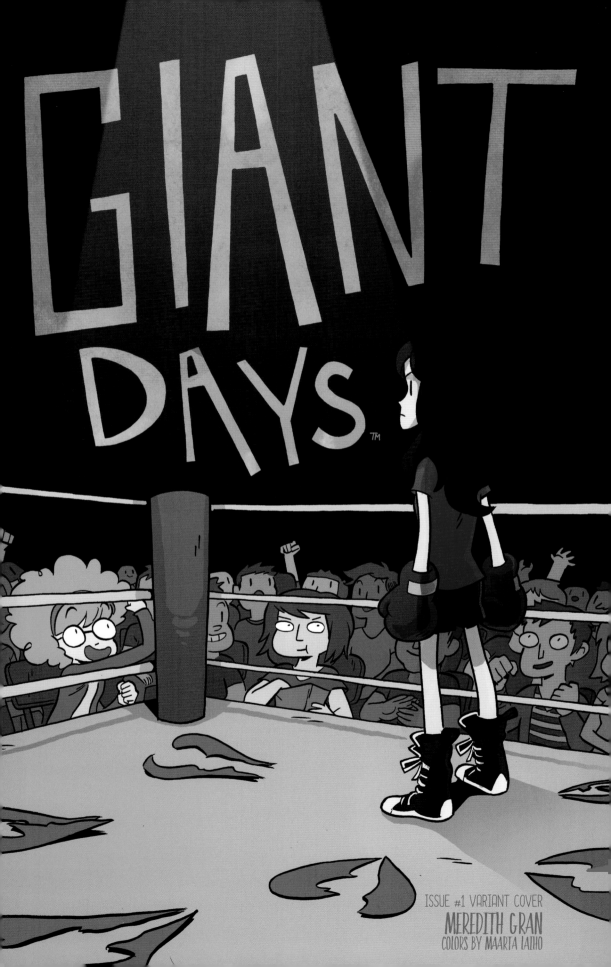

ISSUE #1 VARIANT COVER
MEREDITH GRAN
COLORS BY MAARTA LAIHO

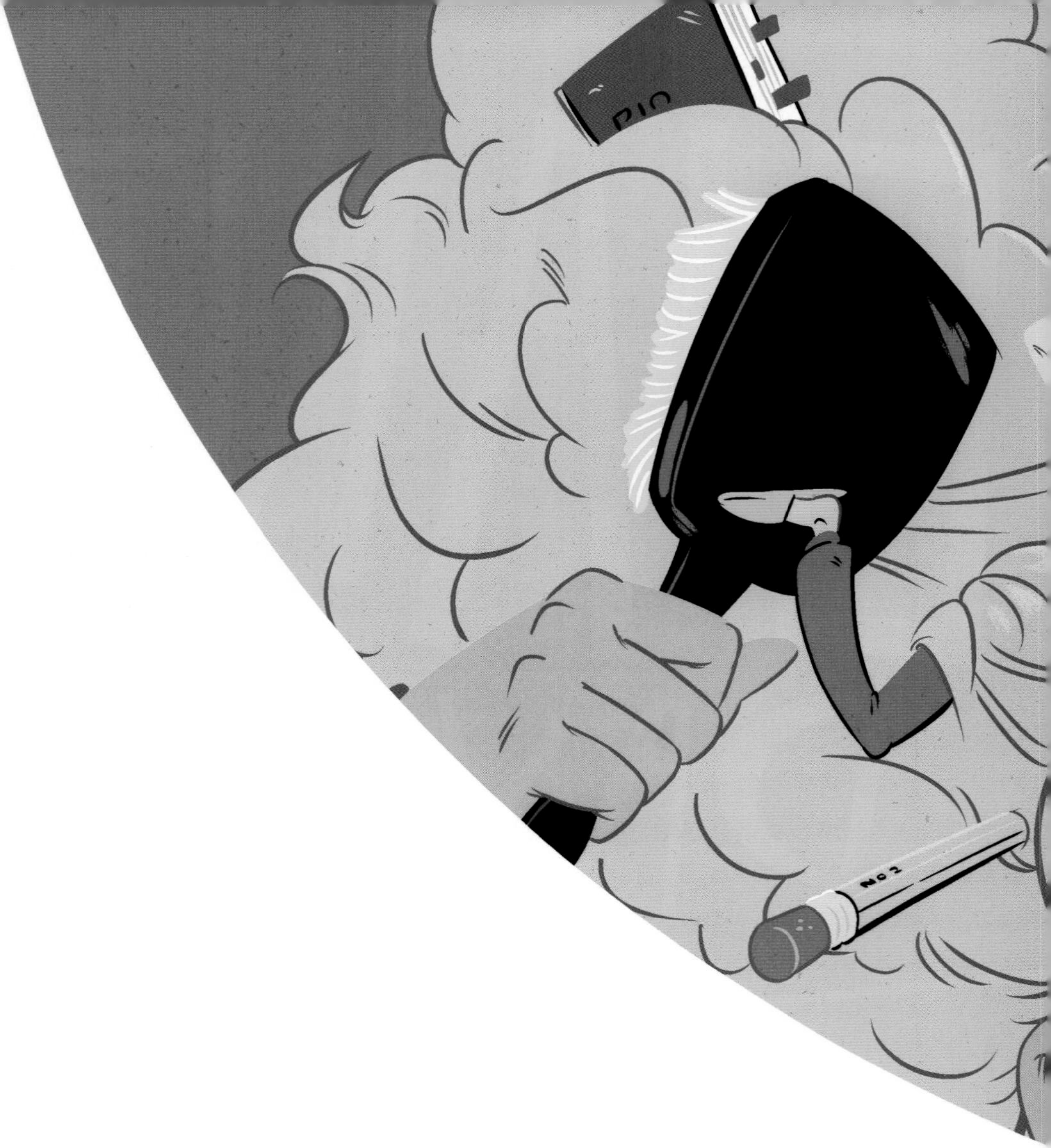

ISSUE #1 BOOM! TEN YEARS VARIANT COVER
SHELLI PAROLINE + BRADEN LAMB

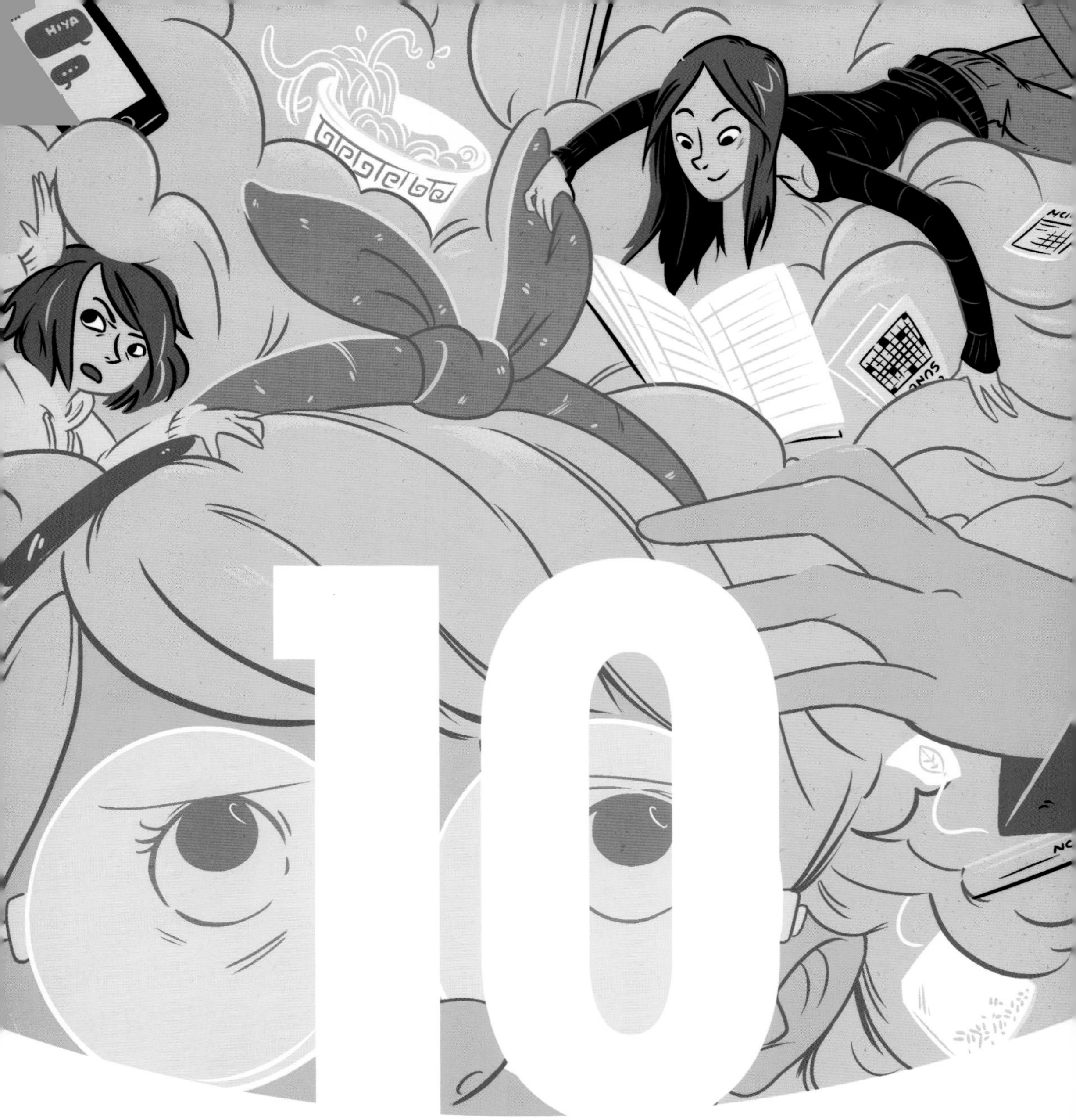
HIYA

10

ISSUE #1 BOOM! STUDIOS EXCLUSIVE COVER
ADAM VASS

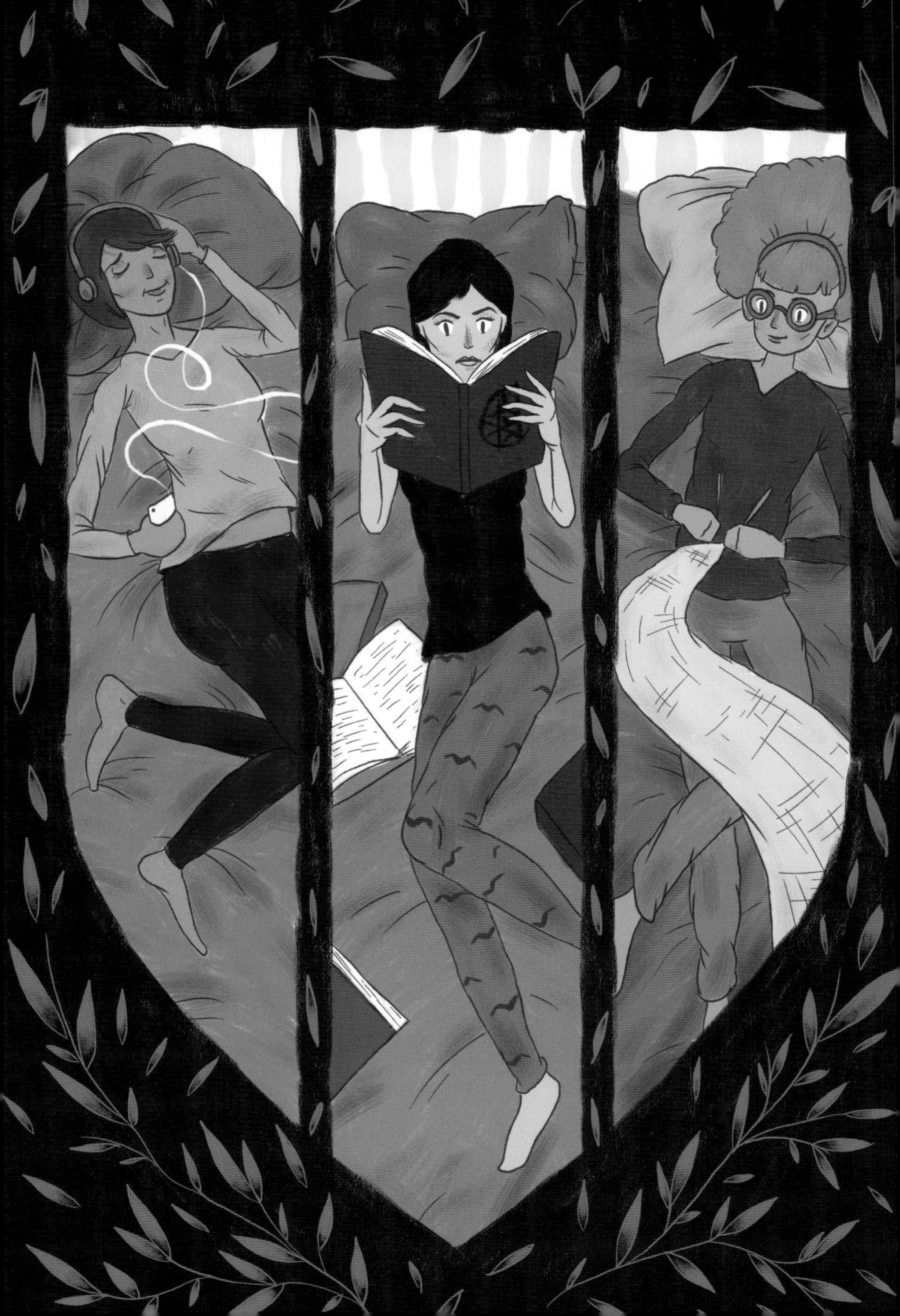

ISSUE #1 2ND PRINTING COVER
LISSA TREIMAN

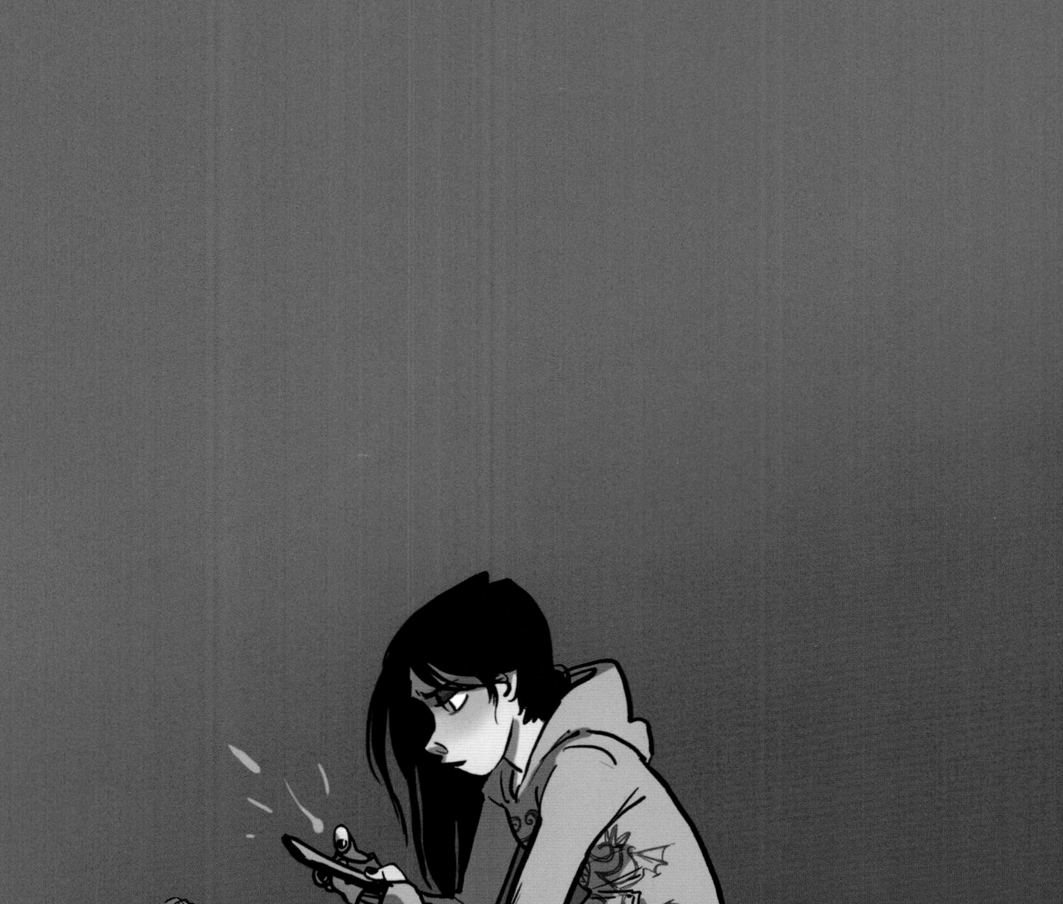
LT

ISSUE #2 COVER

LISSA TREIMAN

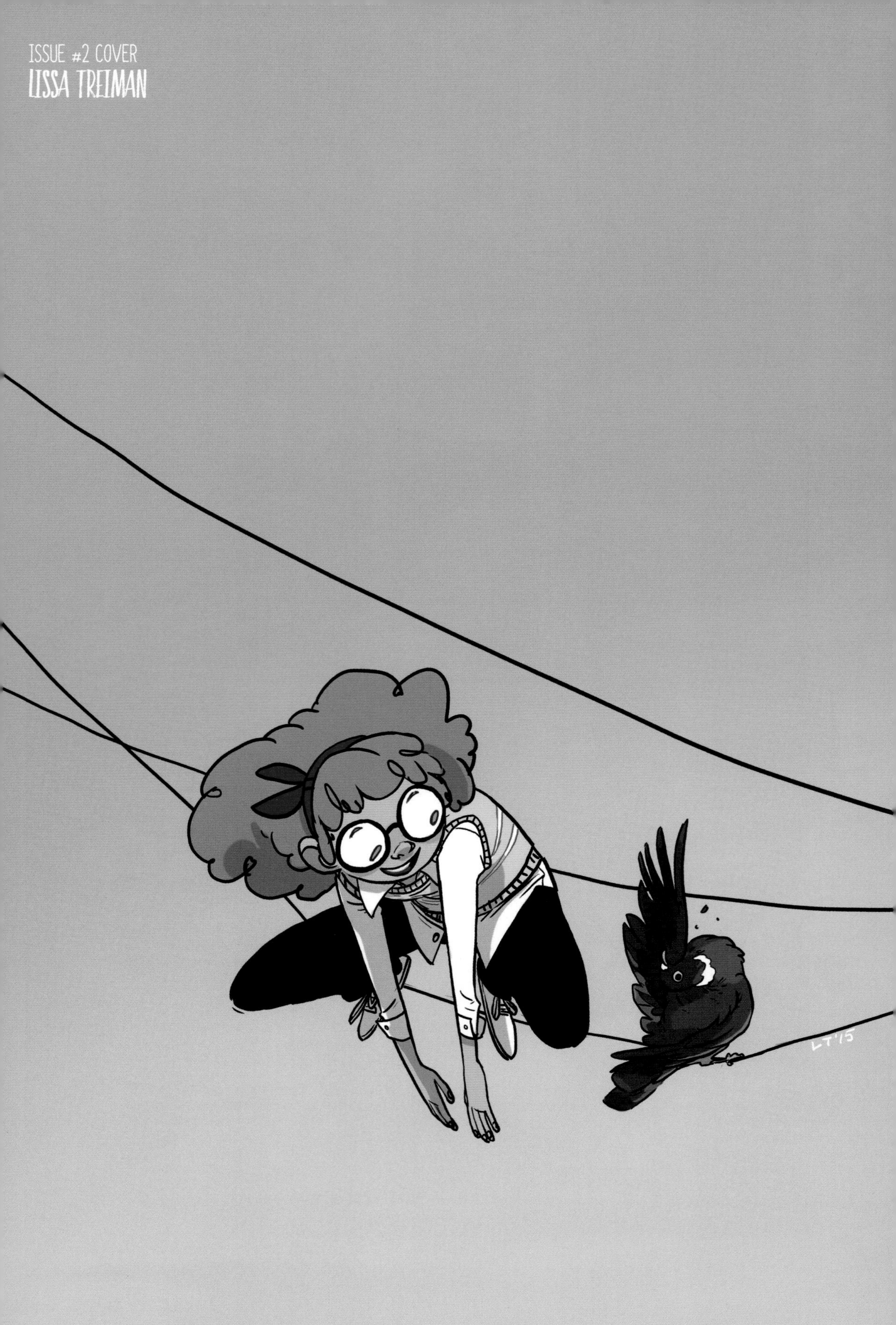
LT'15

ISSUE #3 COVER

LISSA TREIMAN

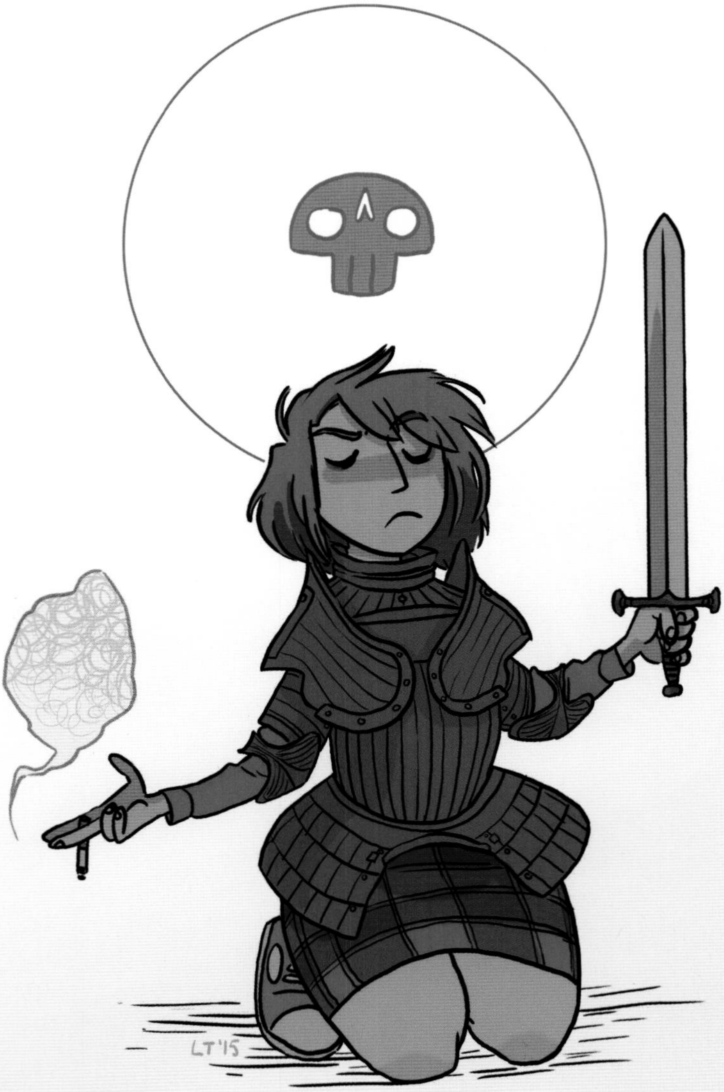
LT'15

ISSUE #4 COVER
LISSA TREIMAN

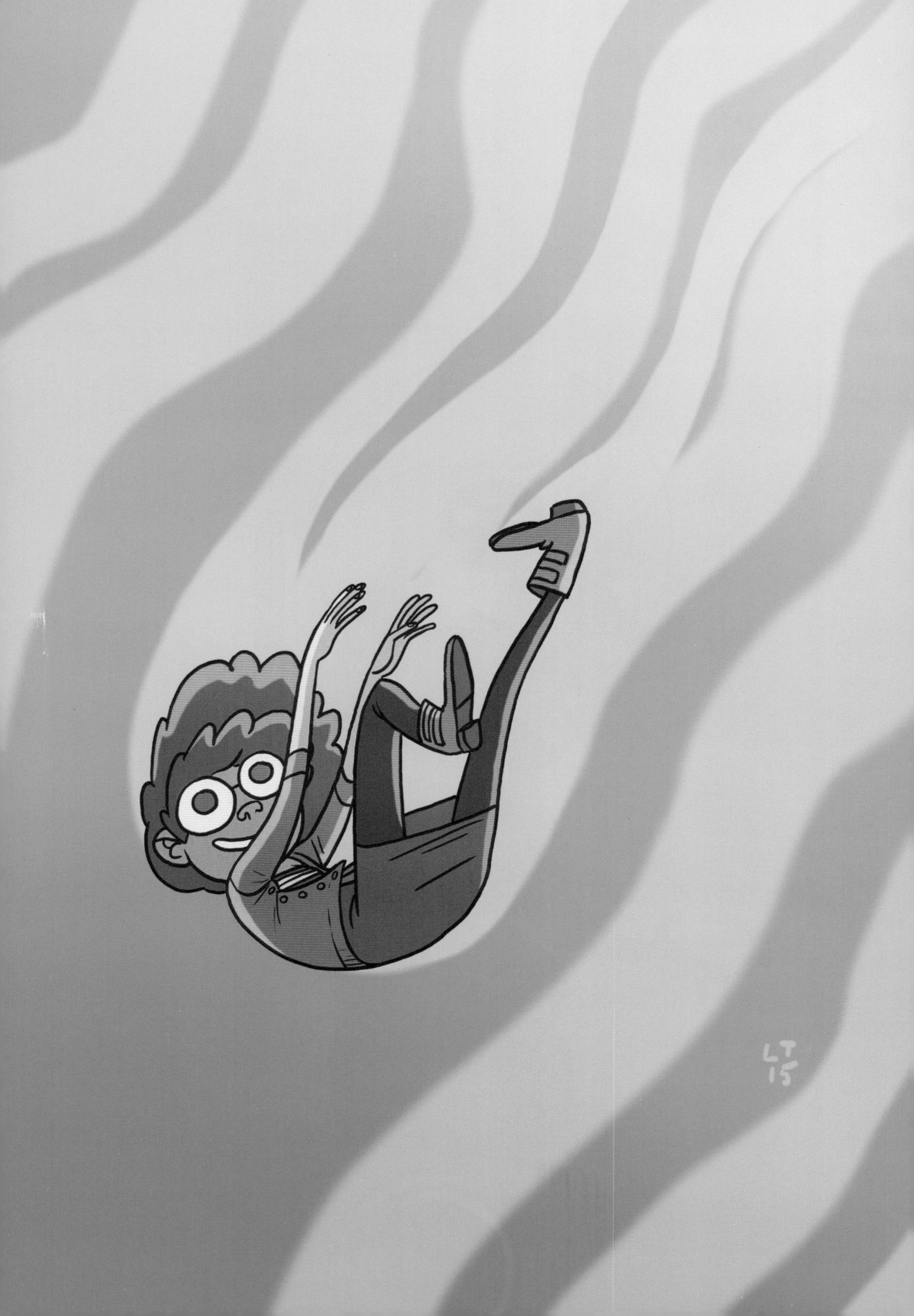
LT
15